# THE GIRL FROM THE FJORDS

ELIZA GRAHAM

Storm
PUBLISHING

To request permissions, contact the publisher at rights@stormpublishing.co

Ebook ISBN: 978-1-80508-596-6
Paperback ISBN: 978-1-80508-597-3

Cover design: Sarah Whittaker
Cover images: Trevillion, Shutterstock

Published by Storm Publishing.
For further information, visit:
www.stormpublishing.co

## ALSO BY ELIZA GRAHAM

*The Girl in Lifeboat Six*

*The Midwife's Promise*

*The Weight of Goodbye*

*You Let Me Go*

*The Truth in Our Lies*

*The Lines We Leave Behind*

*Another Day Gone*

*The One I Was*

*The History Room*

*Jubilee*

*Restitution*

*Playing with the Moon*

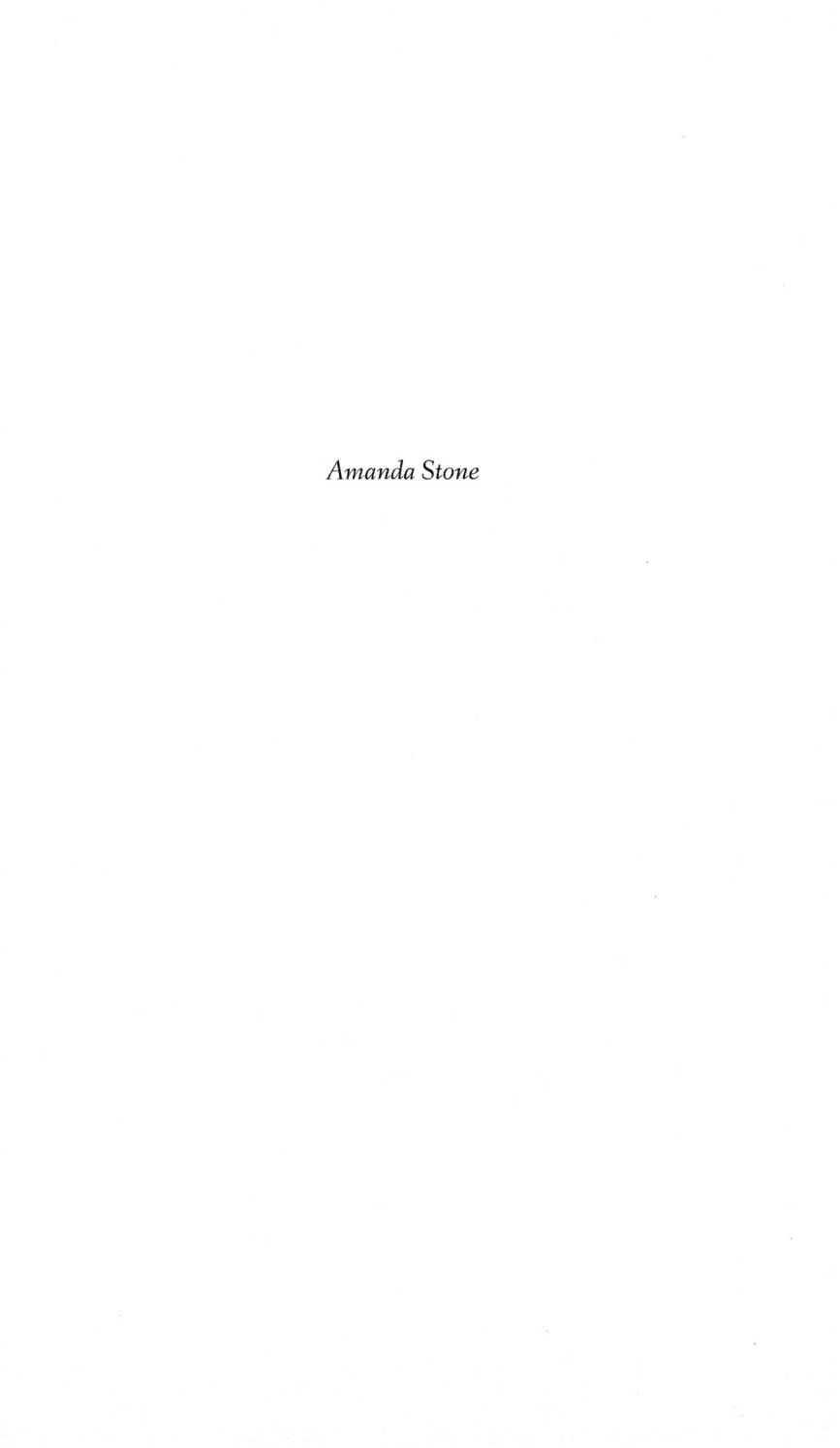

*Amanda Stone*

# PROLOGUE

## NORWAY, APRIL 1940

'Where's your thick pullover?' Asta pulled the drawer out and threw the woollen jumper at her brother. 'And socks, too. Remember how you hate cold, wet feet, Arne?'

'I'm going to fight the Germans, Asta, not setting off on holiday camp.'

'Soldiers need dry feet. Here.' She found his pyjamas. 'You've got your toothbrush? Razor? Change of underwear.'

'Yes.' Arne looked at his watch. 'The boat won't wait for me.'

Time and tide wait for no man, or whatever the saying was. Nor did the German army that was sweeping across the country.

They ran down the wooden stairs. Pappa was waiting by the door. 'Don't come with me, you two,' Arne said. 'It's better to say goodbye now.' He bit his lip and looked like the boy he was, barely twenty.

Pappa nodded. 'Goodbye, my boy. Take care of yourself and let us know you've got to Scotland safely.'

'I'll find a boat coming back to take a message.' He hugged his father and turned to Asta, a question on his face.

'Don't worry, I'll keep things going here,' she told him. 'It will all be over soon. I'll look after Pappa.'

'I don't need looking after,' Pappa said.

Arne bit his lip. 'I hate leaving you and Pappa. Part of me feels I should stay.'

'You're needed to fight with the Allies,' she said. 'Pappa and I will be fine.'

'I'll come back as soon as we've driven them out,' Arne said. 'They're not going to take our country from us. If I can't fight them on Norwegian soil, I'll fight them anywhere else in the world I can.' His blue eyes blazed in his tanned face. He was only eighteen months older than her, but Arne had always been fierce about protecting Asta. Not that she needed protecting, she was no delicate flower, but it was good to know she had Arne as a brother, even if he would be so far away for months, perhaps years to come.

When Mamma had been dying, just a week ago, and they were both sitting with her, she'd woken briefly, smiling at her children, making them promise to look after one another. 'That's all I ask,' she whispered, barely audible. 'Be good to each other and to your father.'

'I'll always do what's best for Pappa and Asta,' Arne said, voice shaking. 'You can trust me, Mamma.'

Mamma had given them a smile that made her look, briefly, like herself and not the woman dying of a disease gnawing her insides. 'No quarrelling. Or I'll come back and haunt you both.'

'We won't fight,' Arne said. 'No point, when I could pick her up and throw her over my shoulder.' He grinned at Asta and she made a face at him.

'And keep those punches of yours to yourself, my boy. Or save them for when they matter.' Mamma's voice was growing fainter.

Arne had always been quick with his fists. When he'd been younger, Pappa had given him stern words about self-control, pointing out that Arne's powerful build meant he didn't have to use the force he threatened. 'You don't need to do much more than fold your arms and set your chin.'

'Asta, you should...' Mamma sighed. Whatever she thought Asta should do was lost as her mother fell back into the sleep from which she wouldn't awaken again. Pappa came into the room and took his place at her bedside. Asta and Arne went out to take a breath of fresh air.

When they'd returned, Pappa was gently removing the rings from their mother's fingers and crossing her hands on her chest. A breeze played on a stray hair falling on her brow. Arne had leant forward to tuck it behind her ear, his fingers as delicate as a girl's, for all their size.

'She slipped away so peacefully I wasn't even sure she'd gone,' Pappa had told them.

As they watched Arne walk down the track towards the village, it felt as if they were losing not just him, but Mamma again. April sunshine bathed them. Overhead a bird was warbling, but their family of four was now just two.

Pappa cleared his throat. 'Those new chickens should be arriving soon. We should check the coop, Asta.'

No point letting a fox or stray dog take the hens. But the Germans were the new foxes now and Norway the henhouse. They'd attacked as suddenly as a cunning predator.

No wire fence could keep them out.

# PART ONE

NORWAY, 1942

# ONE

The young German soldier coming out of the post office held the door open for Asta. She glowered at him until he let it go, blushing, and walked away. She felt the familiar rush of anger tinged with guilt that she was even feeling bad about not thanking him. Why should she be courteous? He didn't belong here.

'How can you bear serving them?' she asked the post-mistress, Marte.

'How can I bear not to keep my job?' Marte replied, reaching under the counter for two parcels. 'These arrived for you.'

'Sorry.' Asta knew she was lucky that she didn't actually need to work outside the home to keep herself fed and housed. 'You can't control who comes into the post office. I know it's hard for you.'

'Work is a useful distraction, most of the time.'

'Perhaps that's what I need, too.'

'The back-office job in the hotel is still open,' Marte told her, pushing two parcels across the counter, one for Pappa, one for Asta herself. 'I heard they hadn't found anyone yet. You should take it, Asta. I know it's a step down for someone with your education, but it would be something to do.' Marte leant across the counter. 'Winter will come around again, less work outdoors. You know what it was like this year. And the year before. You'll be bored stiff again.'

'I'd rather die than work there.' The Germans had commandeered the hotel. Some of them slept there while they waited for their barracks to be built. They used the reception rooms to hold their meetings and conferences. Imagine having to serve them coffee and nod as they ordered you around. In Oslo before the occupation, Asta had studied linguistics at university, her eye on a proper career when she'd finished. Why not? Women were making inroads into all kinds of professions, or had been, before the war. Yet again she wondered about returning to her studies, sitting in lecture halls, working in book-scented libraries, writing essays at night, hand aching. And spending time with the friends she'd left behind in Oslo.

'If you don't take the position, someone else will, Asta.' Marte threw up her hand. 'Look at me, I thought I'd be doing something better than working here.'

Asta looked at her inquiringly. She'd never pictured Marte elsewhere.

'A secretarial job in Bergen. Smart office. Wardrobe full of fashionable clothes, rather than this drab old skirt and blouse, sitting in a draughty old post office.'

'You're brilliant at this job. Everyone likes coming into the post office.' Asta hesitated, not wishing to say it was because of the gossip Marte passed on. The girl seemed to know what was happening everywhere for miles up and down the fjord: who'd had a baby, whose cow had died, who'd been arrested for painting an anti-German slogan on a wall. 'Anyway, nobody else has shown much interest in the hotel job so far, have they?'

'They will. Eventually. When they realise German rations

can sometimes find their way to staff. And it's a hotel, not a prison camp.'

'Not really. Not since *they* took it over.' Trips to the hotel for coffee or a meal had been family treats when the Nilsens had holidayed on the fjord. The hotel had meant conversations about what had happened out on the boat, whether the water really was a little warmer today. It had meant celebrations, old family jokes, her father teasing them, she and her brother Arne complaining that the other had cheated in a card game or race. Not anymore. In the last month, more of the occupiers had arrived. Apparently they were building up sea defences against the Allies, part of their Atlantic Wall, trying to fortify every one of the thousands and thousands of coastal kilometres from the north of Norway down to the French border with Spain to keep the Allies out.

'All the same, it would be something.' Marte paused. Asta knew what she was going to say. 'Berit would have worried about you being so isolated here, Asta, a bright young woman like you.'

'I'm glad Mamma died before the visitors came.' It was a politer term for the German invasion, except that visitors usually showed respect and interest in their destination, instead of helping themselves to whatever took their fancy.

The postmistress nodded. 'At least Berit was spared the occupation.'

Berit Nilsen had been dying of cancer when the family had come up here for that last holiday, experiencing a lull in her pain and nausea, longing for a last holiday on the fjord while she still had some energy. Pappa, Arne and Asta had managed to excuse themselves from their studying and work commitments for what was supposed to be a few weeks here, the four of them tacitly hoping the tumour would magically reduce in the clear air. In fact, the cancer had speeded up its advance, like that other army had.

'You're up there with your father,' Marte continued, 'barely seeing a soul apart from him.'

And her shadow. But Asta didn't mention Magnus Haugen and the way he popped up seemingly out of nowhere. While his name was unspoken, he might remain a minor irritation, like the rain.

'I have you, Marte.' The postmistress was Asta's closest friend here, her age. They'd known one another for years from the Christmas and summer holidays the family spent here.

Marte smiled. 'I'd be bored stiff without you. And it's wonderful for Petter to have you here, of course. Especially while your brother...'

While her brother was presumably still in Scotland, across the North Sea. They knew he'd arrived safely – word had reached them when the fishing boat had returned. Asta shivered when she considered what Arne was doing now. Anxiety kept her awake at night. Sometimes she heard her father pacing around in the bedroom he'd once shared with her mother and knew he'd be worrying about Arne or the occupation and what the future would hold for them all. During the day Asta and Pappa could distract themselves. Sometimes they even laid two places at the dinner table without a pang.

'Anyway,' Marte said. 'Think about the hotel job.'

Asta put the parcels into her canvas bag, feeling Marte's eyes on the smaller, slimmer one addressed to Asta herself. Her cheeks burned a little. Had Marte guessed what was inside it?

She cycled up the track home, stopping at her favourite viewing spot and dismounting to take in the scene. The breeze blew Asta's hair around her face, defeating her attempts to keep it tidy. She drew in a breath of the clear air, feeling it relaxing every cell of her body, driving out the anger. The mountains and water worked as they always did, clearing her head of sadness, anxiety and loneliness. The scene in front of her was as enchanting as always, if you ignored the grey German warship. This little settlement on the fjord felt more like home than the spacious family house in Bergen or her student residence in Oslo. But the fjord had changed. Her life had changed. Everything was different now, since the Germans had arrived two years ago. Back then, she'd imagined the crisis would end quickly. The Allies would liberate Norway. For a few months she'd clung onto this hope.

Yet again, anger at the Germans and the British and at her fellow Norwegians rose inside her, a warm wave of bile. How had the occupation been allowed to happen? But what use was anger? Ignore the warship. Pretend the occupiers weren't here. She pushed the bitterness aside. This was a perfect late-spring morning. Sunshine dappled the water and when she looked away from the warship, she couldn't help but feel her spirits rise.

Her errands this morning had been productive. They'd have a good midday meal today. The carrots, swedes and potatoes her father had produced through the winter and spring, backed up with milk from the cow and occasional fish from the boats that still went out, meant their diet was monotonous but probably just about nutritious.

She'd have to open her parcel before she reached home and Pappa asked about it. Shame mixed with anticipation. Asta sat down on the grass and opened it up. Stockings. Just one packet, a little battered. Proper, silk stockings. A luxury and a total folly, she would have no use for them up here in the wilds. Christa, her friend in Oslo, would certainly have rolled her eyes as she'd bought them for her from a black-market contact. Christa had written a letter and enclosed some kind of flyer.

*Asta, I may not be able to do this again, it's harder and harder to get hold of anything like stockings and, to be honest, it doesn't*

*seem right to use the black market when it's not an essential item.*
*I hope Petter is doing well and you'll come back to the city soon,*
*though you'll find it all changed. Even in spring, it feels at best*
*flat and at worst frightening. Margrit has left Oslo, did you*
*know? After they had their identification cards stamped with the*
*Js in January, her father said things would only deteriorate*
*further for Jews, just as they had in other occupied countries, so*
*they managed to get papers for Sweden. They had to leave behind*
*her brother, who's still in the prison camp near Tromsø. Doesn't*
*it seem like a different world from when the three of us were*
*having almond cake with a cup of real coffee and laughing about*
*the lecturer with the sticking-up hair?*

Coffee and cake, taken for granted, as was the laughing and
joking with the other students, Margrit and Christa teasing Asta
because she'd bought yet another hat or lipstick. Back then,
examinations were the only threats looming.

Asta pushed the memories to the back of her mind.
Tormenting yourself never worked. It was self-indulgent and a
waste of energy. Images of Margrit fleeing her home with her
parents, leaving behind most of her possessions in that beautiful
house of theirs, made Asta feel even more helpless. What use
was feeling guilty about black-market luxuries when such awful
things were happening in Norway. She packed up her stockings
again and put them back in the bag, hoping the scent of the
small piece of cod wouldn't taint the silk. It was late in the year
for the cod catch, but fortune had smiled on the fishermen
today, even if they weren't allowed to go out as far these days
and the Germans usually took the pick of the catch. Asta
stopped herself again. She wouldn't think about the visitors. Or
*the grey worms*, as they also called them in these parts. Along
with other, more explicit names.

She'd continue on home. Help her father with the garden.

Try to open her university books again, though each day syntax and morphology seemed harder to concentrate on and less relevant to anything happening in the world. Perhaps go out for another walk. Play the piano. In the evening, when the forbidden Norwegian-language BBC programme broadcast, she and her father took it in turn to stand by the kitchen window, keeping an eye out for Germans or strangers while they listened to the wireless. Listening to the BBC could mean imprisonment, perhaps death. Asta and her father clung to each word with a mixture of sadness and hope, longing for news while dreading the truth they might learn about the world outside this small settlement, this occupied country of three million souls.

Each day blended into the next, marked out only by the rare sunny spells that western Norway could sometimes enchant you with. Asta needed a job, something that would get her out of the house. But not at that hotel, among grey worms. She'd have to try once again to use her mother's spinning wheel, do something useful with the hours that weren't spent trying to find or grow food on the family *småbruk*, smallholding, or prepare what they harvested. Mamma had been so talented at spinning and all the other domestic skills. Her only daughter had turned up her nose at these interests, imagining there'd be years ahead of them to change her mind and beg for instruction. Time had run out for Asta's mother before that could happen. Whenever the spinning wheel caught her eye, Asta felt a pang of guilt and longing for her mother. If only she'd sat down next to her and watched while Mamma produced her threads of yarn, which she then balled and knitted into the garments they wore. Asta's red and cream cardigan, with its traditional pattern, native to this part of Norway, was one of her mother's creations. Now there was nobody to teach Asta to knit something like this herself.

Work outside home would distract her from such thoughts,

but anything on offer around here would bring her closer to *them*.

Something below on the rocks caught her eye. A head, grey-brown, sleek, eyes alert. Asta held her breath. The otter ran across the rocks before diving into the waves and vanishing back into the fjord. Fishermen complained about the otters taking fish but Asta had always found the creatures enchanting.

A shadow fell behind her. She started and turned. 'Oh, Magnus.' She felt her sinews tense at the sight of him, though he was just an ordinary looking young man.

'Asta Pettersen.' He always insisted on calling her by the old-fashioned version of a Norwegian surname, using the patronymic, based on her father's first name, a form they'd never used in the family. 'What's in your parcel?'

'Nothing much.' She wanted to tell him to mind his own business, but that would make him even more curious. 'Women's things.' She looked him directly in the eye until he blushed. They'd been friends as children. Magnus had joined in with the Nilsens and Marte, his gruff awkwardness not mattering as much when they were playing up on the mountain tracks. As they'd grown up, Magnus had seemed to stay as he'd been as a child: fixed in his views, slow to interrupt social cues.

'Your rear tyre looks soft. I'll pump it up for you.' Without asking, he took the pump off Asta's bicycle frame, pulled out the tube and screwed it onto the rear valve. Asta knew by now that any protest simply prolonged the encounter. Best just to smile and nod. 'That's better.' He unscrewed the tube and replaced the valve cap. 'You don't want to damage the rubber. Tyres are hard to come by now.' He always addressed her as if she was a complete dolt, which was unkindly amusing, as Magnus himself wasn't renowned locally for what was between his ears.

'So I've heard.'

He was looking at her, waiting for a *takk*. If she thanked

him, he'd take it as encouragement to offer further unwanted help.

She looked at her watch. 'Pappa will wonder where I am. Must go, Magnus.'

He held on to the handlebars. 'If you can't pump the tyres yourself, I'll come up to your place and do them for you, Asta.'

'I can manage.' She didn't even try to mask the rolling of her eyes.

'Do you remember how your mother would cook us all those huge meals when we'd been out on our skis? Those were good times.' He looked inquiringly at her, waiting for her to invite him up to the house. Asta knew that as soon as she invited him in for as much as a mug of herbal tea, he would appear on the doorstep almost every day, staring at her with those grey-blue eyes of his that lingered on her chest.

She nodded and gave a brief smile. 'Need to get on now.' She pulled more assertively at the handlebars, and he let go. The track was steep at this point and normally she'd allow herself an easy start. Today she pushed down hard on the pedals, standing up to pull away, thankful Magnus was on foot and wouldn't be able to keep up with her once she'd got some momentum going. She could almost feel his gaze on her back-side as she pedalled.

It was a hard climb home with the added weight of the shopping and her heart thumped fast. She didn't want to stop in case Magnus caught her up. Her breath came in gasps. The war was certainly keeping her fit. The slope levelled out and she allowed herself to ease off the pedals.

She turned a bend. There was the little, red-painted wooden house in front of her. The sight of it always made her want to smile, no matter what was happening: Mamma dead of cancer, Arne away fighting, Pappa and she uprooted from their lives elsewhere, the house remained, its decoratively trimmed windows and doors and white lace curtains greeting her like something from a toy set. It had come down the family line from her mother, once at the heart of a full-time farm. Over the decades the family had sold off parcels of land. After they'd inherited it, her parents used it for holidays, only growing what could be harvested in the summer months, before they returned to Bergen. Since the war had started, Pappa had taken the smallholding far more seriously, buying chickens, planting vegetables, taking advice from the group of local middle-aged men he met a few times a week to drink home-brewed beer. He'd added hens, a few goats and a cow, swapping eggs and surplus milk for other foodstuffs.

Millions of other people in Europe – bombed, homeless, traumatised – would envy their quiet existence here with views over the fjord and the clear mountain air. Sometimes warships thundered out to sea, or flocks of Luftwaffe planes blazed across the sky, in pursuit of enemy shipping or aircraft. Occasionally they heard guns firing far out at sea, but nothing had been bombed out here. What was there to attack in such a small settlement? Perhaps that would change when more Germans arrived here to work on the Atlantic Wall.

As she propped up her bicycle in the lean-to beside the barn, Asta spotted her father in the wired-off vegetable patch, hoeing away at the weeds. The slugs had attacked the spinach and radishes. Without constant vigilance, the weeds would choke what was left to death. Both Asta and Pappa had blisters from the hours spent in the vegetable patch. Perhaps life in the city would be easier. The pastries and real coffee in the cafés might be scarcer, but presumably people still did ordinary things: went to the cinema, strolled in the park, laughed, gossiped?

She certainly couldn't leave Petter here alone. He'd laugh at her concern, saying he was a vigorous man of fifty-two, fit from his love of the outdoors and working on the land. He'd miss her, but he'd understand why she wanted to return to the city. Petter had found solace in the rhythms of the seasons. Once a week, he met up with a group of similarly aged men to drink the beer they brewed, while discussing vegetable production, animal husbandry and exchanging advice and tools. 'You should hear us on the subject of hoes and spades,' he said. 'It can get just as heated as an economics seminar or tutorial.'

Asta remembered when he'd held tutorials for his students in the spacious front room in the Bergen house with its view over the harbour, Mamma knocking on the door to bring in a plate of biscuits or cakes for his students, claiming they looked hungry and he was working them too hard. Pappa had relinquished his academic post when the Germans had arrived in Norway, telegramming the School of Economics to say that he would stay on in the fjords indefinitely. Neither Asta nor Pappa could summon the willpower to leave the red house and return to Bergen. Slowly they'd built up the smallholding, buying the animals, harvesting hay for the winter, finding solace in the rhythm of their days. For the first six months or so, it had been all Asta needed. The crisis would pass, she told herself. She'd return to university. Or move back to Bergen to find a job.

The Germans hadn't requisitioned the Bergen house yet. Yet the thought of living there all by herself with the memories of happier family times was unappealing. On the other hand, if the Germans gave her permission to return to university in Oslo, she'd probably struggle to find lodgings with so many grey worms in the capital. Yet again, competing alternatives whirled around in her head, making decisions feel impossible to make.

Her father spotted her and stood up, hand on his back, grimacing as he straightened himself.

'What have you done to yourself, Pappa?' she asked.

'Spot of arthritis, that's all.' He walked towards her, mouth twisted. She hoped that was all it was. He was fit for his age, but life here could be so tough in the winter.

'Not your heart?'

He glared at her. Around the time of the occupation, the local doctor had warned that his heart had an irregular beat. 'As I told that doctor, I can tackle any steep slopes by foot or on cross-country skis as fast as men half my age. I dig in the vegetable patch for hours at a time.'

'Of course you do, Pappa.'

His moment of irritation passed. 'Apart from Marte, did you see anyone?'

'Just Magnus Haugen, hanging around.'

'That young man needs a job. Apparently the Germans still won't take him to work on the Atlantic Wall defences.'

'You'd think he'd be relieved.'

'Perhaps his pride is injured.'

He followed her into the house. 'I have a letter for you, Pappa.' She took it out of the canvas bag, along with his parcel, keeping her own package out of sight. The letter looked official, in a brown envelope, stamped with a government mark she couldn't make out.

He opened it, skimming the letter, and laughed drily. 'Oh, of course.'

'Of course what, Pappa?'

'We're to have a houseguest.'

Coming in that brown envelope, this announcement could mean only one thing. Asta's blood turned to ice. 'A German?'

Petter sighed. 'Yes. I suppose we should be grateful they don't want the entire house and aren't booting us out.'

'We can't have a German here.' Eating at this table? Sitting by the stove?

Petter sat down at a chair, looking pale, perhaps from reading the letter, but she knew it was more than that.

'You do too much.'

'I'm not ancient.'

She decided not to push the point.

'He's a soldier, this German?'

'The wording is unclear. I can't tell whether he's a serving officer or here in a civilian capacity, but he is referred to as *leutnant* Brandt.' He pushed the letter on its thin grey paper towards her.

'So they'll expect us to cook this German's rations while making do with our own paltry scraps.' Asta pulled out a chair and sat down so abruptly the windows rattled. 'And do his laundry too? They can think again. I will not be his maid and cook.' She thought again of escaping to Oslo. But that would mean leaving Pappa here alone with the German, which seemed a bleak prospect for her father. How could he spend evenings with whoever it was, just the two of them? Some of the things she'd heard about German lodgers... She skimmed the letter, which was just a list of orders with no useful information, a dictate from the occupiers.

'We should be grateful they left us in peace for as long as they did.' Pappa took back the letter and folded it into the envelope. 'And yet again, I'm so relieved your brother escaped when he did.'

They'd heard that the fishing boat had taken Arne up the west coast to a rendezvous with a larger fishing boat. From there, he'd made the hazardous crossing of the North Sea to Peterhead, near Aberdeen in Scotland. Petter and Asta had spent a tense couple of weeks wondering if he'd ever arrived or whether the Luftwaffe or a storm had sunk the boat. Word had finally reached them via the network of fishermen and the mail boat, Marte running up the track to the house to burst in and tell them she'd heard Arne was well and joining a Norwegian unit based in Scotland.

Pappa always said it was tougher to be stuck in an occupied country and unable to fight back. Perhaps it explained his sympathy for Magnus. Arne, though exposed to danger, would feel he was doing something positive for his country. Sometimes when loneliness washed over Asta and she missed her brother, she found a little comfort in picturing him in uniform, learning how to shoot Germans or throw grenades at them.

Pappa was watching her. 'Asta,' he began. 'This is going to make things even more difficult for you. We should try to get you back to Oslo. If it's for educational purposes, there's a good chance they'll let you return...'

She shook her head. 'Only if you come with me. I can't leave you here alone.'

Petter looked down at the table. 'I've made some solid friendships. We may just talk about brewing beer and defeating slugs, but they've become valued friends.'

'But you still have friends back in Oslo, don't you? They'd be thrilled to have you back. You were there for years before we moved west to Bergen. Come with me?'

'I couldn't possibly leave the smallholding.'

'Someone else would take it on. They'd be keen to have the produce in exchange for keeping it going and sending us a fair portion of the food.'

His fatigue seemed to leave him. He stood up. 'I think we both need a cup of coffee.' In a jar they stored coffee grounds – brown diamonds, Pappa called them, drying them out on a cotton cloth, and reusing them. Pappa added a spoonful of roasted-pea coffee substitute to the dried grounds to make them go further. 'Each day, it tastes more like mud and less of coffee. Soon, calling it coffee will be sacrilege.'

'We could barter something for real beans.' She knew of a woman up the valley who reportedly still had coffee. Might she exchange a packet of the precious substance for a box of eggs?

'It's more about the ritual itself, isn't it?' He smiled. 'Though your mother would tell us off for spending too much time sitting around.'

Asta would give anything for Mamma to tell her off for daydreaming, wasting the best of the day by sitting inside with a book. If Mamma was still here, she'd deal with this German interloper.

Arne would have expressed his feelings about the new lodger, too, just as he did about everything. A word from Arne would also have seen off Magnus. Memories of how Magnus had insisted on blowing up her bicycle tyre slipped into Asta's mind like a cold draught in a warm room. She was going to be more assertive with him, make it clear that she didn't want him hanging around her.

'When we've drunk this, I'll go down into the cellar to check on things,' Pappa said, breaking into her thoughts.

Their eyes met. By 'things', Pappa meant the hiding place he'd created behind the shelf they used to store potatoes and cakes of peat for the stove. Pull the shelf out and a cavity was revealed, large enough to conceal a forbidden wireless and a metal box for anything else they didn't want any Germans coming to the house to see. Many Norwegians would have had hidey-holes like this. Until now, it had seemed like an insurance policy. Now it felt essential.

When he was out of sight, Asta took out her own parcel, folding up the brown paper to use again. She hadn't read Christa's other enclosure, the small pamphlet, more like a miniature newspaper, really. *NORWAY FIGHTS ON... BRAVE NORWEGIANS ARRESTED AND TORTURED... DO NOT JOIN NEW PRO-NAZI UNIONS... What can* **you** *do for your country?... Atrocities against Norwegian Jews and other citizens...*

What could she do? Not much. Suppose this publication had been taken out while their new houseguest was in residence? Talk of resistance to the occupier and to Quisling, the pro-Nazi prime minister of Norway, could get you sent to one of those camps Christa talked about in her letter. Was Christa urging her to take some sort of stand? What could she do, alone in this small settlement, with a German about to arrive on their doorstep?

Asta tore up the pamphlet and put it into the stove, feeling a mixture of guilt and relief as the edges curled up, blackened and vanished into ashes.

She needed to hide her new stockings in her room before Pappa came back up from the cellar. She took them up to her bedroom.

# TWO

The new lodger arrived the following Tuesday, dropped off by a truck, carrying a duffel bag and a cardboard box, which he presented to Asta. He wasn't wearing uniform. '*God Dag. Mitt navn er* Max Brandt.' She smirked at the Norwegian pronunciation. He extended a hand. She ignored it. He shrugged and pushed the box at her. 'For the household.'

It was heavy, seemingly housing cans and jars of food. 'We're allowed to eat your rations too?' She allowed herself a quick look at him. Tall. Young. Typically Germanic in appearance. Probably attended Hitler Youth summer camp every year as a boy. She felt her lips curl.

'The food's supposed to be just for me, but I can't see how that would work unless you cooked everything separately. It's not practical. Could you show me my room, please?' He spoke in faltering Norwegian, looking down at his boots as though uncertain as to whether he should take them off.

'Outdoor shoes off inside,' Asta said, folding her arms. Start as you mean to go on, don't let them take an inch. Crouching down, he undid the laces. She noticed that his left hand was missing both ring and little fingers. Combat injury? Hopefully from a Norwegian bullet.

He slipped the boots off. His socks were dark grey, the wool as yet unbobbled. 'I have indoor shoes, which I will put on when I have unpacked. It's more practical.'

Practicality seemed to matter to Max Brandt. He was dressed for outdoor work, but his clothes were obviously good quality, the type that Arne wore for hiking. She couldn't help wondering about this man, who he was, what he did. He looked normal, but men like him had seized innocent Norwegians like Margrit's brother and thrown them into concentration camps.

She shrugged. 'Wear what you like, as long as it's not outdoor footwear.' She set his box of food down on the rug. 'Follow me.' She'd made up Arne's old bed for him. At first she'd been going to store Arne's model boats and books in a box, out of the German's sight, but then she'd thought, no, it's Arne's room he's invading. Let him be reminded of what he's doing, the life his people had ruined. But perhaps the German wouldn't care.

Max Brandt looked at the model yacht on the chest of drawers and an expression she couldn't read flashed over his face, a look of recognition. 'Your brother's room?'

'Yes.'

'Where is he now?'

She wanted to tell him to mind his own damn business but confined in the small room with him, it seemed hard to assert herself. 'We aren't exactly sure.'

He blinked. 'With the Norwegians in Scotland?'

She said nothing. Brandt wasn't Gestapo or even a Norwegian policeman. She didn't have to answer questions like this.

Brandt nodded. 'It's not necessary for me to know this information.'

Yet again she felt thrown off balance.

'We eat our main meal at lunchtime, but I imagine you'll be

detained at your... work?' Whatever that was. She told herself she couldn't care less what he did. He was a German. Enough said. He put his duffel bag down and took off his coat. He managed well with his maimed left hand, she noted.

'I can't fire a rifle easily but I can undertake other roles in a civilian capacity.' He said it mechanically. 'I was studying civil engineering before the war and luckily I am right-handed.'

'I thought German males weren't allowed to be left-handed? Don't you all have to be perfect in every way?' The questions popped out of her mouth in German before she could stop it. Damn. Now she'd made it clear she spoke German. She should have kept that to herself in case he ever said anything to his friends in her presence that he thought she wouldn't under-stand. A flash of something, irritation perhaps, passed over his face.

'Your accent is very good.' The statement sounded like a question.

'We're from Bergen. It has a history of trade with Germans.' Bergen was one of the Hanseatic ports, an ancient trading league stretching across the north of Europe into the Baltic. 'Though the trade is a little less balanced these days.' She couldn't resist the last part. He didn't seem to notice.

'It will be more practical for us to speak German, if your father can manage it?'

'He studied in Frankfurt as a young man.'

'Good. A dinner in the middle of the day works well for me. I'll let you know at breakfast each day if I'm staying down in the village.'

'Very well.'

'In which case I won't need you to cook for me in the evening. The sausage and cheese I will provide will be adequate for a supper at around eight.' He shuffled. 'You may leave me here to unpack now.'

He frowned at something on the window.

'Is something bothering you?'

'If you have sandpaper, you could sand the wood on the inside there where it has splintered.'

'I don't have the time to do that,' she said, flushing with indignation. Did he think she was his servant? That's how the Nazis treated civilians in the countries they walked into: as labourers at best; at worst, like slaves.

He looked her up and down. 'I could do it for you.'

'I wouldn't want to put you to the trouble.'

'No trouble.' He looked approvingly around the room. 'This is all good. I will need two towels, one medium, one smaller. Perhaps you forgot to put them out on the bed?'

'I didn't forget.'

'I see. If your linen isn't adequate, you should tell me so I can bring towels from the barracks.'

'I... Yes. Towels.' It annoyed her to have to supply linen for him, but she wasn't having him think they were a bunch of peasants. 'We use a tin bath. We can bring it in when you need to, erm, use it.'

'I can shower down at the barracks.'

She felt relieved. 'The *utedo* is in the little log outhouse.' She watched him to see if the thought of an outdoor privy bothered him, but he was impassive. 'You can bring hot water up here to wash.' Arrangements here had always been simple. Mamma had talked about building a bathroom extension with an indoor lavatory, but they'd never got round to it. This house was for holidays, for a simple, outdoor life with less fuss. When Mamma had entered her last weeks, the arrangements had been hard to manage, even with the local doctor and nurse making calls every day.

The lieutenant stared out of the window. 'If you and your father cut back that larch, you'd get more light in this room in the mornings.'

Asta bit her tongue and left the room, finding the towels in the linen press and returning to place them on the bed. He took things out of the duffel bag, extra bits of uniform, a few books, a cake of soap, using both his hands, she noticed.

'I lost my fingers during training.'

Asta blushed.

'Sometimes people don't like to ask.'

Especially not when the person they were asking was an occupier.

Pappa was downstairs when she returned to the kitchen. 'I see our guest arrived while I was cleaning out the chickens. What's he like?'

'I found it all a bit awkward.' She couldn't think of a better word.

Pappa stiffened. 'Was he aggressive towards you, Asta. I swear to God—'

'Not aggressive. Just... particular in his requirements. They can ask for anything they want, can't they?'

'Those are his rations?' He frowned at the box.

'He says we can share the food, too. It's more practical, apparently.' They looked at one another and Pappa shrugged. 'He also says we should trim the larch. Apparently it blocks the light.'

Pappa's lips twitched. 'A horticulturist as well as a lodger? Blessed are we.'

Asta heard her own laughter with astonishment. She couldn't remember the last time she'd laughed. It felt as though it must have been years and years ago. Yet she'd always been the one the teacher scolded for giggling in class. And the cause of her laughter was a German of all things. She craned her neck to make sure Max Brandt's door was still closed. 'He'll be lunching with us. I'll have to prepare the meal.'

Pappa's relaxed expression tensed. 'You shouldn't be skivvying here instead of being with interesting people, talking about lectures and books.'

'Neither should you. But it's not so bad here.'

'At least we enjoy one another's company,' he said. It was true. Pappa was easy-going, widely read and did his best to make her life as bearable as it could be.

From Max Brandt's box of groceries Asta pulled out a tin of pork and one of lentils. The aroma of real coffee swept the kitchen, filling her with nostalgia. She roasted potatoes and boiled and grated a suede. He appeared at half twelve seeming to know this would be their lunchtime and asked where he should sit. Asta pointed to the place setting that had once been her brother's, trying not to see Arne's shock of blond hair and rosy cheeks there. 'You said we could share the food, but I wasn't sure if you meant it.'

'If I hadn't meant it, I wouldn't say it,' he answered.

Pappa came in, removing his cap and boots, looking Brandt direct in the eye. 'I'm Petter Nilsen,' he said, without extending a hand, pulling out a chair. 'This is our family home. I trust you will treat it and my daughter with respect.' Like Asta, he spoke in German, too.

Brandt stood up and bowed his head. At least he didn't click heels. 'We were ordered to behave well in your homes.'

'They needed to order you?' Asta placed a plate in front of him and pushed the basket of bread towards him.

'Better to spell things out.' He cut a small piece off his pork. 'Did you want to ask me questions? Where I'm from? What I'm doing here?' His eyes, dark for a German's, more grey than blue, assessed them. 'I'm a stranger in your home, after all.'

Pappa and Asta looked at one another. 'Very well, where are you from and what are you doing in our little settlement? Defending the coast?' Pappa made it sound like everyday conversation.

'My family home is in a town in Brandenburg. About 30km from Berlin. I was sent to basic and then officer training while I was at university studying civil engineering.' He gave a wry smile. Another person whose education had been disrupted, but Asta didn't want to acknowledge any common points with this man. 'You are very courteous, *mein herr*,' he went on, 'but I see you looking at my left hand. I lost two of the fingers in an incident during training.'

An incident? Not an accident? Or was Asta's German a little rusty?

'So now I'm a non-combatant, but at least I can work in my area of interest.' He turned his attention to his potatoes. She wanted to ask him if he'd studied the design and construction of war machinery at university, but bit back the words.

'The Nazi party likes its officers to be physically perfect, doesn't it?' she asked instead, so sweetly even her father was almost taken in. She heard Pappa take a breath as her meaning hit him. Max Brandt nodded.

'I have other skills they can use.'

'I'm sure you have. The German army seems to be adept at finding and deploying talent.' Asta said it without a hint of sarcasm in her voice but perhaps the slight smile on her lips gave her away. Brandt looked puzzled but finished his meal, arranging his knife and fork on the side of the plate. He looked at his watch. 'I have no more time to eat now, but you could make me some coffee.'

Usually they waited an hour or so after their midday meal to serve coffee, as was the custom in Norway. Asta looked at Pappa. He nodded.

She rose to brew it. She needed to make it clear she wasn't his servant. 'I may return to Oslo. My father won't be able to cook for you. You'll have to use the kitchen yourself.'

In fact, Pappa handled kitchen duties with ease, but Brandt wasn't to know this.

'You have essential work in the capital, Frøken Nilsen?' he asked.

'I was a student. At the university in Oslo.'

'*Ach.*' He nodded. 'Your education was disrupted, too, like mine was.'

She didn't like him placing the two of them in the same category. His education had been interrupted by his own country launching an unprovoked attack on its neighbours. Her country had done no such thing. When he'd drunk the coffee she made, he gestured towards the pot. 'You two should finish that.'

Asta and Petter watched him through the kitchen window as he walked up the path to the lane. 'Curious young man,' Petter said. 'I suppose it could be worse. At least he's courteous.'

'He's still a German.'

'Obsessed with practicality,' Petter said. 'I suppose that's Germans for you.'

'How can it be practical for them to station so many of their troops in Norway? You know there are a third of a million German troops here now. Don't they need them on the Eastern Front?' The illicit broadcasts from the BBC Pappa and Asta had listened to before Brandt had arrived had claimed the Russians were tying up large numbers of German soldiers.

'They need to—'

'Protect their sea access for the iron ore they export from Sweden and attack British merchant ships and starve the British out.' Asta stacked plates. 'But it's more than that, isn't it?' She tried not to slam the dishes against each other in her anger.

Pappa looked at her.

'They're just bullies. Norway isn't Norway any more with grey worms swaggering around everywhere.'

'I hate seeing them around our village, knowing they're all over our country.'

'Everyone does, Pappa.'

'Sadly not. I hear our own Norwegians are doing most of the administration for them.'

'That can't be true.' Norwegians in offices making the occupation run smoothly for the Germans?

'Word has it there are only 800 German administrators in the whole of Norway. Our people are heavily involved in occupation work. And that's without all the men who've signed up to fight in their Norwegian divisions and those working on the Atlantic Wall.'

Asta felt sick. 'And all the time, men like Arne do whatever they can to fight the Germans. They should be ashamed of themselves.'

'If they're unemployed, the labour exchanges offer youngsters the choice between fighting or working for the Germans, or going hungry.'

'We're finished as a country if that's what they choose.'

'Norway is not finished.' Pappa spoke sharply, then cleared his throat, looking more like his mild-mannered old self. 'Must get going. Peas and beans to plant out this afternoon, onions, too, if there's time.'

Once his presence had been sought at academic conferences all around the world. Now he worked the small plot of land like his farmer forebears. He turned by the door. 'One day, the Germans will be gone, Asta, I promise. And things will go back to how they were before.'

'I can't wait until we see the back of every last one of them.' She'd be cheering and shouting.

But things couldn't go back to how they'd once been. Mamma was dead. Arne mightn't return from the war. She herself was no longer a carefree student. Their family had been smashed up. How could they glue it back together again?

# THREE

'He's quiet enough, takes himself off for walks in the evening or reads in his room if it's raining. He could be worse,' Asta admitted. Marte made a face. The two of them sat on a rock between Asta's house and the town, enjoying the sun, which had remembered it was summer. Western Norway could never promise days of unbroken sunshine so you grabbed it when you could.

'All the same, not a houseguest you'd choose. Even if he's not actually a soldier.'

'We were told he was a lieutenant, but it seems he's posted here in a civilian capacity, as an engineer. Not that it makes it better. It's worse on the days he's not working. He just hangs around, offering to help indoors or outdoors, doing bits of carpentry or repairing things.'

'Do you let him?' Marte looked surprised.

'No. But Pappa sometimes lets him hold a fence post or hoe the vegetables.'

Brandt's injured left hand didn't prevent him from using tools, she had to admit. 'I just keep praying he'll get leave back in Germany or he'll take it somewhere else in the country, Oslo perhaps, and we'll have a break from him. It's awkward having him in the house. We can never relax with him around.'

Now the radio was hidden in the cellar, they couldn't listen to the BBC. Asta decided not to tell Marte that part, though. Following Brandt's arrival, some of her father's other activities were also more difficult to continue. Pappa still headed down the track into the village to meet his friends, but the group no longer met at the Nilsens'. A young boy was stationed outside whichever house they chose, always seemingly occupied changing the tyre on a bicycle or kicking a ball around, but primed to warn those meeting inside the house if Germans were on the way. Asta had observed all this without comment. What she didn't know couldn't hurt anyone else. Or herself. Pappa never said a word to confirm he was up to something that could have sent him to a prison camp for aiding resistors. If only she, too, could do something to resist. Sometimes she thought of asking Marte if she'd picked up anything in her post office about Milorg, the name given to the Norwegian resistance, short for *Militær Organisasjon*. But she could never think of a way of phrasing what could be a reckless or downright dangerous question. She'd have to wait for the right moment to bring up the subject. She'd wondered if her friend Christa was involved with the organisation in Oslo? But again, this wasn't a question she could ask, not in a letter.

'What happened to your lodger's left hand?' Marte asked. 'I saw it when he came into the post office a few days ago.'

'The fingers were apparently shot off in a training incident. Perhaps he annoyed someone.' She'd purposely refused to show any interest in Brandt or ask him any questions, ignoring his occasional conversational openers. She had no interest in his home in Germany or his family. Not that he had said much about them. He'd talked about his family and friends, admitting he missed home. Pappa had looked more kindly at him then, but

Asta wouldn't be lulled into regarding the guest as anything more than an imposition. An intruder.

Marte laughed. 'You're a hard woman. Still, at least he's not too... German.'

She knew what Marte meant. Max Brandt didn't swagger around and issue orders, for all he was one of them. 'True. I just want all the grey worms to wriggle back into their dark German hole and be gone.'

'Or a big fat crow to pick them up and swallow them,' Marte said, with real venom in her voice. She blushed. 'Sorry, it's a lovely day, I shouldn't let them spoil it. It's just hard when you hear things.'

'Things?'

'Something the skipper said when the mail boat came in. Things happening in Bergen.'

'What things, Marte?' Asta had lowered her voice, although they were alone.

Marte took a moment to reply. 'Arrests. Young men, boys, actually, still at school. Picked off the street for some alleged resistance activity. Tortured. Horribly.' She shivered. 'I doubt they'd done more than deliver messages by bicycle. Or paint slogans on a wall.'

'They torture school kids?'

'Sometimes assisted by our very own home-grown Norwegian Nazis.'

Asta thought again of the pamphlet Christa had sent her. Was this the kind of thing Christa was doing to help the resistance? And there was Asta Nilsen, begging her to find black-market stockings for her. Princess Asta, Christa and Margrit had called her, affectionately before the occupation. The girl who liked the finer things, whose father doted on her. She opened her mouth to ask Marte if she knew anything about Milorg.

Something distracted her, a dark shape moving on the slope beneath them. Asta squinted at it.

'What's wrong?' Marte asked.

'I thought I saw someone down there.'

Marte peered in the same direction. 'You're right. There's a man down there. Not a German. He knows we've spotted him. Must be shy.' But the way Marte said it revealed tension. Asta studied her. Marte wasn't worried about the man, whoever he was, she was worried *for* him. Concerned for him? Did she know men who needed to stay in cover? She took a closer look.

'Don't worry. It's only Magnus again.'

'Magnus Haugen?' Marte's face relaxed.

'He tends to pop up when I'm walking or cycling around.'

'An admirer?'

'If you can call him that.' Asta groaned. 'I know life's hard for him, he's lonely, his friends have all gone, no work, but it makes me feel on edge when he's everywhere I go.' Yesterday evening, when she'd gone out of the house with a bucket of kitchen peelings for the chickens, Magnus had been standing on the track below the house. Asta had been wearing a pair of shorts because she'd just scrubbed down the inside of the henhouse. He'd stared at her bare legs until she'd folded her arms. Then he'd nodded in her direction, before turning and carrying on his way. Just a coincidence? Plenty of people liked to take a stroll in the long early summer evenings. He hadn't come as close to the house since Brandt had moved in – a silver lining to having a German lodger? Max Brandt had come back from work a few minutes later and had also stared at her legs, but blushing and looking away before she could say something cutting to him.

'He drives me mad. He complains about the occupiers but then complains that the Germans won't take him on as a labourer on the Atlantic Wall,' Marte said. 'Why would he want to work alongside slaves from all over Europe? Those poor people, they're treated like dogs.'

Asta had heard about the ill-treatment of Serbs and Russians, people regarded as less worthy than native Aryan Norwegians. She hadn't quite dared to bring up the subject over the dinner table with Max Brandt.

'Talking of missing friends, no word from Arne?' Marte sounded casual but her eyes were turned down to the ground, as though she didn't want Asta to see what she was feeling. Arne and Marte had spent time together before Arne had fled on the fishing boat. Arne'd laughed off Asta's teasing, saying he and Marte were just good friends, but he'd blushed all the same. If something had been blossoming between the two of them, it had been yet another victim of war.

'Not a word. I just hope he's found something useful to do over... there.' Even though Marte knew Arne had crossed the North Sea to Scotland, it was best to be discreet. The Germans harassed fishing boats and their crews enough as it was. Anyone smuggled in and out of the country for secret action against the occupiers could expect bullets. So could those who transported, fed or sheltered them. Before the wireless had been hidden in the cellar, Pappa and Asta had enjoyed trying to decipher the cryptic, sometimes almost poetic messages to those carrying out secret operations. 'See, things are happening, Asta,' Pappa would say. She'd feel a little prick of guilt that she wasn't doing anything.

Marte might well be helping resistance activity, passing on verbal and written messages herself, using her position as postmistress, putting herself in danger. But why add to the risk by telling her more than was strictly necessary about Arne?

'I wonder how long this will all go on for?' Marte's voice sounded sombre.

Asta shrugged. 'Doesn't seem that anything will change in Norway.' The occupation had already lasted two years.

Predicting its end seemed impossible. Yet America had entered the war and Hitler was fighting the Soviets on the Eastern Front. She tried to take comfort in the fact that more and more men were taking up arms against the Nazis.

Marte pulled at her waistband. 'Oh well, at least we don't have to worry about keeping our figures these days.' The moment for talking about acts of resistance seemed to have passed.

'I had to take in my waistbands, too. They kept sliding around my waist.' She rolled her eyes. 'My mother kept an old sewing machine at the house. I've managed to work out how to thread the needle. One of these days I might even manage to sew an apron.'

Marte laughed but her eyes were shadowed. Was she still thinking about Arne? Asta pulled a pack of cigarettes and her lighter out of her skirt pocket and offered them to Marte.

'Let's make the best of the sunshine.' Marte lit a cigarette.


When she returned home, Brandt was in the chicken wire-protected vegetable patch attacking weeds with the hoe, managing to balance it on his left hand while his dominant arm worked. 'The weeds grow almost overnight this time of year,' he said, as she approached.

'Does my father know you're doing this?' Brandt was wearing a short-sleeved vest, his shirt tied around his waist. She tried not to look at his arms, which were muscled and lightly tanned.

'He felt a little breathless. I said I'd finish it off for him. But I can tell it is making you angry.' He said it neutrally.

'Yes.' No point in beating about the bush.

'It feels intrusive to have an invader in a space that belongs to your family?'

'Of course it does.'

'These feelings are natural but not entirely rational.' He stood against the wire fence on the side of the goat field. One of the kids eyed him with interest, coming closer.

'Not rational?' She'd broken her own rule about never exchanging more than essential words with this man or his kind.

'You're angry that the Germans are protecting your coast against the Allies? But if we weren't here, you'd be exploited by the British and Americans.' The kid stuck its nose through the wire, nibbling at Brandt's shirt.

She gave a sarcastic smile and bit her tongue, deciding not to warn him about what was happening to his shirt.

'And who's to say their forces would behave well?'

'I'm confident they would.' *Careful*, she cautioned herself.

'Are you? Think of what happened at Narvik.'

The Germans had invaded the northern town of Narvik, an iron ore export port the Germans needed for their war effort, in 1940. The British had recaptured it. Fierce battles had raged and the rest of Norway had fallen by the time they left, leaving the port as a smouldering wreck, and its inhabitants punished for helping the British.

'Protecting the coast by dragging your slaves in and working them to death? We hear about what you do to Russians and Serbs, you know.' Too late, she wished the words unsaid. His face darkened.

'I don't work with Russians and Serbs. The work I do is highly technical and my colleagues are fellow professionals, from Germany and Norway. A few from Denmark. All remunerated for their work.'

'Who lugs the stones up to the gun emplacements and bunkers? I hear it's not the Germans.'

'I feel this is a conversation we should leave for another time.' But he looked rattled.

'Do you approve of the exploitation of your prisoners? The beatings? The lack of food?'

'No.' He said it so quietly she almost missed it. 'I hope things will improve for them. As I said, I don't see much of the labour deployments—'

'You mean, slave labour.'

'Anyone I work with is treated well.' He looked her directly in the eye. 'I can assure you of that.'

She shrugged. 'You might want to move away from the fence so the goat can't eat more of your shirt.'

He gave a start, turning to look behind himself. The kid hadn't done much damage, it seemed. 'Luckily, just a button gone,' he said, tickling its nose through the wire. 'Or you and I would have had words.'

'Make sure you fasten the gate behind you when you finish so the rabbits don't get inside.' It felt good to issue the occasional order to the visitor. Just to remind him he wasn't a guest, but someone forced upon the household and nation, just another grey worm. No reason to make him too welcome here. She was no slave labourer, forced to work for him.

'Your chest isn't any better?' she said, observing Pappa across the kitchen table as she came in. He was chopping carrots.

'Just something caught in my throat. Made me feel a little breathless for a moment. Those peas in the vegetable patch are doing well now. Still a few carrots to keep us going, too.'

The deflection made it clear Pappa wasn't going to discuss his health. Perhaps it really had just been a coughing fit brought on by something minor. Or maybe the climate here was too damp for her father. She didn't like to think about the other possibilities. Pappa was a hearty man, always active. Until the last year or so, she couldn't remember him falling ill or seeing a doctor.

They had cousins inland in one of the drier parts of Norway. Ordinarily she'd suggest they pay a visit, help look after the live-stock grazing in the uplands, give Pappa a change of scene. One of his friends would tend the vegetables and animals here in return for the produce. But of course, getting permits for travel might be hard – the Germans were twitchy about people moving inland from the coast, perhaps suspecting them of carrying messages back and forth. Surely health grounds would be considered favourably? Asta made a note to ask Marte. Her friend had become the natural information point for almost everything.

'I don't think I can bear having him around,' she said, words spurting out before she could stop them.

Pappa set down the knife. 'Go back to Oslo. Be with your friends, Asta.'

'They're all dispersed now. Margrit's in Sweden. I haven't heard much from Christa in the last month or so.'

'And Margrit's brother is in a camp, you said.' He sighed. 'We've only got about two and a half thousand Jews in Norway, what possible threat could they be? I had Jewish friends at the Institute in Bergen. Sometimes I've felt a coward, staying out here, not protesting about them being sacked. I wondered about offering them shelter here, thinking it might get them out of sight, out of mind.'

'Not with him here.' She nodded in the direction of the vegetable garden.

He coughed, putting the knife down to cover his mouth. 'Brandt certainly makes it hard to do what we might like to do to oppose the occupation,' he said.


'Wouldn't your lodger put in a word for Petter if the grey worms won't issue him a travel permit?' Marte asked in the morning, when Asta visited the post office.

'I think passes need signing by a German official. Though I've heard of girls who've gone on cycling trips without bothering much.'

'Girls showing off their legs in shorts always have special privileges.' Marte leaned forward on the counter, looking relieved to stop for a chat. 'Put those shorts of yours on and go down to the hotel and find some fat German clerk.' She smiled at Asta's expression. 'But seriously, going to Bergen to see a specialist would probably be approved. The Germans always say we should trust them, they're not enemies.' Her lips twitched.

'I've tried...' Asta stopped. How to explain that she'd tried to anything she could to behave as though the Germans weren't here, having as little to do with them as possible, avoiding places where they congregated, not regarding any of them as human beings, just as grey worms. It had been almost impossible and now, of course, they had their very own occupier in the house. Try as she might to see him as a worm, Max Brandt was very much a living, breathing human being. It made her uncomfortable to acknowledge the fact.

'Oh, we all try acting as though they aren't here. But sometimes to get what you want, you have to just go along with them. Play the game. Hang on for the bigger things.' Marte rolled her eyes. 'Don't look at me like that, Asta. Exploit them where you can. It's called surviving.' Her expression grew darker. 'We live in a little oasis here, really.'

'How are things in Bergen?' Asta asked quietly. They were alone in the post office, but Marte looked around.

'Arrests. More rumours. Some... activity. But groups aren't coordinating. Nothing will change while it's all groups here and there. Being patriotic isn't enough.'

'The sooner they're gone the better.' Asta wished she was brave enough to ask if Marte knew how she could help. Perhaps if she'd taken the job in the hotel, she would have been useful to Milorg. She might have overheard useful snatches of conversation. But she'd turned up her nose at the prospect. And now she had Brandt in the house. Or was that a convenient excuse to sit back and let others risk themselves?

Marte frowned. 'Talking of people you'd rather not see...' She gulped.

Asta groaned. 'Not Magnus again?'

'He came in here earlier on, asking if I'd seen you, if you were all right with the grey worm in your house.'

'I don't know which of them I find more annoying, to be honest. At least I can be rude to Brandt with a good conscience. With Magnus, it feels like being cruel to a puppy.'

Marte laughed. 'Tap him on the nose with a rolled-up newspaper and he'll slink back into his corner. There's no malice in him. He wasn't cooked long enough as a baby, his mother said. Born prematurely,' she added, seeing the confusion on Marte's face.

'I feel sorry for him.' She groaned. 'Then guilty for finding him annoying when we used to spend time with him as children.'

'No need for guilt. He's an odd one, for sure.'

On her way back home, Asta found herself eyeing each shadow, each tree, as if her admirer might be about to spring out. Was there no escape from unwanted males? Spending precious free time outside in this rare sunny weather should have provided a break from anxiety. She cursed Magnus silently for taking away this small pleasure.

When she reached home, Pappa and Brandt were both standing outside the house, pointing up at the roof. 'Definitely needs looking at,' Pappa said. 'Before the next storm. I'll fetch the ladder and have a look now.'

'No.' Brandt shook his head. 'I should go up there, Herr Nilsen, not you. I'm an engineer after all, or would have been, when I'd finished my studies. You can trust me to see what needs doing.'

'Trust an engineer?' Pappa laughed. 'Have you seen the monstrosities some of them inflict on cities?'

'It's like trusting an economist to tell you how much money you can spend each week,' Brandt said. The two of them laughed.

Brandt must have seen the surprise on her face. 'Oh, I can take a joke against myself, you know, Frøken Nilsen.'

'Just as well.' She wanted to say it would be essential if you were a German with a leader as ridiculous as Herr Hitler with his silly moustache and madman's eyes.

'But you don't seem to find me very amusing?'

'The occupation of my country hasn't provided much to cheer me. Deportations? Torture? Imprisonment?'

'Asta...' Pappa began.

'It's all right, Pappa, I'll hold my tongue.' She turned back to Brandt. 'You shouldn't be here, in our house. It's difficult for us. When you help us, it feels even more awkward.'

'It would be better if I didn't help?'

'Better if you weren't in the country at all.' She felt herself turn cold. What had she done, saying these things to him? He might look like a helpful young man, but he was a German, a representative of a cruel, vicious regime. If he took offence and reported her, the consequences could be harsh.

But he nodded. 'I understand.'

She felt herself let out a breath. He hadn't said he disapproved of the atrocities, though, had he? He'd claimed before that he treated everyone he worked with properly.

'I like it here,' he continued. 'I'm trying to do what I can to fit in.'

Hearing him say he liked it here made her feel unsettled. 'How could you fit in? Don't you see that you're not wanted?'

He looked as though he was about to disagree then blinked. 'You should not ask me these questions, Frøken Nilsen.'

'You're right.' She folded her arms. 'Best we limit conversation to essentials.'

'On the other hand, what's the harm in telling you there are things from home I miss very much. Friends. Family. Our house.'

'Your Führer?'

He shrugged. 'I know I'm fortunate to be here, not in Russia or in a U-boat like several of my friends.'

Pappa had been watching them both silently, a look of concern mixed with curiosity on his face. 'You two finished? If you're too busy debating, I'll fetch the ladder and climb up to look at the roof myself.'

'No.' They both responded in unison and looked at one another awkwardly.

'I'm not a doddery old idiot.' He sounded exasperated. 'I can still do jobs around the place.'

'I believe you have a heart condition, sir.' Brandt said it gently.

'And your medical qualifications are what, exactly?' Pappa sounded casual but Asta could see his jaw setting, just like Arne's before Arne landed a blow. Pappa wouldn't do that, but he might say something he'd regret.

Brandt seemed to hesitate a moment before continuing. 'You remind me of someone.'

'I do? Someone in particular, young man?'

'My mother, the blue around your lips, the breathlessness, before she saw a doctor and started medication.'

Pappa's face softened.

'If I took your pulse, I imagine it would be fast.'

'You are certainly not taking my pulse, Brandt.'

'Fair enough, as you say, I'm no physician. You should see a doctor, perhaps in Bergen. Or I could ask our medic—'

'Who do you think you are?' Pappa was suddenly fuming. 'Interfering in personal medical matters?'

Max Brandt looked down. 'It's natural you're angry,' he said quietly.

'Stop telling us what is natural or normal. Nothing has been either natural or normal since you Germans occupied Norway.'

'I know. None of us chose this situation. I apologise for over-stepping the mark.' He nodded and walked off towards the track leading up the mountain. At least he had the sensitivity to remove himself from Pappa and not continue the conversation.

'All the same, Pappa,' she said, putting a hand on his arm. 'He has a point. You probably should sit down for a moment.'

'It's a warm day, that's all.' He gave a resigned sigh, glared at her and went inside.

Brandt hadn't walked far up the track. He'd gone to the barn and returned with the ladder. 'If you hold the bottom, I can climb up there and have a quick look.' He patted his pocket. 'I found the hammer and nails. It will take minutes and as your father's so angry with me anyway, it won't make much differ-ence if I carry on. At least we'll know what's going on with the roof.'

She found herself wanting to apologise for her father and felt anger herself. Why should they feel guilt? This situation wasn't of their making. Unlike the Germans, Norwegians hadn't elected a madman in 1933 and then smashed their way into other people's countries. It wasn't of Brandt's making, either, a voice inside her told Asta – he'd have been a child when Hitler was elected. Throughout his formative years, he'd been strictly monitored by the state, his schooling and pastimes proscribed. She clutched the ladder tightly as he climbed, unsure whether she was clinging to it to support herself or to keep him steady. 'It doesn't look too bad,' he called down. 'A few nails is all that's needed and I have them in my pocket.'

'I can imagine my own father in the same circumstances,' he said, when he'd climbed down. 'It's hard having others do things you've always done yourself for your family.'

'Pappa's always been stubborn,' she said. 'Thinks he's still a young man. Wants to do everything himself. Self done is well done, he always says.'

A scintilla of understanding sparked between them. Then she remembered who Max Brandt was and turned her back on him.

A truce fell on the house for the rest of the week, Pappa regaining his normal cheerful composure as days passed. He offered Brandt a glass of his beer one evening. If Brandt was surprised by the gesture, he hid it well. The next day, Brandt brought a bar of chocolate for Asta, dismissing her gruff thanks with a wave of the hand. 'It's just what we have in our rations, not like the chocolate we had at home before the war. We used...'

A faraway look came over his face. She was about to ask him to continue but stopped herself. She didn't want to know anything about him that would make him seem even more of a human being, a boy not so very different from her own brother or the students she'd laughed and flirted with in Oslo.

'Norwegian chocolate has a very good reputation.' He gave one of his curt nods and went upstairs before she gave an equally curt nod in reply. She knew he liked to read at Arne's desk in his free time if the weather wasn't good. At first it had irked her to think of him invading even more of her brother's space, but it was better than having him read downstairs with the two of them. The rain was lashing down this evening, so he mightn't want a stroll.

Asta unwrapped her bar of chocolate. It mightn't have been the rich and creamy chocolate she too remembered from just a year or so ago, but the hit of cocoa, sugar and fat in her mouth almost made her weep. It was all she could do not to eat the entire bar, but to put some aside for Pappa. How often

Mamma had pulled out a bar of sweet, creamy *Melkesjokolade* as they took a break on a cross-country hike or ski. Asta felt the weight of her loss – Mamma and Arne, both absent, both missed – fall on her shoulders yet again as the last taste of the German chocolate became a memory. Hurriedly she folded the wrapper around the bar. Memories should stay neatly tucked away in their place, too, so they didn't take you unawares.

'I ate the chocolate,' she said the next morning, trying to make it sound less like a thank you and more of a statement of fact.

'I noticed you saved some for your father.'

She'd put the half-eaten bar on a plate. Only after wrestling with the part of herself that wanted to hide it away for herself.

'There's nothing you don't notice, is there? It's like having a watchman in the house.'

'A watchman?'

'Just a throwaway remark.'

Max Brandt looked confused. 'You think I'm an informant? I don't do... that. That's the Gestapo, not ordinary people like me.'

'I didn't mean you were literally spying on us.' Though how could she tell? People informed on one another, Norwegians on Norwegians, sometimes. The traitor Quisling, who'd welcomed the Germans and been happy to run the country for them, had found plenty of people to help him.

'I don't think I would be a very good spy or informant.' He said it very matter-of-factly.

'So you're not going to let them know down in the village that I've despatched a battalion of German soldiers?' She regretted the silly words as soon as they fell out of her lips. This man seemed to bring out something ridiculous in her. It was as though she wanted to taunt him until he responded and proved himself to be what she secretly accused him of being: a typical Nazi bully.

'For a start, you haven't the guns to do that. Even if you did, there are no signs of burials around here. So you'd have to take the bodies up the mountain to bury, and, well, you don't have the fuel.' He scrutinised her face.

She couldn't resist the laugh. It came as a shock to her, almost frightening. Asta felt her chest muscles moving for the first time like this in months, probably years.

'*Ach*, it's amusing to act along.'

'Yes, I was being foolish, just seeing...' She paused, shaking her head.

'Whether I really do have a sense of humour.' He shifted his weight from one foot to the other. 'All the same, you should be careful making jokes like that.'

'Indeed I should. Especially to the occupier.'

His face pinkened. Asta told herself off. She'd gone too far. Again. Refusing to play nice with the Germans was one thing. Provoking them was something else. It was folly. She felt suddenly vulnerable. Until very recently she'd thought of Pappa as a still vigorous man, not that she needed protection from anyone. When Magnus appeared, hinting that she needed him to keep an eye on her, it needled her. All the same, she and Pappa lived alone up here with Brandt. If, for whatever reason, he decided they were acting suspiciously, he could make their lives difficult.

'What kind of person do you think I am?' he asked.

'Well, you're here with the occupying force, so it doesn't really matter who you are.'

'I think it does.'

'The German occupying force has behaved well to Norwegians.'

'Other than to those it's rounded up or tortured, like the Jews, for instance.'

'That's the Gestapo.'

'Ah.' She nodded. 'Of course. Nothing to do with you.'

'No.'

'So you don't approve of what they do?' She folded her arms, looking at him.

'I have no power to approve or not. And it's not just the Gestapo you need to watch out for,' he said quietly.

She frowned.

'Not all Norwegians oppose us, Asta. The NS is popular among some of your countrymen.' The NS was the Norwegian Nazi party.

She gave a half grunt.

'They see merit in the things the Germans are doing.'

'Remind me of all the worthwhile projects you've worked on for our benefit since you invaded?' She thought of the people rounded up, Jews, opponents, sent who-knew-where, often executed without anything resembling a trial. The slave labourers working on the coastal defences.

'Today I will be reviewing plans for strengthening the little bridge over the stream a kilometre north of the post office,' Brandt said. 'I don't just work on fortifications. Bridges fascinate me, actually.'

For as long as Asta could remember, people had been fretting about that bridge, claiming it would wash away in the next bad storm, meaning a long drive around to cross the stream higher up.

'No slaves working on the bridge?'

'Just Germans and some locals. Who seem happy enough to take the extra rations. One of the men in the village positively begs us to take him on, but we can't find anything for him to do.'

Magnus. Could she toss back the argument that German troop movements had probably weakened the bridge? She'd never noticed much more than one of their motorcyclists driving over it for months. It was only eight in the morning but already she felt weary of the constant need to bat arguments back and forth with Max Brandt.

She turned her back to him and stacked breakfast plates. They needed water from the pump. If any other houseguest stood in the kitchen she would have asked if they could fill the pail for her. Before the war, Pappa had talked of piping in water to the house, reducing the amount of effort it took to carry out household tasks.

'Talking of non-military projects, I don't specialise in wood-burning stoves, but I believe the stove in the other room is incorrectly installed,' Max said. 'I'll have a word with your father.'

'It burns very well enough.'

'I don't think the flue is drawing properly.' Brandt was picking up the iron pail. 'It will only take me a few minutes to bring in water. You should have filled it up last night, really.' Perhaps he noticed her shoulders stiffening. He added, 'You were busy. I know how much you have to do in the house and outside.'

'*Takk.*' She couldn't remember having actually uttered a thanks to him before. At best, she'd given him a sullen nod. Asta sensed a line being crossed. It made her angry to think that she'd softened towards him. She banged the plates together so hard that the stray cat dozing in a patch of sunlight outside started and jumped away.

# FOUR

As summer progressed, Asta and Max Brandt formed an uneasy truce. 'It could be worse,' she admitted to Marte, as they hiked up the track to the top of the mountain while taking one of their favourite walks. 'If we must have one of them in the house, I suppose he's not the worst. Straightforward enough. And generous with his rations.'

'He seems to help your father quite a bit?'

'I have to admit he's good that way.' She flicked a stray hair out of her eyes. 'He's even been advising Pappa on how to refit the stove flue, but we can't get the spare part for now. And he has an idea for piping water into the kitchen. But again, getting the pipe is another issue.'

'He did a good job on the bridge, apparently.'

'I heard. At least...'

'What?'

'He doesn't seem to have much to do with the defences at the moment. He's working on some improvements to the barracks at the moment. I don't have to look at him in the evenings and wonder if he's witnessed those poor men from eastern Europe and Russia being starved and punished.'

'Some of them escape,' Marte said. 'People give them food.' People? Did that mean Marte herself. She looked down when Asta stared at her, clearly unwilling to say more.

'Well, at least the farm wagons won't end up in the stream when the autumn storms come and the water rises.' Asta shivered, even though the sun felt warm enough and they were walking briskly up the steep track. Summer felt so sweet but lasted for so little time.

Already the late-afternoon air held a nip of the turning season, even though it was still only the third week of August. Asta felt restless. Autumn meant studying, lectures, stretching your mind, feeling yourself relish the intellectual challenge. Yet here she was, facing yet another winter in such a small settlement. The waters of the fjord, changing by the moment, always captivating, wouldn't be enough to feed her curiosity about the world. Nor would the white beauty of the mountains, seen from her skis, be enough to enchant her. She couldn't leave Pappa alone here. She cast around for solutions. They had cousins inland, she recalled. Could one of them be persuaded to make the journey to the coast to help out? It had always been the way in rural Norway that extended family would travel to assist at times of childbirth, illness or death. The cousins had written, extending condolences, offering help at the time of Mamma's death. But would they regard Asta abandoning her father for her studies as a selfish act? And what would they feel about taking on the role of housekeeper to Max Brandt?

She must have groaned aloud. Marte looked at her, head tilted. 'It's not so bad, is it? The soldiers leave us alone.'

'They regard Norwegians as a fount of good genes, that's why. Members of the Aryan super race. Not like the Poles or Russians.'

A girl in the next village had already taken up the offer of food and clothes in return for reproducing and had herself impregnated by an SS officer.

'Like Liv, living in comfort in that hotel up in the mountains for the last months of her pregnancy.' Asta looked at Marte. 'Liv's pretty but not like you.'

'I don't have those requisite blue eyes and golden hair. I'm actually grateful. And I'm not going to prove myself fertile by sleeping with a grey worm.'

'I'm sure they like auburn hair, too, Marte. You wouldn't be tempted, not even for proper coffee and a decent butter ration?'

'Not even for that. Let's not spoil the walk thinking about slaves and women who sleep with occupiers.' Marte stopped, hands on hips. 'I need a moment. I always forget how steep this is.'

'Worth it, though.' Beneath them, the fjord rippled and glistened, the clouds changing its colours by the second. The sun burst through and lit up the scene. Both girls let out a gasp of delight, smiling at one another. 'Nobody can take this from us,' Asta said fiercely. 'This is the true Norway, and it doesn't belong to the Germans.'

'You'd miss it if you went back to Oslo, Asta.'

'I'm not even sure they'd let me go back there. I might be a spy with information about enemy shipping, passing it on.' She remembered Brandt's warning about saying things in jest. 'Just a joke, you know.'

'No need to tell me that. But you're right to be cautious. Enough Quisling supporters around, even here.'

The Quisling supporters thought that the collaborator prime minister held sound views. Some of them had supported *Nasjonal Samling,* his version of National Socialism from the years before the war.

'It's not just pro-Quislings. People inform on their friends and neighbours for all kinds of reasons,' Marte added. 'Sometimes they're scared. But some just want special treatment.' Her face hardened. 'There's a woman from further up the valley who had a huge box of what looked like chocolate and pastries sent up by ferry from Bergen last week. The box had split and I had to tie it up with string.' She shrugged. 'Perhaps there's a good reason someone sent her those things.'

Asta thought guiltily of the stockings Christa had sent her from Oslo. It reminded her of the pamphlet Christa had enclosed. If the parcel had split in transit or someone had opened it, both of them would have been in trouble.

Around here, everyone knew a lot about one another. Would life be freer in Oslo, with more people around to give you a cloud of anonymity, less of a sense of everyone knowing your business?

Marte peered intently at her, as if there was more she could say. Was she actively working for the resistance? Asta wondered again. She knew the skippers of the mail boats, the fishing boats, the farmers who came down from the mountains. All these people brought intelligence, warnings, rumours with them.

'I wish I could do more for my country,' Asta said quietly.

'You have Brandt living with you. Sometimes I'm glad for my little house with just that one tiny second bedroom you could barely squeeze a child into. No German would want to sleep in there.' She pulled out her cigarettes and lit two for them. Asta wanted to ask if Marta had heard more from the post-boat and the fishermen about what was happening in Bergen. Was the resistance developing into something more cohesive? What was the news from the wider world?

'And what of your admirer, Asta?' Marte spoke before she could ask, passing a lit cigarette to Asta.

'Magnus? He's not been around as much. I wondered if he'd gone inland, to help with livestock up in the pastures.'

'I've seen him in the village often enough. Your German must be keeping him at bay.'

Asta felt an unaccountable rush of gratitude towards Max Brandt.

Marte's attention was drawn by something else. She pointed. 'The golden eagle's back again, look.'

They watched the bird until it vanished, gliding on its wide wingspan, unbothered by the doings of the humans below.

They finished the walk on a lighter note, joking about the Germans and their mangling of Norwegian words and their failure to appreciate the local sense of humour. 'Does your lodger enjoy our local jokes?' Marte asked.

'He's not immune to humour.' Asta sighed. 'And he's polite and appreciative. I just never imagined I'd end up as a house-maid to any male, let alone a German.'

'Ah, listen to yourself. Too good to do housework, are you, Asta Nilsen?' Marte was firmly in the mould of the traditional woman of the fjords, practical and hardworking, scornful of anyone who wasn't just the same.

Asta laughed. 'I avoided it when we were growing up. I always preferred reading or going for walks. I wouldn't even let poor Mamma teach me to spin. And she despaired of my knitting and sewing.' Talking about her mother was both a pleasure and a sorrow. It hurt to let her go unmentioned, as though she was now tidied away in the past. Only last night she'd nearly dropped one of the hand-painted bowls her mother had bought from a pottery just before the war. She'd heard Mamma's exclamation and uttered an apology aloud before reminding herself that she was alone in the kitchen, Brandt and her father both out working, her mother gone.

'You miss your mother, of course you do.' Marte said it as a statement. 'When things are difficult, I pine for my father. He would have known how to turn the Germans into a big, fat joke. And he always had good advice.'

Marte's father had been in Bergen during the bombardment by the Germans at the time of the invasion two years earlier. He'd only been in the town to visit his bank manager, delaying the trip a week because of a sick cow he wanted to watch over.

The randomness of his death felt so harsh. 'Just bad luck,' Marte had said at the time of his death. 'The joke was on him, he'd tell me.'

The houses came into view. 'Your hardworking lodger's not working on the smallholding today?' Marte shook her head. 'I fantasise about making them muck out the pigsty.' Her face took on a harder expression for a moment. 'Perhaps one day, that'll be what they're forced to do as a punishment for their war crimes.'

'War crimes? More than slave labour and arrests?'

Marte looked sideways. 'It's just rumours, from Sweden, passed on by word of mouth.'

'What rumours?'

'From Poland and the countries to the east of there. Mass shootings of civilians. And some say the Germans are experimenting with other ways of killing large numbers of people. They want more efficiency.'

'Efficiency?' Something about the word was so cold. Asta shuddered.

'There are always rumours about the enemy in times of war. Some people say it's just hearsay. But there's whispering that the Nazis are planning something truly awful.' Marta sighed. 'I hear things from the ferry skippers and the fishermen. And sometimes I wish I didn't hear them, Asta.'

Asta wrestled with herself, half wanting to know what was being said, half wishing to remain in ignorance.

The village below them came closer into focus, the houses and little church, mostly white-painted buildings, broken up occasionally with red, wooden houses like the Nilsens' home, arranged like a children's toy set, so bright and innocent. Asta never tired of looking at this view, even though nowadays it was like a beautiful prison as well as a refuge.

She waved goodbye to Marte at the spot where the track

continued down to the village and found her father picking blackcurrants inside the fruit nets.

'Looks like a good year,' he called. 'If we can get hold of more sugar, we should be set up for the winter.'

'A big if.'

'Max thinks he can help.'

'He's Max now, is he?'

Her father shrugged. 'Hard not to call him that. He's got the afternoon off work and he's gone down to persuade a colleague to exchange tobacco for the sugar we need.'

Asta counted slowly under her breath. Max Brandt was making himself far too at home here.

'I know you find having him here difficult, Asta. I wish I could make it easier for you.'

Pappa's eyes, gentle, warm, rested on hers. She felt a pang of guilt. She was making things harder than they needed to be. And if she was honest, part of her hostility was caused by the fact that she didn't find the lodger unpleasant. Not anymore. When she heard about German arrests, murders, torture, her stomach turned, but she couldn't object to Max as a person, only as their representative.

'It's hard,' Pappa said. 'If he was a typical strutting Nazi stereotype, we could just hate him.'

Asta nodded.

'But he actually reminds me of my students and that makes me irritable because how can a German, a citizen of that terrible state, be anything like that?' Pappa wiped his brow on a handkerchief. 'It's a warmer day than I thought.' His eyes opened in surprise. 'Magnus? What are you doing up here?'

The man was coming from behind Asta. He must have been lurking in the trees. She tried not to shiver, picturing his eyes on their backs as they chatted and laughed. Why wouldn't he leave her alone? She'd never encouraged him, treating him only in the same friendly way she had all their neighbours.

'Do you need my help, Petter Halvorsen?' Yet again, the insistence on using the patronymic, as if it made someone more Norwegian. Everyone knew that Pappa was Petter Nilsen, Professor Nilsen, to be exact. Not that Pappa stood on ceremony. He'd never been given his father's first name, Halvor, as his family surname.

'I can manage with my daughter's help, Magnus, *takk.*' Pappa nodded at Magnus. 'How are things with you? Your mother's doing well?'

'She misses my brother who went off to fight. I do what I can for her.' Magnus's eyes went to Asta. 'Would you like me to bring down some cloudberries for you? I've picked pounds and pounds this year.'

She was going to say that she was planning her own expedition to pick cloudberries, but perhaps letting him do her a small favour would be a good idea? Or would it just encourage him?

'We're running out of jars and sugar,' Pappa said, coming to her rescue. 'So *nei takk* for now, Magnus.'

He didn't seem to mind Pappa's intervention but stared at him. 'You are very hot, Petter Halv— Nilsen?'

'I do feel warm, yes.' Pappa ran a sleeve across his brow. 'It's a humid day.'

'You need something to drink, Pappa. Let's go inside.' She wished Magnus a polite goodbye and took her father's arm, leading him inside to the kitchen. 'I told you not to overdo it.'

She poured them both water from the jug. Pappa sat down and reached for his thick jumper and put it on. 'You can't be feeling cold?' She frowned at him. 'You were just so hot a moment ago!'

'It's strange.' He shivered and took a long draught of the water. 'My legs don't behave as they did when I was younger. They ache a bit. I'm becoming a doddery old man, Asta.' He laughed, but his voice was shaky.

He was only fifty-two, hardly old. She felt his brow. 'You

say you're cold but you're burning to the touch. Pappa, I think you should lie down.'

'Lie down? In daylight? Like an invalid? What utter nonsense, child.'

The door catch rattled. Brandt was back, carrying a brown paper parcel. Sugar for the blackcurrant jam, perhaps. He looked at Pappa and then at Asta. 'You seem to have a fever. Apparently, several in the barracks have taken sick, influenza, they think.'

'Too early in the year for influenza,' Pappa said, his teeth chattering so much his words were hardly audible.

'That's what the doctor said: it's come very early in the season, when most are still spending so much time outdoors, but you remember that film last week? Everyone crammed in. They think the illness spread among the audience.'

Neither Asta nor Pappa had gone to the film-screening, but Pappa had seen his friends as usual this week. One of them had perhaps been in the packed audience.

'The medical advice is to go to bed, drink fluids and maintain a warm, yet well-ventilated bedroom,' Max said.

'Go to bed? Rubbish. Asta, is there still aspirin in your mother's emergency tin? All I need is a few of those and I'll be just fine.' Asta cursed herself. She'd meant to check on supplies last week. Fortunately, the bottle still yielded half a dozen pills. It wouldn't last long. Would Marte have any? Or the local doctor?

She gave a couple of pills to Pappa and tried to remember what else her mother did when one of them was unwell. 'Hot tea,' she said, getting up to put the kettle on to boil. Mamma had made a concoction out of wildflowers and herbs, drying the plants and then storing them in a jar. Her father watched her take the jar out of the cupboard. 'Not that awful tea,' he groaned. 'Do you want to finish me off, Asta?'

'It's what Mamma made us drink when we were shivery and achy.'

He attempted a rasping laugh. 'I used to tell her she'd kill us before the sickness did.'

'Go to bed, Pappa, I'll bring it up to you.'

Max stood up. 'Let me help you upstairs.'

Pappa looked as though he wanted to protest, then nodded, allowing Max to take his arm. When Max came back downstairs, he was frowning. 'Several of our soldiers and workers have been ill for a week, a few almost two. It's lucky you don't have too many livestock to care for, Asta. I fear your father's not going to be doing much for several days at least.'

Just the goats, a single cow and half a dozen chickens. 'It's really just the harvesting of fruit and vegetables that's time consuming at the moment.' She smiled drily. 'This smallholding used to be a hobby. We didn't worry too much about growing as much as it was capable of producing. My parents felt guilty at times that we didn't get the most from of it. They even talked about renting out land. Since the war Pappa has planted more and more each year to help with the rationing.'

She looked out of the window, where the rows of beans and soft fruit seemed to taunt her. The pig was promised to a man up the valley, who'd slaughter it in return for a share of the meat. How had Pappa planned to get the pig up there? Probably by setting up a complicated arrangement based on mutual favours. She'd have to ask him what to do. Her English and French novels sat on the table, teasing her. No more reading in her spare time. Mamma's spinning wheel would gather more dust, as would the knitting needles.

Max took the kettle off the range. She hadn't noticed it boiling, distracted by the prospect of so many responsibilities. 'We should let this brew for three or four minutes, that's what my mother does at home.' He found an enamel mug hanging over the sink. She nodded. Max grinned.

'What?'

'I'm suggesting something and you're agreeing without argument.'

'And that surprises you?'

'Sorry, you're understandably worried about your father. I would be the same. Would it reassure you to know the men in the barracks are recovering well.'

She was about to snap back at him, saying they'd be younger and have better food, before she reminded herself that she and Pappa hadn't been eating too badly at all in the last months, thanks to Max's supplies.

'It will be all right, Asta.'

'His heart.' She blurted out the words. 'The strain of an infection, it might...'

Better not to say the words.

'Your father's heart has got him this far and I'm sure there's enough of the vigorous Viking in him to keep it going now. Don't seek out trouble before it comes knocking on your door, Asta.'

It sounded like a repeat of something his parents might have told him as a child. 'Tell me about your mother and father.' She hadn't asked questions before and he seemed surprised but not displeased.

'My father's a chemist working on industrial processes at the steel works near our home in Brandenburg.' He poured the tea. 'My mother used to be a teacher but has been at home for... for some years.'

Since the Nazis had changed the school curriculum? Or because mothers weren't allowed to teach after marriage, as was often the case in Norway? She didn't like to ask. She might be assuming too much about Max's family. They mightn't share their son's seemingly detached view of the Reich.

'You mentioned a sister?'

'Clara was a schoolkid when I left. A bit of a dreamer, likes music and reading. Her other main interest was teasing me.' He rolled his eyes.

'I like the sound of Clara.' Asta remembered how she'd gone through a stage of tormenting Arne, provoking him into outbursts when their parents weren't looking, and then putting on an innocent face. She couldn't usually fool her mother.

'She'll be finding home very dull without me to torment.'

'I'm sure you gave as good as you got.'

He grinned, looking years younger. 'That's my job as her older brother.' Then he looked more serious. 'But I worry about her, all the same.'

'Have they conscripted Clara? Do women serve as auxiliaries in German forces?'

'Military service is only voluntary and she's too young. But Clara...'

'Clara what?'

'Marches to her own drum.' He grimaced. 'Or more accurately, doesn't march. Likes her own company, has her own views.'

'And that's bad? I'm guessing it doesn't meet with approval to be like that in Germany?'

He looked at his watch and removed the tea strainer from the enamel mug, sniffing the contents. 'Smells better than it looks. Let's hope it makes your father more comfortable.'

She took the mug from him, breathing in the aroma of past summers, of her mother in holiday mode. Juniper? Lingonberry? She ought to have paid more attention to Mamma when she'd explained what she was picking when they stayed here, and why. Asta had always imagined there'd be more time, and gathering herbs and berries wasn't as much fun as going out in the boat or cycling.

'There were so many things I needed to teach you, Asta,' Mamma had whispered a few days before she died. 'I always thought there'd be time. I'm leaving you so unprepared for life.'

You only knew what you'd lost when it came too late. She'd been such a self-centred, immature girl at the beginning of the war. So keen not to miss out on anything. Even when they'd come out here for Mamma's last holiday in April 1940, Asta had felt a pang that she was missing the fun she and her student friends had planned as the days lengthened and warmed. Even the occupation hadn't seemed an impediment to their enjoyment of spring and summer.

She wouldn't allow her father to succumb to illness. Max's expression showed he understood everything she feared. 'It will be all right,' he said. 'We'll get him through this, Asta. I'll come home every lunchtime this week, more often, if I can.'

She nodded, reassured because Max Brandt was here in the house and would help her. Admitting she couldn't manage alone had seemed such an admission of weakness, but he made his offer of help feel so natural.

# FIVE

Petter Nilsen's fever reached its peak four days later. He'd seemed to rally briefly in the morning, even insisting on getting up for a short time to wash and change his clothes, talking about coming downstairs for a few hours, before Asta herded him back to bed. To her relief, there'd seemed no need to call for a doctor for what just seemed like a regular case of influenza running its course. That night she woke to hear him talking loudly. She almost bumped into Brandt on the landing, holding an oil lamp. 'Your father's hallucinating,' he said, matter-of-factly. 'We must get his temperature down, Asta. Otherwise he may have fits.'

He followed her into her father's room. Her heart sank when she saw Petter, skin white but with hectic red cheeks, sweat falling off his brow. 'He needs the doctor,' she said, feeling panicked. She tried to persuade Petter to drink a little water and take the last aspirin in the bottle. Mamma had used willow bark herb for fevers, she remembered. Perhaps some remained in a jar downstairs. She could only recall it being used for minor aches and pains. Max poured water into the basin and wrung out a muslin cloth, wiping Pappa's brow gently. He shook his head.

'I think this is beyond us. I'm going down to fetch the doctor.' He made for the stairs.

She opened her mouth to tell him she'd be the one to cycle down to the town for speed, but her father's appearance shocked her. She couldn't leave him, not even for the half an hour or forty minutes the return trip would take. 'Take the bicycle,' she called. 'It will be quicker.'

An hour passed. Asta wiped her father's brow and found the willow bark. She brewed tea but couldn't persuade her father to sip it. He groaned, shaking his head. Where was Brandt? A motorbike engine purred outside. Asta looked out to see him sitting pillion behind a figure she didn't recognise. The two men came inside. It wasn't their usual doctor, but a German.

'Your own local doctor is out on a call at a farm and isn't expected back for a few hours,' Max said, knocking on the bedroom door. 'This is Doctor Friedrich Klein, one of our medics.'

'Field wounds are more my speciality,' Klein said in German, obviously aware she could speak it. 'But I've treated a variety of ailments since I came to Norway. May I?'

She stepped back from the bed, to where she'd moved protectively to stand by her father, who still moaned. He took out a stethoscope and checked Petter's heartbeat. 'I can hear something here.'

'Pappa has a suspected heart weakness.'

'Suspected? He hasn't had it investigated?'

'My mother was dying and then the occupation happened before we could make it back to Bergen.'

A flash of something like sympathy passed over Klein's otherwise stern features. 'There's nothing much I can do apart from prescribe what I have in my surgery at headquarters. Brandt here can collect it tomorrow. In the meantime, I'll bring the fever down a bit. Usually I'd let it run, as the temperature can kill the infection. But we want to relieve the strain on the heart.'

'Pappa always seemed so fit and hearty.'

'Sometimes the fit and hearty ones respond too vigorously to a viral infection. After the last great war, it was the young who suffered most from the influenza. But I'd cautiously say that if he doesn't get any worse in the next few hours, he'll recover.'

Asta nodded. 'It's good of you to come up here, *Herr Doktor*,' she said, finding she actually meant the words.

'We live here, in this community. And we have a duty to curtail civilian infections that might compromise our troops,' the doctor said, fastening his bag. It was the soldiers who'd first gone down with the influenza, but gratitude to the doctor made Asta hold back the words.

'*Vielen Dank*,' she said again, at the door.

'You should sleep, Asta,' Brandt said gently, as she came back upstairs. 'Let me sit with your father for a while.'

'You have to be at work. I can sleep during the day when he's calmer.'

He looked as though he wanted to argue, but nodded, with a last glance at Petter.

Petter Nilsen's fever broke just before dawn. Asta had dozed off in the armchair beside his bed and woke to hear him whisper her name in a hoarse voice. He smiled at her, too weak to say very much, but desperate for water. 'Let me make you a bowl of porridge or soup, Pappa.'

He shook his head. 'Just help me out of bed so I can wash and change. I don't need you to help with that.' She noticed how much weight he'd lost in the five days of his fever: his arms and shoulders looked thin. He'd need to eat a good diet to regain the lost weight. No hope of that happening, even with Max Brandt's ration supplements.

When she returned, Pappa asked about the animals, seeming concerned. 'Don't worry, Pappa. I will manage them.'

'...Brandt?'

'He's been helping. He brought their doctor up here, too.'

'Think he's... a good man.'

Asta nodded. 'Yes, I think he could be worse.' They exchanged guilty smiles, as if saying something positive about an occupier counted as treason. 'But then I think about all the terrible things his country has done.'

'And you wonder what he thinks about them?' Pappa smiled, too weak to say more.

She almost fell into her own room and crashed out on top of the bed. Sleep claimed her almost immediately.

When she woke, the sun shining through the window onto her face told her morning was almost gone. The chickens. The cow. Someone knocked on her door. She propped herself up on her shoulders.

'It's me, Max. I've done everything outside. The animals are all taken care of. There's coffee in the pot and I brought you up bread from the mess. I'm going back to work now.'

'My father?' She rubbed her eyes.

'I looked in on him and he managed a small piece of bread and honey. He seems better.'

He'd made breakfast for her father. 'Could... could you come in, please?'

The door opened slowly.

'I wanted to thank you, Max.' She used his name for the first time, feeling the change this marked. 'You didn't have to do all these things for us.'

He gave a shy smile. 'Sometimes it's good to behave as we would do outside war and occupation. If my father was ill I'd want to help.'

'I just want to forget about the occupation.' She sounded like a petulant child. Kindness seemed to come naturally to Max Brandt in a way it didn't to Asta.

'Perhaps we can.' He took at a step into the room. 'Up here, with you and your father, it's as if we're outside the war.'

'Yes.'

'Let's try to exist in this other world, then,' he said. 'For as long as we can.'

No doubt it was foolish – they couldn't pretend the war, the occupation, hadn't happened. But it would make it easier, she reasoned, to regard Max as just a houseguest; helpful, sometimes in the way, but not a bad sort.

'In the meantime, you should eat your breakfast, because the beans really do need picking.' He looked abashed. 'Does that make me sound as if I'm giving you orders again?'

'Yes.'

'But you're not angry about it, Asta?' He gave her a teasing smile.

'I'm too tired to be angry. And you are in credit at the bank of my good will. For today, at least.'

He guffawed. 'I won't waste my credit.' He closed the door quietly behind himself.

Asta's tiredness left her as she worked outside, harvesting beans and spinach, pulling out radishes and the last of the lettuces. The pig needed to go up the valley to be slaughtered at a local farm, she remembered. She found her father sitting up in the chair in his bedroom, pulling on his socks. 'I need fresh air.'

'You need to rest, Pappa. How are you going to get up the stairs if you feel faint again?'

'Being outside will do me good.'

It seemed far too early for him to be moving around like this, but the set of his jaw told her that he would bat away objections, so she walked down the wooden steps with him. He slumped into a chair in the kitchen. 'Just need a moment.' With effort, he stood up and headed slowly out of the door. 'You managed the animals?' He looked out at the chickens scratching around in the yard. 'I was worried. It's so much for one person, looking after me and everything here.'

'Max came back up at lunchtimes and helped me.' She bit her lip at the use of that name but Pappa didn't seem to notice.

'I knew he would. Asta, the pig...'

'Needs to go up to be slaughtered, yes.'

'If you go down to the post office, Marte will pass the message on to the man who'll drive him up for us in return for some of the meat.' He turned back to the house.

Max had brought her bicycle back up from the village for her. As she cycled down, the breeze blew over her face like a tonic, washing away the sickroom and the lack of sleep. Marte stood behind the counter. 'Haven't seen you for a while.' She frowned at Asta. 'Everything all right? I heard Petter had influenza.'

Asta told her about the panic her father's illness had caused.

'I'm glad he's better. It's a lot for you to manage with him out of action.'

'Max helped.'

'Max now, is it?' But Marte's eyes weren't unkind.

'He's been helpful. More than helpful, really.'

Marte laughed. 'I can see how much it costs you to admit it of a grey worm.' The bell rang on the door. 'Oh, Magnus.'

Asta's shoulders tensed at mention of the name.

'I heard that influenza had stricken Petter. I'll come up to your smallholding to take your pig to slaughter, Asta.'

'Oh.' She swallowed. 'Good of you, Magnus, but I've already made arrangements.' She looked desperately at Marte.

'I've found someone to help Petter and Asta.' Marte smiled at Magnus. 'Kind of you to offer, though.'

Magnus stared at Marte, who folded her arms, challenging him to question her.

'I see.' He turned and left the post office.

The two of them looked at one another. 'I need to be blunter to make him understand when his help isn't wanted,' Asta said. 'Sorry to drag you into it, Marte.'

Marte shook her head. 'Don't worry about me.' She leaned forward, her voice taking on a more intense tone. 'Asta, your German lodger works on the fortifications. Does he...'

'Does he what?'

The door opened again. Another customer. Marte looked as if she wanted to say more but then smiled. 'I think you should go and put your feet up for an hour or so, Asta. I really will sort out the pig for you.'


The following day wasn't a work day for Max. The trailer arrived for the pig and he helped her load the pig into it. The driver acknowledged his help with a nod. Not all the locals hated all the Germans, Asta reflected, as she watched the pig vanish up the track, its eyes watching her solemnly from the trailer.

'I feel bad even though I know we gave him a good life,' she said. 'How silly is that, when millions of people are short of food?'

'It's never silly to feel empathy for another living creature.'

She looked at him.

'Oh, I forgot. I'm not supposed to have finer feelings.' Max rolled his eyes. 'Because I'm a German.'

'Some of your countrymen seem to repress their more sensitive side. Which is strange when you think of all that great German music and poetry, all that feeling for mankind.'

'We still have those feelings.' He paused. 'Many of us.'

'Then why? Why Hitler?'

'Some of the people of my parents' generation had harsh memories of life in Germany after the last war, when the Allies blockaded our ports and people starved in the streets. And then again, the years of the great inflation were harsh. Militia were clashing on the streets. My parents thought there might even be a civil war. Hitler put an end to the chaos, that's what older people say.'

'That's no excuse.' She spoke without fear now but warned herself to be careful. Max was bound to his country.

He smiled at her.

'What?'

'You remind me of someone.'

'A woman? Your sister?'

'No, not Clara. A friend at officer training.' The smile turned solemn, his eyes clouded.

'What happened in training, Max? I've never liked to ask about your injury.'

He flexed the remaining fingers and thumb. She'd made a mistake. He was going to clam up, tell her to mind her own business. She was starting to apologise when he put up a hand, stopping her. 'Nobody is supposed to ask and I'm supposed to forget about how it happened.' Max gave a droll laugh. 'As if I could. Just say it was an accident, if pressed, they told me. Accidents aren't uncommon at training.'

'So it wasn't an accident?' She frowned. 'It was done deliberately?'

He looked away.

'It's all right. You don't have to tell me.' She touched his arm gently and moved away to the pump, filling a water bowl for the chickens.

'I haven't even told my family what happened.'

Asta waited, not looking at him.

'I didn't want to go for military training. I was happy doing my engineering degree. I hadn't minded the camps at school, the sports. I didn't even care what I was singing and chanting. Clara told me I was a dolt, I should pay attention to what was happening in Germany.'

Clara had been right, Asta thought. 'You must have noticed people being persecuted?'

'At school, some mornings, teachers and friends didn't turn up. Everyone knew it was because they were Jewish. I remember going home once and asking my mother where my friend Paul was. She was obviously shaken but didn't want to talk about it.'

Asta turned around to look at him. 'And at university?'

'Studying in Berlin, playing tennis in the summer, swimming in the lakes in hot weather, it was enough for me. It was clear that some of the academic staff weren't as good as they should have been. They'd taken the jobs of the Jews who'd been dismissed. But the war started and I felt no urge to go and fight. I had a friend on the same course. Karl. He hated the idea of military training, but there was no choice.' Max laughed harshly. 'Karl said it would be bearable if we stuck together.' Max gulped. 'They thought highly of the two of us in terms of physical prowess and things like map reading, knowledge. We both qualified for officer training when we finished basic training. That's where they look at this.' He tapped his head. 'Whether you're quick-thinking. It's more than just physical fitness and compasses. It can be intellectually demanding.' He shrugged. 'I didn't mind that. To be honest, studying military history and the tactics used by great military leaders was interesting.'

She looked at Max's slim yet sturdy frame. He'd obviously always been a fit young man. And he was an engineer. Lectures, problem-solving, these things wouldn't be hard for him.

'But the correct political and racial attitude, well, that's harder. Karl had one of those faces that can't hide thoughts, views. He'd voiced criticism of the regime when we were alone.'

So Karl knew that Max was not unsympathetic to his views? Asta stopped pumping the water, still silent, aware that questions might dry up the story Max was telling her.

'One evening we were on the range with a particularly obnoxious training sergeant. We were both good shots, but something about us seemed to irk him. Karl couldn't miss the target that night, but he just shrugged, couldn't care less that his score was perfect. I laughed when I saw his face. The sergeant started haranguing us, shouting, that he was preparing us for war, he wanted to see seriousness. When he turned away, Karl said the worst thing was there was no way out for us. We couldn't leave training. We couldn't avoid fighting. Years of our lives would be lost. Unless we were lucky, we'd take part in acts of aggression for war aims we didn't believe in.'

Surely Karl and Max had known this since childhood? Hitler had made no secret of his plans for conflict.

'On that shooting range I suddenly grew up. I'd seen people beaten up on the streets. I didn't like it, but I didn't feel it was my business to oppose it. But now I realised I wouldn't just be a bystander, an observer. I'd be taking part.'

'Did you think of leaving the country?'

He laughed. 'Where would I have gone with a war on? If I'd managed to get out of the country, they'd simply punish my family. When we were walking back from the range, as a black joke I said to Karl, one of these days I'll just have to do this, it's the only escape.' He mimed putting a gun to his temple. 'I laughed. He did, too. I never...' He swallowed.

'Karl took it seriously?'

'I planted the idea in his head. Karl had done his best to evade all the Hitler Youth camps and rallies. Always a good excuse, an infectious illness, a doctor friend of the family who'd sign a letter saying he'd broken a bone. But he couldn't escape training for war. When I told him shooting myself was the only way out, something inside him must have latched onto the idea.'

'You couldn't have predicted that. It was a throwaway comment.'

'Yes, I should have.' Max's voice shook. 'He was falling deeper and deeper into... a kind of melancholy. He still managed the sessions on tactics and navigation. He answered questions in strategy lectures. But he didn't eat. And he was very quiet. Until he suddenly cheered up. More like the old Karl, reminiscing, making me laugh. I thought he'd come to terms with everything. I relaxed. And then...'

He stopped.

'And then Karl got hold of the gun?' she said softly.

'We had easy access to guns and ammunition. Anyway, Karl went missing one suppertime. Told them he wanted to put in an extra hour in the gymnasium. They approved of that kind of dedication. I made him up a plate of food and brought it out to the gymnasium. But he wasn't there. He was behind the stables. "Don't stop me," he said. "You were right, there really is no other way." And then...' He closed his eyes. 'I grabbed the pistol he was aiming at his temples, but the bullet fired through my hand. They told me I'd prevented a huge crime against National Socialism.' Max's voice dried up.

'You were wounded. And Karl survived?'

'If you can call it that. He wasn't injured when they dragged him off. But next day, when they drove him away to a camp as a punishment for cowardice and anti-social behaviour, well, his face was... a mess. God knows what will happen to him in one of those places. And worst of all, before he went, he saw what the gun had done to my hand. I could tell from the horror on his face. I shouted at him that it was all my fault, not his.'

Asta inched closer to him. 'You did a brave thing, Max.'

'I ruined his life. But in a twisted kind of way, I was given an escape from fighting for them.' He flexed the maimed hand again. 'Another reason to feel guilty.'

'You couldn't know Karl would take a throwaway comment

to heart. He was more disturbed than anyone knew. Perhaps you'll see him again one day.'

He sighed. 'I hope so. I've been able to forget it up here. It's like a *märchen*, a fairy tale. The mountains, the sea, it's magical. But the guilt is always there.'

She had to ask him something. 'So what's happening in Norway, the camps, the arrests, you don't approve of it?' Asta willed him to say something more than he'd hinted at. His answer, his agreement with her, seemed to hover in the air between them so she could almost hear the words spoken.

He turned away from her. 'I'm going for a walk.'

What happened next between Asta and Max started almost imperceptibly. Afterwards Asta couldn't pinpoint the exact day it, whatever 'it' was, started. Thinking of him as Max, not Brandt, calling him that. Was that the start? Or was it when he brought the German doctor up to examine Pappa? Or when he took care of the livestock so she could sleep? When did he first touch her fingers? Then her hand, her shoulder, always when they were engaged in a household task or working outside together, in a way that could have been casual or even accidental but she knew meant something more? He was shy; it wasn't more than a hand lingering a little longer on her shoulder or back each time, but the expression in his eyes, fixed on hers, made it clear what he meant. All the same, it would only have taken her stepping back or looking away for him to desist and never repeat the approach.

One lunchtime, after they'd cleared the table, washed the dishes and he was helping her outside in the yard, their bodies touching sometimes in passing, but not really connecting, she grew impatient. Waiting until they were out of sight of the kitchen window, where Pappa might see them, Asta moved so he stood between her and the pigsty. 'I know you want to kiss me, Max, so we might as well just do it.' He was no longer a German, an enemy, but a living breathing, warm-skinned male. And she couldn't deny she wanted to be with him. She wanted his mouth on hers, to feel his breath on her face.

He looked away.

'You changed your mind? Well, that's flattering.'

'Of course not. Why would I change my mind? You're... I hardly know what to say about how I feel.'

She sighed. 'If you feel the way you're suggesting, there's nothing to say, is there?'

'I think it's important. Of course I want to kiss you, Asta. But we both know it would be unwise.'

A frivolous comment came to mind, but what was the point? 'You think you'd be taking advantage of me?'

'You're a civilian whose home I have been billeted in, against her will.'

'Oh, that was just at first. I've got over it.'

He laughed. 'You told me many times. You did not choose to have me billeted on you and my arrival was an unpleasant event for you.'

'It became less unpleasant.' They'd moved aside. Asta turned her attention to the water pump and bucket, uncertain how to proceed. She wasn't going to throw herself at any man.

'Whereas for me, it never felt unpleasant coming up here.' He said it softly. 'For the time since I left for military training, I felt at home. I could forget...' He glanced at his left hand.

She put down the bucket and moved closer to him. His arm circled her waist. 'You're beautiful, Asta.' His voice shook. 'They told us Norwegian girls were goddesses but you're more than that. Sometimes when I'm with you, I can barely breathe.'

'Don't put me on a pedestal. You've seen me at my worst.'

'You've put me in my place a few times, certainly.' He grinned.

'Even when you tried to help us.'

His arm tightened around her waist. 'Nothing about this will be easy.' He placed the other, injured, hand on her shoulder. She looked down at the fingers, fleetingly reminding herself how he'd come by the injury.

He swallowed. 'Asta?' His voice rasped as he called her by her name. He'd spoken it before but now it felt like the first time she'd ever heard it. It sounded like a question and a claim, both at the same time.

Without saying a word in response, she moved her lips towards his. The kiss was long. Tender, almost shy, at first, it became more demanding. Only when Max moved away, minutes or an eternity later, did she remember they were in view of the house.

'I checked before I kissed you. Your father is still at the kitchen table. He can't see this wall from that angle.'

'You're so romantic.' She pinned back her hair, which had somehow unfastened itself from the clip. 'It's your training, I suppose.'

'Your hair's like a golden waterfall.' He smiled at himself. 'Listen to me. An engineer trying to be lyrical.'

'You're more romantic than you give yourself credit for.'

'You're changing me.' He ran the fingers of his good hand down her cheek and groaned. 'I should be going back to work.' His face shadowed. 'Asta...'

'What?'

'We've been rash.'

'I might be the second rash thing you've ever done in your life.' She felt her voice choke, unable to deny what he was saying. 'Hopefully I won't cause you to be injured again.'

'I meant more that it's rash for you. Local people won't like this happening between us. Nor will your father. Think about it, Asta. Perhaps we should stop this now.'

All they'd done was kiss. So far.

'Perhaps I should move out. I'll have a word with the

billeting officer. The barracks are nearly ready and they'd find me a bed down there.'

She watched his strong, upright back as he walked away. He was right. A relationship with her would risk nothing for him. Asta remembered the conversation with Marte about girls being positively encouraged to take up with Germans, to have children with them. Well, she had no intention at all of letting things with Max go that far. Why shouldn't the two of them enjoy a relationship that might realistically only last as long as he was billeted here? She needed him. Realisation of this need struck her forcibly in the chest, like a blow. She couldn't live this life without Max, without his sometimes frustrating calmness, his strength. And she found him physically almost too much to bear at the moment. It wasn't just Asta who responded to him like this. She'd seen girls looking at him in the village, then looking away again, ashamed of their instinctive reaction to a handsome man they ought to hate. This was what war did to people. Normal attractions became something to be ashamed of. Something to fear.

Asta trudged back to the water pump. Real life meant attending to increasingly difficult everyday tasks: getting hold of enough food and clothing, tending sick people like Pappa. She oughtn't to be diverting herself by kissing a German, no matter how his presence drove away all the anxiety, the drudgery and boredom. No matter how much the feel of his lips on hers thrilled her.

She pumped the water as though her life depended on it and her arm ached. Still worried her father might have seen them, she glanced over her shoulder in case he stood behind her, arms folded, frowning. The sensation of being watched was strong but Pappa wasn't there.

·   ·   ·

An autumn storm one Sunday when the three of them sat over their supper, took everyone by surprise, though, as Pappa said, nobody living on the west coast of Norway should be surprised by heavy rainfall and winds. The roof had held up well since Max had mended it.

A crash outside made them all jump. 'The barn door,' Pappa said. 'Probably blown off its hinges.' They grabbed oilskins and went out.

Pappa and Max managed to fasten it back on, with Asta helping them hold the door steady. 'You should go back inside now, Pappa,' Asta said. 'We'll tidy up the tools.'

The rain seemed even more intense now. Between Asta and Max and the house sheets of water fell from the leaden sky.

She realised she'd left her oilskin hat in the house and cursed gently under her breath. 'A fine Viking girl like you shouldn't mind getting wet hair,' he teased, when she told him.

'I only washed my hair last night.' She made a face. 'I'll look like a wet sheep rather than a fierce warrioress. Let's wait it out. Often the rain doesn't persist. If it dies down, we can sprint for the door.'

They sat on the hay bales. 'It smells so good,' he said, sniffing. 'Like the summer has been captured. I could almost eat it.'

'I imagine some people might try,' she said, more seriously. Max nodded, his eyes on hers. The smell of the hay made something inside Asta feel reckless. She moved closer to him. Max hadn't talked again about moving out or stopping the relationship. She hadn't raised the subject either. Pappa had been around and tacitly they seemed to have agreed they didn't want to behave like errant schoolchildren behind his back. But Pappa was in the house now and wouldn't come out while the rain was flinging itself down like this. They'd be undisturbed.

The urge to touch him became irresistible.

She placed a hand on Max's thigh, strong beneath the serge trousers, feeling the muscles beneath her palm, watching him closely, she ran her fingers up his leg towards his body. Her blood seemed to warm in her veins, as if she was waking up from a deep and cold hibernation.

'Asta...'

'Nobody can see us in here.' He felt so warm under her fingers.

'Your father will wonder what we're doing.'

'He'll be in front of the stove with his pipe, engrossed in some economics book.'

'I can't...' He swallowed, taking her hand. 'If you keep doing that, it's going to be very hard to stop.'

'Do you want me to stop?' Watching him intently, she pulled her oilskin and jumper off. 'Max?'

She heard his sharp intake of breath. For a moment he watched, silent. 'No, don't stop. Take off the shirt.' The words were choked up.

'I don't...' She wore nothing underneath the shirt. It didn't usually bother her because war hadn't rounded her figure out enough to make it worth it. She shrugged and unbuttoned the shirt, keeping her eyes on his, hearing his intake of breath as she exposed her naked skin, nipples hardening in the cool air of the barn.

'Should I stop now?'

'No.' It came out as a gasp.

She pulled off her boots and started to roll down her trousers and underwear. 'Or now? I can't hear you, Max.'

'No.'

'Is that no, stop, Max? Or no, carry on?'

His answer was to push her back onto the hay bales and cover her mouth with his.

They emerged, half an hour later, after tidying Asta's hair and fastening shirt buttons. The rain had stopped. In the house, Pappa sat in his chair, sleeping, a book on beekeeping open on his lap. Asta felt a pang for the deception of her father, dozing innocently in here, with no idea what was going on between them.

Perhaps Max sensed her feelings. 'I'm going up to my room,' he muttered. 'I have letters to write.'

He needed to compose himself before facing her father. She felt the same way.

Asta tidied the kitchen. When she'd finished, she found her mother's sewing basket and started the job of darning and mending she'd been putting off for months. Trying to ease a guilty conscience? Probably. But she already knew that guilt wasn't going to stop them repeating what had just happened. The last two years, the death of her mother, the departure of Arne and arrival of the Germans, everything she'd feared and mourned, being with Max made it bearable. Images of what had just happened between them in the barn made her catch her breath. Their bodies, two distinct objects, coming together, awkwardly at first and then as if they'd always known one another. The physical sensations, the thrilling strangeness and inevitability of it.

Yet he was an invader, even if he wasn't wearing the field-grey uniform and carrying a gun. How did she really know what kind of man he was?

# SIX

On Christmas Eve the house smelled of juniper and pine. Asta grated a precious lemon and the combination of scents made memories stir inside her. Christmas still wielded its power. For a moment, the anxiety inside her ebbed.

Max had only just returned from Bergen the previous day. He'd been working on submarine pens, she guessed, though she hadn't asked him. He'd handed her a sack of food. 'Not as much as I'd hoped, sorry.'

'Better than nothing, *takk*.' He'd promised cigarettes, but the bag contained tins of meat, chocolate and an orange.

'I gave the cigarettes away. I'm sorry.'

She used them for bartering, but she'd manage without. He was staring out of the window, seemingly mesmerised by the falling snow.

'I'll do without.' She peered at him. 'What's wrong?'

'It was something you accused me of, when I first came here – ignoring the labourers brought here. Mostly, I don't see them, or at least not those from the east. But this time, there was a group of Yugoslavs. Carrying boulders. Singing carols.' He paused. 'They sang well. I couldn't understand the words, but it was... poignant. And I couldn't just walk past them. I stopped. I saw them flinch, waiting for me to shout at them, threaten them, the look of utter surprise when I asked them about the words. We even laughed because they said they were too early with their carols. Christmas in the Orthodox church is later.'

'So you gave the men the cigarettes?'

'And three bars of chocolate. Easier to hide in their coats and exchange for bread or meat.'

'I'm glad you did.' She went up to him and rested her head against his shoulder. She knew he'd given food to the labourers before, always seeming half angry when he did, as if it hurt him that it was necessary. But there wasn't time to think about the slave labourers any longer. Now was the moment to talk to him about something more personal and pressing, while they were both in a reflective mood, while Pappa tended to the goats and finished up outdoors. He was keen to begin the celebration of Christmas together as darkness fell and candles were lit.

She was opening her lips to start the conversation she needed to have when Max broke away. 'On a happier note, I must give you this.' From his jacket pocket, he handed her a small box, wrapped in tissue paper and tied with red satin ribbon. He put a finger to his lips. 'Don't say a word until you've opened it, Asta.' His eyes were wide with anticipation.

Asta undid the ribbon and opened the box. Inside nestled a gold chain with a single pearl hanging on it. The chain dangled heavily from her fingers and the pearl gave off an effervescent glow. 'It's beautiful. How on earth did you manage to find this, Max? I haven't seen anything like it.' He'd been in Bergen recently, but the city was best known for its silverwork.

'It came from Paris. Friedrich Klein was on leave there and I asked him to find something like this for you.'

'A pearl necklace from Paris.' She said the words with

wonder. It was hard to imagine a place like Paris still existed, that people could still purchase jewellery.

'It's not practical for you to wear it in public, I know. But it was pretty. Like your skin.' He looked awkward. 'Some of the silk... garments from Paris the others bought there were more... personal.' He looked down at the floor. Asta checked that her father was still outdoors.

'Silk garments. Underwear?' His grin confirmed her suspicions. 'I see. You didn't want to look at me in Parisian lingerie.' She silenced his spluttering objection with a grin. 'What did this underwear look like? Was it very... covering?'

'No.'

'Did it conceal all of this?' She pointed at her breasts. 'And was it in a sensible colour, like washed-out grey?' She stared at him. 'You're not answering?'

'It was... I don't know, pale pink, oyster. And no it didn't look as if it would be very warm.'

She had to put a hand over her mouth to stifle her laughter, knowing she was letting herself be distracted from more serious matters, but finding it irresistible. 'Probably hard for me to wear and launder in this house with my father living here, too. Anyway, I love my pearl.' She put it on.

He moved towards her, taking her hands, speaking in a low but intent voice. 'I have a dream that you and I might go to a hotel, Asta. Perhaps not Paris, but somewhere we aren't known. For a night or two. Somewhere where we don't feel so bad about your father being around.'

She sighed. 'How could we possibly do that without people finding out what's between us? It's bad enough that we have to keep it a secret from Pappa.' The deception still hurt her.

'I know. But when we tried to end things, it didn't work, did it, *schatz*?'

For a few weeks in early November she and Max had tried to cool the relationship, agreeing to revert to being friendly companions, avoiding one another whenever possible. The attempt hadn't lasted long. He'd come back one dank evening and found her outside, struggling to round up the goats, who'd escaped. Laughing as they attempted to persuade the animals back into their field, they'd found the amused looks they exchanged becoming longer and more intense, found themselves embracing. It had been shortly after that night that her first suspicions had become more concrete fears.

He groaned. 'I know, I know. But it feels wrong that we can't be together for a few days without worrying that someone will see us.'

The thought of what they might do, alone in a hotel room with nobody they knew anywhere near them drew blood to her face. 'If they gave me a travel permit, we could travel separately, on different days, perhaps. To somewhere out of the area.' She imagined herself lying on a bed in a hotel room, Max coming in and discovering her either completely unclothed or wearing the kind of oyster-coloured silk underwear he'd described. Although the image was no longer as arousing as it had once been. Her body didn't respond the same way now. To distract herself from the unsettling thoughts swirling inside her, she gently released her hands and stood up. 'I must give you your present.'

'You have one for me?'

One of the things she loved about Max was his humility. He'd bought her a present but had no expectation that she'd reciprocate. Germans were supposed to be arrogant and greedy, but he smashed the stereotype. If Pappa served him home-brewed beer he was genuinely surprised and gratified.

'Of course I have a present for you.' From the kitchen drawer Asta pulled out a small box wrapped in brown paper. She'd bound sprigs of pine in the red silk ribbon to make it look festive. He unwrapped it, face brightening.

'A compass.' He opened the lid, gazing at the symbols on the inside of the lid. 'With, what are they, runes?'

'They say they are ancient runes to give you protection and help you on a journey.'

'It's wonderful. I have never had a compass since I was in officer training and I certainly didn't want to use that one.' He smiled at her. 'I'll always be able to find my way back to you, won't I?'

'No chance of escaping me now.' She forced a smile. Telling him was now imperative.

'But it's valuable, Asta. You can't give it to me.'

'I can.' For a moment her voice quivered. Originally she'd intended the compass for Arne, spotting it in a Bergen shop just before they'd left there with Mamma on their last family holiday. It would be a wonderful birthday or Christmas present for him. But Arne had been gone for years now. Who knew when he might return?

'It's the best present I've ever had.'

She checked her father was still out of the house and leaned forward to stroke his face. 'One day we're going to walk out together openly in some grand city. You're going to take me to the best restaurant there is. I'll wear my pearl necklace and you'll wear a civilian's suit and shirt. Instead of talking about ration cards and repairs, we talk about books and opera.' It didn't take much for Asta to see herself in some white-table-clothed restaurant, waiters buzzing around, Max in front of her, glasses of wine, no, flutes of champagne, in their hands, large menus to choose from. Max laughed.

'I used to think I had no imagination, except for bridges and roads, but I can imagine this. And what happens when we go to our hotel room together.'

She had asked him so little about the dreams he'd had before the war. 'What kind of bridges did you dream of when you were studying?'

'I thought they'd be suspended in the sky, above the water, almost held up by magic in the clouds. Not that I believe in magic, of course.'

'Of course not. But we can dream anyway.' But Asta needed to stop daydreaming and start facing hard facts, instead of letting them both drift away into fantasy land. Max needed to know what was happening. She placed a hand over her abdomen.

'If we can't dream on *Weihnachten*, Christmas Eve, we never can.' He took her by the hand towards the small upright piano. 'Shall we?'

'Carols?' A memory flooded her of the times they'd been here for Christmas, rather than in their Bergen house. Yesterday, on the day Norwegians called *Lille Julaften*, the day before Christmas Eve, Pappa had brought in a small tree to decorate but Asta hadn't had the heart to find the box of decorations. While she was peeling potatoes, Max had quietly asked Pappa where the box was and the two of them had decorated the tree with heart-shaped paper baskets and pinecones painted in gold paint. The smell of the tree had filled Asta's heart with the memory of past Christmases, half sad, half consoling.

'Probably not the most artistic arrangement,' Max had said. 'But the tree would be wasted otherwise.' Looking at it now, she admired his handiwork again.

He sat down at the piano and played the opening bars of 'Stille Nacht'. She joined in, in German. She knew the words of this carol well. When she was little, they'd had German friends in Bergen. Evenings this time of year had often been spent singing one another's Christmas carols. Max's voice was a fine baritone.

He switched to a Grieg version of a Norwegian folk song played at Christmas, smiling at the surprise on her face. 'When I was in Bergen, I walked up the mountain to admire his summer house.'

He played on, switching to Schumann. Asta was some-where else now, somewhere outside war and hardship, caught up in melodies that took her somewhere consoling and other-worldly. She put aside the secret she was carrying inside her, one that needed to be shared with Max, and with Pappa, too. Not on Christmas Eve. What difference would one more day make, anyway?

Pappa came into the room, carrying a pile of logs. 'It's good to hear that poor piano having its moment,' he said, when Max had finished. 'It's been silent too long. We only need Asta to start spinning on her mother's wheel and life will seem normal.'

'You'll wait a long time to see that,' she said. 'That spinning wheel despises me.' Thinking about her mother at the spinning wheel made her smile tonight, rather than feeling sorrowful. Perhaps Christmas Eve could be healing, even if, or perhaps because, it was spent with a German sitting at the piano and singing Christmas carols in a lovely voice.

'I forgot to give you your post, Max.' Pappa stood up and took an envelope out from the table.

'My family,' Max said, taking it. 'A Christmas card, and letter, too, by the feel of it.'

He opened it and read, brow furrowing.

'Is everything all right?' Asta asked.

He sighed. 'My sister.'

'She's ill?'

'Not ill, no.' He bit his lip. 'She just causes my parents anxiety.'

Asta wanted to ask more, but he turned back to the piano, playing something that sounded like a Chopin nocturne he must know by heart, melancholic and thoughtful.

'I'll make us something to eat,' she said, going into the kitchen. She was always so hungry now.

Someone rapped softly on the window, making her jump.

Marte, bundled up in hat and scarf, stood outside, snowflakes falling behind her. Asta went to the door. 'Come in. We're getting cosy here by the fire.' Asta beckoned her inside.

She shook her head, a finger to her mouth. 'You have to come with me now.' Asta opened her mouth to protest. 'Please, Asta.'

'What's wrong?'

'It's important.'

Asta pulled on boots, hat, gloves and coats.

Marte led her towards the barn. 'What's happening?'

'You've got to keep this quiet. Can I trust you?'

'Of course.'

'That German of yours?'

'He's playing Christmas carols and Chopin on the piano.'

Marte's mouth twisted into a dry smile. She didn't know how feelings between the two of them had blossomed since summer. Asta had been so careful never to be seen alone with Max, never to talk about him apart from in the most general terms. When she and Max hiked together, she was always watchful, insisting on meeting him far up the track and away from the village, one of them peeling off, if she spotted anyone. She'd even crouched behind rocks if she thought someone was approaching. Magnus was always on her mind when she was outside with Max, but she hadn't seen him, not for months now. She opened the barn door.

'You can come out now,' Marte whispered to someone Asta couldn't see. 'It's safe.'

A man, filthy, freezing, crawled out from behind the bales of hay.

'My God, Marte! Who's this?' Asta whispered.

'Never mind what he is, who he is. He just needs food and warm clothes. I can't take him down to my place because my cousin is staying for Christmas. And she...'

Marte's cousin was engaged to a Quisling supporter.

'How long for?' Asta's reply came out automatically.

'Two nights. He missed a boat. Or the boat missed him. But another one's coming for him. That's all you need to know.'

It was more than enough. Asta glanced towards the house. Any moment now, Pappa or Max would come to the door, wondering where she was, if she needed help.

'I know this is about the worst place we could choose, with your lodger, but he can't walk any farther tonight.'

The man seemed beyond the point of even being able to shiver.

'It's dangerous.' It was more than dangerous.

'Please, Asta,' Marte said. 'For Arne?'

She blinked. 'Does this man know Arne?' Was Marte hinting that Arne was involved in something clandestine and dangerous, like this man? Perhaps even working with him?

Marte was silent.

'I need to know what you're doing, Marte.'

'All right. But it would be safer for you if you didn't. I help transfer British and Norwegian operatives up and down the coast.'

Asta felt as if she might be sick. Operatives? Men who brought weapons or trained Milorg members for the day when they would engage in combat?

'Sometimes they can't make their rendezvous points and I need emergency shelter for them. I know it's dangerous but I sense you want to help, Asta. To do your bit to resist.'

'I do.' Christa had finally got in touch, sending Asta another pamphlet from Oslo folded inside a Christmas card, this one with a short article on resistance operations in the Bergen area. The hint couldn't have been stronger. How could Asta want to help throw the Germans out of Norway when she longed to keep Max with her always, though?

'Your man can stay here.' The words came out of Asta's

mouth before she could stop them. 'I'll keep the others out of the barn and bring some warm food and blankets. You go, Marte, it'll look odd if they see us both out here.'

Marte squeezed her hand, relief and gratitude plain in her face. 'It's better if I knock on the door and wish your father a Happy Christmas. It'll give you time to fetch blankets and food you can spare. I don't think my companion's eaten for days.'

Asta nodded.

'Go back behind the hay,' Marte whispered to the man. 'We'll make you more comfortable.' The wind had risen and blew Asta's hair around her face as she ran back to the house, dark shadows dancing across the snow, making her think fleetingly of old Yule legends.

At the front door, Asta heard the piano playing continuing, her father's bass voice joining in. 'Guess who's here, Pappa,' she called. 'Marte's come to wish us *god jul*.' She lowered her voice. 'Go through, Marte, I'll heat up something to drink.'

The two women slipped off their outer garments, Marte going into the other room with a final grateful look at Asta. Quickly Asta ran upstairs and pulled blankets off her bed. Arne's winter clothes were now stored in a trunk under his, now Max's, bed. Feeling treacherous she slipped into the room, pulled out the trunk and grabbed the warmest clothes she could see, finding an old belt to make a bundle of the thick trousers, socks and jumpers. Marte was still chatting to Pappa, even exchanging a word or two with Max. 'Oh, Asta thought she saw a stray dog or a fox or something outside. She's just looking around. No, no need for anyone else to leave the warm house. I'll check on her on my way home in a minute.'

Marte was a good actress, full of Christmas spirit and good sense. Asta heated milk quickly and found a flask. Pulled out a loaf of bread and a hunk of cheese. It wasn't much. She sliced a piece of the *kransekake* she'd baked, made from rings of ground almonds, sugar and egg, arranged to look like a Christmas tree.

It was hard to cut a wedge out of it and preserve the shape, but she did her best, placing it all in a basket and remembering the old stoneware hot water bottle in the kitchen cupboard. The water on the stove was still hot and she filled the bottle. She'd go out again when she had time to find more for the visitor to eat. Asta tugged on boots and coat again, not wasting time on her gloves and hat, breaking a rule Mamma had set about more haste and less speed in winter.

In the barn, she called quietly to the fugitive. 'Don't come out. I'm leaving warm clothes and food for you. Wait until it's quiet. I'll come back with more later when it's safe.'

'*Takk.*'

He answered in Norwegian, but the accent wasn't a native one. Questions burned on her tongue, but it was rash to even think about the answers.

Closing the barn door behind her, she found the sleet had turned to snow. Marte was coming out of the house, Pappa with her. 'There she is. No stray?'

'Nowhere to be seen, but I'll look again later.'

'Where did you see it, Asta?' Pappa asked. 'I haven't noticed any dogs or foxes around here recently.'

'Probably just a shadow.' She smiled.

Max frowned at her, perhaps thinking it was unlike Asta to mistake shadows for animals.

She shrugged, keeping the smile on her face. 'Christmas Eve. It does things to your imagination. Too many old Norse myths read to us as children. Your fault, Pappa.'

'The old stories and ways are the best.' Pappa smiled at Marte. 'Your father always knew how to make Christmas Eve a most enjoyable night. I remember some good evenings with him.'

Marte's expression grew very soft. 'He loved Christmas.'

Max was still looking puzzled, as if he had more questions.

She gave a casual shrug. 'Anyway, all's well outside. So we can just relax by the fire now.'

Wishing them the season's greetings, too, Marte went on her way. 'Any more snow and you'll need skis to get down to the village,' she called, pulling up her hood.

'Let's eat some of the cake I made.' Asta went into the kitchen to take it out of the tin. She cut three slices there, out of sight, so she didn't have to account for the missing piece.

She had swapped cigarettes for the almond flour with the woman down the track. The hens were about to stop laying, but had provided just enough eggs to make the cake. 'You didn't bring it out here to show it off to us before you cut it,' Pappa said, reproachfully, when she came in with the laden plates.

'Sorry, I forgot.'

'Tastes delicious,' he said, eating it. The three of them sat by the stove with coffee and cake. It almost felt like a peacetime Christmas. Pappa lit his pipe and told Max stories about the old days in Bergen. 'Plenty of Germans or people of German-extraction lived in the city.'

'That's why you both speak German. Just as well as I am not making much progress with Norwegian.' He ate the last piece of *kransekake* on his plate.

'You wouldn't have had contact with many Norwegians where you've been working,' Pappa said. Max's face fell at the reminder that he was here in Norway as a result of war, of German aggression.

'I wish we had more candles for the tree.' Asta changed the subject. 'But it's almost like a pre-war tree. I wonder if we'll ever go back to having all the old things again. All the food and drink and indulgence.'

'At least we'll have butter on our *lefse* tonight.' Pappa was trying so hard to make this Christmas feel merry, as if the pancakes they'd eat would wipe away every other memory.

'And you said you had cinnamon and brown sugar. Just like old times. And the Christmas beer I brewed is waiting for us.'

'I'm glad your regular Wednesdays are so productive,' Asta said, regretting the words as she spoke them. No need to alert Max to the fact that Pappa still met his friends once a week, as if he hadn't already noticed. She had no hard evidence that they were doing anything to help Milorg but she knew Pappa well enough to read something in his face when he returned from the meetings, to note the determination in his eyes. Those men hadn't just been talking about brewing and pig husbandry. She wished he'd confide in her. But then again, knowing as little as possible was better for her.

She felt a return of the bitterness in her mouth. She was keeping too many secrets, pulled in too many directions. She glanced at Max, who was gazing again at the card his family had sent, frowning. He seemed to feel her eyes on him and sat up straight, smiling.

'Tell me about your family Christmases,' he asked. 'Did you always come out here? Or did you spend the holiday in your Bergen house?'

'Depended on Asta's mother,' Pappa said. 'Sometimes she'd just decide she'd had enough of town life and we'd be packing up all the presents and chocolate and rushing for the ferry out here. Other years she'd say we needed to stay in Bergen and catch up with all our friends, and there'd be a burst of energy, decorating the house, shopping, baking, preserving.' He sighed. 'Asta's mother had so much energy and she loved this time of year.'

'What about you?' Asta asked Max. She tended not to talk to him directly any more than she needed to in front of Pappa, anxious she'd give away some sign that their relationship had moved beyond that of just friendly acceptance of one each other, that there'd be some giveaway in how they spoke to one another. He told them about *Weihnachten* in Germany, the

Christmas tree and singing, presents, food and drink. So many things in common, she thought. And yet the Germans wore their green-grey uniforms and the Norwegians were their subjects. That would always stand between them. No matter how much she loved Max, she could never really forget that he was a grey worm, too.

Once again, she put a hand on her lower belly. Miraculously she barely showed, even now, at eight months. Her height gave her a torso long enough to hide a first baby for longer than she could have imagined. Winter weather meant loose jumpers. A long scarf draped around her neck during colder months, masking her abdomen, received no comments. She hadn't known for long. Never having been regular in times of stress and food shortages, she hadn't thought anything of missing a month or two. Easy to tell herself it was just lack of this or that, perfectly explicable, nothing to fret over, not yet. Easy to put a worry to the back of your mind.

She and Max hadn't spent a precious hour together in bed, or in the barn, for more than a month now because he'd been sent to Bergen. In the hours he'd been back, Max hadn't noticed her changing shape. Why hadn't she told him? Written to him in Bergen? No answer came to Asta's mind. Every day since she'd been sure what was happening, Asta had woken and vowed to herself this would be the day she'd finally reveal the secret to Max. Yet every night, she pulled the sheets and blankets up over her swelling body and felt shame that the secret still remained untold. It couldn't be left any longer. He needed to know she was expecting his child.

She only had to tell him and he'd find additional food and give her support. He'd be shocked, of course he would, but she knew him well enough to know he would help her. He loved her, she never doubted it. Perhaps this was why telling him seemed such an enormous thing. She'd inflict such a shock on him.

The three of them talked for longer in front of the stove, Asta praying her distracted frame of mind wasn't obvious. 'I must make another attempt to find a replacement flue for you,' Max said, frowning at the stove. 'It's not drawing properly.'

'Ah, don't worry about it. The stove and chimney will outlive all of us.' Pappa sounded more relaxed than he had for ages, since Arne had left for Scotland. 'Let's finish the beer and then I'll pour some akvavit, that's our traditional Norwegian spirt, Brandt. You might find it better than German schnapps.'

Asta returned to the kitchen to peel the potatoes for the *lefse*. These potato cakes were a dish she'd traditionally prepared with Mamma. She could hear Mamma telling her she'd taken off too much peel from the potatoes and singing carols in her rich mezzo voice. Christmas this year had taken on its own irresistible ancient rhythm. If it hadn't been for the stranger in the barn and the stranger growing inside her, she would actually be enjoying herself.

She peered into the next room. Max and Pappa were deep in conversation. Quickly she wrapped a few of the hot potato cakes in a cloth before grabbing the tin of ham Max had brought up from the barracks and a can opener, plus more water.

She closed the door as silently as she could and made her way across the snow to the barn. 'Only me,' she whispered in Norwegian. 'I have hot food for you. Pull some of the hay out of the bales to cover yourself. It will keep you warm.'

'Thank you,' a muffled voice replied in English, this time. 'I don't want to bring trouble down on you. I'll keep out of sight.'

She hesitated, wanting to ask him more. Had he come across her brother in Britain? What was happening outside Norway? The rumours Marte had shared, and which Pappa had also referred to, about terrible things happening to Jews in eastern Europe, deportations, harsh work camps, executions, were they just propaganda? Was the Norwegian King Haakon still in London?

But the less she knew, the safer everyone in the red house would stay.

She was halfway across the yard, the dark shadows blowing across the snow and reaching out at her. The first pain struck her. Not sure at first what was happening, Asta forced herself to lurch towards the house, opening the door and closing it, resting against it until the pain moved.

This couldn't be happening to her now, not tonight.

# SEVEN

Asta managed to kick off her boots and take off her coat and hang it up, before Max came into the kitchen. 'Your father asked me to bring in the bottle of akvavit, he says it's time... Asta...?'

'I'm fine.' This wasn't supposed to be happening. It was too soon. It wasn't how she had planned Christmas Eve. Maybe the pain wouldn't develop into anything more. From the few books she'd found in the house with information about childbirth, Asta had learned that women sometimes had fake contractions before the real thing, a kind of dress rehearsal.

'You're not well. Sit down.' He pulled out a chair. On the stove the kettle she'd put on to make more coffee boiled and spat. Max dealt with it before turning back to her. 'Have you eaten something bad? What's wrong?'

'Not wrong, exactly.'

'What do you mean?' He frowned. 'Ever since I came back from Bergen you've been very quiet and you look tired.'

She forced a smile, more of a grimace. 'I'm... I'm... I think I may be having a baby.'

'What?' He looked puzzled. 'You're pregnant?'

She nodded.

'You can't be. You'd have told me.'

'I should have told you, before, yes.'

'But there was no sign...' His face was losing its colour.

'This time of year you've barely seen me undressed in daylight because you've been away, only by oil lamp when it's dark. And I actually haven't put on much weight.' Most of her clothes still fitted. She'd always had good muscle tone and perhaps that had held the developing baby in place.

'Why didn't you tell me before?' He knelt down in front of her, holding her hands.

'I only found out while you were in Bergen. But yes, it's really happening. And it's too soon.' Suppose the baby wasn't right? She felt cold.

'When is it due?'

'I'm not completely sure. About another month.' She'd tried working it out and this was as accurate as she could be.

'Have you seen a midwife?'

Asta shook her head.

'Nobody at all?' Concern had made him raise his voice. She put a finger to her lips.

'I told you, I only found out a few weeks ago. I was shocked.' She was thirsty and stood up to pour herself water, trying to remember the last time they'd been together in bed. Some weeks ago now, before he'd gone to Bergen. She'd already been in bed, having undressed quickly when Pappa was safely out of the house, meeting his friends, and she could hear Max coming in the front door. She'd called out to him as he came inside. They hadn't bothered switching on the oil lamp. Had he noticed her swelling stomach, the fuller, more sensitive, breasts? Perhaps he'd thought it was just good German rations. She'd told herself that, too. It had been cold in the room. She hadn't got out from under the covers until she'd pulled on some clothes. He wouldn't have seen her changed shape.

'Let me.' He poured her a glass of water. 'Of course you were shocked. I should fetch someone now. The local midwife? Where does she live?'

Asta tried to remember anything she had been told about the midwife. She lived in one of the houses above the church. Her work took her up into the hills and sometimes by boat along the water. She'd probably be at home tonight celebrating Christmas with her family, unless any other woman needed her help.

Another contraction racked Asta. Max caught the glass before it could fall to the floor. When it passed, she noted that her father had come into the kitchen. Max was muttering something to him. Confusion, doubt and anger passed over Pappa's features in quick succession. He grabbed Max's collar. 'I trusted you to live here honourably with my daughter under the same roof and you have done this. I should throw you out into the snow. You're a dog.' He pushed the younger man against the stove. 'All your fine pretence at being better than the rest of the Germans down there, and you're just the same.' Max was making no attempt to defend himself, his head hung low. 'And for months you've kept your nasty little secret? You pretended to be a decent man but you're just as loathsome as the rest of your countrymen?'

'Max didn't know,' Asta shouted. 'Nobody did, apart from me and I couldn't face up to it. I tried to hide the baby. Perhaps I thought if I ignored it...' What had she thought? That ignoring the situation would make it go away? She, Asta Nilsen, prided herself on her realistic approach to life but she'd fooled herself. Tears ran down her face. Pappa let go of Max with a final shake and came over to take her hands.

'We need you to be calm.'

'Yes, and I need *you* to be calm, too, Pappa. No more shouting. No more raging.'

'Of course.'

'Help me upstairs. One of you could ski down and see if the midwife's home.'

'I'll go,' Max was already moving towards his outdoor clothes.

'Stop,' Pappa said. 'Before you go, fill the stove in Asta's room with wood. I don't want her to be cold.' She usually kept the stove unlit, relying on the heat rising from downstairs. Her father's face told her not to argue. Putting up an objection was beyond her, anyway. All her energy was drawn into her own body, to what was happening to her.

'We need to move you upstairs before the next one starts.' Her father's anger seemed to have left him. His quiet energy moved from him to her. 'Take each step slowly. I'll look after you. I remember how it was with your mother. She had you in this house, did you know?'

'I was born here?'

'You were born a little ahead of time, before we could get back to Bergen, where we were supposed to be for the delivery.'

'Seems to be a family tradition.'

'And everything turned out fine for you and your mamma.'

Asta had been the second baby, though. They said the first-born was more difficult, didn't they? The woman's body didn't always know what it was supposed to do.

Somehow she made it up the stairs. 'I'll fetch towels,' Pappa said. 'Get yourself as comfortable as you can, *kjære*.' He was speaking gently to her now. Pappa's temper had always been short-lived. But something like this, this terrible secret Asta had been keeping to herself, surely he must be furious with her?

The next pain hit her more intensely. Asta moved herself forward. Lying down flat seemed intolerable. She shuffled to the edge of the bed and from there, onto her knees, propped herself forward onto her elbows, which relieved some of the agony. 'Mamma.' She found herself muttering the word, hoping against hope that her mother might appear in the doorway with firm words and good sense. Who would Max find to assist her if the midwife was out on a call or the doctor couldn't be found?

The room felt warm. She thought of the man outside in the barn. The temperature had fallen even more. She'd meant to bring him out an extra blanket.

'Pappa,' she said, when her father appeared with another armful of wood for the stove. 'There's something else you need to know.' She stopped herself. At the moment he could honestly claim to know nothing about what was going on outside. As soon as he did, he'd become complicit. On the other hand, now was the time to tell him, while Max was away. 'In the barn...'

'Who's in the barn?' His eyes were searching. 'I know there was no fox or stray out there, Asta.'

'Someone...' She didn't say more. He knelt down in front of the stove, silent. 'I thought I should tell you.'

'So that's what Marte has been up to. I'd heard word that she was...'

'And there was someone else out there. I saw a shadow, but the pain started and I couldn't see who it was.'

Her father looked up at Asta and his expression softened. 'Never mind about it now.'

'Marte never told me she was involved with... you know.' Marte hadn't told Asta about her resistance activities. She hadn't told Marte this huge secret of hers. Perhaps the two of them hadn't been as close as Asta had thought them to be.

He stood up again. 'That should throw off a good heat now. Don't think about the barn. I can do what's necessary.'

'Don't leave me alone, Pappa.' The thought of being left alone in this room with what was happening to her, this fierce, wild surrendering of her body, terrified her. If only her mother were here now.

'I'll stay with you until help comes. Of course I will.' He did his best to make her comfortable, wiping her brow, turning his back when she managed, between contractions, to pull off her clothes and put on her nightgown.

'At least you had practice with the livestock.'

He let out a deep bark of a laugh. 'I didn't imagine I'd be using the knowledge on my own daughter.'

'I'm sorry. Max and I...'

'If I'm honest, I sensed something was going on back in autumn. I told myself I was just imagining it.' He sighed.

Another contraction passed over her. He held her hand.

When it passed, he stood up and fiddled with the shutter. 'When I had flu, you and Brandt were pushed together. I can understand how that might happen. But not to say a word, Asta, when you must have known you were having a child far earlier than a month ago?'

'I must have sensed the reality deep down, even if I couldn't accept it as hard fact.' She gave a harsh laugh. 'I didn't seem to change physically as much as I thought women usually did, I...' She stopped, unable to explain. 'I'd planned to tell Max as soon as he was back from Bergen. But when it came to it, I just didn't want Christmas to be overshadowed. I wanted us all to have a few days when life could feel like it used to.'

Petter's sigh was a long one. 'It's going to take some time for it to feel like that. The thought of Brandt living here under our roof and doing...' He turned back to her. 'No point reproaching ourselves now.'

The pain was starting up again but she had time to let out a few last words. 'Pappa, you have nothing to reproach yourself for. This is all my fault.' She let the contraction sweep over her, trying to be brave and silent but then finding it impossible not to cry out.

'I've been selfish,' Pappa said, when it was finished and he was wiping her face again. 'I should have insisted you return to Bergen or Oslo instead of staying here, wasting years of your life. Your mother would have done better.'

'No she wouldn't have. I could have gone if I'd really wanted to.' The next contraction was on the way.

'For all my regrets that you stayed, I've loved seeing the woman you've grown into since everything changed.'

She recognised the change in herself, too. Before the war and Mamma's death, she'd been devoted to having a good time, not taking life too seriously. Arne, for all his brashness, had been the clear-sighted older child, Asta quieter but less steady.

Her father swallowed. 'I can't pretend what's happening to you now isn't a terrible shock and I'm not...' He shook his head. 'But we will manage the situation somehow.'

It wasn't a situation, it was a child, a new human being, who would be cursed in the eyes of many in the community from the moment it first drew breath. Her father took her hand. 'What matters now is getting you and the child through the next hours. Everything else must wait.'

If she had changed in the last few years, so had her father. He'd always relied on Mamma to manage any family issues, which was normal, of course. But he'd taken on more of her mother's attributes, a resoluteness when it came to doing what needed doing for the family. And tonight, that meant being here with Asta when she needed him. Thank God.

Two hours passed. Pappa looked at his watch yet again as she asked him the time. At one point his mouth twitched. 'What is it?' she asked.

'It's past midnight, so it's Christmas morning. The Christ child was born today and now my first, half-German, grand-child will be, too.'

Christmas Day. A special day for a child to draw its first breath. But it was weeks too early. Would the baby be strong enough? They were so far from a hospital. She longed for her mother's calm presence to make her calm, too. Perhaps Pappa knew what was on her mind.

'We can go back to Bergen once you've had the baby. I'm

sure we can persuade the Germans to issue a pass. Max will make it happen if the child needs hospital care.' Pappa's tone when he said Max's name was cold. But did they really know that Max would respond in this way? Who knew how he'd really react to so suddenly becoming a father. He might plan a permanent transfer to Bergen or another part of Norway, even if it meant going north to Tromsø, where darkness lasted months and the Soviets were so close. He might even ask to be transferred to another German-occupied territory, escaping from what had happened here.

The contractions were so close together now. Asta felt different, in a way she couldn't describe. Nauseous. Angry. On edge. 'Something's changed,' she said.

The door downstairs opened. Max. She heard another voice, a woman. He'd found the midwife. When the two of them came into the bedroom she recognised the woman, who must have come into the post office. Max's face was red with exertion.

'Asta? Are you all right?'

She managed to nod. The midwife looked at Asta with sharp, but untroubled eyes. 'Both men out. Bring me soap and water.'

She spoke briskly, but her washed hands, as she pulled up Asta's nightgown, were warm and gentle. 'You're in transition.'

'What's that?'

'The baby will be born very soon. I understand you think it may be coming early? You certainly are presenting with a small baby but that might just be your abdominal tone, which is excellent. We will have to be vigilant and careful in case the child is vulnerable. But this room is warm and the position is optimal. Delivery shouldn't be complicated.' She was so matter of fact, as if an unexpected baby on Christmas morning was nothing out of the ordinary.

In a quiet tone she coaxed and urged Asta in how to

breathe, how to push. How could the woman be so calm when Asta was being torn in two? Anger made Asta push. Let her kill herself but this child would be born now.

And suddenly she was there – first her head, the hair damp and curling, then the rest of her. 'A girl,' the midwife said, catching her in a towel. The baby cried.

'She's all right, isn't she?' What harm might she have done the child without knowing she was carrying her?

'Looks perfect to me.' With a muslin cloth from her bag, the midwife wiped the baby's eye gently with some liquid from a small bottle and tied the cord with thread before cutting it. 'She seems almost at term. Your dates might have been inaccurate, Asta. With a first baby, and nobody caring for you, it can be hard to know for sure. Here, I need to deliver the placenta, then I'll weigh her.' She handed Asta the towel-wrapped infant and started massaging her abdomen.

Asta stared at the face in the towel looking up at her. Navy-blue eyes, fixed on her in an unfocused way. Small mouth, a lock of damp hair over her brow. One hand with tiny fingers escaping her wrappings, raised up as if in greeting. A person unknown to her only minutes ago but now very much here, claiming Asta, as if she'd always existed. Already it seemed impossible to imagine that this baby hadn't always been here. She felt she should say something to her daughter. '*God jul.* Merry Christmas, little one.'

Lifting her head from her work, the midwife lifted her head, frowning. 'I suppose that's one way to greet a child who will cause you nothing but heartache. I could see from the anxiety on that German's face who this baby's father is.' The woman's weathered face softened. 'But look at her, pure and perfect as the snow outside, poor little thing.'

'She isn't a poor little thing, but you're right, she is pure.' Asta put her lips to the baby's forehead, the rush of fierce love cutting through the exhaustion and confusion of the last hours.

Weeks, really. 'Kari, that's your name.' *Kari.* The Norwegian word for something pure. Whatever this child's parents had done that was wrong and treacherous, their child was like the snow: untouched, untarnished.

'Do you have anything to dress her in?' The midwife asked. 'Did Berit leave any of your old baby clothes up here?'

The midwife was about the same age as Mamma would have been. 'I can't remember. I'll ask Pappa. Did you know my mother?' Asta asked.

She nodded, looking softer again. 'A fine spinner and knitter, Berit. And she could grow anything in that vegetable garden of hers when she had the time and wasn't rushing off to Bergen. If Berit was here now, I wouldn't be worrying about you and little Kari.'

'You needn't worry. Kari and I will be all right.'

'A German's child.' The midwife shook her head. 'The Germans won't mind, they like our old Viking blood. Some in the village will just shrug and ask what would anyone expect, all those young men here and so many girls without Norwegian men, it's just nature.' The midwife washed her hands again. 'But others will judge you and Kari harshly, Asta Nilsen. And that's why I wish your mamma was still here to protect you both.'

At the mention of locals judging her harshly, Asta thought of Magnus. But he'd left her alone recently. Must have found another girl to obsess about.

The midwife held out her hands for Kari. 'Let me weigh her now and then I'll show you how to latch her on to you for feeding. I'll come up again to check on you tomorrow, but you must work hard on positioning her correctly so she feeds properly. If your German offers you extra food from their stores, you must take every ounce you can get, for her sake.'

Tins of milk were scarce. At least they had the goats and

cow. Thank goodness. If she couldn't feed her daughter herself, they would manage.

It seemed harder to feed a baby than the animals here found it, however. Asta bit her lip with frustration and pain as Kari cried. 'Feeding a newborn takes practice, like most things,' the midwife said. 'Don't fret, Asta. I'll make you some tea.' She patted her bag. 'I have one in here that's good for encouraging the milk to come in.'

Max knocked and came in as Kari was dozing in Asta's arms, wrapped in a napkin fashioned from Asta's old vest and swaddled in her spare nightgown, a blanket draped around them both. Asta was sipping the tea, which seemed to be based on milk thistle and anise. Max's eyes were wide. 'Come and meet your daughter,' the midwife said, more gently than Asta might have imagined.

'My daughter?' He stood at the end of the bed staring, eyes wide. 'We have a girl?'

Asta beckoned him forward. 'Come and look at her.'

'I'm going to see what Berit kept in her chest of drawers.' They heard the midwife talking to Pappa, asking for permission to go into the bedroom he'd shared with Mamma and search for old baby clothes.

'Kari,' Asta said. 'That's the name I would like for her.'

Max nodded. 'That's a good name. My mother's name is Karin, so I like it even more.'

'I'm pleased.' Though what would Max's mother think about having a granddaughter born in such circumstances, so far from home? 'It means "pure" in Norwegian.'

'It suits her. She's a new human being. May I hold her?'

'Of course you can.' She handed Kari to Max. He held her carefully but looking at ease. Strange that Max Brandt, completely new to fatherhood and a newborn, could behave so naturally with his tiny daughter like this.

'Perhaps we could give her a second name to do with Christmas. Krista. Nicola.'

'We don't give middle names as much in Norway. We're not fancy people. But yes, perhaps Lucia. For the saint we associate with Christmas.'

'Kari Lucia Brandt.'

'Kari Lucia Nilsen.'

'I want to marry you, Asta. I want you and Kari to be my family so we can be together after the war. You could come to Germany. Or I could come to Bergen.'

'I'm not sure.' Marriage seemed unimaginable.

'It's too much to think about right now. You must be exhausted.' He bent his head down to the baby and kissed her brow. While they were alone in this room, they held the whole snowy world in their hands. Nobody could come between them.

Apart from Pappa, who cleared his throat outside the door. 'Asta? How are you, *kjære*?' He sounded so anxious.

'I'm just fine and so is your granddaughter. Come inside and meet Kari.'

He entered, looking years older since the afternoon. Poor man. What a terrible shock he had had. He'd been sitting drinking Christmas beer by the stove with his pipe, feeling relaxed for once, thinking that life could be manageable, war tolerable. He had seemingly recovered from his influenza and was back to his old energetic self. Suddenly this bomb had exploded in his life. It wasn't just Asta's existence that had been blown apart. Other people were going to face hard times because of what she had done, because of her lack of morals. 'I'm sorry,' she said again. 'The shock. I... I was frightened, I think. Couldn't face up to it.'

'I only wish I'd known, Asta,' Max said. 'I could have brought you extra rations, helped with more of the heavy work so you could rest.'

Arms open, Pappa approached the younger man, who passed over Kari. Pappa held his granddaughter and nodded without looking up. 'She is beautiful, and I'm so relieved you're both safe.'

'I can't believe I didn't notice,' Max said. 'And that you've been through this worry with me, *schatz*.'

'Things have been different for me since food became scarce. I haven't had...' She felt awkward in front of her father.

The midwife came back in. 'Girls don't have their usual cycles, is what she means.' She shot a look at Max. 'When food's scarce, nature changes things for women.'

Her father was still giving Asta his piercing stare. 'We'll say no more. The child is here. From now on, she matters more than anyone else in this room. Her life will be very hard because of who she is, but that isn't little Kari's fault. She is as deserving as any other infant born to a Norwegian woman, even if not everyone accepts that.'

'Fine words. In the meantime, I can't find any baby clothes,' the midwife said.

'I remember Berit putting some of the old clothes in a box under our bed.' Pappa handed Kari back to Max. 'Let me look.'

He reappeared a few minutes later. 'I didn't realise we had these here,' Asta said, delighted at the sight of napkins, little nightgowns, woollen trousers, jumpers and caps.

'No moths and not damp,' the midwife said, examining them quickly. 'No time to be too fussy, anyway. Let's get Kari warmly dressed.'

Pappa was still gazing at the bundle of clothes. 'Berit always imagined there would be time to sort through that box.' He looked away.

The midwife made shooing motions with her hands. 'Time for you men to leave us alone, and for mother and baby to change and rest.' She might have been addressing a Wehrmacht soldier, an occupier, but this room was her domain. 'Find Asta something good to eat. She will be ravenous and she needs feeding up for the baby's sake, too.'

'The food I brought up for Christmas will be excellent for her.' Max bounded out of the room, blowing Asta a kiss. He seemed to have broken out of his usual awkwardness. How was it possible that he'd recovered from what must have been a huge shock? She thought of the tin of ham she'd taken out to the stranger in the barn and hoped Max didn't ask questions as to where it had gone.

Pappa followed him more slowly. Asta didn't like to imagine the kind of conversation he and Max would have downstairs. Pappa had come to like Max, having resented him as a grey worm forced upon them. Their relationship could be irretrievably ruined now. *What had she done?* She'd been so selfish and rash, giving in to impulses that she should have resisted.

Yet when the midwife handed Kari back to her, dressed in warm layers like a proper Norwegian baby in winter, complete with a woollen bonnet in the softest possible yarn, an invisible silk thread tying Asta to her daughter seemed to tug at her insides. Whatever the sins of her mother, the infant was perfect. From now on, Asta would abandon her selfish ways. Her daughter would be the centre of her world. Keeping her safe would be the priority.

PART TWO

NORWAY, 1943–1945

# EIGHT

Max ran a tap and nodded with approval. The new pipe from the spring to the kitchen meant Asta no longer needed to pump water several times a day. 'It's the best thing you've done since you arrived in Norway,' she told him.

'I don't think so.' He smiled but looked over her shoulder through the window. Out in the yard, Kari slept in the pram Pappa had found in the barn, cleaned, oiled and presented with delight on his face. 'She is. And we did it together. Asta...' A particular expression came over his face.

'You're going to ask me again, aren't you?'

'Ja.'

He wanted them to marry. As soon as they did, she'd effectively be giving up on her Norwegian identity. 'You don't know that for certain,' Max said each time she pointed this out.

'I'd become a German citizen through marriage. You'll understand that the prospect isn't inviting? I love you but I don't want to be a German.'

This morning, he sighed. 'I do understand. But it would make Kari's life simpler. And perhaps you'd only be giving up your Norwegian citizenship temporarily, just until things are easier.'

A time when things were easier. Neither of them liked to express what that kind of future would look like. A total German victory, meaning they didn't need to keep all these troops on the Norwegian coast because the Allies were defeated? Also meaning Max could stay, but the Germans would continue their murderous occupation? A German defeat, meaning the troops, Max among them, were driven out and the Norwegians they'd imprisoned and tortured could be freed? What then? Neither scenario seemed particularly rosy for them as a family. Yet being what Max termed a proper family meant so much to him.

Kari had already been christened. Not in a traditional ceremony, with everyone local in the church, Asta wearing traditional dress, but quietly, the minister in the church looking at the few people in front of him with a mixture of compassion and concern. Asta had worn a dark dress and jacket. Marte was Kari's godmother. She'd accepted with grace, but perhaps a hint of nervousness. Telling Marte what had happened, the morning after Christmas Day, when she'd appeared at the door was possibly one of the most difficult experiences Asta had ever had. 'I don't believe it,' Marte had said, again and again. 'How could this happen, Asta? A German?' She had softened at the sight of Kari, but still barely uttered a word to Max since that day. And although she had recovered from her initial shock and was still warm towards Asta, a reserve had set in between them. Hardly surprising. All those times Asta had complained about grey worms and look what she had done.

They never talked about the man hiding in the barn. Asta had no idea as to when he'd left or where he'd gone. If Pappa had helped Marte move the man on, neither of them had ever told her as much. Not that she'd asked. Secrecy still mattered. They were a family, but Max was always still a German. Asta knew he'd never willingly betray anything he saw or heard, but he had trained as an officer in the Wehrmacht. And even if he tried to protect Asta's family, the worms would blackmail or torture any information out of anyone they suspected.

Marriage was a ceremony too far, just as unthinkable as accepting any money from the occupiers in support of Kari. Max still wanted her to take the money offered by the Germans. He said she could at least put it aside for Kari, in case she needed it in the future. Asta continued to refuse.

'I wish you were less of a Viking, Asta,' he said. 'Accepting help isn't an insult.'

Perhaps he was right. Everything had changed, anyway. Asta had become one of those women she'd never wanted to be, her life revolving around a child and the household. She even knitted in the evenings. She couldn't yet master her mother's spinning wheel and produce the yarn herself, but women in the neighbouring farms would exchange yarn for produce. Nights by the stove producing a warm wool jacket for Kari were more satisfying than she could have imagined. Sometimes Pappa started when he looked at her. 'You remind me of your mother,' he'd say. And yet, even though he smiled, there was sometimes a puzzled look in her father's eyes when he watched her around the house and farm, feeding the baby, washing her clothes. He probably thought life had intended her as more than a mother and housewife, satisfying as those things were. He'd hoped she might graduate and make her way into some professional voca-tion. Pappa was forward-thinking, liberal in his views. But it hadn't made any difference, had it? Asta now lived a life not so different from that experienced by women fifty years ago: tending livestock on the farm, cooking, raising a child. Since Christmas morning, everything had changed. She could never again be that carefree girl.

If she and Max went to live in Germany after the war, as he

would surely want them to do, what kind of life would await them? The Nazis hadn't exactly encouraged women to flourish outside the household. Even if they were swept away, Asta couldn't imagine herself juggling a child and university in a foreign land. And to live in Germany? A country that had committed terrible acts, whose citizens seemed indifferent? She and Max didn't often talk about the Nazis. The arrival of Kari meant there were always more pressing demands. She knew he worried about his sister. She needed to talk to him about Clara, find out what was on his mind.

The door creaked. Max went out to the yard to peer into the pram at Kari, adjusting the blankets to make sure she wasn't cold, checking that the net was safely fastened so the farm cat couldn't jump on top of her. He fussed over the baby as if she were porcelain, Pappa often told him. Max came back inside and sat down at the table.

Pappa had found a box containing toys and books dating back to Asta's own childhood and put it on the table for Asta to look through. Max took books out and flicked through them. 'Your old schoolbooks, Asta?' he said. 'I thought you were at school in Bergen?'

'Mostly. One year we stayed on here for a term. Pappa was on sabbatical, writing a paper, so the two of us went to the local school.' She sat down next to him, peering at the book as he flicked through the pages. 'I'd forgotten we had these.'

He was thoughtful, looking at the book. 'They're so different from the books my sister had at that age.'

'How'd you mean?'

'Clara's books seemed... politicised. Slogans. Racial material.'

'Antisemitic?'

Even now, Max paused before nodding. He frowned, as though seeing the printed pages in front of him.

'You seem thoughtful today?' She squeezed his forearm. 'What's brought this on?'

'I have been thinking, yes.'

'Clara?' She spoke the name softly. 'I know you were worried about her some time ago.'

'Christmas Eve. Just before my life changed forever.' A smile brightened his face. She felt herself melt as it did.

'We never had the chance to talk about her, did we? And life has been so busy since.'

'Clara has always been a girl to do her own thing. She wouldn't join any of the Party youth organisations for girls. In Germany, that's not a wise thing to do. My parents worried it would bring the wrong kind of attention to her. She objected when some Jewish pupils in her class were told they couldn't come back to school.'

'That was brave.'

'Brave and probably foolish. I wasn't there when it happened, I was at university. But my mother and father were summoned to the school and told that they would be under close observation from then onwards because they were obviously not doing their duty to their daughter and the Fatherland.'

Asta didn't know what to say.

'This goes no further, Asta. Not to your father or Marte.' His voice was stern.

She nodded. 'Of course not.'

'Last autumn, Clara fell in with a group who were vehemently anti-Nazi. They based themselves on a group in Munich run by students. They distributed pamphlets and told the population what was going on, the treatment of the Jews, for instance.'

Asta felt a chill run down her spine. 'That sounds very dangerous.'

'The founders, young students, were caught and executed.

Clara was lucky, the authorities didn't find a link to her group in Brandenburg. They disbanded. Of course, she can't say much in her letters, but we have a kind of family code. She dropped some hints, some dates. I found old newspapers from Germany down in the mess and looked up the reports of the arrests and executions.'

When he'd read out the letters and cards from home, what his mother and sister wrote sometimes sounded oblique. Asta had wondered whether her own German wasn't as good as she remembered because she seemed to be missing something. Those references to Clara's interest in floristry, such a strange wartime pursuit, that must have been a code for the organisation she'd joined. 'After I wrote in January with the photograph of Kari,' Max continued, 'my mother hinted in their reply that they were being watched.'

'Gestapo?'

He nodded. 'My mother was careful to praise Kari's fine Nordic features.'

'I remember that.' The praise, sounding so clinical, had made Asta raise her eyebrows. She'd thought it was just the shock of finding out that their son had had a child.

'In case anyone opened the letter. She wanted to use expressions that would reassure the authorities that they could be trusted.' Max sighed. 'My mother hinted at other things, too.

'Other things?'

'The news from the east.' He looked Asta straight in the eye. 'It's not good since we were beaten at Stalingrad. I hear gossip down from the Wehrmacht soldiers and officers. But my parents are now seeing men, boys they've known all their lives, returning from the front terribly injured, hearing what it's like.'

The German army was in retreat now. Things had changed since they'd invaded Russia last year.

'I wonder if they might...' Max stopped.

'Who? Might do what?'

'Re-enlist me. Send me to the Eastern Front. Tell me I'll have to fire a gun in any way I can manage.'

'I see.' She closed the schoolbook, giving herself a moment to take this in.

'We should get married, Asta. We might be separated. If something... worse happened to me, you'd be eligible for a widow's pension.'

'Don't talk like that. Nothing's going to happen to you.' She couldn't bear the thought of Max in Russia or the Ukraine or Belarus or in any of the other terrible places. And a widow's pension, how could that make up for having her heart wrenched out of her? She shivered.

'Even if it's not as bad as that, being married is the best way of keeping us connected to one another. Even if they send me somewhere... far from here. You'd be my official next of kin.'

Asta's heart thumped hard. She focused on the daffodil poking its head through the grass by the paddock outside, the yellow brightness incongruous against the tone of Max's voice.

She'd just assumed they'd continue on with him heading down the track each day to work on various projects in the area: the barracks – well, that was complete now – the road repairs. 'I thought they were involving you in the new gun emplacement up the coast?'

'They are. But that's only a few months' work. If they send me north, to Kirkenes, for instance, we would be separated. I wouldn't be able to help you all out with rations.' He frowned. 'As my wife, it would be easier to provide you with extra food.'

'I wouldn't take it. I never have, not from them.' She had taken Max's food, though, a little voice inside her reminded her. And Max was a German. 'And Kirkenes? Really?' She felt sick. The German naval and air force base was in the far north-east of Norway, just kilometres from the Soviet border and constantly bombed by the Allies. She certainly couldn't take a child up there and she wouldn't leave Kari here to accompany Max.

'There'd be plenty of work for me to do on defences and bunkers. Probably other things I haven't had to do here.' He looked away.

Working on prisoner of war camps? Execution sites? Max had managed to spend much of his time out here on the coast supervising gun emplacements, occasionally spending weeks in Bergen to work on the submarine pens or anti-aircraft batteries, proving himself useful but not drawing attention to himself. Those higher up didn't seem to have noticed that their trained officer-engineer was not committing himself fully to the great cause. How much longer would their luck last? Any day now, Max might be told he was returning to active service, maimed hand or not. As he said, they might send him to the Front.

'It may not happen, Asta.' He attempted a reassuring smile. 'But if it does, it'd be better for the three of us to be legally bound together as a family. People get lost in times of war.' He saw her face. 'I don't mean they die, just that they can be separated, split up, with little warning.'

If not the Eastern Front, they might send him somewhere else along the Atlantic Wall, the German defences against possible Allied seaborn invasion, stretching from northern Norway all the way down to the Spanish border.

'In the meantime, I'll put myself forward for more projects in Bergen, make myself as useful as I can. But think hard about marriage.'

Out in her pram, Kari was kicking more forcefully now, a wrist rising above the blanket, too, as her vague sense of hunger became a more definite need for food.

'It would also mean my family and you were linked. I know what you think about Germans, Asta.'

She made a sound that was neither agreement nor disagreement.

'My parents aren't bad people. They always worried about keeping Clara safe so it's only been recently they've started making it clear they share some of her views.'

All across Germany people who'd regard themselves as decent, Christian, respectable, had turned blind eyes to what was happening? She looked out at the baby in the pram. Could she really say that she wouldn't do the same, if she thought Kari was in danger.

'My mother and father would help you and Kari if something happened to me. They would love you both.'

She nodded. She'd fallen in love with Max because there was something innately loveable about him. That quality must have come from those parents of his, mustn't it?

'We don't need to make a huge fuss about a wedding. The chaplain down at the barracks would conduct the service. It wouldn't be the first time he's done it.'

No, she and Max weren't the only Norwegian and German to marry. The thought didn't make her feel any better about it, though.

'Think about it, Asta.'

She nodded slowly. 'I must bring Kari in.'

He took her shoulder. 'But most importantly, *schatz*, I want to marry you because I love you.'

They fell into one another, desire burning hotly as it always did. Their kiss was long. A wail from outside in the yard broke it up. 'I really must feed her.'

'I'll fetch her for you.'

She smiled. Any excuse to hold his daughter.

Kari's face was a knot of purple rage when he handed her to Asta. Once she'd latched on and was feeding greedily, Asta had more time to think about what he'd proposed. Marry Max? Marry an invader, an occupier? She'd borne his child and they lived together, though they went through the pretence of sleeping separately for the sake of Petter. They never appeared together, not even in the village. All the same, everyone knew that Max was Kari's father. Who else could possibly have fathered her child? There were few young men in the village now. Some had fled for Scotland, others had been forced to take up whatever work they could find elsewhere. So far, angry or vicious words directed at Asta and Kari had been few. Not that Asta often visited the village these days. In truth, she felt wary of everyone apart from Marte, even if Marte was so stiff towards Max.

If she married Max discreetly, perhaps things could continue as they were? Marriage would be an insurance policy, just in case something went wrong. Kari paused in her feeding and looked up at her mother, lips moving into one of her frequent smiles. Sometimes the feelings Asta had for her daughter seemed so powerful they took her breath away. This child had not chosen to be born into this situation. She was healthy and loved and was thriving, war or no war. But when peace came, it would be harder for Kari. If the worst came to the worst, would she be prepared to leave her home and take Kari to Germany, if it was safer for her there? Leave behind everything that meant so much: father, home, brother, assuming Arne returned? Suppose the Norwegians never let her come back home? Yes, she'd do it if she had to. For Kari's sake. But it would be so hard.

She would tell him she'd agree to be his wife.

Asta clutched the small bouquet of sedum, poppies and saxifrage Marte had picked and arranged for her, adding fat, pink peonies that must have come from Bergen or even further afield. Marte had responded to the announcement of the engagement with silence, followed by a nod of acceptance. 'If you didn't have Kari, I'd be shocked,' she said. 'But having a child changes things. You have to do what's best for her.'

Marte smiled at Kari, who was trying to reach forward from her arms to pull at one of the peonies in Asta's bouquet. 'You like your mamma's flowers, little one.'

'We so appreciate what you've done for us, Marte,' Max told her. 'And for being a witness.' Marte gave him a brief nod in reply.

Marte, Pappa, Dr Klein, who'd come out to help Pappa when he'd had influenza, and the army chaplain were the only people standing up with the bridal couple and their child in the small chapel. As a young girl, Asta had always imagined herself marrying, if she did at all, in one of Bergen's splendid old churches. If she'd thought of a ceremony in the village, it would have been in the little wooden church down by the fjord, surrounded by water and mountains, arriving by boat perhaps, or in a flower-decorated wagon, wearing full traditional Norwegian dress. The makeshift military chapel she stood in was decorated with just a single vase of lupins for the ceremony. The chaplain was kind enough, though, appearing sincere in his attempts to make the wedding both joyful and solemn. His affection for Max appeared genuine, too.

Dr Klein shook hands with Pappa after the service, looking him up and down with professional concern. 'I'm glad to see you've recovered well, Herr Nilsen. I'll write you a travel permit whenever you wish to have your heart examined properly in Bergen, though.'

Petter took Klein's hand with a nod and thanks.

'We caught Dr Klein just in time,' Max said. 'He's going back home on leave.'

Pappa asked him whereabouts in Germany he lived.

'I grew up in Kiel.' He smiled. 'Another old Hanseatic port. Bergen feels familiar in that respect.'

Making small talk with Germans. How compromised they were, how little they'd kept to the standards she and Pappa had thought they'd maintain when Max Brandt had turned up on the doorstep last year. Little by little their position of having nothing to do with grey worms had been compromised.

Marte handed her Kari. 'I just need to adjust your crown for the photographs.'

With her simple dress and the silk stockings Christa had sent from Oslo two years ago, unworn until today, Asta wore a typical Norwegian bridal crown borrowed from Marte's family. Mamma's crown was stored in a box in the Bergen house, something which had caused Asta to feel a pang. Berit's only daughter would not be honouring her by wearing her crown today. But what would her mother have thought about the marriage, the child born to a German?

Unsettled by the contradictions in her own emotions, Asta had been unsure about putting on the Norwegian, *bunad*, traditional dress, today, but its dark-red folds and embroidery were so beautiful and not too flamboyant, she told herself again, setting off the lustre of the pearl Max had given her for Christmas. One day, Kari might look back at the few photographs and feel proud of her parents on their marriage day. Asta loved Max, he loved her, and they were both devoted to Kari. There was nothing shameful in this union. Let people think what they might.

The mess had provided two bottles of champagne, which were opened in the small private function room Max had reserved in the hotel. Dr Klein proposed a toast to the bridal couple. The cook at the base had been delighted to produce something reminiscent of peacetime catering and provided a cake, which they cut, to a discreet round of applause. And that was that, married and legal, as Max put it, putting an arm around her waist.

'My beautiful wife,' he whispered. 'I'm so proud of you. I don't know how I could be so lucky. My parents will love the photographs.' Now he could tell his family that the union was formalised. Max, Asta and Kari were a proper family. With a kiss on her cheek, Max went to thank the chaplain for officiating at the service.

Marte drank the last of her champagne and smiled at Asta, who'd reclaimed Kari. 'That crown suits you far more than it did the last cousin of ours who wore it.'

'I'm so grateful to you.' Though Asta felt another pang for not being able to use her mother's crown. Never mind, when Kari was old enough to marry, she could resume the family tradition.

'I'm so glad you wore it. I have to go, Asta.'

'So soon?'

'Something I need to do.'

Fleetingly, Asta wondered whether Marte was still involved in the resistance work that had brought the stranger to their barn on Christmas Eve. She felt bad at not asking her questions, but the arrival of Kari had made her wary, cautious of involving herself in anything that might bring danger to the family. Christa hadn't sent any more pamphlets from Oslo. She hadn't answered Asta's last letter, telling her about Kari. Perhaps she was shocked, disgusted. Or perhaps she'd had to go to ground.

With a wave and a kiss to the top of Kari's head, Marta left the reception. Max came to Asta's side.

'Our car will be with us shortly, *liebling*.'

Asta felt a cold nervousness. They'd be visible going through the village and up the track to the farm. Not that word about the wedding wouldn't already have spread through the community. Nothing here stayed secret for long and she hadn't expected the marriage to be the exception. Walking back to the house or sitting up in a horse-drawn wagon would have been more traditional, but the car felt safer. Nothing mattered apart from their little family, she told herself again. Nobody was going to harm her child. The three of them were watching over Kari.

Max held the car door open for her and handed Kari to her

when she was seated. The baby stared up at her mother, seemingly still entranced by the bridal crown, which must look like a beautiful toy to her. 'Perhaps one day we'll be watching her get married,' Max said, as the car pulled away from the hotel.

The splatter of mud and pebbles landed on the window next to Asta. Kari gave a cry of surprise as her mother jolted forward. 'It's all right, I've got you.' Asta tightened her grip on the baby. 'We're all right.' Kari examined her mother's face and then seemed reassured that all was well.

Magnus Haugen. He was running away now, but she'd glimpsed the rage on his face. She shivered. The driver stopped, asking Max if he wanted him to pursue the attacker. Max was pale with anger. She hadn't seen him look like this before, the remaining fingers on his maimed hand clenched in anger. Her hand went to his arm. 'Please, just leave it, *liebling*. Not today.'

'You know that man? I didn't catch sight of his face.'

'Yes.'

'Who is he?'

She hesitated.

'Tell me. I want him punished for scaring you and Kari.'

'We're not scared.' She smiled at him. 'Let's not waste time. I want to get Kari home for her sleep so we can celebrate the rest of our wedding day without her being grumpy.' Her smile almost certainly looked forced.

'There's a special brew of beer waiting for us,' Pappa said. 'Champagne's all very well, but beer is what you need on a day like this, Max.' Pappa was putting on a cheerful front, but Asta knew he'd be unsettled by what had happened.

After a moment Max nodded.

'Very well. Take us home,' he told the driver.

Kari would be married in a time and place where they didn't have to watch out for stones being thrown at them or people spitting. 'It won't always be like this,' Asta whispered to

Kari, who smiled a gummy smile at her, completely unaware and unworried by the things that made her parents so anxious.

'She has such a sunny nature,' Pappa said, watching the child. 'It will get her through life. She keeps us all cheerful, too.'

Kari turned her head towards her grandfather's voice and grinned at him. The three of them laughed at her.

# NINE

Since the marriage ceremony, Marte had softened towards Max. Nowadays, she'd come up to the house to see Asta, even exchange a few brief words of greeting with him. This morning, the two women were off for a walk up the mountain, Asta with Kari in a makeshift carrier on her back. They'd go up the track, past the waterfall, to gaze out at the sea. 'Isn't Max working today?' Marte asked. 'Or has he taken a day off to help Petter?'

'He's packing for a trip to Bergen, taking the afternoon ferry.'

'Ah. The submarine base again?'

'I suppose so. He didn't say.'

'Doesn't it bother you that he's helping the German war machine? Those U-boats cause havoc in the Atlantic with Allied shipping.'

'Yes.' Asta didn't like to think of the merchant and naval ships the U-boats had sunk, the supplies and human lives lost to the Atlantic. 'Often he's just doing something mundane, like advising on a new underground shower block for the submariners.'

'Still helping the Nazis, though.'

'He has to do the work, Marte. Or else they'll send him somewhere where far worse things will be required of him. Like the Eastern Front.'

'I thought he was barred from fighting because of his hand?'

Asta glanced over her shoulder before answering. 'I think things out there are so bad they'll take any man who can stand up and just about fire a gun, which he probably could, given how handy he is with tools.' It mightn't have gone unnoticed that Max Brandt could use a hoe or a saw. Max himself felt guilty, she knew, that so many of his old friends had been sent to fight the Soviets, even while he was relieved not to take up arms himself.

'If only he wasn't a German,' Marte said, sorrowfully.

'If only, yes.' If only she and Max had met in another time and place, all this, all they had, Kari, their life together would be so simple. They'd just be a man and a woman who'd fallen in love and started a family.

'If Max wasn't Max, Kari wouldn't be Kari.' She looked Marte in her face. 'I would find it impossible to be without her and one of the reasons I love her is because of her father. He's part of her.'

'I know, I know.' Marte made a funny face at Kari by rolling her eyes and sticking out her tongue. 'She's perfect, she really is.'

'The best thing I ever did.' They'd reached the waterfall, and stood for a moment, watching the silver water cascade down.

'One day you might go back to Bergen or Oslo, Asta, and all this will seem like, I don't know, a dream.'

'I don't think there can be anything more beautiful in the world.' Sometimes Asta felt a funny tingling in her back, as though something was warning her to take note, pay attention, because nothing could be taken for granted.

They walked on up the track. Kari, at nearly eighteen

months, was more of a weight now, and Asta mused that she would be very fit if she carried on using the carrier with the child in it.

'I suppose we might move back to Bergen. I don't know about Oslo.' Her university days felt like they belonged to someone else now.

'A shame to throw away all that education of yours.' Marte spoke lightly but sometimes Asta detected a wistful note in her voice. Life hadn't offered her the same chances.

'Let's sit down for a moment.'

Asta released Kari, who toddled off to investigate a stick. She chuckled at a butterfly and Asta's heart gave a flip.

Asta stretched out her legs in the sun. 'When the occupation started, it was all I could think about, the resentment at losing that life of mine. I suppose I still have ambition, but on days like this, when it's actually sunny and I look down at that view, I wonder whether it really matters.'

'On days like this when we have fresh lettuces and radishes and possibly some fish. And we're not freezing. That's what your Max's people have brought down on us.'

'I know. Sometimes it feels as if I've split my brain in half.'

'Sounds painful.'

'Half of me is so happy with what I have. The other half still hates the grey worms and what they stand for.'

'But not your own personal grey worm?'

Asta laughed, but feeling the bitter conflict inside her, all the same. 'I could never hate Max, even when he always has a better way of doing everything around the house. Pappa's just about given in now, lets Max sort out a lot of the more strenuous repairs. They're fretting about a pipe for the stove they can't get hold of and every mealtime is spent discussing it.' It was a gentle, if austere, domestic existence, rare in Europe now.

'One day Max'll go away, Asta, for whatever reason.'

Marte's voice was gentle. 'The Allies have landed in Normandy.'

She stared at Marte. 'What? When?'

'Yesterday. I heard it from... well, never mind. But it was a good source, someone who can listen to the BBC news. If they can hold the ground they took and move further into France, it means the Germans are fighting on two fronts now.'

They'd be even more desperate for fresh men. Even those who were formerly considered too disabled.

'It means the end is coming, Asta. What happens to you and Max then?'

Kari was making fretting noises. Asta lifted her up onto her lap and jiggled her around. 'I don't know. We talk about it, we make vague plans, but that's as far as it goes.'

'What do your vague plans consist of?'

'Kari and I possibly moving to Sweden. It seems the most obvious neutral country that would take us.' She shrugged. How to explain the tumult that raged inside her when she thought of the future? At home, the three of them didn't talk about the Soviet advance into Poland and Belarus. If Pappa still ever listened to the BBC on the radio, he must be doing it at a friend's house because their own wireless was still stashed behind the shelves in the cellar. He couldn't have heard the news about Normandy yet.

'Complicated, eh?' Marte said, offering her a cigarette.

'So complicated.' They smoked in silence for a few minutes before Asta looked at her watch. 'I should be going back. This one needs her nap or else she'll be grumbling for the rest of the day.'

Kari protested at going back into her carrier. 'She wants to walk,' Asta said. 'She thinks she's got longer legs than she has.'

'Must be hard being one and a half and longing to explore the world.'

They walked back down the track. 'There's something I

need to ask you,' Marte said casually. 'It's something similar to what you did back when the little one was born.'

Asta stopped.

'I know. It's a lot to ask. It would only be during the day, tomorrow. I need to move someone out of the area. I've got places lined up to take them, but I can't use the... the place I wanted to use because the owner's come back.'

'Don't tell me any more.'

'Asta?'

'How can I? You know my situation. I live with a German, remember? And I have a child who needs me. The risks...' She shuddered.

'It's because you live with a German that you'll be safer than other people would. It would only be sheltering someone for one night.'

'In our barn? With my father going in and out this time of year?'

'He's concentrating on the vegetables at the moment, isn't he? And he won't need the hay because the animals are out.'

Marte had obviously thought it all through. 'Pappa keeps all kinds of tools and pieces of twine and netting in there.'

'This person would be careful to stay out of sight.'

'Pappa has eyes like a hawk. Last time, when I helped, we were lucky because it was Christmas Eve and Kari made her appearance and so he wasn't paying attention.'

'Asta, please. We're desperate.' Marte's words were coming out in a rush now. 'I wouldn't ask you if we weren't. And I wouldn't have said anything if you hadn't told me Max was going off to Bergen today. This person, well, if they caught him, he'd be taken straight to one of the Gestapo torture cells in Bergen. He could give away a whole chain of people. And he would talk. Eventually. He's the bravest man I know, but nobody can hold out for ever.'

Marte's desperation made Asta even more certain she didn't

want to be involved. 'If you're desperate, it's because things are very dangerous.'

'That's true,' Marte said quietly. They'd reached the waterfall again but this time, neither of them slowed to admire the shining water. 'Forget I asked. I'm sorry.'

She looked at her friend. 'Are you all right, Marte? You're not in trouble, are you?'

Marte swallowed. 'I'm fine. This person, well, I've just grown to feel responsible for them.'

Asta looked at her sharply. 'Do you have feelings for the person concerned, Marte? She smiled. 'I think you might?'

Marte blushed. 'Pretend I never mentioned it. I'll find somewhere else, and I completely understand why you feel the way you do. You have a—' She stopped talking abruptly, putting out a hand, halting them.

'What?'

'Thought I saw someone in the trees.'

Asta sighed. 'I honestly thought he'd stopped spying on me.'

'Magnus Haugen? Still? Even though you're a married woman of a year now?'

'I thought it had put him off.' Asta peered into the trees. 'If it's him, he's gone now.'

'Asta, it wasn't—' She stopped as they rounded a bend and the smallholding came into view. This time both women stopped. 'Oh God.'

In front of the house, a truck was parked. Asta knew what those trucks meant. Germans. And not just the regular soldier variety. 'What should we do?' Her mind was whirring. Could Max see them off?

'Stay up here with Kari,' Marte said, sounding unusually authoritative. 'I'll go down. If you see me drop my hat, it's safe to come down.'

Asta had no idea what she ought to do if it wasn't safe. With a toddler on her back, she wouldn't be able to run away and hide in some remote shepherd's hut. And Marte had particular reason to be wary of the Germans.

'I'll go. You stay.' She sounded authoritative. 'It would look suspicious if I stayed away from my own house.'

Marte looked as if she wanted to object.

'Marte, given your latest activity, you don't want to be anywhere near them just now, do you—' She broke off. A man in a grey uniform with a flash of black on the arm came out of the house. 'Is that Gestapo?'

'Yes,' Marte whispered. 'We're staying up here.'

Kari emitted a wail and wriggled against Asta's back. 'I'll have to take her off or she'll make too much noise.'

'Let's walk back up into the trees. They won't hear or see us there.'

Glancing at the dark shadows, Asta prayed that Magnus had gone.

'I need to see what they're doing to Pappa.' Asta's stomach churned, but she allowed Marte to pull her behind a fir tree on the side of the track, where they were less visible. Kari seemed to have found something to look at, keeping her occupied. All the same, if the truck drove up here, they'd find them quickly. With Kari to carry, Asta would never outrun them.

'Look,' Marte said. 'Max.' He came out of the house and said something to the man in the grey uniform. Where was Pappa? Already pushed into that truck, hands cuffed?

Then she saw him, pulled out of the door by a soldier. 'Why are they taking him?' she asked. 'What's happening?'

'Shh, stay quiet, don't draw attention to us.'

Max seemed to be pleading with the man with the black band round his arm. The pleading wasn't going well. The Gestapo officer poked him in the chest. Max wasn't backing down, he folded his arms. 'Stop it,' Asta muttered. 'Don't provoke them.'

'I think Max'll be all right, Asta. He's one of theirs.'

She turned on Marte. 'Doesn't mean they can't arrest him, threaten him. He's at risk, too.'

'Max might be the only person who can stop them taking your father.'

Two soldiers came out of the house, empty-handed. The Gestapo officer nodded at the truck. They were going to take Pappa away.

'They aren't just looking for home wireless sets,' Marte said. 'This is something else.'

Hidden transmitters, foreign agents, resistance people? Asta shivered.

The soldiers dropped Pappa's arms. The three of them got into the truck and drove off, leaving Max and Pappa standing by the open door of the house. Marte grabbed Asta's sleeve as she moved forward. 'Give it a few minutes. Sometimes they double back, see who's popped out when they think it's safe.'

Kari was crying now, quiet, desperate sobs. She was over-tired and needed her cot, followed by her lunch. Asta rocked back and forth on the spot, trying to soothe her.

'Come on,' Marte said, when ten minutes had passed. 'I think we're safe now.'

Asta looked sidelong at her friend. 'You're not just hiding the odd man on the run, are you? You've been doing more.'

'You know not to ask questions, Asta Nilsen. And no, I'm careful never to take on more than I think I can manage. Arne always—'

'What about Arne?'

'Oh, nothing, before he left, he just said to do what we could to help the struggle. But keep it quiet. No unnecessary risks.'

Asta hadn't known that her brother was spending time with Marte in any more than a casual way, flirting with her, perhaps, when he visited the post office. She had always imagined he'd go for a more urban, cosmopolitan girl, the kind he'd known in Bergen.

Shame washed over her. Marte might not be sophisticated, but she was kind and loyal, with a good sense of humour. Without Marte, life would be unbearable, even with Max on the scene. Arne had shown a maturity in counselling caution that she hadn't remembered in him back in 1940. Her brother had been such a live wire. It had been heartbreaking to watch his joie de vivre fade under the double burden of losing their mother and the capitulation of the country. Nature hadn't intended Arne to be one of life's solemn citizens.

At the door, Max and Pappa greeted them with relief. 'What happened? What did they want?' she asked.

'I couldn't get them to tell me what they were looking for,' Max said, putting his arm around her shoulders. 'They've torn the rooms to bits, I'm afraid. I've been tidying up.'

The kitchen dresser had been emptied, all the drawers taken out, contents spilled onto the floor. Mamma's pottery bowl was smashed. In the living room, books lay scattered on the rug. Handing Kari to Max, she went upstairs to find things just as bad: the bed sheets ripped off, clothes thrown out of wardrobes, chests ransacked.

'It's going to take hours to tidy it all up,' she said, coming down again, discouraged. 'What about the cellar?' She daren't look her father in the eye in case Max noticed.

'They didn't find the beer, if that's what you're worried about.' Pappa twinkled at her.

'Our evenings by the stove are safe,' Max said. 'This one is asleep in my arms.' He smiled down at Kari. 'She's unbothered by it.' He sounded so relaxed, yet she could tell that he was rattled by what had happened.

She went down to the cellar, needing to see with her own eyes that all was safe down there. The potatoes were scattered on the earthen floor and the cakes of peat used for the stoves trampled by boots. Straining her eyes in the gloom, Asta lifted the oil lantern and shone the beam at the shelf on the far wall. The hiding place behind it had not been discovered.

Someone was coming down behind her. 'It's all right,' Max said. 'I know you and Petter must have things you wanted to keep hidden. Not just beer.'

Her blood ran cold.

He took hold of her shoulders. 'You're my family. Petter is my father-in-law.'

'When did he tell you about the hiding place?'

'When he was ill that time with the terrible fever. You were sleeping. He was delirious, thought I was Arne, kept telling me to have some beer, to pull the shelves out.' Max smiled, then his expression became more serious. 'They could come back, you know. And I'll be in Bergen, unable to help you.' He turned his attention to replace cutlery in a drawer, jaw set. 'There've been raids on farms up and down this part of the coast. They found a British agent sheltering in a shepherd's hut. He'd obviously received help from the local population.' Max looked up from the drawer. 'They shot two Norwegian Milorg members in a farmhouse not that far from here, a man and a woman.'

Asta's blood ran cold. She didn't even bother asking what would happen to the men and the woman as, by now, everyone knew of people who'd vanished into a prison or camp, to be shot or deported to another country, to an uncertain fate.

'You've got to be careful, not to do anything that brings you to their attention. I can't work out why they came up here, why they thought it was worth searching the house and the barn.'

She murmured something vague in response. He hadn't mentioned the Allied landings in France, she realised. Probably didn't yet know.

Marte was in the farmyard beside Kari's pram when Asta went back upstairs.

'I put her in and she dropped right off,' Marte said. 'She

must have been exhausted. One rock of the pram and she was away. The sun was in her eyes, so I moved her round behind the woodpile.'

'*Takk.*'

'Is everything all right in the house?'

'They didn't find... anything, not even the beer.'

'They pulled your barn to bits, too. I put the tools back against the wall and covered up your hay bales again the way Petter likes it.'

'You can hide that man of yours in the barn, if it helps.'

'What?' Marte stared at her. 'After what's just happened?'

'They've pulled the house and barn to bits and found nothing. Max has spoken to them. Why would they come back here? You could say we're the safest place around for the moment.'

'Should you speak to your father?'

'Perhaps later.'

'Well.' Marte seemed lost for words.

Asta looked down at her sleeping daughter. 'I don't want her to grow up like this, scared police are going to raid her house. She shouldn't be afraid of people who shouldn't even be here, who have no right to be here.'

Marte wasn't going to spell out the irony; she didn't need to.

'And yes, I know that I'm the last person with a right to claim to be a patriot. Perhaps I am, though. I'm pulled apart inside, Marte. Half of me wants Max to stay here with us for ever, not go back to Germany. The other half of me wants to drive the Germans out, to do anything I can. I wish I could cut myself in half and be two versions of myself.'

Marte squeezed her arm. 'This won't be forgotten, Asta.'

Did she mean when the Germans left Norway? When they were finally driven out? When the locals might look at women like Asta and want a reckoning with her because of what she'd done?

The sun went in behind a cloud. Asta shivered. 'I must go

in and start work on lunch. At least they didn't take our potatoes.'


After lunch, Asta tried to slip out to the barn to make sure it was ready for Marte's fugitive. 'Just going out to look for a handkerchief I dropped,' she called to the others.

'I'll come with you,' Max said. 'Kari's sleeping soundly. Let's have a stroll up the track before I have to go and catch the ferry.'

'All right. Meet me out in the yard.'

She smiled and went to the door before he could say anything in reply. Quickly wriggling her feet into her shoes she laced them before he had time to follow. While the men were eating she'd wrapped a bottle of water, hunk of bread and piece of cheese in an old shawl, stashing it out of sight by the door, behind their shoes and boots, until she could slip out by herself.

The barn appeared unoccupied as she shone her torch around. No sign of anyone here. Good. Glancing over her shoulder, she dropped her handkerchief on the ground just inside the door. 'Are you here yet?' she whispered to the invisible guest. 'I'm leaving something for you to eat and drink. My father will probably come in, so stay hidden. I'll come and lock the barn myself and bring you more food.'

She put a hand behind the hay bales and placed the shawl gently onto the ground. 'Food and water.'

'Takk,' a male voice said, so quietly she couldn't tell whether it was a native Norwegian speaking or not. Marte had smuggled him in here so quickly and quietly, nobody had noticed. It struck her that of course this must have been the shadowy presence she'd spotted out on the mountain this morning, the person she'd mistaken for Magnus.

'Are you all right? Do you need anything else?'

'No, I'll be gone before dawn.' The words were so mumbled she could barely make them out.

The door to the house creaked open. Asta returned to the open barn door, stooping down to pick up her handkerchief. 'Knew it was somewhere around here. I took it out to wipe Kari's nose and must have dropped it.'

Did he believe her? 'It was my mother's handkerchief.' This was true. She'd taken it out of Mamma's old chest earlier on. The fewer the lies she told Max the better. 'See the embroidery?' She showed him the delicate silk roses. 'She did this. Shame I didn't inherit her sewing talent. I could be making Kari the most beautiful clothes.' A lump formed in Asta's throat. Strange how the longing for her mother could ambush her, how regret that Kari would never know her *mormor* could creep up on her. Berit Nielsen would have been such a wonderful grandmother to Kari.

'Our daughter does very well.' He put an arm around her shoulders. 'You're wonderful the way you manage, *schatz*, keeping her so well clothed.'

'At least I can knit a little better now. Kari's not discerning enough to notice any mistakes I make. Some of the women around here can probably spot a dropped stitch from a mile away.'

'I sent Clara a pullover from a local knitter when I first came to Norway, before I moved up to the house. She was so impressed with the pattern. I think she's been glad of the warmth in the winter.'

She wondered if his family knew about the Allied landings.

'Let's play the game,' she said, to distract herself, squeezing his arm. The game was an alternative life they'd invented one idle night, creating different versions of how they'd met, which didn't involve being a German and a Norwegian in the 1940s. 'We're both in Buenos Aires.'

'Argentina tonight, is it? I like it.'

'I'm a Norwegian journalist, covering a story about, ooh, I don't know what.'

'Civic regeneration, of course.'

'And you're a civil engineer, emphasis on civil, not military. You and I meet when I'm taking photographs and you lend me...'

'A light meter.'

'We chat and then go out for dinner that night.'

'We fall in love and never go back to Europe. We both become naturalised Argentinian citizens through some miracle.'

'We're both outstanding at our work and they're desperate to keep us.'

'We're in a neutral country so nobody expects us to be one another's enemies. Kari grows up...' her voice shook. 'Kari grows up never having to worry about one or other of her parents being hated for who they are and what they've done.'

His arm tightened around her. 'This needn't be just a dream. We can live in Sweden,' he said. 'Or Switzerland. Or yes, even Argentina. We'll find our way to one of those countries when all this is over. I know you'll be sad to leave the fjords, but it would be worth it.' He looked at her seriously. 'We need to make plans.'

That was the prompt she needed. 'Max?'

He looked at her.

'The Allies have landed in France. Don't ask me how I know.'

He grew pale. After a moment he nodded. 'I suppose we always knew it would happen. I wonder if that's what made the Gestapo officer so angry this morning?' He blew out his cheeks. 'It will be interesting at the submarine base this evening.'

The breeze had picked up and a few slivers of cloud covered the fjord below. They came to a halt at the waterfall, just visible as a silvery ribbon. 'I'll remember how it sounds for the rest of my life,' Max said. 'Wherever I am, I will think of being here, at this waterfall, with you.'

They held one another. She knew he was thinking of what would happen to him now it was impossible for Germany to win, with the Americans and British in France and the Russians pushing east. When the war ended, what would they do to the men like Max, who'd not even been old enough to vote for Hitler in 1933, who'd been subjected to his propaganda for so much of his childhood? Having only half a left hand wouldn't be enough to spare him any retribution.

Think too much about the future and the present became intolerable.

Max broke away to look at his watch. 'I should go back and collect my things if I'm going to catch that ferry,' he said. She wanted to cling to him, grab Kari and escape up to the highlands, somewhere miles away inland, where the three of them could hide away, where the closing stage of the war, bloody as it was going to be, could wash over the world, leaving them untouched.

Marte and the fugitive made their way out of the Nilsen barn just before dawn. She had the feeling he was tearing himself away, staring into the dark fields as if noting the fences and the just-discernible shapes of the cow and goats. Marta had brought a flask of warm coffee for him, the real stuff, and the bread was fresh. 'Local cheese, too. I remember how much you like it. And look, chocolate. Proper Norwegian chocolate.'

He tried to smile as he thanked her. 'I'll eat it when we're clear of the village. We should be in good time for the tide.'

Her stomach flipped. If he missed this boat, she didn't know what they'd do. There hadn't been time yesterday to ask him what had gone wrong and whether there was still a contingency plan. She barely knew how many people they'd lost, either.

Marte forced herself into the moment, ears pricked for the sound of an engine or boots pounding towards them.

The track led down to the quay and then there was a path out through the far side of the village leading alongside the fjord. People here rose early. Should they have gone the long route up the mountain?

He must have been thinking along the same lines. 'It would take too long to go over the mountain. It's only a matter of a hundred metres where we have to pay attention. You should go home now, Marte. Let me go through the village by myself. Less risky to do it one at a time.'

He was right, of course, but it hurt to let go of him. For all his tan, his face looked washed out this morning. 'What happened yesterday?' she asked gently. 'How bad was it?'

'I reached the Jensen farmhouse. It looked fine, smoke from the chimney, bicycles outside, just as it always was. But something...' He shook his head. 'There were tyre marks on the track outside the house. No car. They didn't look like the ones a farm vehicle would make and the Jensens didn't have mechanised vehicles and their car's been off the road for a year. I crept on my belly behind the wall, you remember that low stone wall around the field and garden?'

She nodded. 'So you could look in the back door?'

'Couldn't see much, so I dropped over the wall, still very low on my belly. No dog barking.' He gave a hollow laugh. 'I realised why, when I saw it lying with its throat slit.'

'And the Jensens?'

'I didn't really need to see any more, but something made me go closer. At first when I looked through the window, I thought they were just sitting there, very still. But they'd been propped up in their chairs at the kitchen table. Mickel was missing an eye.'

Marte felt her muscles grow rigid.

'I couldn't see what they'd done to Hanna and I dared not

wait. There might have been Gestapo inside, waiting for me to arrive, or watching the house from up the track. Their mistake was killing the dog. It would have warned them I was there.'

'You were lucky.'

'I waited until the sun came out behind me before I climbed over the wall and crawled to the window. It's surprising how dazzling it can be.'

Of course. He'd been trained in all the tricks in Scotland when the British had chosen him for this role, liaising with Milorg units, teaching them combat skills, exchanging intelligence.

'And of course, I'm absolutely filthy, covered in mud, so I blended in well.' An attempt at humour, almost successful. They'd both known the Jensens for years. Marte felt herself shaking. Mickel and Hanna, both gone?

'Mickel and I loved all the same things,' he said. 'Sailing, skiing. He was a good man.'

And Hanna had always loved coming into the post office for a chat, bringing presents of food for Marte. Marte was glad he hadn't told her until this morning. It would have made it even harder to sleep.

The two of them had reached the last bend before the track descended to the village, the riskiest part of the walk. 'You should go ahead now, Marte. I'll wait here until you're indoors.'

She started to protest, but Arne cut her short. 'I'm glad I caught a glimpse of Asta, if not my father. I really wanted to talk to her, tell her it was me, ask how she was. It was hard but good when she came out to the barn. I kept hoping Pappa would need to come in, too.'

'Asta kept everyone else out of sight.' Marte bit her lip as the words came out. Damn.

'Everyone else? It was just my father there?'

'That's who I meant.'

Arne hadn't made contact with the Jensens. One of Marte's

concerns had vanished in the blackest and saddest of all ways. Hanna and Mickel wouldn't have been able to let it slip that Arne's sister had married a German and had his child. Before Arne had come down to the smallholding, Marte had moved Kari's pram out of sight behind the woodpile so Arne wouldn't see it. And Max had gone off on the trip to Bergen before Arne had come down from the mountain. Arne had not seen signs of either husband or child. Someone could still tell him what his sister had done, the fisherman whose boat they were trying to meet. She prayed he wouldn't find out and could return to Scotland, mourn those he'd lost and keep fighting.

'Someone betrayed the Jensens,' he said. 'We have informants very close to us. I'll find out who it was, Marte.' He kissed her on the cheek and held her closely, before lifting her chin and kissing her again, more forcibly. 'I would be in custody now, too, if it wasn't for you.'

Arne let her go and she forced herself to walk away from him, wiping her eyes.

# PART THREE

NORWAY, 1945

# TEN

Max was saying goodbye to their daughter. It would be a long time before she saw him again, they told Kari, uncertain as to whether she really understood, but he'd write to her when he could. She was two and a half, barely more than an infant. It felt so unnatural that he had to leave them.

The Allies had pushed further and further into France and across into Belgium and the Netherlands, then Germany. It hadn't been smooth progress; there'd been bloody battles where the Germans had fought back. The Russians had continued their attrition in the east, sending hordes of frightened German civilians running west to escape the vengeance. Max had feared for his family in Brandenburg, but they'd heard nothing since the winter.

Now the Norwegian resistance had occupied the main police station in Oslo, an administration was set up and the Allies were in Norway, supervising the capitulation. For weeks Asta had half prayed that some miracle would occur, that Max could find a way to stay in the red house with them.

Max held Kari tight and kissed her forehead, before handing her back to Asta, who hadn't said a word and whose arms were rigid as she took Kari. 'I don't want to leave, Kari, but I have to,' he said, his eyes taking them in, as if he was pressing the image into his memory. Asta prayed she'd understand that her father wasn't willingly going away. 'I promise I'll come back as soon as I can.'

He pulled Asta into an embrace. When he released her, her hands went out to stop him from leaving, to have one more moment, one more second, together. But that would only mean they'd go through this burning pain of separation one more time. She couldn't let Kari see her distress. Asta forced herself to smile and blow a kiss to Max. When the occupation had started she'd claimed she'd be cheering the Germans' departure, hurling insults at their grey-green uniformed backs. Now it felt as if her heart had been torn out of her.

Then he was gone, a hand raised, with a last backward look over his shoulder, walking away to join the other men, wearing a uniform they'd ordered him to put on again in the last few months, in preparation for active service. The bombardment of the coast had delayed his deployment because they'd decided he was needed to supervise repairs, no longer as a civilian, but as a Wehrmacht officer. She hated seeing him in that uniform.

Civilians and soldiers were heading to the ferry, which would take them to Bergen, where they were to surrender to the Norwegians, now that the war was coming to an end and the occupation ending.

'Pappa.' Kari tried to wriggle free and go after him. 'Pappa, wait.'

'He has to go.' Asta held her more firmly.

'No, Pappa has to stay.'

Asta put her down and took her hand. 'Come, Kari. We need to go home now.' Her voice was strong, almost stern. 'We have things to do at home. Animals to feed. Remember how Morfar wanted you to help him today?'

They climbed the track and the scent of the sea made Kari

want to run and play, her father almost forgotten. Asta knew how she felt. This part of the walk home always lifted her spirits, too. Even today, when part of her heart seemed to have been cut out of her.

'Look for seals, Mamma!' Kari demanded, but Asta didn't want to turn back to the fjord and risk catching sight of the ferry taking Max away from them.

A shout behind her broke into her reverie. She stopped, listening. The warmth of the sun seemed to cool.

'Get that whore now her grey worm can't protect her... How much farther up the track...?' Voices she didn't recognise.

'She's not far ahead of us, we'll get her before she reaches her house.'

Magnus's bass tones.

'And she's not with her father? Now's our chance then, come on.'

Footsteps pounded below.

She pulled Kari forward. 'Let's pretend we're being chased by a troll.' Kari loved the troll stories, which were frightening but funny, and ran with her. The first stones hit the road beside the two of them. At first Kari thought it was a game and turned, smiling.

'There's the Nazi slut.' More stones landed, closer to them now.

She looked behind them, and saw they were still out of sight of the men below them. Could she pick Kari up and make it to the safety of home before they caught up with them? No. The track was steep. If the men caught up with them, Kari would be terrified. Better to leave her somewhere safe and run up and find Pappa.

Asta pulled Kari off the track, behind a rock, finger to mouth. 'Wait here a few minutes quietly. I'm going to run home quickly and find your grandfather.' Kari clung to her. 'They won't hurt you.' To herself Asta added, 'It's me they want.' She forced her voice to steady. 'Silly men. We're going to play a game.'

'Game,' Kari echoed.

'You have to be as quiet as a mouse in a hole.'

Kari smiled. 'A baby mouse. Or a baby hare?'

'Yes, one of those. I'll come back very soon,' she told Kari. 'See how quiet you can be.' She kissed her on the top of the head and ran uphill through the trees.

The men below her on the track had made more progress than she'd expected. She paused, wondering whether she too should hide in the trees. What would they do if they reached the house and she wasn't there? She'd heard stories of mobs burning collaborators' houses. Better not to be in the house or better to be in it to protect it?

No time to dither, she sprinted out of the trees and up the track. She was fit from years of walking and cycling up here. Shouts followed her but she knew she could maintain the distance between herself and them. Pappa would come out, perhaps with his shotgun, if necessary, and scare them off. Then he and she would run down to collect Kari.

The shouts grew more distant. Asta allowed herself to slow to a walk, heart thumping, breaths coming in spasms.

A shadow took shape on the track ahead of her.

Magnus.

'I saw where you'd hidden Kari and guessed what you were doing.'

He'd run past her on the track while she was settling Kari, got ahead of her so he could cut her off from help.

'Don't you touch her, I'll kill you—'

He'd already grabbed her sleeve. 'It's you we want.'

'Why? What did I ever do to you, Magnus?' She tried to pull away. Her sleeve tore.

'You led me on, smiling at me, all friendly.'

'We were friends, just friends, you used to go sailing with us when we were here in the holidays.' For a moment, his grip loosened. Asta twisted away. He grabbed her more tightly.

'Don't, Asta, you're making it worse for yourself.'

'You have no right, my father—'

'Petter and Arne are good men. Patriots. They fought the Germans. You let them down.'

She pulled away. 'I'll scream.'

'Petter's not in the house, I saw him go up the track, probably gone out to help someone mend a fence. He's a good neighbour. He won't hear you. Nobody will except perhaps Kari.' Magnus's hand caught her wrist. It felt like a vice around her. She twisted her arm but his grip only seemed to grow stronger. 'Don't try to get away, Asta.' He sounded almost sorrowful. 'Take your punishment, show some shame.'

'My punishment.' She pushed at his chest. 'What are you talking about?' But she already knew. The group of men below her were coming closer. She didn't recognise most of them. Strangers who'd come to join in the shaming.

'We're taking you down to the harbour now. It's important that people see what's happening, Asta. It's part of the judgement.'

'You have no right to judge me, Magnus.'

He pulled her down the track towards the men, whose jeers rose in volume. Not just men, but a few women she vaguely recognised; not people who lived here, but from other villages along the fjord. People who'd known what she'd done with Max and had stored the information away.

One of the strangers, a man missing a front tooth, produced a roll of twine and tied her hands roughly behind her.

'What are you scared of?' she asked. 'That I'll hit you?'

'Shut up.'

'I hid men from the Germans in the barn,' she shouted. 'Christmas Eve 1942, and then again around the time of the Normandy Landings.'

He hit her round the cheek. 'Hold your tongue, whore.'

They'd reached the quay now. More people clustered around. Asta looked from face to face, her mouth opening as she saw Marte. Marte's face was pale, her eyes on Asta. *Say something*, Asta willed. *Tell them to stop. Show me that one person here will speak up for me.* Marte looked down.

Magnus produced a pair of scissors. 'That fine hair of yours, Asta Pettersen. It must have been what caught the eye of the grey worm. Let's see how pretty you look without it.' He pushed her down onto an upturned bucket that stank of fish guts.

It was only her hair, she told herself. Losing hair couldn't hurt her. Magnus's cuts hacked into the locks. He caught the side of her ear and she winced. He flinched and for a moment she thought he might stop, might show her mercy, but he carried on. Her hair fell onto the ground in front of her, catching the spring light, some of it blowing away into the water.

He stood back. 'Lucky for you we didn't shave you, too.'

'Not too late to do that, I've got a razor,' a man called.

'Let me go now, Magnus, you've made your point.' She tried to sound reasonable.

Something wet and stinking hit her on the head, sliding down her face. Fish guts.

'Not so pretty now, are you?' The crowd roared with laughter. Her hands were still tied so she couldn't wipe it off.

'Norwegians like the Jensens were tortured and killed and women like you just spread your legs with the Germans.'

'My brother never came back from detention in Gimli.'

'You're just German-loving whores, girls like you will be deported.'

Words fired at her like bullets.

Asta shook her head, trying to flick off the mess, her stomach turning, bile in her mouth. While they were here with her, they weren't looking for Kari. The thought kept her standing straight, maintaining eye contact with Magnus.

'Shame on you,' she said, so quietly only he could hear her. 'What will my father say when I tell him that Magnus Haugen took part in this?'

His face turned puce.

'Let me go, you've had your fun.'

Magnus looked at one of the strangers for guidance. The man nodded. Magnus took out a penknife. Asta's stomach lurched. He was going to cut her face with it, scar her so she was marked for life. But he went behind her and released her hands. She turned to look at Marte, saying nothing, but staring at her, trying to see a sign of shame in Marte's eyes. There was something, concern, anguish, but Marte still said nothing.

Walking briskly away, desperate not to humiliate herself by running, taunts still shouted at her, Asta rubbed her wrists where the twine had cut them before she wiped her face. She stank of fish guts. A stream ran down the side of the track towards the fjord. Crouching beside it, Asta rubbed her face. Her ear was bleeding but didn't hurt. Her cheek stung. She touched it gingerly. Magnus's scissors must have cut her there, too. Ever since she and Max had kissed in the farmyard, she'd known this punishment was coming for her. Now it had fallen on her.

Kari was shivering when she found her in the hiding place. She'd wet herself because she hadn't moved, following Asta's instructions. 'I left you for too long, *kjære,* I'm sorry.' She dropped down beside the child. 'You're frozen. Let's get home. They've gone, you're safe now.' Kari stared at her.

'Your hair, Mamma?'

'It's all right.' Asta forced a smile. 'I've just got shorter hair.'

'Like Pappa?'

'A bit like Pappa.' She knew she didn't look like Max though. She looked like Kari's Mamma, but frightened, shaken. Kari's lip trembled. 'My hair will grow again. I'll be like Rapunzel.'

Kari's face brightened. She loved the fairy tale.

When they reached the red-painted wooden house Pappa was standing there. 'What happened? I thought you'd be home before now.' His face grew pale as he looked at her. 'Asta? Did they...?'

He grabbed Kari from her mamma's arms. 'She's not hurt?' He looked Kari over. '*Gudskjelov*. Thank God, you're all right.' Kari leant against him, burrowing into his warmth and strength. 'Your hair, Asta...' He broke off. 'We'll say nothing about it now. There's food on the table for you both.' He sounded like Pappa again. 'And the chickens will need you to collect their eggs, Kari, when you've eaten.' He set her down gently, as though he didn't want to let go of her. She wriggled out of his arms and ran up the track. Her father had gone. Her mother had left her and reappeared looking dishevelled and scared. But her grandfather was still here and the chickens still needed feeding. Everything else was forgotten.

# ELEVEN

At night, when Kari was tucked up in her wooden bed and her door closed, Asta and Petter talked. Her face stung, but she'd applied disinfectant ointment to both it and her ear, and the cuts would heal up. As for her hair, she was trying to ignore it. Magnus had cut chunks of it so close to her scalp he might as well have shaved it. In other places it hung in jagged locks above her cheekbones. 'Do you want me to cut it all to one length?' Pappa asked.

'Not tonight. Let me see how I look when I've washed it. Do I still smell of fish?'

'Only very slightly. I'll heat up more water for the tub. You can have a good soak.' He opened a cupboard and pulled out the bottle of akvavit and poured her a glass. 'Drink this. Your mother always said it was good for the nerves.'

Nothing could help her, but she sipped the powerful spirit anyway. 'They hate me, Pappa.'

'And most of the crowd were strangers?'

'Magnus was leading them.' The spirit was doing its work, making her feel less shivery.

He shook his head. 'He's known us for years. Why turn on you like this?'

'He was a little over-attentive before Max... appeared. I sensed he wanted to be more than friends.'

'Ah.' Pappa nodded. 'Sometimes I wondered. He seemed to hang around the house.'

But Magnus wasn't the one on her mind. 'Marte was in the crowd, too.' It hurt to tell him this, to acknowledge that her friend had been standing there, watching as Asta was humiliated. Asta blinked hard, trying not to let tears fall from her eyes.

'Marte?' He sat up straight. 'Surely not?'

'She didn't actually throw anything.'

'I should think not.'

'But she watched as they cut my hair.' Her voice trembled.

'Scared, probably.'

Too scared to stand up for her friend? But seriously, what could a single female have done to stop that angry gang of men? Asta rubbed the place where a stone had hit her forehead. 'Do you think that's that now? They've vented their anger, had their revenge and now we can move on?'

Her father looked over her shoulder towards the front door. 'So much anger is being vented now that the Germans are finally going. Some justified. Some not at all. You know how the last years have been?'

Of course she did. All Norwegians had friends and family who'd been rounded up and sent to camps in Norway, or to faraway places in Germany and further east. Many wouldn't return.

'Some in that crowd probably need to deflect attention away from what they did or didn't do in the war.'

Pick on a woman like Asta so to distract attention from their own behaviour during the occupation?

'And others...' Pappa gulped.

'Others what?'

He sighed. 'You're not naïve, Asta. You knew I was going down to the village to meet my friends. You must have guessed we weren't just playing cards or chess.'

'What were you doing?'

'We passed on information. Troop movements, new vessels on the fjord, more aircraft than usual. We passed it up a... line to people who sent it over the sea to the British. But some of the intelligence we sent were warnings.'

'What kind of warnings?'

'People to avoid. People around here who couldn't be trusted, either because they were our own Norwegian Nazis or because the Germans had some kind of hold over them.'

So many secrets.

'Some of those people who attacked you this morning might fear I'd let slip names,' Pappa said slowly. 'A warning to me to keep what I knew to myself, as much as punishment for you.'

'But Magnus wouldn't fall into that category? He was no collaborator.' Nor was Marte.

'I imagine they used Magnus to find out more about the people in the area.'

'They won't attack you, Pappa?'

He gave a scornful laugh. 'No. Why attack a man when there's a woman you can pick on? A defenceless woman with a small child. It's despicable, whipping up anger into an attack like that.' His eyes showed his hurt and dismay.

Something was on her mind, something it was time to say while they were talking freely and admitting the rawness. 'You were angry with me, too, when Kari was born. When you realised just how poorly I'd behaved with Max. I deserved the anger.'

'I was very shocked,' he admitted. 'And frankly, livid. I thought of you as a sensible girl with morals and Max as an honourable man, despite being what he was. You hated it when he was billeted on us, almost to the point of rudeness. Yet then the two of you went behind my back and...' He glanced at her and fell silent.

That was what had hurt Pappa, the deception. Which was why she and Max had tried to halt the relationship in the first weeks of its existence. But once the flame had been lit, it had proved hard to extinguish. Once she'd known how Max's skin felt against hers, the softness of his lips, the scent of him, she couldn't unknow it. After the first time he'd slept with her, she'd found ways to be alone with him on the farm. And even as each example of German brutality had reached her ears, she'd carried on, managing to detach those horrors from the man she loved. More personally and critically, she'd known her father would hate what she was doing, but still she'd continued. Desire could wind its fingers round your common sense and conscience, grip you tight, pull you away from what had mattered before.

'I'm sorry,' she said. 'For everything. You could have thrown us out, but you didn't.'

'How could I throw out my own daughter? And my grand-daughter?' Pappa let out a deep sigh. 'Despite everything, I saw that what was between you and Max was stronger than just a passing passion between a lonely girl and a handsome, kindly man. It was huge adjustment to make, all the same.' He swallowed.

Had she in some way damaged her father's heart further by inflicting such a thing on him?

'Yet when my anger passed, the three of you seemed so right together. And little Kari, well... how could I possibly think that her arrival was anything less than a gift?' His face softened as he mentioned her name. 'You married Max and that showed you wanted what was best for the child, even though I fear marriage has made your situation more difficult now.'

For a moment they sat in silence, the only sound the ticking of the kitchen clock.

'Our marriage must have been the final straw for Magnus,' Asta said, her mind going back to her former admirer. Marrying the occupier, instead of living shamefully in sin – she couldn't have done more to inflame him. The Norwegian state agreed with Magnus. Women like her were threatened with deportation to Germany, told they had chosen their nationality by marrying Germans. They weren't Norwegian, not any longer.

'You married for Kari's sake,' Pappa said. 'I know it was a difficult decision to make.'

'I couldn't bear her to think she was just the product of something casual. Max and I meant the world to one another.'

*Meant.* Was she already looking at her marriage of two years in the past tense? Max was just one more defeated enemy, with no agency over his future. He might be her husband, Kari's father, but in war, individuals counted for little. They'd pushed that hated uniform back on him and he'd be imprisoned with the other combatants.

She'd pushed a harsh truth into a dark space, as if it was a wireless to be hidden behind shelves in a cellar. 'Perhaps Max and I shouldn't have married. Kari and I could have moved out and waited until memories faded.'

'This is a small country. People would sniff the truth out.' Pappa was right. People's kin stretched across the mountains and fjords, farm to farm, fishing boat to fishing boat. For all the lack of roads in remoter areas, gossip and news seemed to spread on birds' wings or on the crests of waves.

'I'm still glad you made the relationship official,' Pappa said. 'Even now. You made a promise to one another. That still counts.'

She hoped he was right. She was flailing, all instinct deserting her. She might have been a small girl again, needing someone to tell her the answer. Everything had fallen apart today.

'I don't know what to do. Spotting Marte in that crowd, it's made me see this place very differently.'

Pappa nodded. 'I'm going to arrange a boat for you tomorrow. Quietly, but quickly.'

'What?' She sat up.

'We'll get you up the coast. And then there's someone I know who'll help you leave for Scotland.'

'Scotland?'

'Not sure where they'll take you. Aberdeen, Peterhead, perhaps Shetland.'

Where Norwegians had trained for special projects there, a rugged and remote place in the middle of the ocean.

'I can't possibly leave Kari.'

'All across Europe people have had to leave children for periods of time. For the children's sake.'

'How is it for her sake? If I go, she should come, too.' Separating from Kari would be like asking her to remove a limb. Impossible.

'You can't take her on a fishing boat across the North Sea. Not even in summer.'

He was right. The voyage would be difficult, possibly dangerous, even in good conditions. The fjords could still be mined.

'Kari's safe here. She loves the animals. And you know I'd take good care of her.'

Of course he would.

'It would only be for a matter of months, until things calm down.'

'But it's so far away. And it won't change what people here think about Kari. She'll still be here for them to abuse.'

'If you aren't here to remind them, *kjære*, if it's just the two of us, they'll soften their tongues.' He sat back in the chair, looking tired. He still wasn't quite right. That heart of his... 'I don't think Kari herself is at risk. For all that happened today, Marte won't let anyone hurt her.'

She'd protect her friend's child, even if she wouldn't stand up for her friend? Asta didn't think she'd ever get over seeing Marte watch her being humiliated without saying a word.

'How will you manage on the smallholding without me, Pappa?'

'Men are drifting back here now. I'll hire someone to lend a hand when I need it. Or write to our cousins and ask if they can spend some time here. They might be glad to see the fjords again.'

Her hand went to one of the cropped tresses on her neck. She couldn't stop touching her hair, as if her mind hadn't caught up with it being slashed off. Magnus, with that look of triumph in his eyes as he wielded his scissors. Marte, just standing there, a hand placed over her mouth, turned to stone. Asta had been waiting for her to scream at them to stop. 'Are you really sure you and Kari are going to be safe here?'

'If it becomes too bad we'll think again.' Pappa stood up to serve the supper. 'But without you around, there's less of a reminder to everyone. A child's just a child, after all.'

Asta was now a danger to her own daughter. She had to face that fact. Asta blinked hard and stood up.

'Let me do that, Pappa.' But he shook his head and pushed a bowl of soup towards her.

She sat down again and ran her spoon through it, brain registering that it smelled good and she was hungry, but unable to lift the spoon to her mouth.

'I could take Kari away for a while,' he said. 'Until memories are less sharp.'

'You love it here, this house, Pappa. You had your happiest times here with Mamma.'

His solemn expression relaxed. 'We certainly had some good times out here before the war, didn't we?'

'And what would you say to people who know us in Bergen when you reappear with a grandchild?'

'I could say she's a cousin's child I'm looking after.'

'Why would you take on a distantly related three-year-old, Pappa?' She tried to say it gently. 'They'll know it's Kari living with you and who her parents are. Bergen's no distance away from here at all. Everyone finds out the truth about everyone. Everyone is someone's kin.' She spoke the last words with bitterness dripping through.

Yet she could understand some of the anger against women like her. Deaths. Deportations. Some of those suffering the beatings, the electrodes, the maiming and executions had done less than she had sheltering those two men in the barn. It might have been her, picked up, imprisoned, shot. She and Max might have dwelled in sunlight, but they'd been two fools playing in front of a dark veil.

'Asta, this is your best chance. And Kari's, too. You don't have to stay away for long.'

'I can't leave her.'

'The child is all that matters.' Petter's voice was heavy, sad. 'Just a few months, six at most, to let things settle down.'

'Kari and I should have gone to Max's family in Brandenburg when he offered to organise it for us. He said they'd be good to us. It just seemed such a... I couldn't see us living in Germany, away from you.'

'Some of those Russian soldiers...' Pappa looked away. Brandenburg was in the Soviet zone. Word had reached the fjords of the widespread rape of women.

It seemed doubtful they'd hold back from violating a woman just because she claimed to be Norwegian.

'Anyway.' Pappa slapped his thighs. 'Enough of all the should-haves and regrets. Let's look to a brighter future. We can start again in Bergen when you come back, the three of us. Open up the house, make it our home. It's a big enough place.

Your mother and I were happy there, with the two of you growing up. We can thrive there again. Kari can go to school there. If Bergen's too quiet for you, you can return to Oslo, Asta. Finish your studies.'

He sounded upbeat but his face betrayed the intense strain of the last years. The death of his wife. The silence from his only son. His daughter falling in love with a German, marrying him, bearing his child. Opening the family up to the hatred of the neighbourhood. It had always meant much to Petter Nilsen that they were respected in their community. He'd done his utmost to be a good neighbour to those around them. So had Mamma. And their daughter's passion for a German had threatened everything they'd built up for their family.

What were a few months, perhaps a year at most, away from Kari if it was for her benefit and Pappa's? One fewer person to feed, too, albeit one able-bodied person fewer to work on the smallholding.

Everything rational pointed to her going away. If she could only numb the part inside her that was screaming out that she couldn't leave Kari.

'Think about it,' her father told her. 'But go to bed now, child. You look exhausted.'

In the morning, when she was washing her face in front of the mirror, Asta felt the shock at her changed appearance all over again. Her hair, so taken for granted, gone. She put a hand to her neck, as if it might still be there, invisible. Kari came running in and blinked at her. 'My hair will all grow back,' she told the child again, forcing a smile. 'Just you see. It will be longer than yours.'

Kari held up her arms so Asta could lift her to the mirror and she could look at the two of them together. She shook her head. 'Poor Mamma.' She stroked her mother's cheek in consolation.

'I'll go to Scotland.' She waited until they'd finished eating. Kari ran out into the yard, where they could watch her from the open door. Asta smiled at her father over the breakfast table. 'You're right, Pappa. Things will settle down again and I can come back and start again, find work. Perhaps even finish my studies.' His face brightened. He'd always hated the fact that her time at university had been cut short. A scholar himself, he'd accepted that Arne was always going to be a practical person, a bright mind that needed action to feel engaged, was how Pappa had put it. Asta was more like him: fond of books and discussion.

Exile to Scotland or England would only be temporary, but Asta would need money. She'd be in a foreign country without an income. During the war, money had seemed barely relevant. Life had revolved around the currency of rations and the produce from the smallholding. What would she do during her exile in Britain? Office work? Would they actually let her work over there? Just how good was her English? She needed to start brushing it up. Too much time had been spent speaking German to Max. If necessary, she'd take a domestic service job. The British liked their big houses and servants, didn't they? Well, she certainly knew a lot about running a house, cooking and sewing as a result of the war. She had practical skills. Farm work was a possibility, too. A fleeting pang hit her as she remembered the plans she'd had before the war, how she'd work in some interesting and well-paid job and travel the world. Now she'd be grateful for a job as a maid or milking cows. As for returning to university, that was just a daydream.

Pappa stood up.

'Where are you going, Pappa?'

'To see someone about a boat.'

'What, now?' She heard the shock in her voice. Somehow she'd hoped there'd be a bit more time to think about this.

'The sooner the better.'

Through the window she watched him walk down the track, perhaps to see one of the same contacts who'd smuggled Arne out of Norway in 1940. Now Pappa would be begging them to help Arne's treacherous sister with her hacked-off hair and half-German child. Those contacts mightn't have been in the crowd that had attacked her yesterday, but they might approve of the punishment dealt out to Asta.

Kari was trying to persuade the cat to let her stroke it but the cat politely evaded her attentions, moving out of her range and jumping over the wall into the paddock. She gave up and ran up to a group of hens, who scattered. Asta went outside to her daughter. 'You have to approach the chickens gently.' She scooped Kari up. 'How would you feel if I ran up to you like a big bad wolf?' She tickled the child's stomach. Kari roared with laughter. She was a child who seemed to have been born with the sunshine always shining on her, as Berit Nilsen would have said. Certainly Kari had brought light into Asta's own life. She put Kari down and took her hand. 'Let's go for a little walk, kjære.'

'Walk,' Kari agreed, pulling at her hand. 'Come on, Mamma.' She seemed to have forgotten about her time hiding behind the rock yesterday, showing no signs of still being upset by what had happened. Were the memories still lurking in Kari's mind, ready to frighten the child again when they reappeared? Should she talk to her gently about the events? Or was it better to encourage Kari to forget? All she *did* know was that something like that must never happen to Kari again. Asta's resolve strengthened again. She could do this, leave Kari, choose the best course for her child.

Kari let go of her hand and ran ahead. She was so adventurous, so keen to explore, reminding Asta of Arne. Kari would be fine with her *morfar* while her mother was away.

She ought to be preparing for the trip. Kari needed enough serviceable clothes for the coming summer and beyond, into the colder months. The child was growing fast and had barely anything in a larger size. She needed to finish knitting the hat for Kari she'd started, red with a white snowflake pattern. Another pair of shoes would be needed soon, too. If she was going to leave her child, she'd leave her well prepared for the year to come. She must check that the berries she'd attempted to preserve without sugar last summer would still be safe for Kari to eat. And Asta's clothes required attention, too, holes in jumpers darned, her jacket sponged and aired. She wasn't going to go to Scotland looking like a downtrodden war victim, even if she did have this closely cut hair. It would grow again, she reminded herself. Patience was all that was needed. Soon she'd look more like her former self again. A memory stirred inside her. Her silk stockings, bought on the black market, only ever worn on her wedding day. She'd take those with her.

The sun was out. The clothes could all wait. Who could tell how many more walks there would be along this track into the hills? 'Let's go up to the waterfall,' she called to Kari.

She wanted to stare at the sparkling ribbon of silver, point it out to Kari, try to imprint it on her daughter's mind so she remembered standing there with Asta. She wanted to tell Kari how much her father had also loved the waterfall, its noise, its shimmering.

Her eyes felt sore as she tried to burn the scene into her heart.

Petter and Kari watched Asta until she was only a little dot in the boat, waving and waving until she vanished. 'I'll come back for you,' Asta called. 'Be good for Morfar until then.' Asta had left her before with Morfar so Kari waved cheerfully back at her.

Petter led her gently away before the boat disappeared, his heart aching both for the child and for her mother. His pride in his daughter mingled with sorrow. And anxiety. Asta had been a girl who loved her family but had firmly put herself first. Perhaps that was natural for a youngster. Even as her mother had died and the Germans had arrived, she'd been fretting about stockings and cosmetics, books left behind in Bergen or Oslo. At times he'd wanted to snap at her.

Yet she had risen to the challenge of the occupation like a champion, toiling with him on the smallholding, learning to cook the often meagre rations.

She'd fallen in love with the wrong man, made a terrible mistake, but somehow turned the relationship into a little family. His family. Petter had seen Max leave with genuine sorrow. And now Asta was going, too, proving herself capable of sacrifice for her child's sake.

Just him and this small girl left in the little red house, now.

'All will be well,' he said. 'It will all work out.' He'd said this all Kari's short life, even when inside, he'd felt a tumult of emotion. 'Perhaps we can stay,' he went on, in a quiet voice. 'People are reasonable, after all. A child's a child, an innocent, and now Asta isn't here to remind them, a line can be drawn. Those who cut off her hair were mainly outsiders.'

Kari hadn't a clue what her grandfather was talking about, only that his voice was low and his shoulders hunched. 'Feed the goats?' she suggested.

He looked down at her. 'Good idea, *kjære*. We can't do all we'd like, but that we can do.'

# TWELVE

Asta clung to side of the bunk and forced herself to open her eyes. It might be well into spring now, but the North Sea crossing pitched and tossed the fishing boat as if it wanted to smash its passengers and crew to pieces. The other passengers barely let this dent their high spirits. Two were returning British men, possibly involved in operations they would keep secret for the rest of their lives. A couple were Norwegians heading for Scotland to rekindle longstanding seafaring connections or to take their leave of people they'd worked with clandestinely during the occupation. From what she'd gathered, all these men had made the voyage across the North Sea under threat of fire from German planes or patrol ships. These were brave, patriotic men. They'd despise women like Asta. Pappa had urged her to keep her woollen hat on, hiding her hair, and say little about herself. The captain knew she was a contact of Petter's, that was all. In Scotland, wherever the boat docked, she'd have to make herself known to the harbourmaster out of earshot of the others.

Asta kept herself to herself, letting them believe she was suffering from seasickness or shyness at being a lone woman thrown into a group of men. Shyness wasn't a quality she associated with herself, but she'd let them believe she was some kind of blushing maiden if it meant they didn't ask questions. They probably thought she was lovestruck and desperate to reunite with a man she'd been parted from. That much was true, but if she'd told them the object of her passion was probably now a prisoner of war, on the wrong side, that she had succumbed to his charms while men like them were fighting for freedom, their good humour would turn to contempt.

Her wedding ring hung around her neck on its chain next to the pearl Max had given her. She fingered pearl and ring, as if they were lucky charms. Pearls came from oysters, formed around a tiny piece of grit. It had been like that for Max and Asta, finding something in one another that transcended the hatred and the everyday privations of war. His looks, his strong body, his way of moving had undoubtedly been hard to resist, but his kindness had made him irresistible. Seeing him wipe her father's brow that night Pappa had been so ill had made something melt inside her.

While wearing the ring would spare her unwanted approaches from the men, it would raise too many questions about the identity of her husband. She dreaded bumping into someone who was in contact with Arne and might pass on the news about his sister's wartime marriage. If she could find him in Britain, she'd tell him herself. Otherwise Pappa would break the news when Arne returned to Norway. She and Pappa could explain that Max was a good person.

They hadn't heard news of her brother for weeks now, other than a short message passed on via one of Pappa's friends, saying he was well and would return as soon as he could demobilise. Pappa had let out a long sigh of relief. Both his children had survived the war fit and healthy. More than many families in Europe could say. Asta tried to feel the same way: she and Max and Kari were healthy and had so much to be grateful for.

They just had to get through the next difficult part and all would be well.

At least when she was alone in the cabin, she could remove her woollen hat. She peered at her reflection in the tiny square of mirror above her bunk. It could just be her imagination but surely her hair was already regrowing? As long as the British didn't suspect she'd had it chopped off because of an infectious illness and quarantine her. Her need to find paid work weighed down on her as the boat pitched and rolled.

She reached inside her jacket pocket to pull out the photograph of Max, herself and Kari, sitting on a wall in the farmyard last winter, smiling, the snowy whiteness all around them, reflecting light up onto their faces. She and Max had been living in a fool's paradise. When this picture was taken, they'd known the Germans' time in Norway was finite. What exactly had they imagined would happen when the surrender finally took place? Max had made plans, writing a careful explanation of exactly where his family home in Brandenburg was, giving the telephone number, assuming the lines would still work. He'd told her the best way to go from the railway station – again, assuming trains even ran in Germany. From what she'd heard, people weren't allowed to travel much, even if they could find trains still operating. Max's notes listed family and other people who'd help her and Kari. He'd made sure she had all the paperwork, their marriage certificate, Kari's birth certificate, everything, and it was all stored in a metal box in Pappa's hidey-hole. Yet still she hadn't faced up to what was going to happen. Her image in the photograph was one of a happy young woman enjoying her small family on a beautiful wintry morning.

Kari had been a smaller toddler then, her expression one of wonder at the snow. How much she'd grown these last months. Her sunny nature didn't seem to be changing. Asta prayed her daughter would keep it. Max looked relaxed in the photograph, too, his cross-country skis neatly arranged against the wall beside the group. He'd just returned from an excursion hunting for hares up on the mountain when Pappa had taken the photograph.

Where was Max now? The Germans had marched to surrender points to hand themselves over. She'd heard that some had simply put down their guns and turned in the direction of Germany without bothering to surrender. Perhaps Max had done this? He hadn't held a combat role. Who would think it worth imprisoning a civil engineer with a maimed hand? Perhaps he was already at home with his parents and sister, of whom he'd spoken so fondly, showing them photographs of his time in Norway. Would he be pulling out his copy of this very same photograph, telling them about his wife and child? Would he proudly list all the things that Kari was doing now, how every day she learned some new skill? How strong she was, how full of energy and mischief, and such an affectionate child.

She could barely think of Kari without feeling that her chest was being crushed. Pappa would care for his granddaughter, of course he would, but how could he protect the child from the contempt falling on her? That heart condition of his, down-played but untreated during the war... He'd promised to take care of himself, to find someone to help out on the smallholding.

Had she been rash to do what her father had suggested and make this voyage? Part of her saw the logic in removing herself, severing the constant reminder of Kari's parentage by leaving. Now, in this pitching cabin, instinct screamed at her that only she could protect her daughter and she should have stayed with Kari. This was all wrong. As soon as she landed in Scotland she'd return to Norway as speedily as she could, even if she had to lie her way onto a boat. Nobody else could look after Kari as well as her mother could.

Someone stomped past the door to the cabin, lurching into the door. Asta froze as it opened slightly. An apology was shouted and the door closed again. There was no lock. If whoever it was had barged in they'd have seen her on the bunk with her cropped hair. They'd know what cropped hair meant on a woman. Infectious illness wouldn't come to mind. They'd treat her like a whore.

Asta closed her eyes and tried to channel her thoughts back across the sea, to the track up from the village and the house where Kari might be waking up now, ready to let out the chickens, anticipating a day out in the garden with her grandfather, perhaps a stroll up the mountainside to the waterfall later on. But perhaps there'd be more people waiting to ambush them, to taunt the girl, throw stones at her. Kari's morfar would scare them off, but what would it be like, living with this kind of response to you every day? How could she start school when she was old enough? All the children in the classroom would have heard the whispers. Children could be vile to one another if adults didn't monitor them.

This separation was going to wrench Asta's heart in two. *I will be back*, she called silently across the sea to her child. *Your morfar will take great care of you while I'm away, I know. We will start again. I haven't left you, Kari, not really.*

PART FOUR

# THIRTEEN

## PETTER

Kari seemed accustomed to her mother's absence now. The letters they received were always a highlight, with their little drawings of things Asta had seen in Scotland and London. Bearskins on the soldiers guarding Buckingham Palace, the red buses, telephone boxes and post boxes in London. A Scottie dog in a tartan collar.

*I've got a job as a clerical assistant in an insurance company in the City of London, in one of the few offices in the area the Luftwaffe didn't flatten. We suffered during the occupation, Pappa, but we didn't see destruction like this.*

*I tried to contact Arne in London. When I went to his last-known address, the landlady said he'd moved on. Do you know if Arne knew about Max and Kari? I really want to tell him myself before gossip reaches him. As weeks and months pass, chances are he's going to find out and it's best it comes from me, not the locals.*

*In the meantime, I'm already making plans for my return to Scandinavia. If I can't come home to Norway, Stockholm would be a good place for Kari and me to live: near enough to home that you can visit, but a fresh start for us until we can reunite with Max. I don't know when they'll let a German move to Sweden, but his engineering training will surely help? I read somewhere the Swedes plan mass urban rebuilding projects in their cities, with bridges over all the waterways. Max would love that kind of work.*

*I haven't had replies to my letters to him in Brandenburg and I'm worried. The Red Cross can only tell me that he was in a prisoner of war camp near the Rhine, but my letters there have gone unanswered. I'm told he falls into a grey area because although he was wearing uniform at surrender, he hadn't got a normal service record because of the years spent working as a civilian. This might make him harder to trace.*

None of these parts of the letters meant anything to Kari, of course. She could only understand the tone in her grandfather's voice as he read and the promise that her mother would come back. If the letters were long, she wriggled on his lap, wanting to do something else.

Of course she was still so young, three this coming Christmas Day. 'I wish your mother was still here, too,' he said, stroking the top of her head. The months that Asta had been away was such a long chunk of her short life. 'I always miss your mother, but she is safe and one day she will return to us. In the meantime, aren't we lucky, with our animals and our little house?'

The people in the village were mainly kind enough to the child. Some of them whispered when they went to the post office and the whispers didn't sound kind, even though Kari wouldn't understand their meaning. Petter eyed them, wondering if any of them had watched the group throwing stones at Asta, without helping her, tempted to ask. Marte would glare at the whisperers. But the whispers didn't stop.

'Don't bring it up,' his friends urged. 'Those men were mainly outsiders, bringing their trouble with them. Let emotions die down.'

'Magnus Laugen was no outsider.'

'Magnus is an oddball, always has been.'

He didn't see his friends as often as he had before Asta had left. Kari needed someone in the house at night and, besides, it felt awkward now. The group had worked hard for Milorg behind the scenes, passing on messages, taking in weapons smuggled into the village and hiding them until they could be passed on. With his friends, Petter had felt a connection to what was going on in Norway and beyond that had given him purpose. Continuing his work with the group while Max was under the same roof hadn't been easy, but he'd still managed to be useful once or twice, taking handwritten notes up the mountain and leaving them in a hut, though with his wretched heart, these exertions had worn him out. If Asta suspected, she'd said nothing.

Peacetime felt hard, even though he'd longed for it so much.

The letters in official envelopes were still arriving for Asta. She'd told him to open them. In stark terms the letters insisted that Kari was a German citizen and would receive no help from the authorities. Damn them, Petter Nilsen hadn't asked for public assistance, wouldn't dream of it. He would provide for his granddaughter. And Kari was a Norwegian child, as Norwegian as her mother.

Worse came the next week. He'd always thought the threat of deportation to be exaggerated, but there it was in black and white in an official letter, instructions to go to a camp near Oslo, for 'processing' before she was sent on to Germany. She no longer had the right to reside in Norway, the country of her birth, the land her parents, grandparents and forebears had lived in. Asta had helped the resistance effort during the war. She didn't know Petter had been aware of what she'd done. Hiding people wanted by the Gestapo was no small matter, it showed she was a true patriot.

Tomorrow he'd talk to Marte, ask her to use her Milorg connections to pass word around, telling people what Asta had done for the cause. Some of those who'd shorn Asta's hair, pelted her with missiles and humiliated her, might feel ashamed when they knew the truth about Petter's daughter.

Young Marte blushed when she talked about Arne. There'd been a flicker of something between Marte and Arne before his son had left, but nothing serious. They'd certainly had a long spell away from one another, but that was the way of things in wartime. The relationship could be rekindled. The prospect made Petter smile. Yes, she'd stood by and watched Asta's humiliation. It had hurt Petter when Asta had told him this, but Marte must have suspected that intervening would make things worse for Asta. Marte was a good person. She'd risked her life for Norway many times. Having her in the family would be something positive. There'd be more of them around the table for meals again.

Talking to Marte was a task for tomorrow. That evening he took Kari up to bed and supervised her teeth cleaning, washing her face and hands, and brushing her blond hair, now almost shoulder-length. Kari usually fell asleep quickly at night, worn out by the days spent outside, even in winter when it was very cold. He read a story to her, fairy tales from the book that had once been Arne and Asta's. Arne had scribbled on the picture of a troll on the title page. Typical of the boy. Berit had been so angry with him.

Where was Petter's boy now? Why wasn't he coming home now the war was over? Arne's letters were vague, something about business opportunities to pursue to 'secure' his future. He mentioned acquiring fishing boats from the British, if they could be found. Seemed a fool's errand to Petter. Norwegian fishing boats were designed for the fjords in a way that Scottish and English boats weren't. Surely the British would need their own fishing boats? Yet he couldn't help but feel proud of the boy. Arne's urge to rebuild was right. Norway was in a dreadful state. The Germans had destroyed so much of Norwegian industry as they'd retreated. Cities like Bergen had been blasted by both sides. Why shouldn't an energetic and brave young man like Arne throw himself into a good business opportunity that would help his country?

Petter kissed his granddaughter goodnight. 'Sov godt, sleep tight. See you in the morning.' As he closed her bedroom door, he took a moment to steady himself before he walked down the steep stairs. Kari was too young to know that at times Petter's heart seemed to be following a rhythm of its own devising, suddenly pounding and speeding up, or that his chest some-times felt tight, as if someone was pressing down on it. Easy to pass off as the effects of overexertion. When things were settled, he and Kari would take the ferry to Bergen so he could see a specialist.

Good to see what state the old house was in after so many years of being left empty. He'd gone there briefly just before the invasion to visit friends, to stock up the medicine Berit needed and bring back a few things to make her more comfortable in this little wooden house. He was distracted by the deterioration in Berit's condition and had hurried around, closing shutters and turning off water pipes.

Kari would enjoy the ferry trip to Bergen. The child had never left this small corner of the fjord and she'd be wide-eyed at being on a boat, seeing more of the waterfalls and then Bergen itself, coming into view. Did the old part of the city by the port still look as it had before the occupation? It had been terribly blasted, Max said. Never mind, Bergen would rebuild itself. He pictured himself and Kari walking slowly up the steep streets behind the quay to the house, stopping to look at the view so her short legs could rest. In the old creamy lemon-walled family house there were still cupboards full of Arne and Asta's books and toys she'd love to investigate. He imagined her running through the airy rooms, exclaiming at the rocking horse and doll's house in the nursery. He'd think of some way to explain who she was to anyone they bumped into who might recognise him and wonder about the child.

Petter made his way slowly downstairs to the chair by the stove. Idleness wasn't good, but he needed to take a few minutes before going outside to check all was in order before he could rest, wireless on – how good it was to listen without fear again – a book on his lap. Asta had done more than he had noticed, quietly insisting on shutting up the animals at night, clearing the kitchen. In the past three years she had changed from being a somewhat self-centred girl and thrown herself into the challenge of occupation. Even what could have been a disastrous affair with their German lodger and the birth of a child had been transformed by Asta and Max into something precious. How Petter missed Max, as well. The arrival of this young man, German occupier though he was, had partly compensated for the absence of his own Arne. Working outdoors with Max holding a post steady for him, or willing to climb ladders, had been a practical and enjoyable companionship, even though Petter had hated everything about the country that Max represented.

Arne. As Asta's letter had reminded him, Arne might still not know about his half-German niece, unless someone in the village had passed the gossip up the fjords and across the ocean. Telling Arne what had gone on in this house would be something Petter hoped, in a coward's fashion, he would not have to do himself. Petter knew his son: kind but quick to respond, sometimes rash. Yet did he really still know the boy who'd gone away to fight all those years ago? Arne would have seen things, done things, that would have changed him. Perhaps it wouldn't be long now until his son was coming through that door, throwing off his boots and coat, asking what there was to eat, filling the house with his energy and laughter. And once Arne met little Kari, he wouldn't help but have his heart melted by her. Even the old woman down the track from here, who'd scowled at them following Kari's birth, now allowed herself a smile when she saw the child running along the track, babbling about a bird she'd seen or pointing out a flower in the grass.

On this particular evening, as well as the usual breathlessness, Petter felt a pressure in his head and a vague sense of unease he couldn't pinpoint, even as pleasurable thoughts of returning to the old house in Bergen and reacquainting himself with the library he'd left there passed through his mind. Everyone was safe. Kari would be sleeping upstairs. All was well here and yet... He was just weary, that was all. He was looking after a small child at the same time as doing everything else on the smallholding. His heart was beating faster now and it was making everything more of an effort. He'd light his pipe and sit for a moment, reviving himself.

The stove needed stoking. Words of Max's floated through his mind, something Max had said, very early on, when he'd just arrived in the house. Something they'd looked at together but hadn't been able to complete. A black soot mark on the wall reminded him of the conversation but he couldn't remember its conclusion. They'd needed to order something, but it hadn't been available. Max had told him he should try again to get hold of the part, but Asta's sudden departure had put it out of his mind. Whatever it was, he needed to resolve it. Max's face was in front of him and he was silently telling Petter to make more enquiries, tomorrow! The stove, something about the stove...

Tomorrow, he'd remember it all tomorrow. For now, he just needed to rest, close his eyes for a moment until his heart rate returned to normal and the headache lifted. It was better when he just sat very still. Was he asleep? He really couldn't tell. He was drifting out into the fjord in a boat, the current drawing him away. Someone was calling at him to pay attention. The wind had changed, but he couldn't remember how to sail the boat, how to turn it back to shore, and the warm breeze was making him sleepy. *Wake up*, a voice told him. He tried to rouse himself but couldn't find the strength. It was a lovely day out on the water, so no harm done if he just let himself go. Just for a little bit longer. Petter smiled as he watched the shore fade into the distance. He'd been alone in the boat yet now Berit was sitting beside him. 'I missed you,' he told her.

In the morning Kari woke to hear the cow mooing. Something in the animal's noise sounded different. The patch of light on the wall was higher up. The sun had been up for a long time, telling her off for being a *syvsover*, sleepy head. Morfar hadn't woken her for breakfast.

She didn't feel hungry. Instead Kari felt something strange in her stomach, as if she might be sick and when she stood up the room spun. Her head hurt. Instinctively she dropped to her knees and crawled to the staircase. Morfar's bedroom door was closed, not open as it always was during the day. She called for him and when he didn't answer she made her way carefully down the wooden stairs, hanging on to the banister as he'd showed her. She was supposed to wait for him to help her down as it was steep. 'I did it!' she called out triumphantly. 'All by myself.'

Morfar was sitting in front of the stove, which had gone out, his mouth slightly open. Kari rubbed her eyes. Outside the cow's moos were louder now. Why was her grandfather still asleep? Where was her breakfast? Was it a game? 'It's me,' she shouted. 'Wake up, *syvsover.*'

She'd never called him that before because Morfar was always awake when she was. He didn't stir. 'Chickens! Cow!' she reminded him. The door handle was a bit high for her to reach. Morfar always joked that she'd be tall enough by Christmas, which was also her third birthday. Kari pushed a chair towards the door, her stomach still feeling strange as she climbed up to push the door handle down. Mamma told her not to do this, but Mamma wasn't here to stop her.

When the cold air came inside, Kari's head felt less heavy. She clambered down and ran back to her grandfather. 'Breakfast time.'

He didn't stir, even when she shook his leg. The game didn't feel as much fun now. Kari went outside, puzzled, looking for someone to help, someone to wake up Morfar and tell him the game was over now. The moos of the cow followed her as she walked onto the track. The older lady who was often stern-faced with Kari but sometimes gave her apples was leaving her house, basket over arm, on the way down to the village. She frowned at Kari. 'What is it, *kjære*? Where's your coat?'

'Morfar.'

'What about him?'

'Asleep.'

The woman looked at her wristwatch. 'He's probably just tired. Go back inside now, you shouldn't be down here alone.' The woman walked a few steps away and turned around. 'You mean he won't wake up?'

Kari observed her, not sure how to answer. 'Asleep,' she said again.

The woman frowned, but she didn't look cross now. 'Oh, come on then, I'd better have a look at him.' She took Kari's hand and led her back into the house. 'Wait there,' she said, going inside.

Then there was shouting, the woman running out of the house saying she was going to call for the doctor, dropping her basket, picking Kari up and running down the track with her. Snow was starting to fall, Kari noticed, putting out a hand to catch some of the flakes.

And all the time the cow was mooing and mooing.

# FOURTEEN
## MARTE

Marte still had nightmares about the day the men had dragged Asta to the harbourside. The mud had struck Asta's face. Marte had watched her friend's eyes widen in surprise. Asta couldn't wipe it off because they'd tied her hands behind her. Marte had bitten her lip, clutching her own hands so she wasn't tempted to strike Asta's tormenters.

Arne's letter, delivered by a fishing boat a few days before the German capitulation, had been stark.

*The war's effectively over, the occupation's ending but you must draw no attention to yourself, you must not tell people what we did. Keep your eyes open for the man we suspect. He isn't local and sounds unremarkable in appearance, except that he received a punch to the jaw in a bar a few months ago. There's specula-tion he might have lost a tooth. But don't confront him. Just watch him, who he talks to, where he goes.*

*It's not just you at risk. The Quisling supporters probably know Pappa has names. Dates. Do whatever you can to deflect atten-*

*tion away from yourself and him for the next few weeks, maybe a month.*

But Arne couldn't know that some of those same men, those traitors, were assaulting his sister like this. He didn't yet know that Asta had had a child. Marte hadn't told him anything about Asta's affair and marriage. It wasn't her place and he'd had enough to worry about on the clandestine operations along the fjords and undertaking the sea voyages between here and Shetland. Marte had half expected word to slip out and reach Scotland on the tongue of a Norwegian. Somehow, the news hadn't reached him.

Every time she recalled the moment when Asta was dragged along the quay, Marte had regretted her silence that day.

*I'm sorry*, she had tried to convey silently to Asta as her beautiful hair was hacked off. *I'm so, so sorry.*


And now Petter Nilsen was gone, too. Marte still couldn't believe it. Although he hadn't grown up in the village, Petter had been coming to the village with his family for decades. During the war he'd been a constant presence up in the red wooden house. Reliable, cheerful, sensible, for all he was a university professor writing books on economics. Marte felt a grief that was perhaps something to do with losing her own father at the start of the occupation. Petter had become her substitute father. When he'd come into the post office he'd always had time to talk to her, and not just about resisting the Germans.

It felt as if everyone had gone apart from Kari and Marte. Asta was God-knows-where in Scotland or England. Letters seemed to take a long time to come through and Petter hadn't heard from her for a few weeks before his death. No other family lived close by. Who else was there to look after Kari other than Marte? The child was so sweet with her large eyes and wide smile. Even if she hadn't been her best friend's daughter, Marte would probably have taken her in. She thought of moving up to the Nilsen property to keep an eye on the smallholding and the animals still up there, but the stove was too dangerous to use. Petter wouldn't have known too much about his final hours, they said. Imagine surviving the occupation with a weak heart and then dying from a faulty flue pipe. Such a waste of a good man.

Marte took Kari up to the house to recover some of her clothes and toys.

'Just as well we took your red hat to keep you warm.' Asta had knitted it for Kari, Marte remembered, proud that she'd finally mastered some knitting proficiency.

It was safe to go into the house as it had been well aired. They tramped through the snow on the track, Kari holding her hand, seeming as settled as you could expect someone of not quite three years old to be in such circumstances, pointing at a robin on a branch of a fir tree.

They rounded the bend and stopped.

'What's that?' Kari pointed at the smoke spluttering out of what was left of the walls, their red timbers turned to charred black. A few chickens ran loose. The goat field was empty. A farmer had taken the cow after Petter's death, but the goats had been a useful source of milk for Kari. Petter's friends had helped with the milking. Now they'd gone.

'We should go back.' Marte turned around, tugging at Kari's hand. Whoever had done this might still be hanging around, watching them. Marte shivered.

'My bear,' Kari said, digging her legs in, refusing to move. 'I want him.'

The floor of the first-floor bedrooms had fallen down on top of the ground-floor rooms. What was left of the furniture was blackened. The rounded shape in the corner might be the remains of Berit Nilsen's spinning wheel.

'Don't worry about the bear, you have Ulla.' Marta had grabbed the doll from Kari's bed when she'd come up here to collect a few things for Kari that she could easily carry in her basket.

'Where are the goats?'

'Someone will find them, don't worry about the goats, they'll be fine.'

Kari's lip trembled but she went back down the track with Marte without complaining. Poor mite. What must she think? Her mother and father gone. Her grandfather dead. And now her home destroyed? Just as well children were resilient. Kari had a lot to adapt to. 'We need to feed my cat,' she told Kari. 'Could you help me?' Kari's face brightened.

Marte took Kari into the post office after the fruitless visit to the Nilsen house. She had nobody to mind her during opening hours. The child sat on a cushion behind the counter, drawing on the scrap paper Marte found for her in her drawer, standing up to run to the window every now and then to look outside. Perhaps she was waiting for her mother and father to step off the ferry.

Mostly those coming into the post office spoke kindly to the child. One or two had muttered under their breath about the Nazi brat. A sharp look from Marte generally shut their mouths. 'And when is Asta Nilsen, should I call her Frau Brandt, returning to her child?' one middle-aged woman from a farm up the valley asked. 'Or have they deported her for good?' She sniffed. 'When will this girl be joining her mother in Germany?'

'I am caring for her and she is going nowhere.' Marte slammed the book of stamps closed and folded her arm. 'If you have a problem with seeing her here, I suggest taking the ferry to the nearest alternative post office.'

Arne knocked on the door a few evenings later when Kari was asleep in Marte's small, second bedroom.

'Oh God, I'm so pleased to see you,' she blurted out, resisting the temptation to throw herself into his arms and letting him inside. The morning after he'd sheltered in his family barn, she and Arne had kissed passionately. Marte had told herself it was the relief of having him off the mountain. But it had felt like something more than that.

'I came as quickly as I could.' He put his arms around her. 'Thank you for all you've done for my family.' Marte's anxiety and exhaustion seemed to evaporate in his presence. They were a good-looking family, the Nilsens, but it was more than just physical attractiveness. They had a charm, a presence. Even when she'd found Asta a little flighty, self-centered at times, there'd always been something about her that had made Marte feel interesting, worthy of attention. You didn't always get that from city folk when you just worked in a rural post office.

Sitting by the stove she told Arne all that had happened. 'If only your father had found the part to mend the stove. I'm so sorry for your loss. And then to lose your home, too, it's terrible.'

'I've been up there just now, though in the dark it was hard to see.' He pursed his lips. 'When I find the people who did that they'll be sorry.' Arne was a powerfully built man now. Marte felt a flush of relief that he was back.

'I'm pretty sure I know who it was,' she said. 'Magnus.'

'Magnus Haugen?' Arne frowned. 'Really?'

'I've seen him hanging around your house. He had a crush on your sister, used to follow her. His heart was broken the day she...' She swallowed. How much did Arne know about his sister and Max.

'The day Asta married a grey worm, you mean.' Arne's jaw tightened.

Marte let out a breath. At least she wouldn't be the one who told him about Max Brandt marrying his sister, fathering his niece. It was a relief, she thought guiltily.

'Word passed up the coast and someone made sure to tell me as soon as I landed.' He folded his arms. 'I'm surprised it took two and a half years for me to find out she'd had a child with a German.' She wondered if he'd already exchanged angry words, or blows, with a busybody keen to taunt him.

'Arne, I, I didn't know whether or not I should—'

'I'm not blaming you for not telling me. Your instinct was right. It would have been a distraction when we were on an operation that was already in danger.' He gave a dry laugh. 'I saw no signs of a child or German husband when you hid me in the barn.'

She'd moved the pram out of sight. It had only been luck that had meant Max had been going away to Bergen on a trip. What would have happened if Arne had seen the baby? Or seen his sister kiss her German husband goodbye? Even now, Marte shivered.

'I can't imagine what got into my sister's head. I would never have thought it of Asta, never. She was raised to have good morals.' There was scorn in Arne's voice.

'Don't judge Asta.' Marte said it sharply. 'She was alone up there with your father, and Petter wasn't a well man.'

'All across Europe women were left to keep things going, in desperate conditions. They didn't all impregnate themselves with German soldiers.'

'Max Brandt wasn't like other German soldiers. He was decent. Kind. And...' She swallowed, unable to express to Asta's brother just how attractive Max was. 'Anyway, your father and Asta doted on Kari. She is a sweet child.'

'The child is an innocent party,' he agreed. 'She doesn't deserve any of this.'

'You'll see her in the morning and I know you'll love her, too.' She paused. 'And Asta did her bit, as you well know. She risked their lives to let you sleep in the barn last year.'

'Yes.' He sounded quieter.

'Asta sheltered you, not even knowing who you were. Because that's the kind of person she is. And it wasn't the first time she'd hidden men on the run from the Germans.'

He looked surprised.

'Asta let a man stay in there on Christmas Eve of 1942.'

'Did she?'

'Again, I asked her to do it, even though it was dangerous for her, and she said yes. But I think the stress of it all brought on her labour.' She told Arne about Kari making her appearance hours after Asta had agreed to hide the man. 'It was lucky that everything turned out all right for her and Kari.' Thinking of Asta made her eyes water. 'And she was brave.'

'Not as brave as you, Marte.' His eyes were warm as they focused on her, making her feel as if she was coming alive again in a way she hadn't since the war had started and the Germans had arrived.

'Plenty of others helped the cause. I was just in a useful job.' In the post office she'd intercepted letters she suspected came from informants, addressed as they were to the Gestapo in Bergen or police. Those people, fugitives from the city hiding out in remote farmhouses, had been able to sleep safely in haylofts and shepherds' huts because Marte had destroyed the letters, risking her job, her liberty and possibly her life. She'd passed on messages to fishing boats going on up the fjord or across to Scotland and delivered agents, sometimes weapons, to remote hideaways. If she'd been caught with guns or grenades in her rucksack, it would have meant a bullet to her head.

So many times she'd wanted to talk to Asta about what she

was doing, to relieve herself of some of the strain. But it was impossible. Asta's loyalties were divided.

But always, the image in Marta's mind was how she'd failed Asta when the mob had grabbed her. There hadn't been time to put things right with Asta before she'd left for Scotland. She'd hoped to see Asta before she left, but she'd obviously found a route out of the village that didn't involve the ferry. Asta probably despised Marte too much to want to speak to her again, anyway.

All Marte could do now for Asta was to protect her child. There was consolation in that.

'How have you been, Marte?' Arne's voice was gentle. 'I should have asked that question first, shouldn't I, instead of going on about collaborators and that sister of mine?'

Marte sat up straight. 'I'm fine.' She smiled. 'Putting the war and the occupation behind me, looking forward to the future.'

You said these things to show that you hadn't been beaten down, that returning men could be proud of you. Her mind went again to poor Asta, banished, parted from those she loved, waiting to return home and start her life again, with her daughter and, who knew, one day perhaps her husband, too.

And Magnus floated through Marte's mind as well, lumbering around, still vengeful, even though he'd driven Asta away and destroyed her home.

Arne moved into Marte's house, officially sleeping in the small second bedroom, with Kari sharing Marte's bed. From the prurient looks Marte received when people came into the post office, it was clear everyone knew what was going on between her and Arne. She didn't care. They could gossip all they wanted.

As well as working on his fisheries project, Arne vowed to rebuild the Nilsen home when materials could be assembled.

He hadn't yet proposed to Marte on his knees, with a ring, but talked about the life they would lead when married and back at the smallholding.

Kari greeted Arne with initial shyness, but quickly accepting him as her uncle, running to greet him when he came back to the house each day, having spent hours up at the Nilsen place, tidying up the remains of the house, mending fences and reclaiming livestock. He took Kari out on Marte's old toboggan, telling her that her mother had loved the snow, too. On her birthday on Christmas Day, he found a pair of small skis in the Nilsen barn. The three of them went up the mountain to introduce Kari to the world of snow. It was like being a proper little family, doing something normal and wonderful in peacetime. 'She reminds me of Asta,' he said, carrying her back inside, red-cheeked and exhausted. 'Barely a complaint.'

'Even when she fell over those few times getting her balance.' Thinking about Asta reminded Marte that Kari wasn't her own child. Asta would be longing for her daughter.

'Kari's a true Norwegian.' His face darkened, probably because he was thinking about Kari's German father.


Arne came home the day after Christmas with a black eye. He grinned at Marte and Kari as they stood, mouths open. 'Do you like my eye?' he asked his niece. 'Isn't it pretty?'

'Funny,' Kari said, laughing at him.

But when Kari was in bed Arne's tone was sombre. 'Punch-up with Magnus, who wanted to tell me what a slut my sister was. I left him in quite a state, but he shouted at me that everyone knew who the father of Asta's child was.'

'I thought it would be better for Kari when you came back.' Marte gave an exasperated sigh. 'After all you did for your country, the likes of Magnus should respect Kari as your niece. But I think it makes them feel even worse about themselves.'

He looked at her quizzically. 'We're making people like Magnus feel guilty or inadequate?'

'Wouldn't take much to do that.' She frowned. 'He never amounted to much, even before the war. Never settled to anything. I remember his father trying to get him into building boats, fishing, farming.' Marte tapped her head. 'Something up here isn't wired for anything steady. And he became obsessed with Asta. She was kind to him at first, felt sorry for him. He read into it more than Asta meant and became jealous when she fell for Max Brandt. Even so, he shouldn't take it out on a little child.'

'Trouble is, it's not just Magnus with a grudge against Asta,' Arne told her.

It was true. And the violence of the war had accustomed some men to settling scores with brutality.

'What is it?' She poured him a mug of coffee. They could buy real beans again now, though the cost made her blanch. Instead of drinking it he stared into the dark liquid, brow puckered.

'It's Kari.'

'What about her? She's doing well.'

'What future does she have here? Or anywhere in Norway? Suppose Asta never comes back for her?'

'Of course she'll come back for her own child.'

'But how? She's regarded as a German citizen now. They won't let her in.'

Marte sniffed. 'You could find her a berth on a fishing boat, smuggle her in.'

'The government won't support the children of the occupiers.'

'Asta doesn't ask for any state support for Kari, why would they worry about her being back in her home?'

'If she comes back here, it won't be easy. Not for either of them. She will be a non-person legally. How can she study or work?'

'Perhaps she could settle in Britain? We could bring Kari to her in London.'

He looked up. 'You mean she might divorce Brandt? I hadn't thought of that.'

'Asta won't divorce Max.' Marte heard the absolute certainty in her own voice. 'She adores him.' She remembered their wedding day, the way Asta and Max had looked at one another as they were proclaimed *mann og kone*, man and wife.

'In the meantime, it's difficult for you to look after Kari.'

A small child was certainly hard work. Finding someone to watch over Kari when Marte had post office duties wasn't easy, either, even now Arne was around. Scrabbling around for enough food, keeping Kari clean and fed and occupied while turning up to work at the post office, it was all starting to feel overwhelming. But surely they could widen their search for help with Kari? Not everyone around here felt animosity for the child, after all.

'We aren't her parents. What happens if my sister never comes back?'

'You're her uncle. In time, people will forget who her parents really are and they'll look on us as her family.'

'They'll always know who she is here.' Arne frowned. 'Nobody will ever let her forget who her father is.'

'Perhaps Max Brandt will want Kari and Asta to go to Germany? Asta said his parents sounded like kind people.'

'Germany's a hellhole, barely any food to feed the population, half the houses in ruins, and will be for months, years yet. Kari couldn't go there. Even that German couldn't ask it of a child.'

'I heard it was bad, but you know the Germans, they'll clear the rubble.'

'They can't feed themselves. The Soviets are taking the best of their produce from their zone. The Germans there haven't even got the manpower to harvest what's left.'

It certainly didn't sound like a safe place to send a mother with a small child. During the occupation Marte had managed to listen to the illicit BBC broadcasts on her wireless set. She'd picked up bits and pieces of information from the boats that docked at the quay by the post office. Her contacts in Milorg brought her news of what was happening in the eastern parts of Germany as the Red Army moved west, carrying out its bloody revenge for what the Germans had done to Soviet citizens. She shivered.

'The Germans did terrible things,' Arne said. 'They brought this on themselves. You know, they estimate millions and millions of Jews, Poles and Russians were killed.'

'So many?' She couldn't imagine such a large number of people.

'I saw some news clips in London about the camps the British and Americans liberated, but it didn't tell half the story. What the Soviets found in Poland was even worse.'

'I heard of atrocities in camps in this country, too.'

'The Germans tortured and killed Norwegian men, women and children.'

And when people looked at Kari, too young to understand any of it, the child represented all this hatred and despair.


A letter to Petter from Asta turned up in the post office mailbag, with a little drawing of a dog for Kari. Marte showed her. 'Open it,' Arne told her. 'What does Asta say?'

Asta was working in London, saving money for her return. She obviously hadn't received Marte's letter telling her about her father's death and the fire at the Nilsen house. She sounded cheerful, saying the office work was dull, but the people were friendly and she enjoyed being in a city, even when it was as grey and smashed up as London was. She was moving into a better flat and would send on her new address shortly.

'Asta always liked city life. No word of when she hoped to come back?' Arne asked.

'She hopes by summer.' Marte skimmed the rest of the letter. 'She says she doesn't want to be a liability when she returns.'

'She needs to know about Pappa,' Arne said. 'I'll have to telegram her. It's not the way I'd want to tell her the news but we have no choice as she doesn't seem to receive letters.'

When Kari asked about her *morfar* they said he was dead, but she didn't understand what that meant. She'd ask the question again. Eventually she seemed to accept that Petter wasn't coming back.

Marte had to stop bringing the child into work with her. A few locals had heightened their complaints, saying they didn't want to have a German child reminding them of the occupation when they came in to send letters.

Arne was thoughtful when Marte told him. 'You have to work. Is there anyone who can watch her for us? You said you've been asking around?'

'No luck so far.' Marte looked out of the kitchen window. Kari was talking to the cat, squatting down so she was face to face with the animal.

'Petter Nilsen was a much-liked member of the community, but nobody will help his granddaughter.' Arne made a scoffing noise.

'I thought they'd soften towards her, I must admit,' Marte said. 'Look at her. She's adorable.'

'Sometimes I wonder...'

'Wonder what?'

'If Kari would be better out of Norway.'

'With her mother in London, you mean?' Marte nodded.

'They'd just think Asta and Kari were a Norwegian mother and child.'

'With the name Brandt?'

'They could change it back to Nilsen. Don't they have deed polls or something in England? I bet other people with German names are changing them, too.'

'I'm not sure about Britain. They had a tough war, too, with bombs and rationing. Asta wouldn't find it easy to work and look after Kari, even if they let Kari join her.'

'So Kari can't stay here, she can't go to Britain, or to her father in Germany.' Marte groaned. 'What do we do for the best?' Sometimes Marte's chest seemed to be filled with a physical pain for the child, so young and bright, yet so burdened by her circumstances. 'We could move.' Marte could hear the hesitation in her own voice. She wasn't like Asta. Everything she loved was here, on the fjord. It was where her family had always lived, generations of them.

'We could go to our house in Bergen,' Arne said. 'But it would be the same there. Everyone knows who Kari is. Oslo would be more anonymous, but it wouldn't work for me.'

Not with his North Sea fishery plans.

Arne took something out of his duffel bag. 'When I was in Bergen during the week, I saw this, in an American magazine, *Time*.'

He handed it to Marte, open on a page with photographs of a group of young children. 'It's a children's home in Stockholm. They're setting up a scheme for families in Canada and Australia to adopt war orphans.'

'Kari's not an orphan.'

'It might almost be better for her if she were.'

Marte gasped. 'How can you say that?'

'A new family would mean Kari wasn't worried or scared by things she can't possibly understand,' Arne said.

'No.' Marte threw the magazine down on the table. 'Not that, Arne. You can't do that to Kari and Asta.'

Sometimes she thought that war had put a hard edge on Arne. He was loving with her and Kari, but there was a ruthlessness to him at times, forged by the harshness of fighting a covert war against the invaders. He had never told her much at all about what he'd done, other than that it had involved training on Shetland and passages on Norwegian fishing boats back and forth across the North Sea. If you saw your companions killed and imprisoned, knew some of them would have been tortured, perhaps it made the fate of one small civilian a matter to examine objectively, not emotionally. Marte remembered him telling her about what he'd discovered at the Jensen farm that summer of 1944, the bodies of his friends left for him to find. Experiences like this had turned a dial somewhere inside Arne's heart. He could play with his niece in the snow but still think about her as if she was a stranger's child. Arne wasn't the openhearted boy he'd been when he'd left for war in 1940. He was a good man, a brave man, but something had been cut out of him. She hoped she could help him grow it back.

He stood up. 'I'm going up to the house.' She must have looked surprised. 'My father had an old metal box he kept important papers in.'

'A safe?'

Arne gave a half laugh. 'Nothing so secure. Before the war it wouldn't have occurred to him that locking it would be necessary. I don't remember seeing it when I looked around the ruins, but I never looked down in the cellar.'

'What important papers, Arne?' But in her heart she knew. Asta wouldn't have taken her daughter's birth certificate with her, would she? Nor her marriage certificate? She'd probably packed in a rush, imagining she'd return to Norway in a matter of months and that her child was safe with her own father.

. . .

Arne lugged the sooty metal box back to Marte's house that night, when Kari was asleep. 'It took me hours to shift the burnt wood to get down into the cellar. But down there everything was almost untouched. This is locked and the key is nowhere to be found, but I can jam it open.' He sat down at the kitchen table and pulled a penknife out of his pocket.

The lock submitted to the knife's blade without too much effort. Arne pulled out a handful of papers, flicking through them, a frown on his face. 'Here we are. Kari's birth certificate. With her German father's name on it.'

'Surely that won't be enough?'

He shrugged. 'I don't know what they'll need. I have my identification papers and my parents' marriage certificate and my birth certificate are here.' He laid them out on the table. 'So I can prove I'm Kari's next of kin. You've got her identification papers, haven't you?'

She hesitated. 'Arne...'

'You think I'm being cruel, don't you? That I can let my niece go without feeling bad? I'm desperate at losing her, she's wonderful. But life here won't get easier for her. What happens when she has to spend more time with other children? Schoolkids can be unforgiving.'

'I think we have to do what's best for Kari, yes. But not this. Think what it will do to your sister?'

His expression darkened. 'Asta's fling meant more to her than her country.'

'It wasn't a fling. She and Max—'

'While Mamma was alive, she made sure Asta knew her duty. Asta wouldn't have taken up with a German if Mamma had been around. Pappa always spoiled her.'

'You're far too harsh on your sister...' She took a breath. 'Asta may have been a little self-absorbed before the war. Lots of people are when they're young. But when the war started and your mother died and you went away, she worked for hours, cooking, outdoors in the vegetable patch, putting up fences for the goats, looking after the chickens, same as anyone else around here. And she nursed your father through his influenza, barely sleeping or eating for days and days. And Max helped her.'

Arne was silent for a moment. 'I accept Asta may have changed,' he said quietly. 'But that only makes me even more convinced she needs to find a new life for herself, too. Asta needs to forget the war. How can she do that with a permanent reminder?'

He meant Kari.

He turned back to the papers from the metal box, arranging them into piles. Something made him sit up straight.

'What is it?'

He was reading a handwritten note. 'This.' He pushed it at her.

*That daughter of yours and her brat won't find a home here after the war. We are watching your family, Petter Nilsen*

'No signature, of course.' He sounded weary. 'I wonder why Pappa kept it?'

'Planning to unmask and confront them?' Marte read the letters with a sinking heart. Upstairs a child was sleeping, unaware that there were people who hated her like this for nothing that she could be blamed for. The injustice made bile rise into Marte's mouth. She had wanted to protect Asta's daughter by keeping her but perhaps Kari would be better off somewhere else. Perhaps Arne was right? 'Do you think it has anything to do with the collaborator you are trying to catch? The man with the missing tooth?'

'Possibly, though he's not the only one with a grudge against our family because of what we know about them.'

.  .  .

'You told them it's only temporary, until Asta comes back or we find another solution?' Marte asked for the second time, folding Kari's nightdress and placing it on the top of the small suitcase.

'I told you, I did.' Arne looked at his watch. 'Where is she? You should be on your way. The ferry won't wait.'

'Saying goodbye to the cat. She wanted to go up to the goats again but I told her there wasn't time.'

Kari knew she was going on a trip by boat and train and her excitement was great, but understanding this would mean separation from the animals had come as a blow. Arne's preliminary visit to the children's home in Stockholm had been successful. 'It's in a lovely old house, Marte, lots of space. With a park nearby for the children to play in. The administrator's a woman well used to children like Kari. She genuinely wants to help them. Provide them with a safe environment. There are other Norwegian kids there, so Kari won't feel out of place.'

Kari came inside. 'Hurry,' Marte called. 'Let's wash your hands and face. I expect you've got them muddy again, haven't you, *kjære?*'

Kari held them out. 'Clean.'

'Where's your doll?'

Ulla was retrieved from the kitchen table. Arne came into the room and swept his niece up into his arms. 'Enjoy the boat and train, little one. And be good for them in Sweden.'

'Sweden,' she echoed. The puzzled look Marte had noted came over her face again. How could Kari know what Sweden was? Was she going to ask about Petter and Asta again? She didn't talk much about her father these days, but her mother's absence still baffled her.

Soon Kari would be with children her own age, constant companions to play with. Her mind would be filled with games and distraction. The war and its aftermath would become distant memories. She'd just be a Norwegian orphan, no questions asked about parentage.

But Kari wasn't an orphan, and it was important to remember that her mother would return.

When they sat down on their seats on the deck of the ferry, Kari could hardly speak for excitement, her eyes wide. Marte felt her own flush of pleasure at travelling freely again up and down the fjords without needing German permission. She lit a cigarette and watched the breeze whirling the smoke away into infinity and felt truly free for the first time in years.

When Bergen came into view she pointed it out proudly to Kari. The city showed the scars of the RAF bombardment of its U-boat bases, but was still noticeably the picturesque place Marte had known all her life. Her spirits lifted as the houses on the harbour front came into view, looking like a child's toy town.

'Your *morfar's* house is just up a side street from here,' she told Kari as they disembarked, pointing up the hill.

'Morfar!' Kari shouted.

'He isn't there, *kjære*. We told you, he's dead. But you'll see where your mamma grew up. Some of her toys are still there.' At mention of Asta, Kari looked puzzled. Perhaps she thought her mother might be in the house. 'Of course, she's not here at the moment.'

Marte was half dreading what they might find in the house after its long closure. Arne had organised a woman to come in and air it for them and make up the beds. The woman had also dusted and cleaned the windows and even found some wood for the stoves, as well as buying some basic food for them. The house was comfortable, so spacious after Marte's own small house.

Marte gazed at a photograph on the piano of Arne and Asta as children around Kari's age. The two of them had their arms around one another's waists, heads close together. Marte remembered them as retaining that closeness as they'd grown up, coming to the fjord for holidays, taking out their boat, arguing and competing with one another, but laughing together.

Asta had won a cross-country race on her skis when she was about twelve and Arne had been at the finishing line, Marte recalled, clapping and cheering on his sister.

Kari and Asta really did look so alike, though Kari's grey eyes reminded Marte of Max's. Max. Where was Max Brandt now and what would he think if he knew his daughter was heading for a home among strangers? Wild thoughts rushed through Marte's mind. She and Kari could stay here in the house. She would pretend Kari was a distant cousin of hers. She'd beg the Red Cross to help her track down Max in Germany. There must be a way... No. Arne was Kari's kin, not Marte's. She and Arne weren't even married yet. She had no right to disobey him. Arne Nilsen was a returning Norwegian war hero. Marte was just a girl who worked in a post office. She was lucky to have him as her future husband.

The night in the old house was distracting enough for Kari to forget her grandfather and grandmother. The next day, they set off by train to Oslo. Kari sat, face pressed to the glass, staring at mountains, trees, animals and fields, enchanted. Worn out by the spectacle, she dozed. Marte covered her with her own coat.

They spent that night in Oslo as it was too late to travel on to Stockholm. The hotel Arne had booked for them was in a back street, smelling of damp and full of sullen men who stared at Marte as she came in. War was over, but it would take more than months for the capital to recover, it seemed. When they were in their room, Marte was careful to lock the door and place a chair under the door handle.

Kari was quieter the next day, barely looking at the border guards who checked their papers when the train crossed into Sweden. Marte expected, perhaps almost hoped, that the men would question her but they merely wished her a pleasant journey. The forests and meadows they passed were beautiful, but as hours went by, Marte longed for the train to pull into Stockholm. The novelty of being somewhere new after years at home during the war was fading. Kari grew restless, bouncing on her seat, wanting to run up and down. She was a country girl, used to being outdoors and on the move. How would she manage in an institution where everyone had to adhere to the same rules? Asta, Petter and Max had brought her up well, Marte reassured herself. She'd fit in. She pushed away the doubts clamouring inside her.

The children's home was a nineteenth-century house of the kind that seemed common in Stockholm, elegant, with its own grounds. Marta paid the taxi and rang the bell at the iron gates.

A girl, young and round-cheeked, let them in. She didn't speak much Norwegian but seemed to be expecting Kari, whom she greeted with a hug and smile, a good sign, Marta thought.

Kari sniffed as they walked inside, across a black and white checkerboard floor. 'It smells strange.' She was right. Disinfectant, lots of bodies, food. Not a bad smell, but not like home.

In the office they were shown into, Marte felt an urge to get this done before the act of separation became unbearable. She knew she was being a coward, but it was too painful.

'When are we going home?' Kari asked.

'Your Uncle Arne thinks this is for the best, *kjære*.' She embraced Kari, feeling her small body cling to her, Kari not understanding what was about to happen but perhaps instinctively knowing it would not be good, that she should resist. Marte tried not to remember the calves her father had raised, how their eyes would show bafflement when you separated them from the cows. 'Just sit here for a moment.' She lifted Kari onto one of the chairs in front of the desk.

A middle-aged woman with her hair tied up in a bun came in, carrying a file. She greeted the pair with brisk politeness, beckoning them to sit. 'You have the paperwork?'

Marte handed her the envelope Arne had given her.

The woman, who hadn't introduced herself, flicked through the papers. 'Birth certificate, good, looks in order.' She opened the file and put the certificate inside.

'This is only temporary,' Marte said. 'So I'll take the certificate back with me.' The doubting voices inside her were now screaming in protest.

'Normally we would keep it here.'

'The child's uncle told me to return it to him.' She crossed her arms. Arne had said no such thing, but how would this woman know?

'Well, I suppose we could always ask you to post it to us, if necessary.' She handed it back to Marte.

'And we will let you know when Asta Brandt can come and collect Kari?' Kari sat up at the sound of her mother's name.

The woman wrote down a brief note. 'The mother's return was explained by Arne Nilsen as a contingency.'

'Contingency?'

'One of a range of possibilities.'

'*Nei.* No. Asta will be coming. I know she will.'

The woman smiled kindly. 'These mothers have the very best of intentions. They're not bad girls, not all of them, despite... They want the best for their children. Sometimes distance lends objectivity to a situation.'

Distance and objectivity didn't seem the words Marte would have associated with her friend's maternal feelings. Again, she thought of the calves separated from the cows and how the cows would do anything, storm through any weak fencing, barge past any human in the way, to return to their offspring.

'If Kari stays in Norway, they might send her somewhere you wouldn't want to see a child go,' the woman said softly. 'Suppose they deported her to a displaced person's camp in Germany?'

'They wouldn't do that.' Marte shivered. 'That would be inhumane. All by herself?'

'They could try to organise things so her father could collect her, but I understand travel across Germany is very hard at the moment. I can see you are a kind and responsible person and the very thought of that makes you see this is the best, the kindest option. We will be in touch when we have news.' The woman stood up. 'What time is your train or are you spending the night in Stockholm? I can recommend a reasonably priced hotel, if so.'

Marte stood, too. She'd wanted to get this over and done with, but now it was all happening too fast. Questions burned on her tongue. 'I don't know about this.'

'Arne Nilsen has signed the paperwork,' the woman said.

The girl who'd shown them in came forward and picked up Kari's small suitcase. 'Don't linger,' she whispered. 'It's best for the child if you just go quickly now. I'll look after her.'

Kari jumped off her chair and clung to Marte's coat. 'Don't go, Marte.'

'Don't make the little one suffer by hanging around,' the girl said.

Marte untangled her fingers from Kari's and walked out.

# FIFTEEN

Asta and Arne met in London. Arne was over seeing someone in Whitehall about the fish processing business he planned to set up, wanting to lease British fishing boats to boost catches. They hadn't seen one another for five years and she clung to him when he came up to her, outside the National Gallery in Trafalgar Square. When had her brother become this focused businessman? Gone was the boy she remembered. He had gained muscle and his face showed a watchfulness that was new.

As they walked to the Lyons' Corner House on the Strand, Asta listened politely to his business plans, desperate to interrupt and ask about Kari. She had her money saved for the trip home. She'd pick up Kari from Marte's and take her back to Bergen to live. Nobody was seriously going to forbid her entry to Norway. If necessary, she'd find a way of using her passport, with her old name in it, rather than any identification showing the Brandt name. Or she'd change the name by deed poll. Why did her brother need to see her now in England when they could surely meet at Marte's? It seemed he was spending all his time there anyway when he was in Norway. Arne had hinted at an engagement.

'So Kari's well?' Asta asked as they walked across the square.

'She is.' He gave Asta a brief smile, seemingly overcome with the emotion of finally seeing her again after all this time.

'She must have loved the snow. Did you take her out on those old skis we had as toddlers? She's just about big enough for them now.'

'She enjoyed the skiing.'

'She must be about this high now?' Asta put a gloved hand out to indicate how tall she estimated Kari must be.

'Something like that. Last time I... Oh, here we are.'

They'd reached the Lyon's Corner house. Conversation stopped while they removed hats and gloves at the table.

'I'm sorry the letter we, I, sent didn't reach you.' He fidgeted with the greasy menu. Arne had always been a fidgeter. 'I need to tell you something.' He was looking down at the food offerings on the menu.

'You said Kari was all right?' She leant forward, heart pounding.

'She is.'

'She's not suffering some long-term effect of the stove fumes?'

'Marte had the doctor give her a thorough examination. She was fine. Any signs of illness, Marte would have taken her to see the doctor again, you know how careful she is.'

'Marte has been wonderful. Kari must have been so shocked by finding Pappa like that.' Something lodged in her throat. 'This is my fault. I should have made sure we found the parts for the stove. It was all such a rush when I left.' She could still remember the race to pack her bag, to prepare Kari's things for the parting. 'Poor, poor Pappa. When you wrote me that last letter that finally reached me, I, I—' Her eyes filled with tears. How could he be gone?

'Pappa shouldn't have died like that, but the flue pipe was impossible to replace.' Arne spoke softly. 'And his heart condition made him vulnerable.' His eyes were fixed on hers, watching her, as he took out a cigarette packet and lit up.

'And you're sure Kari's all right?'

He drew on the cigarette. 'I told you, she's a healthy, sturdy little Viking girl.'

The muscles in Asta's face relaxed. She smiled. 'I've been trying to buy clothes for her, not that there's much on sale in London and I don't have many vouchers. I should have asked you to bring measurements. I bet she's tall for her age.'

'Asta.' He cleared his throat and rested his cigarette in the ashtray. 'Kari is well but quite a few letters have missed you.'

'When I moved to my new place, I asked the landlady to forward on the post but she was always unreliable. I can't believe I missed the letters you sent before about Pappa.' She looked at him, narrowing her eyes. 'What's happened?'

'We had to make some decisions about Kari.' Arne's eyes were on the table's worn surface. 'You know how hard things were in the village when you left? The awful experience you had when those people assaulted you by the harbour?'

Automatically she touched her hair, which was now at a respectable length again. Even now, memories of being grabbed, feeling Magnus's scissor blades against her skin, hearing the taunts of the crowd, could make her shake. 'It was why I left, to disassociate her from me. Pappa said it would be best.'

'You made a selfless choice, Asta. And it worked. Pappa acted as a shield for Kari. But then he died.'

'And Marte took her in, bless her.'

'Marte has received abuse. She had to stop bringing Kari into the post office because people complained.'

Asta stiffened. 'Which people? Magnus?' If she could get her hands on Magnus Haugen, he would regret it.

'It seems likely.' He shook his head. 'I don't know what got into him. I remember him as a decent enough boy but he stirred up local animosity.'

'I remember.' She shuddered, recalling not just the scissor blades against her neck but seeing the mud splatter on the windscreen of the car driving them home from their marriage ceremony, that look on Magnus's face.

'Then we lost contact with you at a crucial time.'

The waitress appeared. Arne ordered coffees and buns for them both in a hurry, so they could talk privately again.

'I was here in London. Before that in Scotland. Marte always knew I'd come back.'

He stubbed out his cigarette with great attention. 'Marte was worried Kari would be forcibly sent to Germany as a German national. She might end up in a displaced persons camp.'

'What?' She felt her stomach flip. 'Surely you wouldn't have let that happen! I thought all the aggression towards me would die down when I left.'

'Unfortunately, not.' He stubbed out the unsmoked cigarette in the ashtray.

She eyed him. 'There's something else, isn't there?'

'Someone burned our house to cinders after Pappa died.'

Asta had been going through the motions of cutting her bun. The knife fell from her fingers with a crash. 'Was anyone in it? Was anyone hurt?' The little red house was gone? It had always been part of her life, somewhere she could return to.

'Thankfully not. Whoever it was, they ripped down fences, trampled on anything that was growing, stole the goats and most of the chickens.'

The house where she and Max had spent those few years together, where so much of her early family life had been spent happily – gone. Pappa's work on the smallholding through all those wartime years, destroyed. 'I can't... I can't imagine why anyone would do it. Pappa had so many friends there. He was always doing favours for people.'

'Pappa knew things about those who were collaborating.'

She remembered Pappa telling her this at the time the crowd had shorn her hair.

'They didn't dare touch him while he was alive, though they wrote some letters threatening Kari. Torching his house after he died was a warning but probably stirred up by your relationship with... with that German.'

'That German? You mean my husband, Kari's father.'

Arne was silent. He would never understand how the arrival of Max had changed her life and Pappa's life. For the better.

'You can't imagine what it was like in the occupation when you were away and it was just Pappa and me there.'

'I saw how you built up the smallholding. It was impressive.'

'What?' She stared at him. 'You mean you had a local contact?'

'I came back, Asta. Four or five times, up and down the coast, sometimes closer to Bergen, once further north towards Alesund. Once to our village, to our home.'

'But you... You were serving with the Norwegians alongside a Scottish regiment?'

'I was working for... other people.' He looked down. She knew he wouldn't tell her what he'd been doing, not even now, with the war over. He'd probably signed official secrets oaths. Asta could only guess what his work had involved. Passing intelligence, organising wireless transmitters. Picking people up, dropping them off, liaising with the locals involved in Milorg.

'Did Pappa know? Did you see him?'

'I didn't see him.' He stared fixedly at the table. 'I saw you though, Asta.'

'What?'

'The summer of 1944. Around the time of the Normandy Landings. I spent a night in the barn.'

'Our barn?'

He smiled. 'I shouldn't have done it.'

'Why not?'

'You remember what happened in Telavåg?'

Telavåg wasn't that far from the smallholding. In April 1942, two Norwegian agents from Scotland had been hidden by the locals. An informer had informed the Gestapo. Fighting broke out when they arrived in Telavåg. One of the Norwegian agents and two Gestapo officers were killed.

She nodded. 'They razed the houses and arrested all the women, children and elderly. Sent all the men from sixteen to sixty to concentration camps.'

'That wasn't the only atrocity they carried out. Just before I came to our barn to hide, I'd been up at the Jensen farm.'

She eyed her bun, appetite gone, remembering what had happened to the Jensens.

'I saw their bodies. I should have stayed far away from you,' Arne said. 'The original plan was that Marte would smuggle me into her own house the previous night, but I was held up at my previous rendezvous. The days are so long that time of year, it would have been impossible to walk through the village to Marte's the next day without people seeing me.'

Marte's house was overlooked by other properties.

'Marte told you about the raid on our smallholding that very same morning?' They'd been on a walk, Asta remembered. On their way home, they'd spotted the Germans searching the house. Max had been there. He'd spoken up for the family and the Gestapo officer had reluctantly left them. Seeing what had happened had shifted something inside Asta. She'd told Marte the barn could be used as a refuge for Marte's fugitive. Who'd turned out to be Arne.

'Marte only told me after I'd left the barn the next morning. Otherwise I would have stayed away. She was amazed you'd agreed after the raid, when the dangers had been made so clear.'

Asta shrugged. 'Nothing like seeing bullies throw your possessions around and threaten your father to make you angry.'

'The smallholding was out of my view up on the mountain. Otherwise I'd never have agreed.'

If she'd known he was just across the farmyard, she could have talked to Arne, hugged him, known he was safe. Instead she'd handed him food and water as she would have a worrying stranger she was keen to have gone, fearing for Kari's safety.

'Marte knew I'd done that, but she still stood back and watched that mob attack me without saying a word in my defence.'

'When Magnus and the group did that to you we were watching people along the fjords, gathering evidence about collaboration with the Nazis by some resistance members. Marte was helping me identify collaborators. She had to keep her head down. I know it hurt her to see that happen to you.'

Not as much as it had hurt Asta to be pulled off the track and dragged down to the quay to be humiliated. But what could a single woman have done to stop the mob, anyway? But this wasn't the most pressing thing on her mind. She lit another cigarette, hand shaking. While they'd talked about Arne's work in the special forces and her small role in helping him, they'd leaned forward across the table towards one another. Now Asta sat back in her chair, suspicion threading its way through her veins like a cold worm.

'What have you done with my daughter, Arne?' She knew her brother. He looked like he had when he'd scratched her new skis on a stone, having borrowed them without permission. 'Arne?' He'd sent Kari to their cousins in the uplands for a few weeks, that would be it. Not what she would have wanted for her small child, but at least it was family.

'Kari is safe and cared for somewhere where nobody can reproach her for what she is.'

'At one of our cousins' farms?'

He shook his head.

'Where is my daughter?' She banged the table and her coffee spilt over the cup onto the saucer. He was going to say Kari was with friends of Mamma's and Pappa's in Bergen, or, worst case, in a children's home in Bergen.

'She's... Kari's in Stockholm.'

'What?' Asta had a sudden need to shake her head, like a dog when you gave it instructions it didn't want to hear. 'Kari's in Sweden? What on earth is she doing there?'

'It's a safe place for her. We didn't know when you were coming back, if you'd even be allowed to return to Norway.'

'You're saying a bunch of criminals and collaborators should decide what happens to me and my child?'

'It's not just Magnus and the locals. Other people across Norway feel very strongly about women who did... what you did. They agree with the government that you should go to Germany and live with your husband.'

She gave a half laugh. 'It's not that simple. I can't take Kari to live in Max's home. It's in the Soviet zone. Even if it wasn't, they're almost starving all over Germany and the bombed cities make the destruction here' – she pointed out of the window – 'look like nothing.'

'Of course the two of you can't go to Germany. Nobody could ask that of you.'

'I wouldn't be a drain on Norway. I'd earn a living and support Kari.'

'Norway doesn't want you, Asta.'

She flinched.

'You've built up a life for yourself in London. You're still very young. This is your chance to recreate yourself.'

'I don't want to recreate myself.' Her voice was rising. The couple at the next table looked over at them. 'I just want my daughter. Why didn't you and Marte keep her with you until I returned?'

'We did what was best. It's not some kind of punishment.'

'How can you say that?' Her voice trembled as the enormity of what her brother had done sank in fully. 'That's exactly what's happened to my child. She's been punished by being sent away from everyone, by her own uncle. I could move to Sweden, too, so we could be with Max eventually. But now...' She dried up, her dreams, her hopes as ruined as the buildings she passed each day on her way to work. Burned out. Smashed up.

Arne looked down at his uneaten bun, seemingly equally unable to say more. She shouldn't be sitting here in this café in London. She needed to head for Stockholm by whatever means possible to find Kari.

Arne reached across the table and touched her fingers. 'Your daughter is safer in Sweden, Asta. Nobody knows who her real father is there. She is just an innocent little girl who can start again.'

Asta snatched her hand away. 'Kari doesn't want a fresh start. She wants me.' Kari would be yearning for Asta with every cell of her body. 'She wants her father, too. Max was a good man. Pappa liked him. Or do you believe that every German is a devil?'

'They certainly acted like devils.' He spat the words out. 'Our people, sent to those prisons and camps. Tortured terribly, day after day. Transported on to extermination camps for more torture, more death. That's what your... man's people did to us. And why? What did Norway do to Germany to deserve all that?'

'You think I don't know what the Nazis did in Norway? What they did in Poland and France and all the other countries?' She was speaking quietly and fiercely now. 'I've seen the news films about those camps, too, the starved people, the corpses. You think I didn't wrestle with those facts? But Max isn't part of that. He never wanted to fight for them. He was almost relieved when he lost part of his hand and they discharged him from active service. And even if the Germans were all monsters, that's no reason for you to have done what you did with Kari.'

His face was still stony, his arms folded in front of him.

'This is personal, isn't it? You're never going to forgive me, are you?' She'd fallen in love with the wrong man and that was all her brother could see. 'This is your way of punishing me. You're not like Magnus, you won't hack off my hair, but you'll still make me pay by taking my child because you think I'm a traitor to my country.'

'I know you're a patriotic woman. Look what you did for me and for that other man you sheltered on Christmas Eve 1942.' He swallowed, looking down at the table. 'I'll give you the address for the children's home, Asta. Send them a telegram saying you're on your way to collect Kari. We always said it might only be temporary.'

'Might?' Scorn dripped from her words. 'You're admitting you were probably sending Kari away for good. Give me the address.'

'Of course.' He nodded. 'Once you've got her back, Marte and I will find a way of keeping you together in Norway or—'

She stared at him. 'I never want to see you or Marte again. We're finished. When I find my daughter, I'll stay with her in Sweden or bring her back here where I know she's safe.'

'I was hoping you'd be there when I marry Marte. We've grown so close.'

Marte had never even told them she was in touch with Arne during the war years. Probably because of Max's presence in the Nilsen house. On the other hand, Marte had never told Arne about Asta starting a relationship with a German, either.

How much Marte's silence on both points must have cost her, Asta didn't care.

'Tell Marte I'll be thinking of her on her wedding day.' She meant the words sarcastically but found she was feeling a fleeting softness towards Marte. 'She'll look wonderful in her bridal crown. She leant it to me when Max and I married, did you know that?'

Arne flinched.

'She liked Max.'

Arne's eyes were softer now, too. 'Sometimes it's the wrong people, the women and children, who suffer most in war. That's not right.'

Asta and Arne had been close as children, only eighteen months between them. She'd missed him so much. Yet sitting across the table from her, he was a stranger. Steam from the untouched cups of coffee rose like a fog between them. She tried to remind herself that when he'd made his dash away from the occupying German forces, she'd still just been a girl. Perhaps he still thought of her as too immature to know what was best. But no, she couldn't make excuses for her once-loved brother. He'd failed her. He had failed his own niece. Something else struck her. 'How did you manage to even do it? Surely even a German's child can't just be given away like an unwanted kitten?'

'Kari's birth certificate was in Pappa's cellar. In the metal box.'

She gave a scoffing laugh. 'He thought his box would protect everything valuable in case of an emergency. Pappa wouldn't have imagined you opening it to do this.' Arne looked abject. Good. She could find no words to make things easier for him. The gentler feelings towards him and Marte evaporated. The two of them had let this happen to Kari. Nothing could make up for it.

Asta grabbed his cigarette packet and took a pen out of her

bag. 'Write down the address of the children's home here. I'm going to book tickets for Stockholm.'

He wrote it down on the packet. 'Asta, won't you finish your coffee? Don't go off like this.'

She walked out without looking back.

# SIXTEEN

## STOCKHOLM

Kari's doll, Ulla, had come with her to this large, echoing house that smelled of cooking vegetables and bodies. Sometimes Ulla was the only person Kari could talk to. Nobody would tell her when her mother would come and fetch her. Even the young woman, who didn't shout, looked down at her feet when Kari asked about her mother. She didn't speak in the same language as Kari and they couldn't completely understand one another. The other adults spoke in loud voices. Their hands were not always as gentle. Briga, the oldest girl in Kari's dormitory, only a year or so older than Kari herself, whispered warnings and advice in Norwegian. *Stay away from her. She's mean. Stay quiet. Don't let them notice you.*

'My mamma will get me,' Kari told Briga. 'She's coming.'

Briga looked at her strangely. 'The mammas never come. They don't let them.'

So it wouldn't be Mamma, it would be Marte who'd come back for Kari. Marte wasn't the same, but she was kind. Kari turned her attention back to her doll, straightening her dress and hair. Ulla still smelled of home.

'I like your doll, Kari,' Briga said. 'She's pretty.'

Briga was pretty, too. Her hair was reddish brown and her eyes almost green. 'I wasn't supposed to look like this,' Briga told her once, pulling at a pigtail. 'I didn't come out right.'

Kari stared at her.

'I was meant to have fair hair, blue eyes. I was going to Germany because a lot of families wanted me. I was a special child. But then the war ended anyway.' Briga bit her lip. 'I wish I was in Germany. They had beautiful homes for us, in castles, with lots of food. We were better than other boys and girls. But now we're here and everyone hates us.'

Mamma had read her stories about castles. And Germany, that word meant something to her. It was where her pappa had gone. He'd marched away and Mamma had said he was going to Germany, to see his parents and his sister and tell them all about Kari.

'They hate us,' Briga said.

Kari remembered the men who'd chased her with Mamma and shouted at them. Her hand went to her hair as she recalled Mamma's hair being cut. It had looked funny. Mamma had laughed but not in the usual way she laughed when Morfar said something funny.

'You're too little to understand. Our mothers are bad. On Sundays, good people come to look at us and we wear our smart clothes. They aren't Norwegian and they don't mind that we're just German dirt.'

Dirt was what you washed off your face and hands before meals and before you went to bed. Briga's words were just one more part of a life that made no sense. 'When's my mamma coming?' she asked Briga again.

Briga stared at her. 'You really don't know anything, Kari. But you'll have a new mother and father soon and you'll be safe. I wish I could go to live in Germany, in a castle, like they said we would.'

Castles were where princesses lived. Kari just wanted her

real home, the red house. She picked up Ulla and found a corner where she could curl up, doll clasped to her, rocking slightly. Every time the door to the playroom opened, she turned to see whether it was her mother coming to collect her.

On Sundays the kind girl scrubbed them with carbolic soap and washed their hair. They wore clean smocks to go into the room where Marte had left Kari: a parlour with freshly painted walls, smelling of the wax that her mother had sometimes used on the dresser at home. People came in and looked at them, walking up to the row of boys and girls, discussing them. 'Some of them want boys,' Briga whispered. 'To work on farms.' No visitors came in the weeks around Christmas and the New Year.

On Christmas Eve they had a special meal of hams, spiced breads and rice pudding. Each child received a clean handker-chief and a prayer book. Briga knelt by her bed that night. 'I'm saying a special Christmas prayer than my next Christmas will be in a family. You should pray, too, Kari.'

Obediently, she'd knelt, opening and closing her mouth silently, mimicking Briga.

Visitor Sundays resumed. Instead of standing with the others, Kari found she was the only one the girl brought in to meet those attending.

'She was three on Christmas Day, of all dates, would you believe. Very healthy child, not a single infection since she's been here.' The same Fru Olsson who'd been here to meet her when Marte had dropped Kari here, was sitting behind the desk again, speaking in her Norwegian accent that sounded strange. The stove had been lit ahead of time. 'Good teeth. Clean. Well brought up. Quite bright. Some say that the mothers who do such things must be suffering mental deficiency, but there's no evidence of a hereditary trait.' None of the words meant anything to Kari.

The couple smiled at Kari. The woman had brown hair, slightly curling. The man was older, with wrinkles. The woman wasn't as pretty as Mamma but Kari liked her dress, with its rose pattern. 'I like your doll,' the woman said, in halting Norwegian. 'What is her name?'

'Ulla.'

The man laughed. 'How very Norwegian. She's been well used, hasn't she?'

Mrs Morgan pointed at a box of toys sitting on the rug. 'Shall we play with those? Which one is your favourite?' Her voice sounded jerky.

Kari hesitated. As she hadn't ever seen these toys before, she had no idea which one she liked best.

'Don't be shy, let's look together, shall we?'

Mrs Morgan sat down on the rug, motioning to Kari to join her, taking out a doll from the box, who was so much cleaner and newer than Ulla, along with a wooden boat, and a puzzle. It had been so long since she'd had toys like this, Kari almost forgot everything else, absorbed in opening the puzzle box, slotting the pieces into the right place. Morfar had done puzzles with her in the evenings, so she was good at them.

'She does seem bright.' Mr Morgan lowered his voice. 'Do we know much about the... the parents, Fru Olsson?'

'Mother was a student at Oslo University at one stage just before the occupation. Father was a civilian engineer, working on coastal defences. We know nothing more than that about him and he would now be back in Germany.'

'Strange that an educated girl like the mother would let herself... you know, behave like that.' Mrs Morgan was whispering, her words floating over Kari, meaningless, but somehow suspect.

'Strange and disgraceful. We suspect she must have had some kind of nervous breakdown. It's the only explanation.' Fru

Olsson stiffened. 'But of course, there's no sign of that in Kari,' she added hurriedly.

'She's certainly a beautiful girl.' Mrs Morgan sat back on her heels and gazed at Kari. 'Tall for her age. Lovely thick hair. I'm so taken with her.'

'You mentioned there was no sign of any... mental disturbance.' The man spoke in a soft voice. 'You're sure there's nothing that might cause issues later on in Kari's life? I mean, her mother probably started out normal, didn't she?'

'As I said, Kari's mother was from a very respectable family. Her father was an academic. Her brother escaped to Shetland and fought with the British against the Germans.'

'Clearly young Asta didn't share the family's patriotism?' Mr Morgan sighed. 'We mustn't judge when the occupation was so harsh for them, I know.'

'We have been very cautious with the child,' Fru Olsson said. 'She has been subjected to the same wholesome treatment as everyone else here. No special treatment for her.'

'Why would Kari have special treatment?' Mrs Morgan asked.

Fru Olsson's voice dropped. 'During the occupation, some of those women and children were brainwashed into thinking they were something special. The mothers were supplying the Nazis with a stock of genetically superior offspring. They received extra rations during pregnancy, would you believe. And extra food afterwards for the children. At a time when food was so scarce for the Norwegian population.' She sniffed. 'While Kari's been with us, she's had no indulgences, just simple food and routine. Nobody is special here. Their old identities are wiped away. That's why the child's birth certificate doesn't mean much, Mr Morgan.'

The words floated over Kari, meaningless. All she could tell was that Fru Olsson was saying things about her that were causing Mrs Morgan to sigh.

'We'll take her away from those bad influences,' Mrs Morgan said, standing up. 'And nobody will fill her head with those ideas.'

'It's good she's going so far away.' Fru Olsson looked as if she'd said too much.

'Nilsen, or Brandt, or whatever the woman's name is, can't try to get her back?' Mr Morgan asked.

'It's possible...' Fru Olsson lowered her voice '...for a biological parent to make a claim. But it would be costly through the law courts where international borders are crossed. Much harder if the child is on the other side of the globe, in a sound family.'

'This little girl will blossom in our home,' Mr Morgan said. 'She will forget about her parents. We have the time and patience to correct any behavioural issues.'

'Kari is a lucky, lucky girl. I hope you know that, Kari,' Fru Olsson said, looking at her.

'Do you have her original birth certificate?' Mr Morgan asked.

'The woman who brought Kari took it back after she'd shown it to me.'

'Will this cause problems, darling?' Mrs Morgan asked her husband.

'We'd have to alter the original birth certificate anyway, to remove details of the birth parents and make her ours completely. I'll have a word with the consul. Everyone's keen that these children have fresh starts so I'm sure problems will be smoothed out.'

'Caroline,' Mrs Morgan said. 'That was my mother's name, and it's so close to Kari. Or Carrie, Carrie Morgan. A new identity.' Mrs Morgan smiled down at Kari. 'Do you like your new name, Carrie?'

The name sounded a bit like hers, but it wasn't hers. Kari looked from one adult to another. Asking questions usually brought answers she didn't understand. They were speaking in Norwegian to her now but it wasn't very clear. So she just kept quiet and nodded.

'You're going, Kari,' Briga said that evening. They were playing in the courtyard after supper. Briga's green eyes were narrow and her mouth pursed. 'You weren't even here for long but you were chosen.' She kicked out at a patch of hard ice.

Going where?

'You'll have your own clothes, not just the ones we share here. And your own bedroom, and they might let you choose the wallpaper and curtains.'

All this meant nothing to Kari.

'You never say anything because you're too small. You just want your mother to come for you. That'll never happen now, Kari. It's not fair. I've been here longer than you, but nobody comes for me.'

Briga was crying now, large tears falling down her face.

'When's Mamma coming?' Kari asked.

Briga looked at her more kindly. 'I told you, you're a *naziynge*, a Nazi brat. She doesn't want you.'

The words were meaningless to Kari. She thought of her mother in the boat, waving a hand, calling out her goodbyes. 'She is coming.'

'You made your mamma's life hard and she made your life hard. "Better for both of us if I leave you here, Briga," my mother said to me.'

Kari made Mamma's life hard? And Mamma made her life hard? What did that mean? The idea clashed with Kari's memories of life in the wooden house: the four of them picking raspberries in the garden, playing in the snow. The emotions crowding her were so confusing she couldn't stand up any longer. She slumped onto the frozen ground, clinging to her doll. 'You go. Not me,' she told Briga.

Yet when they came to collect her, with a parcel of brand-new clothes for her to wear, Mr and Mrs Morgan laughed at her suggestion that they take Briga instead. 'Oh, Carrie, darling, how sweet you are. It's you we want, not any other child. You'll fit into our home so well. We can't wait for our friends to see you.' Mrs Morgan undid the string on the parcel. 'Let's get you changed.'

Her clothes from home had been taken when she'd arrived, even her red knitted hat. She wore a grey pinafore and white smock like the other girls in the home, smelling of everything else in this place. Mrs Morgan's replacements were stiff and shiny. They smelled good, though. A white blouse, a skirt with pleats, a cardigan. Black, gleaming shoes. Kari touched them to be sure they were real.

'And most important of all.' The woman pulled out a doll, too, with brightly painted features and shining golden blonde hair, whose clothes were also new. Kari stared at her.

'We thought you'd like to swap that doll of yours for this one. Ulla's getting a bit sad, isn't she? Let's leave her for the children here.'

'Nei.' Kari clutched Ulla tightly. 'Nei.'

The man and woman stared at her. 'Well, we'll leave it for now,' the woman said, blinking. 'You can have both of them. Doll friends!' She put the doll back in her bag. 'Let's get you changed into your new clothes.'

'Mamma's coming?' Kari looked at the door.

Fru Olsson cleared her throat. 'You're a lucky girl. Do as you're told and go with your new mother and father, like a good child.'

'You're Caroline Morgan now,' Mr Morgan said, pointing at Kari. 'Caroline. Morgan.'

'Let me help you put on the new things, darling,' Mrs Morgan said.

Kari didn't need anyone to get her dressed. Mamma had taught her to do that herself, apart from difficult fastenings and her laces.

Mrs Morgan's hands fumbled with buttons. The blouse smelled good, but alien. Kari raised Ulla to her face, drawing in the scent of everything left behind.

Fru Olsson and Mr Morgan were writing on pieces of papers, talking quietly. '...problem at the border, but the consul will take a telephone call if necessary. Advantages of being in this game for a few years now. Shame we can't take more of the little ones from Norway. Australia's crying out for good Scandinavian stock.'

'Just look at Carrie. Isn't she a little doll in her new clothes?' Mrs Morgan whispered to her husband. 'Aren't we lucky, darling?'

Fru Olsson and the kind girl walked them out to the iron gates, which Fru Olsson unlocked. The girl hugged Kari, saying something she couldn't understand. Wishing Kari *farvel* in Norwegian, Fru Olsson closed the gates behind them.

A taxi stood outside. Kari hadn't been in one of these before. Marte had taken her on the tram when the train had pulled into Stockholm.

'This is the beginning of your new life,' Mr Morgan said.

'When's my mamma coming?' Kari asked.

# SEVENTEEN

## MARTE

Bumping into Magnus was something Marte was dreading. Unavoidable, though, given she was working at the post office and he, like most people, would probably come in at some point.

This morning, he was sending a letter to Stockholm. She handled his business with cool aloofness, taking his coins with just a nod and pushing the change back at him, not making eye contact, willing him out of the post office. He stared down at the stamps she'd given him, with their images of King Haakon on them. 'Do you remember the Quisling stamps during the war?' he said.

'Of course I do. The occupation only ended last May.' The turncoat prime minister's portrait was printed on Norwegian stamps during the occupation. Marte had loathed them, feeling like a traitor when she had to sell them in the post office, occasionally amused, if a little anxious, when a rival government-in-exile stamp appeared on a letter that had been sent from Britain and somehow made its way through the mail system.

'We threw out those devils, didn't we? And the collaborators.' Magnus was nodding to himself. 'The Germans were sent home with their tails between their legs and the likes of Quisling got what they deserved for their treachery.'

She busied herself straightening the pages of stamps in the book so she didn't have to answer, feeling the fury inside her. Magnus would have worked on the Atlantic Wall fortifications if the Germans had taken him. Did he think she was stupid or had just forgotten this? He'd moaned about the unfairness of being turned down when they'd take Serbs and Russians, failing to add that the Serbs and Russians were slaves, ill-treated, half starved.

'I'm going to Sweden, Marte,' he said. 'There's work there for me, my cousin says. Until things are better here. That's what the Germans and traitors did to this country, left us in a bad state so we must go abroad to find better opportunities.'

She was surprised he had the gumption to manage arrangements for the trip, even if it was only to neighbouring Sweden, but felt a rush of pleasure at the news. Magnus had felt like a cigarette stub you couldn't sweep away. She responded with a nod.

'Marte? May I ask you something?'

'It's a free world.'

'You hate me for what I did to Asta, don't you?'

Now she really did have to say something to him and there was no way in hell she could repress the words bursting out of her. 'You were a coward and a bully. You didn't dare grab her like that in front of her father. You waited until she was by herself, and terrified her and her child, and drove her away and then you burnt down her father's house. You were the reason it wasn't safe for Kari to stay here.' She felt her cheeks burn with rage, a rage she had never expressed before, a rage that seemed to ignite into such a fury she could have reached across the counter and shaken him.

'It was wrong.' Magnus shook his head. 'I see that now. I was jealous. I should not have been.'

'Oh? And what brought about this big revelation? Been talking to God or something?'

He looked away. 'I stand by their house and I think of Petter Nilsen, how kind he was to me, always a smile and a word for me. I used to mend things for him, you know, years ago, before the war, when you could get the spare parts. If I'd mended his stove flue for him, perhaps he'd still be alive now.'

'Instead you hacked off his daughter's hair and stoned her and threatened his grandchild.'

He shook his head. 'I didn't threaten the little one. You were there, we didn't harm Kari that day, did we? And I didn't burn down the house.'

To be fair, his powers of literacy probably weren't great enough to write the poison pen letters they'd received, either. And there was no evidence that he'd been involved in the arson.

'Those others, they told me it was justice, what we did to Asta. They'd seen more than I had during the war.'

'They used you, Magnus.' Marte couldn't tell him about the man with the missing tooth who'd almost certainly been whispering his poison into the ears of fools like Magnus.

He nodded. 'I see that now. My mother always said I was easily led. She was pleased when I spent summers with Asta and Arne, sailing in their boat, riding their pony. They were a good influence on me.'

'She was right. And look how you repaid the Nilsens.'

'I wasn't brave or clever enough to see what was what.' He said it matter-of-factly. 'You were brave during the war, Marte. People talk about you.'

'They shouldn't.' The investigation into the Milorg collaborators was still going on. She didn't want Magnus reminding people that she'd been involved in resistance work, she needed to listen in to conversations – just the girl behind the post office counter who'd lived on the fjord all her life. 'And you shouldn't talk about me and my work in the war, either.'

'I will keep my lips sealed. You can trust me.' He looked around, as if he'd mislaid something. 'Where did you take Kari, Marte?' he asked.

'What's it to you? Surely you're just glad she's not here? A little girl like that and she was such a threat to you, wasn't she?' Sarcasm was wasted on Magnus, but she couldn't resist it.

'She was too small to be a threat. Where is she?' he asked again.

'Stockholm.' She slammed the book of stamps on the desk. 'That's how far we had to take her to make sure you and your friends couldn't harm her.' The lump in her throat felt like a boulder. She would never, never forgive herself for leaving Kari in that echoing old building, with strangers.

'Kari's in Stockholm and soon I will be in Stockholm, too.' He said the words as if they held meaning.

'Don't get any ideas about bumping into her. Stockholm's a big place. Bigger than Bergen.' The thought of Magnus seeking out Kari chilled her. But why would he want to see the child he so despised? 'If I discover you've been anywhere near her, I'll send a telegram to the Stockholm police.' The misuse of post office facilities was severely punished, but Magnus wouldn't know that. Doubtful the Swedish police would care about a Norwegian child in a home, either.

'So she must be in a children's home in Stockholm,' he muttered to himself, turning for the door. 'A home for inno-cents.' She could almost see his brain whirring, making sense of it all.

'Don't hurry back here,' she shouted at him. 'Stay in Stockholm, Magnus.'

Marte wasn't even sure he'd heard her as he opened the door and went on his way. Her attention turned back to the letter that had come in today, a letter with a Swedish stamp on it. She was certain she knew whose handwriting was on the envelope. Her fingers burned with the longing to open Max

Brandt's letter. During the war, she'd intercepted letters from people suspected of denouncing fellow citizens for hiding fugitives. It had gone against all her training and values. She'd put her job at risk, but she'd done it. She couldn't open Max's letter to Asta, though. When she closed up the post office, she'd take the letter home with her to show Arne and ask what they should do with it. Max hadn't put his family out of his mind, it seemed.

Marte had a feeling that a terrible mistake had been made and it might be too late to put things right.

# PART FIVE

## GERMANY, NOVEMBER 1945–JANUARY 1946

# EIGHTEEN

## MAX

This might be the house where he'd grown up. Hesitating, Max looked at the faded paint and patchy stucco, the boarded windows. He'd estimated the distance from the crossroads to his old home, a walk he'd made so many times as a child on his way home from school. The outline of the roads had sometimes been the only thing left to guide him through towns on his journey east across Germany.

No telegram or a letter had heralded his arrival. Nobody would be pulling aside the frayed curtains to see if he was coming yet. When he'd left this house in 1941 his parents and sister had stood in the garden, waving him off for his first posting, to Norway. Roses bloomed, not yet sacrificed for growing vegetables.

No roses blooming today in the tentative autumn sunshine. The door had obviously been kicked in and then reboarded. Max felt bile in his mouth picturing how it had happened. The bell was gone so he rapped his knuckles on the boards, the sound vanishing into the interior and echoing unanswered. He walked around to the back of the house, past muddy patches that had been flower beds, then vegetable patches, and since then the sites of skirmishes involving many pairs of boots. Long scraping gouges suggested heavy objects dragged through the garden and out to the road. Furniture? The stove? His heart thumped. For the first time since his military training had ended so abruptly, he wished he had a gun. Though showing a firearm would be madness.

He called out a greeting, not too loud in case there was someone there he mightn't want to meet, but to reassure anyone inside he wasn't a Red Army soldier. The worst of the violence against women had abated now, but he'd seen the faces of girls and old ladies when Russian soldiers passed them in groups, how they folded in on themselves, heads bowed, trying to disappear. None of those women and girls had raped or murdered, but now they were the scapegoats for every German atrocity.

'Clara?' he called again. 'It's me, Max.' He remembered the back of the family villa as just as elegant as the front, well painted and maintained, windows gleaming. Now the external walls looked like the icing on a cake that clumsy knives had hacked into. Still structurally sound and the roof looked passable. Better than he'd feared.

The back door wasn't locked. He stepped inside. The tiles had been wrenched up and the parquet floor leading into the house had also gone. Probably on some wagon heading east.

A noise ahead of him made him halt as he entered the hallway. The banisters on the stairs had vanished, too. For firewood?

'Max?' A voice that was familiar, but not. She'd only been a kid when he'd kissed her goodbye, hair in plaits, trying to evade the League of German Maidens. 'Is that you?'

'I'm home.' He put down his rucksack and came towards her. 'It's taken me so long, but I'm here now, Clara.'

She was in his arms then, though he felt as though he was embracing air. Clara had always been slim, now she was thin, eyes huge in her face. 'I didn't know if you... If you...'

'I wrote from the camp I was first in.' On the banks of the Rhine. But he'd known that the chaos between him and Brandenburg was going to suck the letter into its dark heart. 'And again, later on.'

'I heard on the BBC that our forces in Norway had surrendered. I was hopeful as it didn't sound as if there'd been huge bloody battles. Not like... here.' She shivered and released herself. He'd noted the use of the singular and perhaps the question about his parents was clear in his eyes. 'They're both gone, Max. Mutti in April. Pulmonary infection of some kind. Papi had gone off to fight in the Volksturm in the final months. I never heard what happened to him.'

Their father's body was probably buried somewhere between here and Berlin, just one of hundreds of thousands of Germans, perhaps millions, dying to defend the citizens.

'Papi wasn't fit enough,' she said. 'He could barely manage the walk into the town by the time he left.'

'They forced him? I heard they even pulled boys out of school and pushed rifles into their hands.'

She hesitated. 'He volunteered.'

He stared at her, questions on his lips.

Her gaze didn't meet his. 'Come into the kitchen. We still have the stove.'

'I noticed the banisters were gone. You ran out of fuel?'

Clara nodded. 'We started with the furniture in the spare bedrooms but by the time Papi left we were using anything we could find.'

'And food?'

Clara busied herself filling a pan with water from a jug. Perhaps the mains water was still not working. 'The Soviets issue a ration. It's not enough, but it's not like the early days when they first arrived and it was just...' She shrugged, pulling enamel mugs he vaguely remembered from a cupboard, spotting his surprise. 'The Soviets took the porcelain cups and saucers.'

He'd already seen the plundering as he'd travelled, houses pulled apart, crates of clothes, china, furniture loaded onto wagons, livestock led away, complaining and weeping citizens pushed aside.

'I wrote and told you all about Asta and Kari.' He'd barely spoken their names in the last eight months and now they seemed to echo in the kitchen.

'A beautiful little girl.' She smiled. 'We were surprised by your news.'

He looked at her closely but saw no judgement in her eyes. In the context of ruined buildings, defeat and death, perhaps Max's sudden fatherhood and marriage had registered only as surprises rather than shocks.

'The photographs were lovely. Mama and Papi often looked at them.'

Clara's smile turned to a frown. 'Are Asta and Kari coming here?' When he shook his head, she looked relieved. 'So you'll return to Norway?'

'They won't let me back, but we'll find a way to be together again.'

His words sounded hollow. Asta and Kari were safe, he reminded himself. Petter was looking after them, his respected position in the area acting as a guarantee.

Clara motioned him to a seat. 'Why did you come back here, Max?' The question was almost aggressive. 'You were foolish. You must know that the Soviets deported our soldiers to their prisoner of war camps? Nobody knows when they'll be released.'

In the last camp, they'd advised him to stay in the British sector.

Clara was looking at his hand. 'That's healed up better than we feared. Mama always worried there'd be some infection in the bone.'

'My living conditions were good. I spent a lot of time

outdoors, keeping fit.' *Playing in the snow with Asta and Kari. Mending roofs and fences with Petter.*

'Norway looked idyllic in the postcards and photographs, the fjords and mountains. I wanted to visit you.'

'I wish you had.' Asta would have let Clara stay with them. She'd like his sister, who was quiet and considerate, fond of animals and hiking.

'I was kept busy in the last year of the war, working in an anti-aircraft tower in Berlin.'

'But the other things you did, Clara? So risky.'

'The White Rose?' She frowned. 'You know about that?'

'It was hinted at.'

She smiled. 'It seems a long time ago.'

'You could have been executed, too.' Young people her age had been guillotined for passing on pamphlets denouncing the regime.

'There's barely a day when I don't think about those others who died. The day the war ended I felt an overwhelming sorrow they hadn't lived to see Hitler overthrown.'

'You were lucky to get away with it.'

She frowned. 'Not just luck.'

'What do you mean?'

'It's why Papi dragged himself into the rags that passed as uniform and went off to fight the Soviets.'

He sat back, trying to make sense of it.

'The Gestapo had questioned me once, briefly, a few years before.' She put up a hand. 'They didn't hurt me and they couldn't prove anything. But they never let you off the hook. They keep watching you and your family. You'd think they'd have had better things to worry about as the Soviets crossed the Oder, but the surveillance grew worse. Even when I was in the anti-aircraft tower in Berlin I knew I was watched and so was this house.'

'Papi joined the Volksturm to make the family look patriotic?'

She gave a little laugh. 'I was at home the day he went off. It was almost funny in a dark way. Papi made a great point of kissing us at the front gate, loudly saying how proud he was to fight for his country, knowing his daughter was doing her bit by risking her life in the anti-aircraft tower. The neighbours were watching. Almost certainly one or two of them were reporting to the police on us.'

'Did it work?'

'I didn't see as many random men following me to my lodgings in Berlin – a hostel. They stopped searching my work locker after Papi went off. But perhaps they hadn't as much time, given the country was collapsing around us.'

Gentle Clara, helping to wipe out allied bombers from a flak tower? Papi, an invalid, fighting the Soviets to protect his daughter from her own country?

'So it was my fault he died.' She said it flatly, putting up a hand to interrupt Max's protest. 'Oh, I know he might have been killed anyway or died of hunger or disease. But he didn't need to die fighting when he should have been at home, in bed.'

'He wouldn't have done it if he didn't believe you'd done the right thing, Clara. Plenty of families denounced their own children.'

'I think Mama and Papi felt shame that they'd been taken in by Hitler. And guilt at their culpability, Papi said, and complicity.'

'I didn't know this.'

'How could you, in Norway?'

'Bad things happened there, too,' he said. 'Even by those idyllic fjords. Things I tried to ignore.'

They fell silent.

'And Mama?' he said, after a while.

'After Papi went off to fight, she picked up one illness after another. I came home for good to look after her.' The words were coming out in awkward sentences, as though Clara wasn't used to conversations. Max still had his mother's last letter to him, asking him how tall Kari was, what she was doing, how Asta was, whether they were still receiving adequate food rations. Papi had still been at home then. Having seen what he'd seen coming east across Germany, the casualties, the hunger, it came as no surprise to Max that both his parents were gone, but a blunt ache settled into his chest as confirmation came.

Clara was pouring boiling water over some kind of herbs. 'I wish we had proper tea. There is coffee, but I save it for mornings.'

'You have coffee?' Even now, with so many hundreds of miles walked, with the anxiety he'd felt for Kari and Asta and the family left here in Brandenburg, the prospect of coffee could make his senses race.

'Just a small amount. But it's the real thing.' She looked at her watch and turned away, as if listening out for something, someone. Boots thudded down the side of the house. Clara's face turned pale. 'Max, there's something you need to know. We have a lodger. A Russian.'

'What?' He stood up.

'No.' She put a hand out. 'He's an officer, not in the advance troops, in the occupation force.' She broke off. A man was coming into the kitchen, dressed in a Red Army captain's uniform, a smile on his face. When he saw Max, the smile turned into a frown. Clara muttered something in Russian that sounded like an attempt to soothe.

'You brother?' the Russian said. 'You not in camp?'

'They released me in the British zone. Gave me papers to cross into the Soviet sector.' Max made a movement towards his jacket pocket.

'It's all right,' Clara said firmly. 'Max worked as an engineer during the war, Sergei.'

Sergei was still scowling at him. 'You did not say he would come here.'

'Clara didn't know. Letters haven't got through.'

'Max didn't even know both our parents had died.'

Sergei removed his cap, eyes still on Max.

'Sergei is an administrator for the Soviet occupying force.' Clara made him sound like a respectable civil servant.

'I inspect farms, factories, provide information.'

The job description didn't reassure Max.

Clara motioned both men to sit down. 'I'll pour the tea.'

'Those weeds?' Sergei said.

She poured it from a china teapot and smiled at Max's look of recognition. 'I hung on to some of Mama's things.'

'We took reparations from civilians,' Sergei said, looking hurt. 'For damage to Soviet property and lives. Wehrmacht burned down our houses, killed our animals, murdered our people. But comrades do not take Clara's things, now I am here.'

Clara opened her mouth, closed it and then seemed to come to a decision. 'Look, Max, Sergei keeps an eye on me and the house. You have to understand how it's been here.'

'Even in Norway, we heard reports of what happened when the Red Army arrived.'

'Brutalised men treated us brutally,' Clara said.

Sergei nodded, face expressionless. He drank the tea Clara put in front of him. 'I have bath. Stove is on?'

'I made sure it stayed alight so there'd be water for you.'

Sergei's eyes narrowed at Max as he stood up.

'He likes the bath,' Clara said.

'Do you have enough fuel for the stove?'

'He makes sure I have enough. Sergei...' She lowered her eyes. 'Before he came to live here, I... There were so many Russian soldiers, Max, and...'

She'd been totally alone, no parents, no brother, defence-less. He couldn't ask her what had happened. His hand found hers across the table. How many Russians had burst in here? Had she been violated, perhaps many times? 'Were you hurt, Clara?'

'Just the once, when they first broke through.'

So not only Sergei. Another Soviet had inflicted himself on his sister, left alone in the family home to face the vengeance of those the Germans had brutalised, as she put it. He could have marched up to the bathroom and pushed Sergei's head under the water. He looked away, not wanting her to see the anger. 'I'm sorry.' Such an insufficient thing to say.

'You find your own wolf,' Clara went on. 'And they keep the rest of the pack away.'

In the middle of the twentieth century, a young woman from a professional family had to live like this? He shouldn't have felt as shocked as he did.

'During the day I'm out anyway. Clearing rubble in the town.' She gave a little smile. 'I was exempt, as I wasn't ever a member of the League of German Maidens.'

Clara had been in the resistance. She ought to be feted for her bravery. He wanted to ask what the White Rose pamphlets she'd distributed had said but could imagine. Ill-treatment of Jews and other opponents of the state. Back when she'd been arrested, the extermination camps in Poland had barely started, but Clara and her friends had seen enough to know where the persecution was leading.

'I get free soup for a day's work clearing bomb sites. I'm just relieved it's all over, the fighting, the killing. If you keep your head down, the Soviets leave you in peace. It could be worse.'

Max made his way up the stairs to his old bedroom. The walnut headboard and the dressing table were gone. But on the wall there was still a photograph of the four Brandts, taken before he'd left for military training.

He hadn't been able to help them in their greatest time of need, though. He'd left Asta and Kari, too. Was he always to abandon the people he loved? Asta and Petter were a solid duo, he reminded himself.

Clara, however, only had him to stand between her and that Russian wolf, who'd circled the vulnerable home and picked her out. *I'm going to do whatever I have to to protect her*, he promised his parents silently, as the Russian in the bathroom next door sang and splashed around in the hot water Clara had heated using wood from the family furniture. *I won't leave Clara alone.*

Max's luck ran out when he was looking for food, his father's medals from the First World War in his pocket. Distracted by potatoes on a makeshift stall, he wasn't keeping an eye open for trouble. When a truck of Soviets emptied along the street, it was only seconds before one of them clasped his shoulder. 'You. Papers.'

Automatically, he pulled out his papers, showing them the stamps from the prisoner of war camp he'd passed through. 'The British POW camp allowed me to return home to my family. I'm registered here now.' The soldier summoned a man in a uniform Max didn't recognise.

'You are a civil engineer?' The man's eyes narrowed behind his spectacles. 'Where did you study?' His German was flaw-less. Native. One of the German socialists who'd fled east after Hitler came to power?

'I was a student at the Technische Hochschule in Charlot-tenburg.'

A nod from the man. 'After the Nazis had purged the insti-tute of anyone who didn't like their architectural style?'

'The institute wasn't what it had been in the Weimar years,' Max admitted. 'In Norway I worked on the Atlantic Wall. Bunkers, anti-aircraft batteries and civilian projects such as road bridges,' he added.

'Where exactly in Norway?' Eyes suspicious.

'Up the coast from Bergen.'

'The Atlantic Wall?' The last two words were spoken with slight emphasis.

'They sent me to a small settlement because I wasn't fit for combat.' He raised his left hand. One of the other Soviets shouted at him, brandishing a rifle. Max curled the remaining fingers until the shouts died down.

'Wounded in combat?'

'In training.'

'Your address?' When Max told him, the man nodded. 'Do not leave town.'

At least they hadn't hauled him off immediately, without a chance to tell Clara what had happened. So many people had been picked up, taken away, vanishing for good. It had been going on for years now, Clara said, under the Nazis or their successors.

'Always keep your valuables and papers with you, Max,' she'd added casually. 'Just in case they take you.'

Nobody came for Max after his encounter on the streets. He kept an ear out for boots pounding up to the front door and occupied himself by repairing the worst of the damage to the windows and shutters, fixing the pipes so that the mains supply of water came into the kitchen again. 'What a luxury,' Clara said, turning a tap on and off.

The wolf returned from a few days away looking over a large farm whose aristocratic owner had been dispatched. The farm would be collectivised. Stolen, the owners would term it.

Max froze in his bed when he heard him crashing around as they came upstairs, Clara whispering, the Soviet shouting at her, saying something that sounded threatening. The bedroom door slammed. Rage burned through Max's veins. He wanted to burst into that room, pull the wolf off, beat him up. But then the Soviets would drag him off to some cell or camp and Clara would be left alone again to the mercies of the wolf. He had to take her away from here.

The letter he received the following day dashed immediate hopes of doing this. It instructed him to report to the steel works three kilometres away across the town. 'They'll want you to dismantle the plant,' Clara said. 'It's all going east to the Soviet Union. There've been rumours about it for weeks now.'

The steel works was to be pillaged, to pay for the thousands of razed fields and cities in the Soviet Union the Germans had left behind them. In their occupation zone, the Soviets could help themselves to anything they wanted. Already local factories had been taken to bits and the machinery sent east.

Clara found him a bicycle to get to work. 'The Soviets are very keen on bikes, though they don't always know how to ride them, so they'll try to grab it off you.' Her face twisted into a wry smile. 'Try to hold on to it, though. It cost me 500 cigarettes.'

He noticed that Clara's watch, a present from their parents on her confirmation day, had vanished from her wrist. It reminded him of the compass Asta had given him for Christmas all those years ago, hours before Kari was born. It had steered him back across Germany, on occasions when he'd seen patrols ahead of him and had veered cross-country, over fields and hills. He went to his duffel bag to check it was still there. Gone. The wolf. Fury swept Max, but what was the point? He was powerless. He remembered the expression on Asta's face when he'd first arrived at the red house on the fjord: the barely suppressed fury and contempt, the iciness. The same expression must be painted on his face: loathing of the occupier living in your home.

The cycle to the steel works was a smooth one, with only the wind from the east acting as his enemy. Clara had found an old scarf of Papi's for him to wrap around his face. The cashmere smelled of Papi's bay and citrus cologne, reminding Max yet again of how his father would have trusted him to look after Clara. These reflections were scoured from his mind as the working day started.

On arrival Max's papers were checked and he was escorted into an office, where a thin, bespectacled man in his early fifties greeted him, plans and drawings spread out on huge trestle tables. 'You didn't dismantle anything in Norway, did you?' he greeted Max, saving himself the luxury of an introduction. 'I know some of their plant equipment was brought back to Germany just before liberation. Any ideas are welcome.'

The man, Braun, was a German, too. As the morning progressed and they discussed the task with a Russian engineer, who communicated mainly in grunts and scowls, Max learned that Braun was a returner from the Soviet Union. Not that this was directly conveyed.

'Norway must have been a pleasant deployment,' Braun said. 'Fjords and Grieg?'

'I couldn't complain,' Max said, thinking of Asta and Kari, faces bright on a snowy morning. Something told him not to mention them, not to expose his vulnerability. His left hand stiffened. It felt sore today, probably because of how he'd had to clutch the bicycle handle. Braun scowled at the hand.

'How did that happen?'

Max started the accident story again, then broke off and just came out with the truth.

Braun gave him a long stare. He knocked the ash out of his pipe and looked over Max's head at the clock on the wall. 'Enough time talking.'

He passed the day studying the original plans and diagrams of the steel works, built in the early years of the century, writing initial notes on how best machinery and equipment could be removed. Max longed to ask where in the Soviet Union the parts would go but knew better than to pose questions. The plant had been well constructed and upgraded just before the war. Considering the factory had received a direct hit in 1944, it was in remarkable working condition. 'Machinery like this will vastly improve Soviet productivity,' Braun said.

He was putting on his cap and scarf to return home at the end of the shift when he was called into an office. Two SWAG officers, members of the Soviet occupation forces, sat behind a desk. 'Factory is going to the Ukraine,' the officer said, without preamble. 'You are going, too, Brandt.'

'*Wie bitte?* What do you mean?' Surprise made him forget the usual obeisance.

'You will advise on the reassembly of the plant.'

Heading east would take him further and further away from Asta and Kari.

'You are allowed to take your sister. Possessions you can carry with you. Train is tomorrow.'

'Tomorrow?'

Much of the last six or seven months had felt like Alice in Wonderland but now they'd crossed over into something so absurd it could only have come from a forbidden surrealist like Dada.

'Transport will collect you at 0730.' The officer folded papers. 'Cows and chickens can come, too, if you want.'


Clara laughed when he returned and told her to pack for Russia. 'Are you insane?' She looked at his face and blinked. 'My God, you're serious? You're telling me we're going to an unknown destination in a country we fought for years?' She folded her arms, the strong muscles from clearing rubble standing out under her wool blouse.

The wolf was crashing around upstairs, running one of his interminable baths. There'd be no heat from the stove tonight. Clara would have to abandon the meal of boiled potatoes and the single egg she was planning and serve bread and something from a tin. If there was still one left.

'To get away from the wolves you chose a wolf, Clara. Now you can go and live among people who can protect you from all of them.'

'The apex predators? Really?'

'It will be safe. We will be living in a kind of village by the factory.'

'Why do they need you to go for so long, Max? Surely it's a job that would take months, a year at most?'

It was true. Kari would be eight when he was released. 'Nobody will touch you there, Clara. Women have good jobs in the Soviet Union.'

'If they're not used as slave labourers.'

'By the time we come back here, things will be safer.' He took her hand. 'You'll still be young.'

'But you, Max? Even though you barely served, you have that Wehrmacht service record in your papers. They could still throw you into a prisoner of war camp on a whim. Those prisoners will be gone for years, some say decades. You have to go back to the western zone. Now.' Gentle Clara spoke with force.

'I'm not leaving you alone here with that man,' he said.

'So there's only one answer.' Clara looked around the house. His studious, book-loving sister had always loved her home. During the war, it must have been a haven, even as bombers crowded the skies and their parents were lost to her. Leaving it was going to be a wrench.

'We both leave in the morning, before they come?'

'No. Tonight. Sergei's out drinking. There's a better chance now. They may turn up any moment to guard the house. Pack quickly, Max.'

Max ran up to the wolf's bedroom. The Russian had obviously helped himself to a new coat, because the one he'd worn before was thrown on the bed. Hope against hope, Max put a hand into the pocket and pulled out the compass.

It felt like a sign from Asta to do what Clara said.

'Hurry up,' Clara called from downstairs.

He packed his duffel bag – easy to pack when you had so little. Max removed the family photograph from the wall and shoved it into the rucksack.

Clara was already waiting at the front door, holding a bundle of sheets and cooking pots, along with a bag of tinned food and a rucksack. She gave a tight smile at his surprise. 'We lived in fear of air-raids and the Soviet invasion for so long we grew used to getting ready to go in a hurry.

He instinctively wanted to lock the door behind them, but how would the wolf get out without smashing a window and further damaging the house? Instead he shut the door and placed the key under the terracotta pot on the doorstep long used for this purpose.

'Bring the bicycle around,' Clara whispered. 'It'll make it easier to carry everything.'

'Where are we going, Clara?' he said, when he'd done this. They had no travel papers. They'd shortly be breaking curfew, too.

'One of the ports in the British sector. You need to be on a ship back to a Scandinavian countries. Denmark, perhaps. From there to Norway.'

'Rostock's nearer?'

'Still in the Soviet zone.'

'The Norwegians won't take me. We're pariahs, Clara. Nobody wants Germans.'

'We'll find a way.' They fastened the bundle of blankets to the front basket.

'Come on,' Clara said, leading the way.

They retraced the journey he'd made only weeks ago,

pausing to shelter in doorways or behind the few remaining trees whenever vehicles passed.

'Down,' Clara said suddenly, pushing him behind a wall. Two young conscripts strode past them on the torn-up pavement.

Snow fell lightly now, a warning that winter was here. They trundled through streets with mountains of rubble piled up neatly on the sides, burned-out buildings and craters punctuating the scene.

The town fell away. They were on an open road heading west. When he looked behind them he saw the snow gently erasing their tracks. Again Clara put up a hand. A horse-drawn wagon driven by Russians came towards them. They ducked behind a semi-destroyed cowshed, Clara careful to wheel the bicycle out of sight. 'We should make you look ill in case they question you,' she whispered. 'Paint spots on your face so they don't want to handle you.'

'I've been consistently healthy, even when I was in the POW camp.' He'd lost weight, an alarming amount, but hadn't experienced serious illness. Thinking of the camp reminded him of the doctor from the barracks in Norway, Friedrich Klein, who'd come out to Petter Nilsen that night when his influenza had reached its peak. Friedrich had been a guest at the wedding. He came from Kiel, in the north of the country, in the British sector. Kiel was a major port. Or had been.

'I've got an idea,' he said. 'There's someone who might help us.' He told her about the doctor in Kiel. 'If his house is standing, he might let us stay while we make plans.'

She nodded. Clara was giving up everything for him.

'Are you sure?' he asked again.

She raised an eyebrow. 'Am I sure I want to leave this paradise?'

In Max's pocket, the compass seemed to glow, as if warming

him. All they needed to do was keep walking and find a way back to Asta and Kari.

# NINETEEN

## A WEEK LATER

On Christmas Eve, Max and Clara entered the British sector. Max had expected suspicious questions, examinations of papers, but the British soldiers waved them through without much interest or perhaps in an expression of seasonal goodwill. From his journey east from the prisoner of war camp, Max remembered the British as cold, if proper, occupiers of their chunk of Germany. Not outrightly cruel, on the whole, but sticking rigidly to the non-fraternisation rules. On the road he'd seen them throw away scraps of food from messes and field canteens rather than give them to hungry children, following occupation rules to the letter. He tried not to superimpose Kari's face onto the pinched features of the hungry children.

That afternoon they reached a village where Christmas had arrived, a little scruffy and faded this year, but still old and familiar. Without a word to one another, he and Clara followed a group of villagers entering the church. A paraffin heater gave off a warmth. Candles lit the darkness. They sang 'Stille Nacht'. For the hour the service lasted, Christmas filled the world, made it softer, more full of possibility. Max remembered the Christmas Eve when Asta had told him she was expecting a child. His world had trembled. He hadn't known what he felt: terror, anxiety and excitement. Then, when he'd seen Kari, a sense of nothing ever having mattered as much before as she did. Where was she, this Christmas Eve? Excited by the presents under the tree? Eating a special meal?

Afterwards, the pastor's wife served them warm soup in their presbytery and offered them spaces to sleep on the floor of their sitting room. The other guest that night was a Polish girl of about sixteen, who didn't speak at all. She slept on the floor of the pastor's study and slipped away into the darkness of Christmas morning. From the window, Max watched her open the front gate and vanish, her footsteps covered by a sprinkling of snow almost instantly. 'She shouldn't go off by herself,' he said. Frequently on the journey, he'd pulled Clara behind a building or burned-out vehicle to avoid a drunken group of soldiers or a vengeful band of released prisoners, who'd spurned the security of a displaced persons' camp.

'Whatever's pulling her is stronger than anything else,' Clara said. Was someone waiting for the nameless girl somewhere? All the hundreds of miles away in Poland? He pictured the girl's parents, waking on Christmas morning, wherever they were, willing her home.

'She was frightened of us,' Clara added. 'Terrible things were done to her.'

'You mean, we, our people, Germans, did terrible things to her,' Max said.

'At home, nobody talks about what we did to the Jews, the Poles and the Soviets,' Clara said. 'And all the others, the Latvians, Yugoslavians, Romanians, Norwegians, French, too many to name. Our own suffering from the bombs and the invaders didn't make people feel empathy. If anything, it just made us harder.'

Clara had nothing to feel guilty about. She'd risked her life distributing those leaflets in the war. They stood in silence for a moment until Max remembered something. 'Kari's three today.'

'A Christmas child.' She paused in the folding up of the blankets and tidying of the pillows. 'I wish you were with her. I wish I was, too.'

'The snow makes me think of her.' He explained the meaning of Kari's name. 'I wonder if it's snowing at the small-holding?' Perhaps they were waking up, Kari keen to take the toboggan out, Asta and Petter in the kitchen, preparing something special for Christmas morning.

They moved on after the pastor served them black bread and tea, thanking him. 'I can only take in a few at a time,' he told them at the front door. 'You and the Polish girl looked so weary.'

'Who is she?' Max asked.

'Slave labourer in the local work camp, picked up off the street in Warsaw and transported here. I suspect she was Jewish, though she said she was Catholic. It didn't save her from being worked to the bone. The local displaced persons' camp wanted her to stay while they traced her family, but she ran away. Warsaw is rubble. If they're Jewish, her family will have been murdered.' He sighed. 'All we could give her was the little food we have and warm clothes.'

Clara and Max said nothing for a long time when they left the house. 'We should have done more to stop it,' Clara said quietly at last. Max knew what she meant.

'You did more than most,' he told her.

She looked at him quizzically. 'There was resistance in Norway, wasn't there? Did you see much sign of it?'

'Sometimes I suspected Asta and her father and friends were doing... things they didn't want me to know about. But I never asked questions.' He'd suspected they had a wireless hidden in the cellar, possibly listened to the BBC when he was away, and had noted Asta behaving furtively on a few occasions.

'Sensible. What exactly would you have done if you had hard evidence they were resisting the occupation?'

He'd asked himself this several times during the war and had never known the answer.

'Tell me about Asta's father?' Clara asked.

'Petter is a good man. A Norwegian who loves the outdoors but reads a lot. They're a nation of booklovers. He wrestled with how he saw me. On the one hand, we shared interests. We both liked working outside, fixing things, putting up fences. He knows a lot about Germany and speaks the language perfectly. But then... Then he'd look at me and I knew he'd heard or read something about what we'd done. Some atrocity. And Petter would struggle. He sees me through two lenses, I suppose.'

He could tell by Clara's face that she liked the sound of Petter.

'Perhaps one day you'll meet him,' he said, daring to speak the hope aloud.

They walked on in the snow through Christmas Day.

'We could try to get on a train?' he suggested at last.

She shook her head. 'Those stations, full of filth and people crammed together, no running water, I can't do it.'

He nodded. He knew she meant more than the filth and smell. She couldn't face the desperation, the fleeting hope when a train pulled in, the despair when it didn't stop or wouldn't take on passengers.

In all the days they'd been walking, Clara hadn't pressed him on how they'd find their way onto a ship sailing to Sweden. Nothing would keep him from crossing the sea. Once he was in Sweden, he'd telephone or telegraph the post office in the village, ask Marte for news of Asta. He imagined Marte taking the call, telling him she'd go up to the red house as soon as she'd locked up for the day. Asta and Kari would travel to Sweden to meet him. Kari would be so excited to go on trains.

That night, sheltering in an old barn, stomachs full, as a

result of Clara bartering coffee beans for potatoes on the road, she spoke. 'There's bound to be a Swede coming into Kiel on a ship who'll accept coffee or cigarettes in exchange for their papers. Everything's for sale, if the price is right.'

In the darkness of the barn, his sister was almost invisible. She'd given up everything to head west with him, knowing the risks if the Soviets caught them trying to escape without exit permits. Yet Clara's face showed nothing but determination, and something else, too: purpose. Her eyes were full of curiosity as they walked across the shattered country. He'd left her a shy girl. Now she faced ruined houses and streams of refugees, some burning with anger engendered by years of German persecution, without despair or fear.

Outside the barn, something moved in the dark. Footsteps came towards the barn door. They stiffened. The farmer? Another displaced survivor with nothing to lose and everything to gain from robbing an unarmed pair of Germans? Max gestured at her silently to hide behind the hay bales. Clara ignored the suggestion. The door creaked. A man, young, bedraggled, wearing scraps of uniform, stood in front of them. 'What do you want?' Max asked, eyeing the knife in the man's hand.

'Food. Cigarettes. Water.'

'And this is how you ask, with a threat?' Max frowned. He must be mistaken, this boy couldn't be speaking in a Norwegian accent. 'Who are you?' he asked in that language.

'I don't know what you mean?' the stranger answered in German.

'You're Norwegian,' Max said.

'Former SS,' Clara said. 'A volunteer for the Eastern Front. Those scraps of uniform you're still wearing, you should have got rid of them.'

The young man shuffled, brandishing his knife.

'Whereabouts in Norway are you from?' Max asked.

'Oslo.'

'You're an escaped SS POW and you think you can get back to Norway?' Still eyeing the knife, Max waved the man into the barn. 'Sit with us. Tell us more.'

'Max,' Clara began.

'Our friend's not going to harm us. Why would he make things even riskier for himself? There are British military police in the town we just passed.' Max had looked out for the MPs, watching how they monitored the markets and places where people congregated, trying to pick up knowledge that might be useful in Kiel where he'd need to be on his guard trying to buy Swedish identity papers.

'Give me your knife,' Clara said.

The stranger handed it to her. 'You can buy forged papers in Kiel,' he said. 'Sometimes real ones.'

'You'll certainly need them to avoid arrest for treason as soon as you step foot in Norway.' Clara snorted.

'Yes, I could be executed.' He sat down abruptly on the straw beside them. 'But at least if I'm in jail in Oslo my mother could visit me before they...' He mimicked a rope going around his neck.

'Who do you get the papers from in Kiel?' Clara asked.

The stranger didn't answer at first.

'Listen, you want to stay here with us, you help us,' Max said.

The Norwegian kicked the straw with the tip of his boot. 'I'm heading for the docks. Goods enter Germany, with tariffs. If they can be imported into the British sector without all the paperwork, they can be sold at more reasonable prices.'

'You're going to help smuggle in goods from Sweden?' Max said. 'Food?'

'It'll get me more to eat and help me get home.'

'And you have contacts in Kiel?'

The Norwegian nodded. 'There was a quartermaster while

I was serving. His brother worked on the docks.' He took off his cap, looking younger. 'You help me and I'll help you.'

'You'll introduce us to the quartermaster's brother?' Max folded his arms and looked directly at him.

'You share your rations with me on the road, I'll make the introductions.' The Norwegian looked at Clara appraisingly. 'You, too, *fräulein*. You're pretty. Some new clothes and a bit of lipstick, you can help with the marketing.'

Max had already seen the made-up girls in long coats opening to reveal rows of watches tied to the lining, voluminous pockets concealing cigarettes, soap, stockings, lipstick.

'Paint myself with cosmetics, dress like a tart and sell nylons and butter?' Clara smiled at her brother's disapproving face. 'Things have changed since you went away, Max.'

The Norwegian laughed. 'Your sister has adapted. You must, too, *mein freund*. We find ourselves in harsh times.'

The comradely tone made Max feel sick. But the newcomer was right. Compromises couldn't be avoided.

Clara yawned. 'We need to sleep. Show me what else is in your pockets and rucksack,' she told the Norwegian, brandishing his knife at him.

He tipped out the pathetic array of objects in the rucksack. A photograph of a middle-aged woman, presumably his mother. A toothbrush and hairbrush. A change of underwear. A heel of very old rye loaf and a tin, which he opened and turned out to be filled with cigarette butts. 'Sometimes you can make up a new cigarette or two with what's left in the ends,' he said. Clara nodded, seemingly familiar with the process. Not much to show for one who'd thrown in his lot with the SS to conquer the world and was now sneaking home like a flea-bitten dog.

The three of them slept.

In the morning, the Norwegian was up first, possessions packed, the piece of bread sitting on top of the rucksack. He broke it into three and handed them each a piece. After a pause,

Clara looked at Max and put a hand into her own rucksack to pull out one of the cooked potatoes, which she broke into three as well.

'Why are you interested in Swedish ships?' the Norwegian asked. 'Do you have Swedish family? They won't want Germans there, either.' He peered at Max. 'Or did you leave a sweetheart in Norway?' He smirked at Max's annoyance. 'So many Wehrmacht soldiers in my own country, admiring our fjords and beautiful girls. I should have stayed at home instead of going off to do German dirty work, but at the labour exchange they said we had no choice, fight for them or work on the Atlantic Wall, putting up bunkers and gun emplacements.'

Max turned his back on the Norwegian. 'We leave in five minutes.'

PART SIX

# TWENTY

## ASTA

After she'd met Arne in the Lyons' Corner House, Asta had risked the wrath of her boss in the insurance office, heading straight to a travel agent off the Strand to book the ferry and rail journeys to Stockholm. It would cost more money than she had. Tourism and holidays weren't yet encouraged again for the British. Travel prices reflected this.

'I'll be back,' she told the clerk, her hand going to the pearl necklace. She dashed along the Strand, looking for jewellers, before heading north towards Hatton Garden, where she'd heard jewellery was bought and sold. She found a shuttered office where a man in spectacles and a gloomy face bought it from her for three guineas. Enough, with her savings, for the fares and for a few nights in a cheap hotel in Stockholm. She thought of telephoning the children's home, telling them she was on her way but booking an international call would take too long and cost too much. Explaining who she was and telling them she was on the way would be too complicated to express in a telegram. Asta rushed back down to the Strand to buy the ferry and rail tickets.

'Single or return, miss?' the clerk asked.

She hesitated. 'Return. And please add a ticket for a child for the return journey.'

When he looked at her Norwegian passport, he scuttled to a back office to check visa requirements. 'Does the child have her own passport?'

'No.'

'She's not named on yours. Before you leave Sweden, you'll have to apply for one for her from the Norwegian delegation in Oslo.' He peered again at her passport. 'You haven't changed your name on marriage?' He nodded at her wedding ring. 'Do you have a marriage certificate?'

She met his gaze. 'I am still Asta Nilsen, born in Oslo and resident there all my life until the occupation ended.' She cursed herself for not removing her ring. She couldn't be Asta Brandt, wife of a German, effectively now an enemy alien herself. Germans weren't allowed to travel.

He fussed about ensuring her passport would let her re-enter Britain, filling out a visa application form. Thank God she'd brought the passport with her when she'd left the fjords. Shame she hadn't taken her daughter's birth certificate at the same time. In the foreign exchange bureau, the clerk wouldn't let her change many of her saved pounds into Swedish krone. 'Exchange restrictions, miss.' Britain wanted money to stay in the country; it was bankrupt after the war.

Back in the office, breathless, two hours late from her lunch break, Asta told the office manager that she would be travelling to Sweden for a week in a few days' time. The silence greeting this announcement indicated that her job might not be waiting for her. But perhaps she wouldn't return to London, anyway. That evening, she packed her few belongings in her small suit-case. She'd travel in the suit and warm coat she'd bought from a second-hand clothes shop, along with a hat that didn't look too bad. Asta Nilsen needed to look presentable and respectable. She had nothing for Kari except for a small teddy bear, dressed as a Tower of London Beefeater, a toothbrush, a new pair of pyjamas and set of underwear, from a department store near her flat.

On the ferry across the North Sea, Asta sat upright in her seat, too tense to sleep. It was only later, an hour into the connecting train journey from Goteborg to Stockholm, that she was lulled into sleep for a few hours as they sped past snowy fields and forests. From the central station she wasted no time in travelling on to the children's home, stopping only to pick up a transport map of the city from the information office. She had no money to spend on a taxi and took a blue and white tram to the address Arne had given her in the Corner House. She frowned as she looked at the cigarette packet. She hadn't noticed before that he'd dashed down a few extra lines at the bottom and round the side, the writing small and almost indecipherable.

*I made a mistake. Get Kari back. Return to Norway, there's always a home here with Marte and me for you both. The police arrested the local collaborator who betrayed Milorg, seen assaulting you. Things will quieten down.*

Live with Marte and Arne? Asta laughed aloud as she reread the words on the paper, a bitter, rasping sound. Live with the people who'd given away her child? A businessman in a suit lifted his eyes from his newspaper with a predatory smile. She took off her gloves to reveal her wedding ring. She was part of a married couple, but where was Max? The war was over. Why couldn't she summon Kari's father to help her find their child? Her letters to his family home went unanswered.

Last week, she'd queued at the Red Cross office, trying to find out if any new information about Max had been released. Other than details of his captivity in a camp near the Rhine immediately after surrender, and his release a month later, they knew no more. She had hesitated outside the Norwegian Legation. She couldn't go in there and tell them she was the Norwegian wife of a German soldier and ask for help finding one of the occupiers in order to reclaim their child, could she? The Germans, understandably, didn't have an embassy operating in London. Perhaps Stockholm, being neutral, would have places that could help her track down Max? But first things first.

Finding Kari mattered more than anything. As she approached the children's home Asta's stomach churned, and her heart pounded fast.

She checked her map. They were approaching the stop nearest to the home. Asta rose to her feet before the tram slowed, picking up her suitcase. She jumped off and strode out, the route to the house in her head, each step she took making her heart pound more insistently. The home was situated in a quiet street, a park on the corner, respectable. Did they take the children to play there? Kari had always loved being out of doors. Even so, she'd be looking for her mother, wondering where Asta was, why she'd let this happen. How could she ever explain to Kari that none of this had been her plan, that she was so terribly, terribly sorry?

The iron gates were locked, with a bell pull. Asta gave it a firm tug. Nobody came. She tugged it again. The door to the building opened and a girl in an apron came out, looking confused, saying something in Swedish about visiting only being allowed on Sundays. Asta explained who she was, the Swedish words coming easily to her tongue. 'There's been a mistake with a child who isn't an orphan at all. I am here to collect Kari Nilsen.' The girl looked baffled. 'May I come in and talk to the principal?' Asta asked.

'I don't know.' The girl twisted the apron in her hands, eyes wide.

'I've come all the way from England.'

'England?' The girl sounded startled. 'But you sound Norwegian?'

'I am Norwegian.'

Something passed across the girl's features. 'Come in and wait. I'll find someone to talk to you.'

Asta followed her inside and across a checkerboard tiled floor. It was imposing, apparently clean, but felt cold. No sound of children playing, but this was a large house.

'Wait here,' the girl said, pointing at a chair in a corridor.

Asta sat down. Minutes passed. The girl returned. 'Fru Olsson will see you now.' Leaving her suitcase by the chair, Asta followed her into the office.

The woman behind the desk was in late middle age. She looked up from the papers in front of her. 'I can give you five minutes. What was your name?'

'Asta Brandt. Kari is my daughter.'

'Kari?' The woman's already pale complexion seemed to lose more of its colour. 'You are from the Bergen area?'

'Yes. Where's my daughter?'

'Can you prove your identity?'

Asta produced her passport.

'That says you are Asta Nilsen.'

'Married to Max Brandt.'

'You have a marriage certificate?'

'No, that's at home in Norway. You don't need it. As you can see, there's been a mistake. Kari isn't an orphan. She isn't unwanted. I've come to bring my daughter home.' This was the moment at which everything would be made right, Kari brought out to her. Reason would prevail. She smoothed down her wool skirt. The woman's eyes took in Asta's suit, the stockings that were not darned, her hair pinned back neatly now it was longer again.

She looked down again at her file. 'Kari came to us because of the misfortune of her birth. Her father is a German and you yourself were attacked by a mob, your hair cut, as punishment for your behaviour?'

Her behaviour? Asta thought of herself and Max, leaning back against a warm boulder overlooking the fjord. He was tickling her chin with a piece of grass and laughing at her. She remembered him coming up behind her when she was struggling to hold a post up straight and knock it into place with a mallet, just quietly taking hold of the post for her.

'Your brother, Arne Nilsen, the child's uncle and de facto guardian, felt that violence against the child herself was a possibility.'

'I'll be bringing Kari back to England with me. I have a job there. She'll be safe.'

'At this institution we place the welfare of the child foremost and so it was decided...' She swallowed. 'It was decided adoption would be in Kari's best interest.'

'Adoption? How could she be adopted without my permission?' There were laws, weren't there? The Nazis had taken children away from parents and agencies worked to track down the children and reunite them with their families. Was it so different for Norwegians? Only Kari technically wasn't Norwegian, it seemed, but the responsibility of the Germans.

'Arne Nilsen signed papers saying he was the child's legal guardian, in the absence of both her parents, who were no longer in Norway. Are you saying that your brother was untruthful about your absence?' The woman seemed to be taking the fight to Asta.

'I only left because of what happened to me.' Asta's hand went to her hair. 'Arne would have known I was coming back for Kari.'

The woman observed her seemingly without emotion. 'We can only operate on the basis of truthful submissions. As I say, everything we do is in the best interests of the child.'

'You didn't have adequate procedures to check the information. I am telling you now that adoption is not necessary for my daughter. I am here. I want to take her with me.'

'She has already left.'

The room spun. Asta forced herself to stay in control, not to surrender to the panic inside her. 'Where is Kari now?'

'She is on her way out of Sweden. That's all I can tell you.'

'Someone is taking her to Norway or Denmark?' Or to a country like Switzerland or Portugal where war hadn't ravaged homes. 'When?'

'Yesterday.'

She'd missed her daughter by just one day.

But it was only a day, with a small child, who would slow them down. Asta could go after Kari.

Fru Olsson was watching her. 'Kari isn't going to Norway or Denmark. She will be going to Australia.'

Asta still hadn't been asked to sit. Her legs buckled. She grabbed at the air as though it would hold her upright. The woman shouted something and the girl in the apron came rushing back in with a chair from the corridor and gently pushed her down onto it. They fanned her with papers from the desk and the girl brought a glass of water.

'Australia?' The single word seemed to sum up the emptiness inside Asta. 'Australia?' She said again, trying to fix it in her mind as a place, a destination, but it couldn't be right. 'Were they going back to embark on the ship in England?' she asked, her voice rasping. 'Which port? Tilbury? Southampton?'

'I only know they were catching a ferry from Goteborg to England.'

So they would take the train from Stockholm to Sweden's western port, reversing Asta's own trip.

'They were taking the train to Goteborg today?'

'They were spending last night and tonight in Stockholm to give Mr Morgan time to wind down his affairs here.'

A Mr and Mrs Morgan had taken Kari. At least she now

had names. If they were leaving Stockholm tomorrow morning, they'd take an early train to be in Goteborg for the 7pm ferry to Tilbury. 'Tell me what you know so I can go after them. Where were they staying, do you know the hotel?'

'I do not know the name of the hotel.' Fru Olsson was looking at her more sympathetically. 'You aren't what I thought you'd be.'

'What was that? Some kind of tart? I fell in love with Kari's father and he with me. We are a family.'

'And yet your brother says that the German concerned has returned home to a part of the country now occupied by the Soviets. Assuming he's not in a prisoner of war camp. Your own home was burned down. You have no occupation, no income, in Norway. The Norwegians say you belong in Germany. You are effectively stateless. And you think you can offer that little girl a home?'

Asta got up and slammed her palms on the desk. 'You will tell me the names and address of these people who have taken my daughter before I go to the police to tell them you have stolen a child. The police, the newspapers, I will tell everyone.'

Fru Olsson turned pale. 'We acted within the law. Your brother was the child's next of kin and he gave us permission to put her up for adoption when he signed the papers.'

'You took a child without adequate checks on whether you could legally do it? Did you give the Morgans the birth certificate?' Fru Olsson shuffled in her chair.

'I didn't have the certificate. The woman who brought her here, your brother's fiancée, insisted on taking it back to Norway with her. The adopting couple will contact the registrar in any case, to have it amended.'

Marte hadn't handed over Kari's birth certificate – some instinct had told her not to do this. A chink of hardness towards Marte softened inside Asta. Her anger rose against Fru Olsson again. 'How can you amend the facts? Kari is my daughter, they can't pretend she's someone else's.'

'We were told you were not contactable, that you had abandoned your daughter, that her only blood relative was her uncle, your brother. He still lives in the area where you suffered the abuse and believed it in Kari's best interests to find a good home for her.'

'You made no effort to look for me. I was in England, not Timbuktu. I could have been here in a matter of days, had I known you were about to send my daughter to Australia.'

The woman reached for her writing pad and scribbled something on a piece of paper. 'I should not give you any information, according to the confidentiality we maintain. But this is the full name of the adoptive parents and the address I have for them in Australia.'

Asta took the paper. Sydney.

'Mr Morgan told me they would be moving back to their original home in Melbourne at some point.'

The girl who'd brought Asta into the home cleared her throat. 'Even if you miss them before they get to Tilbury, they'll probably have to wait a day or so before their liner sails for Sydney.' Asta turned to look at her. 'My brother's in the merchant navy so I know some of the timetables,' the girl said, something in her voice suggesting a wish to help.

'Thank you.' Asta stood up.

'We had no way of knowing,' Fru Olsson said, defensiveness clear in her voice. 'Legally, we do our best to check papers and birth certificates. It's difficult after a major war. People move, names are changed, we don't know if parents are still alive. Or interested.'

'Why was that man even in Sweden?'

'Mr Morgan? He was in Norway and Sweden as part of an Australian delegation looking into a large-scale adoption of certain children.'

'Certain children? You mean children with German fathers?'

'Mr Morgan was concerned by reports of ill-treatment of these children in Norway after the Germans capitulated. He believed the best way to protect them was to remove them from those who might abuse them, a belief I share. No child here is treated harshly, and no child is treated differently because of their parentage.'

Asta heard a note of something in Fru Olsson's voice that made her temporarily lose some of her fury. The woman had probably tried to protect children like Kari from abuse.

'Many of the Norwegian children with German fathers were sent to this home. The government scheme didn't work out but he and his wife decided they themselves would adopt from here.'

They'd helped themselves to a pretty little Norwegian girl, as if she was a toy in a shop to be bought as a souvenir – not even bought, picked up for free. Asta closed her eyes briefly. Exploding with rage now would not bring her closer to her daughter. She had to control herself, harbour her energy, her wits. Nothing could be wasted.

'So Mr Morgan is an Australian civil servant?'

'Yes. A good man. A humanitarian. He wanted to help.'

'He's a child thief. And you're complicit in a crime.'

Without another word, Asta walked out, Fru Olsson's apologetic pleas falling unheeded on her back. Picking up her suitcase she stormed towards the door, the girl walking behind her.

'You need me to unlock the gate,' she said, pulling out the set of large keys. 'Good luck. I hope you find your daughter.' Hesitating, she added, 'The hotel will be one near the station. Probably the Anthon because that's where all the foreign delegations put up their people.'

Asta thanked her again.

Asta had memorised the location of the tram stop she had been planning to walk to with Kari. A hotel, more of a hostel, had been booked for them both close to the railway station. It certainly wasn't the Anthon. Instead of going there, Asta was going straight to the station. Suppose the Morgans had changed their plans and weren't staying a second night here with Kari? She'd check the railway timetables there. If there was a night train to Goteborg, Asta would catch them before they could sweep Kari away. If they were on the morning train, she'd be waiting for them tomorrow. Her head was full of railway links and ferries. Suppose they'd cut short their time in Stockholm completely and had already left this morning? She actually might have been in the station at the same time as Kari. Asta shivered.

Even if she had missed the Morgans and Kari, there could only be so many ships sailing for Australia in the next week. She could track them down. And if she didn't? Asta couldn't let herself imagine this but forced herself to make a plan. There was an Australian High Commission in London, wasn't there? She was sure she'd walked past it on the Strand. They might be able to help her track down Mr Morgan if he worked for the government. She had his address. A lawyer would help.

Asta found herself back on the tram, heading towards the railway station. She sat in the concourse, shivering in the cold. Her budget for hot drinks was strict. She'd have to wait until later. A pair of young women walked past her, carrying cross-country skis over the shoulders, heading for a day up in the hills, where they'd laugh and gossip, not a care in the world. Thoughts of herself and Marte came to her. How long ago it seemed that the two of them had hiked up the mountain outside the village, laughing about silly things, lamenting the lack of food, hoping for better days, for peace and an end to the occupation. And here they were, war over. How could it be that things were even more desperate and she felt so very alone, fighting for Kari without any help?

A voice spoke up inside her. So what if she was alone? It would only make her even fiercer. The image of her mother floated in front of her. Berit could be stern with her children if she thought they were being lazy or slapdash, but she wouldn't have let anyone take them away from her without a fight. If Mamma were here now, she'd be pointing out that Kari was either in this city, or on the way to Tilbury. It couldn't be impossible to find her. Asta stood up. She'd check the timetables, note all the departures for Goteborg in the next few days. Then she would stack her suitcase in the luggage office and take a walk, clear her head, buy something to eat and drink, even if it meant she had to sell the wedding ring on her finger. You couldn't fight if you were cold and weak. Max would understand, if he ever found out, that was. Perhaps he'd committed his wife and child to the past.

She stood at the counter of the luggage office, handing over the suitcase, finding the coins in her purse to pay for the locker. In the glass petition the reflections of passengers came and went. A couple with a small child passed as Asta replaced her purse in her bag. The child wore a red knitted hat with white snowflakes on it. She spun on her heel, seeing them disappear towards one of the platforms for regional trains. The Morgans were breaking the journey up, staying overnight in central Sweden?

She burst past the inspector and porters and ran along the platform, in time to see the couple helping the child up the steps into a carriage. 'Kari,' she shouted.

The child turned. A boy, older than Kari, wearing trousers under his long coat. Reindeer, not snowflakes, on the knitted hat. Muttering an apology, she returned to the concourse.

A sense of absolute isolation swept over Asta, threatening to overwhelm her. Everyone, everything had gone. She was alone in this marble-floored concourse. Breathing seemed suddenly hard, as if she was climbing a steep slope. Desperately she looked around, fixing her eyes on one of the water fountains at the end of the concourse. Lions had been moulded into the bowl. Kari would have loved them. A pang for her daughter swept through Asta, so strong it felt as if someone had hit her. A passing woman slowed to look at her, concern on her face. Asta tried to smile away her concerns, but the woman escorted her to a bench, glancing over her shoulder as she walked away.

Her heart was still pounding, her stomach flipping, but the moment of kindness had strengthened her. She had to pull herself together. Go to the hotel she'd booked. Sleep for a little. She only had herself to rely on; Max was lost to her. Kari needed her to be strong and rational now.

Asta stood up.

# TWENTY-ONE

## MAX

Each night, after he'd checked on Clara outside the door of the women's hostel where she was staying, Max made his way to the places where working men congregated, men from across the world: sailors, builders, metalworkers, stevedores, but above all, Norwegians. His excursions took him around the harbour, to the islands, and into the back streets of Stockholm's Old Town. Sweden had strict rules about alcohol. The city wasn't a place where bars littered the narrow alleys.

Emil Mauland, the former Norwegian SS private they'd met on the way to Kiel, shook his head when Max asked him to accompany him on these outings. 'Waste my free time in one of those dismal beer houses, sitting at a long table, eating meatballs and drinking weak beer?' He snorted. They were on their way back to the men's hostel after a day unloading crates of coffee, tea and oranges in a warehouse, almost certainly working illegally. Probably as well that there were only a few Swedish natives here today and no hint of a union representative to object to their presence and the low wages.

'I'll buy the food and drink,' he told Mauland. 'You've got your ration vouchers?'

'Not risking myself being spotted in one of those places with a German.' He stopped to light a cigarette. 'I'd as good as put a noose around my own neck. No, you're on your own now, Brandt.'

'One word from me...' The men locked eyes as Mauland threw his match into the gutter. Mauland was living here under a new identity he'd bought in Kiel before they'd left on a cargo ship returning to Stockholm. They hadn't tracked down Friedrich Klein, whose home was just rubble, but had found work in the Kiel docks, loading cargo and helping with maintenance jobs, Max's maimed hand regarded with scepticism until he proved he was as strong as anyone. After a few weeks, Max had won the respect of the crew and offered himself as a ship's engineer. By then, he'd managed to buy Swedish identities for himself and Clara, using a forger recommended by Mauland. She'd been employed in the ship's galley, ducking lecherous looks and hands, switching to mopping out the harbourside shower house when they arrived in Stockholm, before finding a job cleaning offices.

The Brandts had reverted to their German identities. Nobody would be fooled by them pretending to be Swedes here, anyway, and at least they were committing one fewer offence. The country had been neutral in the war. Germans weren't popular and weren't supposed to leave their own country, but antipathy was limited to mutters. If they kept their heads down, worked in places where nobody examined their work permits too closely, they might get away with it for the time it took Max to contact Asta in Norway.

'You're not going to hand me in, Brandt,' Mauland said. 'You know I'd tell the authorities about your own false papers. And the jobs you've had without the right to work here. They'd probably deport you and your little sister back home to the Soviets. I'm sure they'd give you a warm welcome.'

'You could just give me an idea of where to look for Norwegians. It wouldn't kill you.'

'I said I'd help you get here and I did. Your wife hasn't answered your letter. She's probably trying to divorce you.'

Max bit down the impulse to hit Mauland. He wasn't going to show him that he was bothered by Asta's lack of response to the letter he'd sent within days of arriving in Sweden. 'Just a few names is all I'm asking, man. Places where Norwegian patriots meet up and say what they'd like to do to Norwegian traitors like you.'

He glared at Max. 'I'll give you some starting points.' He pulled an old envelope from his pocket and a pencil stub, tugged off his gloves and scribbled names of beer houses for Max. 'Don't mention my name. If anyone comes looking for me, I'll know it's you. I'll find you and your sister.'

He handed over the note. 'Norwegians are working on construction of the Skanstull tram and road bridge to Söderort, to the south of here. They might drink down there on a Friday night.'

Loose-mouthed men trying to make a watery beer hit the right spot, nostalgic for the fjords, talking about the people they'd left behind, the memories of the occupation.

'But keep your mouth shut,' Mauland warned, as he picked up his rucksack.

'I'd keep yours closed, too, Mauland. The things you did on the Eastern Front wouldn't make you friends.'

'Says the fool who didn't even fire a shot in anger. But you said you'd rebuilt a bridge for the locals. Something like that means a lot out on the west coast. They're a pragmatic lot. Perhaps you could even live there again one day if your wife isn't remarried. As for me...' A look of vulnerability passed over his face. 'Anyway, you won't be seeing much of me from now on.'

Max couldn't think of anything to say. 'I hope you see your mother,' was the best he could manage.

Mauland vanished the following evening, after they'd finished a freezing day's work on the docks. As Max trudged from Clara's lodgings into dark streets and alleyways that made him glance over his shoulder at every passing footstep, he regretted Mauland's absence. The man had done things on the Eastern Front Max didn't want to think about. But he'd been helpful.

Clara's own job in Stockholm, cleaning a small block of offices at night, didn't bring her into contact with many Swedes. 'I'm asleep during the day so I don't speak to anyone,' she said. 'And I don't speak Swedish or Norwegian. I'm not much help.'

'You are.' He struggled to find words to explain to Clara how much it meant that she'd made this journey with him. If she was caught using the false papers, she might be imprisoned, deported, punished by the Soviets on her return to their zone.

His tour of beer houses and places where workers met showed that Stockholm was home to a number of Norwegians, some staying on after they'd taken refuge here during the war, others arriving afterwards to earn money to send home. Norway didn't have a large population, Max told himself. Family connections were strong in rural areas like the one where Asta and Petter lived. If he could find a place where Norwegians from the Bergen area liked to meet, he could perhaps find out what was happening. He hadn't admitted it to Mauland but he'd sent a second letter to Asta, this time to the family home in Bergen.

His plan, unshared with Clara, was to bribe a Norwegian worker to lend him his identity papers for a week, even five days might be enough, for him to travel to the west coast of Norway and reassure himself that Asta and Kari were all right, hand over the money he'd somehow managed to save for them, by half starving himself, Clara said. It was a huge thing for a German to ask of a Norwegian man and would probably land him a punch to the jaw. At worst it could mean a bunch of outraged Vikings digging a hole in the ice in the harbour and throwing him into it. What choice did he have? Longing for Asta and Kari seemed to grow stronger each day. If he couldn't buy papers from someone here, he'd have to steal them or find another black-market forger to produce a Norwegian identity. Any longer separation from his family couldn't be endured.

Each night he told himself he could be close to finding the men he needed to listen in to. Each night he sloped away, usually disappointed, sometimes making a few dumplings last an hour. A whole week might pass where he couldn't pick out a single Norwegian voice.

This evening he opened the door and a wall of Norwegian dialects hit him. So many men, most of them living up to all the stereotypes, tall and fair, sitting on benches at the long tables. He passed over the ration book Mauland had helped him acquire and ordered beer and meatballs, sitting at the end of one of the tables, half in the shadows, waiting and listening. A group of friends from southern Norway sat opposite. Brothers from the Oslo area flopped down next to him. The brothers saw him watching them and frowned. He grinned and raised his half-full glass at them, before dropping his head in the direction of his plate, trying not to draw attention to himself. Just another working man seeking warmth and what passed for drink.

The door opened with a crash. The men at a table opposite shouted a greeting. Workers from the west of Norway. Max thought he heard Bergen mentioned. He told himself to drink his beer, not to stare, not to draw eyes. Asta and Petter had insisted on speaking Norwegian once Kari had arrived, encouraging Max to learn as much as he could. As a result, Max could follow conversations in the language, speak a bit himself. Making out the words across the echoing room was hard. He felt himself frowning as he strained to listen and told himself not to make it obvious. *The foreman at the job needed his face rearranging and the lodgings weren't fit for a dog. Back home was better, always better, we won't be here long, just until we've earned some more money. Norway will do well when it's recovered. The Germans did their best to trash the country, but we'll build it back up.*

Their voices rose as they declaimed, drawing frowns from the more sober diners and the woman bringing food on trays. Max looked down at his glass. The beer barely felt like alcohol at all. He wondered what had happened to Petter's home-brewed supplies and hoped his father-in-law was still enjoying it by the stove, along with his pipe. Distracted by thoughts of Petter, he blinked when he realised someone had asked him a question. A light. He nodded and took out his lighter. The man opposite was rolling a Norskavlet from the familiar yellow and green tobacco tin, asking Max if he wanted one. He smiled and patted his pocket, taking out his own packet of Swedish cigarettes.

The Norwegian frowned at him. 'What did you do to your hand?'

'Lost my fingers in an accident.' Max managed to end the conversation by scraping his fork across the plate, as if he was desperate to eat every last morsel. He didn't want to hold this man in conversation, exposing his nationality; he wanted to listen in to him speaking to his companions.

The group from the south of Norway were making a move. Calling farewells across the room, they poured out of the door. The men remaining inside spread out a little along the benches, enabling Max to shuffle towards the middle of the table.

'Brandt.'

He reacted to his name before he could stop himself. On the table next to his, sitting opposite him now, he saw a face that was familiar, though he'd barely exchanged a word with the man. Magnus Haugen. The local who they'd turned down for work on the coastal defences because he wasn't strong enough. The man who'd thrown the mud at the car on the way back from Asta and Max's wedding.

'*Hva pokker gjør du?* What the hell are you doing here, you German bastard?' Magnus squared up to him, fists raised. Around the room, men lowered glasses and cutlery and turned. In seconds, this was all going to go very wrong. Magnus's name had only once or twice been mentioned by Asta or her father and they'd been studiously casual. It had been Asta's friend, Marte, who'd once briefly referred to the man's obsession with Asta.

*He used to dog her footsteps, hang around the farmyard.* This man loathed Germans. He would know what was happening back at the smallholding but was more likely to incite a lynching than tell Max what he wanted to know. Max put down his knife and fork and stood up.

The brothers from Oslo stood, too, positioning themselves between Max and the door, blocking his escape route.

'You.' Magnus walked around the table and grabbed him by the shoulders. 'You know what you did, how you left her.'

'She is my wife.' He pushed Magnus back. Whatever happened now, it wasn't going to go his way, so he might as well not be taken as a milksop. 'What's it to you, Haugen?'

'This is a German?' The man whose cigarette he'd lit glowered at him. 'You didn't tell me that when we talked.'

'While spoil a pleasant evening?' Max knew he wasn't making things easier for himself.

'You know this man from the occupation?' he asked Magnus. 'He was posted up on the west? What'd he do while he was with you?'

'Got a local girl pregnant. From a good Norwegian family.'

'Slut.'

The word was like a spark burning along a fuse towards gunpowder. Max spun around, his right wrist connecting with the cheek of the man who'd called Asta that word. Beyond reason, he followed with an uppercut from his left hand, the missing fingers not seeming to matter tonight. 'Want to say it again?'

They were on him, pushing their chairs out as they rose, like a pack, kicking and punching him, pushing him down onto the tiled floor, shouts of outrage from the staff unheeded. Pain exploded through his body. He rolled onto his side and kicked out at their legs where he could.

Someone else shouted. Nobody paid any attention. The pain became a constant. Beer trickled down his brow and nose. The shout came again. The kicks and blows subsided. *Get up*, Max told himself. *While you can, before it starts again.* His legs barely worked but he managed to stagger to his knees and then stand up, swaying, a vice around his head. Blood trickled onto the floor. Magnus was shouting.

'Enough.' Magnus made a sweeping motion with his arms. Back on the fjord, nobody would have paid any attention, but in Oslo, he seemed larger, louder. The man who ran the beer house was pushing the door open, shouting at them to sit down and behave or leave before he called the police. The group of men returned to their meals. Food was too good to be wasted, even on a brawl. Magnus and Max found themselves pushed out into the street. Each breath of cool air scoured Max's lungs. His palms ached to make contact with Magnus's face again. Before he could, Magnus raised a hand, palm out. The man had grown in strength and presence since Max had left Norway.

'I don't want to fight. Your child's here in Stockholm.' Magnus said it slowly, as if wanting to be sure the words were completely understood, before switching to a halting German. 'In a children's home. But she won't be there for long now.'

'What the hell are you talking about?' Stars floated in front of Max's eyes, the left one of which didn't seem to be working properly. 'She's at home, with her mother.' A black curtain had fallen over the vision that side. Shocks of pain fired around his body.

'Sit.' Magnus pushed him down against the wall. 'Before you fall. Don't want to be responsible for you.'

From down here he could see the stars above the snow-covered roofs. 'Kari is in Stockholm or are you just trying to see if you can get another reaction from me?'

'I'm telling you, your kid's here.'

'But why? Where's Asta? And Petter?' None of it made sense. 'You said Kari was in a home—' He stood up, lurching.

Magnus held up a hand. 'Petter's dead. Asta's left the country.'

The outline of the backstreet and the buildings was spinning round in front of Max. He squinted and found a lamppost to focus on, so he could concentrate on what this man was telling him.

'Marte...' Asta's friend would have helped Kari, surely?

'Marte and Asta's brother, Arne, sent the child away because after you left, things became hard for Asta and Kari.' There was a silence. Magnus seemed to grapple for words. 'It was difficult... People were... There was trouble. So Asta had to go.'

'What kind of trouble?'

'You and her.' Magnus focused on the trampled snow in the gutter. 'People didn't understand.'

'What do you mean, they didn't understand?' The pain was breaking through the haze. 'Did they hurt Kari?'

'Nobody harmed Kari, but Arne sent her here because they worried about her, growing up with a father like you. I wanted to write to Asta, to tell her, but I didn't have her address in England. But I think it's too late now.'

Names and locations seemed to buzz around in Max's brain as he struggled to concentrate, the throbbing in his head demanding attention.

'So how do you know where my daughter is?' he asked slowly, as thinking became possible again.

'There's a fellow in the Lutheran Working Man's hostel where I stay. He's a handyman and plumber. Goes around schools and hospitals, the like. I asked him if he ever went anywhere there were Norwegian orphans.'

'Kari's no orphan,' Max said fiercely. Magnus nodded.

'Lots of the kids have mothers. Who don't want them. Because of what happened after the war ended, mainly.'

'What did the plumber tell you?'

'I gave him some cigarettes and asked for names, sexes, rough ideas of what kids looked like.' Magnus scoffed. 'He told me there was a girl, no more than three or four, he thought, who'd come in with a red knitted Norwegian hat, clutching a doll. The hat had gone – they take the clothes – but the kid had the doll. I remembered seeing Kari with a red knitted hat the day Marte took her on the ferry. She had a doll, too.'

'Is Kari still there?'

Magnus was silent.

'Tell me!'

'People come to the home to adopt the Norwegian children if they like the look of them. My friend asked a girl who works there and she said an Australian couple called Morgan wanted a little girl, young enough to be made into what they want. They chose Kari.'

'They're adopting Kari? They can't!'

'People say the children are lacking up here, like me,' Magnus tapped his head. 'Because their mothers must have been soft in their heads to have been with Germans. The sins of the mothers are passed on to the children, like it says in Scripture. So adoption and a new country will be the best for those boys and girls.'

Max's hands clenched. 'I'll stop this.'

'The Morgans have already taken Kari. They left with her

yesterday. So my letter back home will be too late.' From his pocket, he removed a scrap of paper. 'This is the name of the home, they might tell you more about where they've gone.'

'Did you hurt Asta?' Max asked quietly.

Magnus looked at him steadily. 'I told the men who wanted to punish her where she was and I cut her hair off. I feel shame for that. But I could cut your throat now and I would feel no guilt, none at all.'

'I could cut yours. Because of you, and men like you, Asta and Kari had to leave their home.'

'I told you where Kari is. We're even now.'

'Why are you doing this, Haugen? Just because of a guilty conscience?'

Magnus looked away. 'Petter and Berit Nilsen were good to me. Asta and Arne were once my friends. Perhaps it took me longer than it should have done to remember this. People always said I was slow to learn.'

Max watched him slope away, eaten up by the darkness almost immediately, before looking down at the scrap of paper in his hand.


Clara, when he roused her, greeted him at the door of her women's hostel in dressing gown and slippers. 'You realise I'll be thrown out now for having noisy male guests after lights-out?'

'I told the woman who answered the door it was a family emergency.'

She shivered. 'Tell me before we freeze to death out here in the street. They won't let you inside.' Quickly he explained. Her eyes widened. 'Kari's here? In Stockholm?'

'The people who're taking her to Australia must be staying in a hotel.'

'Go to the children's home tomorrow and ask for the address?'

'It may be too late.'

'Even if they're still in the city, they could be anywhere.'

'You said there were women in here who work at the hotels?'

'Cleaners and kitchen staff, yes. I'll ask, but I can't wake them up now, Max.'

'If they're taking her out of the city there's no time for me to go round all the hotels tonight.'

She looked him up and down in his working man's jacket and cap, the bruises and cuts on his face, which she hadn't asked about. 'They probably wouldn't tell you, no. What's the time?' She hadn't been able to replace the watch stolen from the Soviets.

'Eleven.'

'So they're probably not going on any train tonight. They'll probably take an early service tomorrow morning.'

'Night porters might be amenable to some ready cash for checking hotel guest books.'

Clara considered it for a moment. 'Wait five minutes for me to get properly dressed. We'll search the hotels near the Central Station.'

'It's freezing, I can't drag you out.'

'People are more likely to talk if a woman's with you.'

She came back down five minutes later. He waited while she argued with the woman guarding the door. It sounded as if Clara had lost her bed for infringing curfew rules. 'I'm sorry,' he said, when she appeared, muffled in a scarf. Yet again, Clara's life had been disrupted on his account.

'I'll find somewhere else tomorrow. Let's go.'

He gave her a sidelong look. 'You've given up too much for me.'

She took his arm. 'You came all the way home for me,

remember? You could have left me alone there. Now, the first hotel we should go to looked promising because there were conference delegates staying there, a girl in the hostel told me just now.'

The Sadler Hotel's concierge brushed them out of the main entrance before they could even enter, telling them no Australians were staying there and he would call the police if he saw the pair of them again.

The porter from the smaller, shabbier hotel around the corner took pity on Clara and went in to reception himself to look at the hotel records, returning with a mug of coffee for her, ignoring Max. 'I've looked at the guest book for you and there's no child staying tonight except for a boy.'

They moved on to the next hotel, now finding themselves on Vasagatan square. Max was too tired to even make out its name. The main door was firmly closed. 'We could ring the bell,' Max said.

'Let's go round to the side,' Clara said. 'There might be a door that's unlocked so the night staff can put out the rubbish. We could sneak in and make our way to the front desk and look at the guest book ourselves when nobody's looking.'

The night was now so cold, the snow taking on a gritty, piercing texture, that the thought of respite from the weather was hard to resist. The white outline of the Central Station faded behind the snow, appearing every now and then like a beacon, warning Max that there might only be hours to find Kari.

The side door of the hotel was locked. 'There'll be another entrance at the back,' Clara said.

A small shadow twisted itself through the snow in front of them. Clara, an animal lover, put a hand down and the cat brushed up against her, miaowing. 'You'll freeze out here, little one,' she said.

The door creaked behind them. A man, almost invisible in

coat and hat and muffler, came out. 'There she is. Got herself shut out of the warm boiler room.' He picked the cat up and peered at Clara. 'You look as if you'd like some warmth, too.'

'I'm frozen,' she said.

He looked them up and down. 'What are you two doing out at this hour?'

'I'm looking for my daughter,' Max said, urgency lending him fluency.

'And what might she be doing in the Anthon?'

'She's been taken from me.' As the words came out of his mouth the horror of the situation seemed to sharpen and stab him.

The porter eyed him. 'And you think you'll find her at this time of night? Thanks for finding my cat but be on your way now.'

'My niece is three,' Clara said. 'We've walked hundreds and hundreds of kilometres to find her.'

He shrugged.

'Could we please come in for just a moment, just to warm ourselves?'

He nodded, unlocking the door.

It was a quiet night, the porter said. January. Not many guests, just a few foreigners, staying here for the convenient walk to the station. He took them through to a room where a few old chairs, stuffing coming out, and a stove provided his den and sat down, cat on his lap. 'I sit down here until the night staff need me for something.' He nodded up at the bell on the wall. 'Sit down for a few minutes.' He took a flask from his pocket and passed it to them. Akvavit.

'My daughter is Norwegian,' Max said. 'I know it sounds extraordinary, because, yes, I'm German. She was taken for adoption after I left Norway. Her mother and I didn't agree to this.'

The man's eyes narrowed. 'German, eh?'

The cat jumped off the porter's lap and rubbed itself against Clara's legs. 'I always wanted a cat,' she said. 'For a while I looked after one when its home was bombed. But she vanished. I kept looking for her on the streets. Never saw her again.'

Max sat completely still, instinct telling him to be silent.

'When someone vanishes, part of you tells yourself to accept it, you won't see them again. But the part of you that can't accept it makes it impossible. That's what it's like for my brother. He knows everything is against his family reuniting. He's taken me on an impossible journey across Germany and the Baltic. Because we have hope. We have to have hope.'

The porter was silent, too. The only sound was the cat's purring.

'Room seven,' he said. 'There's a couple in there with a little girl. I thought she'd be English or something. Australian, like them. But she was talking to her doll and then I realised it was Norwegian.'

'Ulla,' Max said. 'She's still got Ulla. Her grandfather bought her that doll for her birthday last year.'

'Don't cause a scene,' the porter said. 'That would be my job gone, and then where would we both be?' He glanced at the cat. 'Stay down here until morning. Breakfast is served from seven. If they have room service, I'll ask the kitchen to ring the bell and tell me. I leave at half six. Close your eyes now, you can't do anything more tonight.'

He waved his hand as they thanked him.


Sleep eluded Max until the early hours. He heard a clock strike three before sleeping in a way he hadn't since he'd left Norway, falling into an empty, silent space.

He woke to Clara shaking his leg. 'Max! We have to go.'

'What's happened?' He looked at his watch. Eight in the morning.

'The porter's gone. Before he went, he asked the kitchen staff to ring the bell if room seven had breakfast sent to them, but they didn't. The Australians aren't in the breakfast room, either. When I begged the concierge to tell me where they were, he said they'd checked out already.'

He was standing up, reaching for his coat. 'They must be having breakfast on the train or in the station.'

'Hurry,' Clara said. 'The first train for Goteborg leaves in ten minutes.'

# TWENTY-TWO

## STOCKHOLM CENTRAL STATION

Lars Eklund had never considered his cleaning and maintenance job to be less important than any other in Stockholm Central Station. Or than on the Swedish railways themselves. He mattered as much as a train driver or one of the nation's railway engineers. An ill-swept concourse or unemptied litter bins looked unsightly and raised doubts in passengers' minds.

Neatness. Safety. And pride. People thought pride meant jackboots and angry flags. Lars saw it as ensuring cigarette butts were swept up as soon as they were dropped. He'd taken on more than his job, too, directing passengers who looked lost or bewildered to the correct platform. He'd seen it all in his thirty years: weeping women and children, relieved men, harassed teachers shepherding school camping groups.

This morning had started well. By eight, not a single piece of litter besmirched the marble floor of the concourse. The moulded lions and fish on the red sandstone fountains guarded pristine basins. His small team had cleaned the men's and women's lavatories to his standard. Puddles from snow-covered boots had been mopped. The station was settling into a happy buzz of activity: not too busy, not too quiet. Shortly he'd find a quiet place to smoke a pipe and read the ice hockey results in the *Svenska Dagbladet* for ten minutes.

The train leaving for Goteborg was ready for boarding. Lars stood back, propping his mop against the trolley, watching the passengers. Life was returning to normal now the war was over, people travelling to Denmark and Norway and beyond. Some of them wore the faded, threadbare clothes of refugees, people displaced by war, still trying to reach home, or, if home wouldn't have them, find a new home in Sweden, if they were allowed.

The middle-aged couple with the little girl were obviously not refugees, not in those smart travel outfits. Funny how observant you became when you did this job: you could spot the people who belonged together, even when the mother was scolding the children or the father dragging a naughty boy along. This smart woman held the little girl's hand with care, looking nervous, as if the girl might run off. The child herself seemed to go where she was led as if she was in a dream until something grabbed her attention. The lions on the water fountain. She slowed to take a closer look.

The woman pulled a little too enthusiastically on the child's hand, in Lars' opinion as a father and grandfather, and said something to hurry her on. He felt himself smile at her as the kid passed him. She didn't look like either of the couple, being fair-haired while they were both dark-haired. She'd be an orphan adopted and on her way to a better life. He wanted to tell her life would get better, or at least, not any worse, more understandable. She wasn't the first kid Lars had seen heading off for a new life and wouldn't be the last. Perhaps she read something in his expression because her eyes met his for a moment and she looked at him solemnly. Wherever they were taking her, this girl wasn't sure about it, not at all. Her new mamma hurried her on again in a mangled language that might be an attempt at Norwegian because it certainly wasn't Swedish.

A racket at the far end of the concourse pulled Lars's attention away. Across the marble floor came two people, running fast – a man in shabby clothes and caps, like those worn by labourers, and a girl in a respectable but threadbare suit, shouting not in Swedish but in what sounded like German.

She looked at him as if she hadn't a clue what he meant, dodged his detaining arm and ran after her companion. 'There,' the man shouted towards the ticket inspector and porter in a rough approximation of Swedish. 'There they are. Stop them. They've got my daughter!' The two men looked at one another, baffled.

Across the marble floor came a further diversion: a young woman, also in a suit but a newer, better-cut one, entering from the opposite side of the station. Lars had seen her yesterday afternoon, moping around, looking as if she wanted something that wasn't a train. When she saw the pair running towards the platform, she let out a gasp that was almost a scream and ran towards them. 'Max?' she shouted.

The older couple with the kid had been fussing around with tickets and porters. They turned at the sound of the commotion, but Lars's attention was now on the smartly dressed young woman hurrying towards the little girl.

'Kari?' She slowed, as if uncertain, and spoke the word almost as a question, and then again, more urgently. 'Kari!' The shout sounded as though it was coming from a stricken animal. Around the concourse, passengers turned their heads. Lars frowned. Disturbances were not welcome at Stockholm Central Station. Foreigners might make a noise in a public place; Swedes did not.

'Mamma!' The child pulled her hand free and ran towards her, seeming to topple into her mother's arms. At the same time, the man in workman's clothes rush towards the pair. *Kari, Asta,*

*Mamma, Pappa.* Then there were three of them, man, woman, child, bound together like a living and breathing statue, repeating one another's names over and over again in tones of wonder and doubt.

At the platform entrance stood the older couple who had been on their way to Goteborg; the train was about to pull out of the station now. The slight girl in the shabby suit addressed them in what sounded like a stilted English. 'This child is my brother's daughter, Kari Brandt. This is Kari's mother, Asta Brandt, born Asta Nilsen, from Bergen in Norway. Kari should not be leaving with you.'

'Kari is our adopted child.' The man took a step towards Kari, who clung to her parents.

'We did not consent to her being adopted and we are here to reclaim her.' Lars thought that was what the man said. Then there were words about birth certificates and authorities Lars wasn't quite sure he was understanding correctly.

The couple who were about to miss the train seemed to crumple. 'We should call the police,' the man said defiantly.

The ins and outs of foreign adoptions were not for the likes of Lars to understand, but he understood kids. 'I think this really is their child,' he said in Swedish to the middle-aged couple. A few English words floated into his memory. 'Their daughter, not yours.'

'Think what we can offer her, Mrs Brandt,' the middle-aged man said desperately. 'Life in a country that wasn't ravaged by war.'

'You can't offer her more than we can,' the child's mother – her real mother, that was clear from the way they held one another so tightly – said. 'We are Kari's parents. She belongs with us.' She might have been speaking in Norwegian or English, by now Lars couldn't tell but he knew what she meant.

'Perhaps you go to the cafeteria with the police?' Lars

suggested, just flying with his English now. 'Coffee, yes? Discuss it there, not on public concourse by the platform.'

The woman identifying herself as Asta Nilsen or Brandt understood and nodded. 'Yes, the cafeteria.' Her hand tightened on her daughter's hand, eyes blazing in her head. 'And we will call the police.' Lars wouldn't have taken her on.

The Australian couple looked at one another, the man seeming to grasp the situation. 'No need for that,' he said. 'We thought we were doing something good,' he added quietly. 'For Kari. We signed the papers.'

The young German girl in the shabby clothes seemed to understand, nodding, saying something about the war. The Australian's wife still appeared dazed. Asta approached her, still clinging to her daughter, saying words that seemed to mean that she didn't blame the other woman, but making it clear Kari wouldn't be going with her. Kari whispered something to her mother in their own language and Asta nodded. 'She says thank you for her clothes.'

The Australians smiled at the child, looking sad but guilty at the same time.

Lars saw his moment to regain order. 'Now then, this is a public railway station, not a custody court. Move along please.' He spoke the words in Swedish but could see they knew what he meant, as foreigners often found they did when he was firm. 'The train for Goteborg will be leaving in two minutes, so you need to hurry along, sir and madam.'

The two of them blinked, looked at one another and the man seemed to tell his wife that they might as well continue as planned to Goteborg. She bent down to Kari and kissed her cheek.

The porter had already swept their suitcases away and the two of them walked off in the direction of the platform with just a quick glance back at Kari, who lifted a hand and waved. Nice kid, well brought up, obviously been through a bit, like so many children in Europe.

Not that child welfare issues were his business.

The stationmaster approached. 'Trouble, Eklund?'

'All sorted now.'

Asta and her husband, the little girl, and the younger German woman walked away towards the main exit. The husband seemed to be introducing Asta and the kid to her.

It was as if an earthquake had threatened the station, an emotional turbulence. A scene in public. He returned to his trolley, eyes on the quartet until they had passed out of the station, into the streets and alleys of Stockholm. What would become of such a curious group comprising Germans and Norwegians? Where would they live? Here, in Sweden? What would they do?

The German pair probably oughtn't to be in Stockholm. If Lars summoned the police, they'd be interested. Not his business, Lars reminded himself. No damage to the station or the Swedish railway had been inflicted. No other passengers had been threatened. The four of them could be allowed to walk out into the wintry morning, across the snowy paths and along the iced-up waterways of the city to find their future.

Someone had dropped a chocolate bar wrapper by the fountain. Time to stop wondering and start working.


'Where are we going?' Kari asked. Her parents looked at one another and smiled.

'I don't know,' Asta said, picking her up. Her Norwegian home on the fjord was lost. Max couldn't live in Norway anyway. Nor could Clara, who seemed, in the last half an hour, to already be part of Asta's family. She smiled at the German girl, feeling shy. 'I'm so glad you're here with Max,' she said, in German. Clara's face seemed one that hadn't shown much joy in the last year, but a smile briefly lit up her features.

'We can't go home and live in the Soviet zone,' Max said.

'And you and Clara can't live in England, either. That's where I've been.'

'We'll all just have to stay here,' Clara said. 'I like this city.' She shrugged. 'We'll keep ourselves to ourselves for a while so nobody notices Max and me and sends us back to Germany.'

'They'd have to get past me before that happens,' Asta said.

Max rolled his eyes at Clara. 'I told you she was a Viking.'

Still clutching Kari, Asta looked at the water glittering silver in the winter sunshine, the sky a limitless pale-blue dome. Hadn't she pined for life in a city when she'd lived on the small-holding? Now she was being given a city, along with her family. Max caught her eye.

'I promise I'll buy new clothes as soon as I can,' he said. 'This is just what I wear for work.'

'I was more worried about your face.' How was it she hadn't noticed the bruises and cut before? 'You've been fighting?' Max, who barely raised his voice, brawling?

He shrugged.

'How did you both even know to be at the station for that train?' At the time of his appearance, she hadn't had time to wonder about the magic of this happening.

'Magnus told us what was going on with this one.' He nodded at Kari, who was mesmerised by three dachshunds on a lead, sniffing the snow.

'Magnus Laugen?' She heard incredulity in her voice. 'But he...' She put a hand to the back of her neck, feeling the cold bite of the scissors.

'He's here in Stockholm.'

Asta found words failing her. Magnus had finally felt a prick of conscience?

Max told her about a night visiting hotels, finally finding the one where Kari and the Morgans were sleeping. 'Even if we'd missed her, you'd have been there in the station, Asta. You wouldn't have let Kari go with those people.'

'You were there in time, we both were. We were never going to let her go. And we won't be parted again.'

The future was uncertain. Yet, as they walked out of the station, the morning seemed full of light, sparkling off the snow and rooftops.

PART SEVEN

# TWENTY-THREE

## FEBRUARY, 1947

Kari's cheeks were like a pair of large cherries, her father told her, pulling the top off the water bottle and insisting that she take a large drink before she skied any further. 'I'm faster than Mamma already,' she told her parents.

'What?' Asta put her hands on her hips. 'I think you'll find that's untrue, young lady.'

'I see a race coming up,' Max said. 'Oh dear.'

'You'll be last, Pappa.'

'Beaten by the women in my life. Again.' He took the bottle from Kari and offered it to Asta.

'Pappa didn't have the chance to learn when he was little, like you and me,' Asta said. 'You were on skis when you could barely walk. Morfar and I did our best to teach Pappa, and I think he does very well, considering.'

'Yes, poor me. I am handicapped.' Max took off a glove and looked at his watch. 'We should turn off onto that trail through the trees now. It'll take us back to the cabin. The sun's quite low.'

'We've got another forty minutes, I'd say,' Asta said. 'No

need to rush back. And we haven't had the buns.' She opened her rucksack and took out a paper bag.

'Let's save them for when we're back in front of the stove.' He replaced his glove. 'First one back to that big rock on the right, Kari?'

Kari appeared torn between the cinnamon buns and the chance to race her father. 'Two buns if you can beat me,' he called, striding forward on his skis. She propelled herself off, naturally seeming to understand the movement and breaking into a skating motion, too young to use poles yet, though it wouldn't be long before she would be safe to have them.

Asta returned the buns to her rucksack and hurried to replace it on her back and pull her gloves on. Unlike Max to cut short a family outing. Perhaps he was tired after a busy week in the office, poring over plans for yet another Stockholm bridge. It didn't take Asta long to catch him up. Living in Sweden could never be like living at home, but at least they could spend weekends out here, exploring the countryside on their skis, renting a cabin. During the week, she had city life, even though they had little money to spend.

The track climbed gently. Asta caught up with Kari and gave her a gentle push. 'I can manage,' Kari shouted, herringboning her skis to get up it. She squealed with joy as she reached the top and picked up speed. Asta stood at the top, motionless, looking down at the cabin. A lantern was lit in the window. She hadn't left it alight.

Max had reached the cabin and was removing his skis, leaning them up in the overhang to one side of the door. He glanced back at her and something in his expression was serious. Asta's heart thumped and she pushed herself on towards him, passing Kari. 'Is someone in there?' she asked. 'Did Clara change her mind and leave her books for some fresh air?' Clara was studying in Stockholm, doing well.

'Asta.' He put a hand on her shoulder. 'We have visitors. They've come here specially to meet you.'

'Who?' She removed her skis. 'Why didn't you tell me?' He let her stack the skis in the overhang to the side of the door but held her sleeve to stop her going inside the cabin.

'It's Arne and Marte. And... someone else.'

She felt a wash of nausea. 'What on earth have you done?'

'You've been writing to one another, haven't you?'

'Yes. But I haven't heard a word from Arne since before Christmas, not even a card.'

Kari had reached them now, face puckered. 'I don't like it when you both go and leave me behind.'

Max stooped down to help her with her skis. 'We have special guests, that's why.'

The door opened. A tall, fair man stood in front of them, a hesitant smile on his face. He bent down to Kari. 'Hello, Kari. Remember me?'

Kari shook her head.

'You were very small, but we went skiing together. I bet you're fast now?'

'Faster than Mamma.'

'She won't like that.' Arne grinned at her and something inside Asta uncurled. They'd been writing to one another for a year now. Arne had sold the house in Bergen and needed to transfer Asta's share of the proceeds to her. The sum had helped them rent the Stockholm apartment she, Max, Clara and Kari lived in. Since then, Asta and her brother had slowly tried to find a way back to one another. She'd never been able to invite them to stay in Stockholm, always worried that something would be said that would be hard for Max to hear. Or that her own bitterness towards Arne would erupt, she'd say things that could never be unspoken. Then there'd been that silence from Arne and Marte. Asta hadn't known how to break it. Had the weight of Asta's marriage to a German once again become too heavy? Perhaps Arne had to distance himself from her to maintain good terms with his Norwegian clientele and suppliers.

Arne stood back to let them inside. 'We took the liberty of stoking the stove,' he said. 'And putting on some coffee.'

Marte was coming out of the small living room now, carrying something her arms. A baby, wrapped in layers of blankets, sleeping.

'Oh,' Asta said, understanding now why there had been a silence.

'Meet Petter.' Arne beamed at his son.

'Two months old,' Marte said proudly. 'That's why we didn't write any cards this year. He came a few weeks early and had the doctors worried at first, but he's doing well now.' The sleeping baby uncurled a mittened fist briefly, as if in confirmation.

She offered Petter to Asta. 'He's absolutely perfect,' Asta said, cradling her nephew. 'And I think his grandfather would be very proud.' She crouched down so that Kari could admire the baby, too. 'Look at your cousin.' She glanced up at Marte. 'I still can't believe this.' She blinked hard. Arne couldn't really be here. With a son.

Max had been silent until now. He cleared his throat. 'I told Arne where we'd be this weekend. I thought it was time for you all to meet and that it would be easier out here, in the forest.'

She wanted to shout at him that he had no right to interfere. The baby stirred briefly, as if sensing the discord.

'I wanted to see you, Asta. I wanted you to see little Petter. So I wrote to Max at his office.' Arne swallowed. 'I didn't know what else to do. Marte suggested it.'

Arne and Max, men on different sides of the war, with so much bitterness between them, these two had managed to communicate.

Asta handed Petter back to Marte, their eyes meeting.

Marte's held a question in them. Asta smiled. 'I'm glad this cabin has plenty of rooms.'

'I'm going to show that niece of mine how to ski like a Norwegian,' Arne said. 'And I'll race you, too, little sister.'

'I look forward to leaving you behind.' She placed one hand on his shoulder and he put his hand on hers, before pulling her into a deep hug. Arne felt as solid and warm as he always had. Asta blinked as he released her, not wishing to show tears in front of Kari.

'Am I forgiven?' Max asked Asta quietly, as they took off their coats and helped Kari remove her boots. 'You and Arne seemed stuck, both wanting to meet up but not knowing how.'

'The Nilsens are a stubborn lot,' Marte said, overhearing them.

Asta found being with Marte again was sweeping her with emotion. It wasn't just about Arne, it was about the lost friendship that had sustained her for those years during the occupation. 'If I'd known, I'd have bought more buns,' she said. 'Mamma used to say Arne could eat a house empty if you let him.' She felt herself letting go of something that had been clamped tightly around her insides whenever she thought of Arne. She'd despaired, thinking she could never forgive him for what he had done to Kari, who'd never spoken of her month in the children's home, perhaps no longer remembered it or had buried it deep inside her.

Asta couldn't forgive her brother, perhaps never would, but she had finally found her way to leaving the anger behind. Kari needed her uncle and his family, that new cousin of hers. And if Max and Arne could find a way to sit in a room together eating buns and talking about skiing, ice hockey and football, then she could, too.

'I missed you, Asta,' Marte said. 'When I had the baby I couldn't stop thinking about you and the Christmas when Kari was born.'

'I missed you, too.' Asta might never be allowed home, but a little bit of home had come to her today. 'I wish I'd been there to help.'

'We're rebuilding the red house,' Marte said. 'It will be a little larger, and modernised inside, but it will look very similar. One day you'll see for yourself, Asta.'

Asta hoped that her country would forgive her in time, that her exile might end. 'Life's not so bad in Sweden,' she said. 'I've got the museums and shops I always loved. And I'm studying at night school. But I miss the fjord. And I'd like to see the new house. My parents always wanted to put in a bathroom. You'd find it useful, with a baby.'

The child in Marte's arms was stirring, head turning side to side, lips opening a little before his navy-blue eyes did. 'I need to feed him,' Marte said.

'Let's sit down by the stove.'

A baby needed feeding. Kari needed a glass of warm milk and a bun. The mundane, the ordinary business of tending children and catching up with family news was sweeping aside war and bitterness.

Outside the shadows on the snow were lengthening. Time to be indoors, around the stove, all of them together.

## A LETTER FROM THE AUTHOR

Dear reader,

Huge thanks for reading *The Girl from the Fjords*. I hope you were caught up in the story of Asta and Max and their family. If you want to join other readers in hearing all about my new releases, you can sign up here:

www.stormpublishing.co/eliza-graham

And if you would like to sign up for my regular newsletter, please click here:

www.elizagrahamauthor.com/newsletter

If you enjoyed this book and could spare a few moments to leave a review, that would be hugely appreciated. Even a short review can make all the difference in encouraging a reader to discover my books for the first time. Thank you so much!

Thanks again for being part of this amazing journey with me and I hope you'll stay in touch – I have so many more stories and ideas to entertain you with!

Eliza

 facebook.com/ElizaGrahamUK
instagram.com/elizagraham1

# AUTHOR'S NOTES

In October 2024, I went on a short research trip to Norway, took a boat trip from Bergen up a fjord and fell in love with a country. Norway is a very easy country to love, with its scenery and its friendly, down-to-earth people.

Norway was neutral during the war, but its location between Sweden's iron ore supplies and the North Sea, coupled with Hitler's fears that the coast could be used by the Allies as a landing point onto the continent meant that in April 1940, Germany invaded the country. Much has been written about the Shetland Bus, the crossings of the North Sea between Shetland and western Norway by Norwegian and British Special Operatives during the occupation. I've found these accounts fascinating, but as I watched a waterfall from the deck of the boat taking me up a fjord and admired the small settlements with their wooden houses and churches, a different story seemed to take shape in my mind, a story about the people living alongside German invaders.

Novels that paint invaders, representatives of vicious regimes such as Nazi Germany, as fully human can be a tough proposition. I remember being moved by Irène Némirovsky's *Suite Francaise,* with its sensitive depiction of a relationship between a German officer and the French woman who must house him while her husband is a prisoner of war in Germany. What had played out in occupied France must surely have played out in occupied Norway, I thought.

During the occupation, German men and Norwegian

women formed relationships. Some were transactional, encouraged as part of the Lebensborn 'enrichment' programme for Germany's racial stock – Nordic blood being admired by the Nazis. Female participants were rewarded with food and comfortable accommodation. Other liaisons were simply the result of lonely women falling for men who were a long way from home.

Children were conceived and born. Many were not well-received, to say the least. One of the most famous cases is that of Anni-Frid Lyngstad of Abba fame, child of a Norwegian mother and Wehrmacht father. Anni-Frid, her mother and grandmother were forced to move to Sweden as a result of ostracism by their village. Anni-Frid only met her German father decades later for the first time. They certainly had reason to fear life in post-war Norway. The *Tyskerbarnas*, German children, were often scapegoats and ended up in harsh, sometimes brutal, institutions. Their mothers, if married, could be equally abused and even deported to Germany. In 2018, Norway's Prime Minister Erna Solberg issued an official apology to Norwegian women who were mistreated over World War Two-era relationships with German soldiers.

# ACKNOWLEDGEMENTS

My thanks again to all the Storm Publishing team for their never-ending encouragement with my writing, especially when I needed an extra month this time round to deal with a pressing family matter. In particular, thanks to my editor, Kate Smith, for understanding what I wanted to do with *The Girl from the Fjords* and helping me do it. My gratitude also to Liz Hurst, yet again, for her attention to detail during her copyedit, and to Shirley Khan for doing that crucial proofread. Naomi Knox worked magic with file conversions and corrections, and Alexandra Begley juggled so many publishing balls: audio, ebook, printed book production. Elke Desanghere, Anna McKerrow and Chris Lucraft are owed sincere thanks for their marketing and digital operations support. Sarah Whittaker produced another wonderful cover, so evocative of the book's theme and location. And finally, my thanks as ever to Oliver Rhodes and Kathryn Taussig.

Closer to home, Johnnie, Mungo, Eloise and Lewis continue to provide support for my books, not blinking when I vanish off with short notice to Norway, Lisbon or Corfu or somewhere else. I couldn't do it without them.

# BIBLIOGRAPHY

The following books and websites were useful references for me while writing this book.

## Norway under the Germans

**Norway 1940–45**
**The Resistance Movement**
Olave Riste and Berit Nökleby

**Heartfelt Greetings From Nazi-Occupied Norway**
Sophie Peterson
Letters and Diaries Compiled by: Barbara Peterson Schutte, Karen Peterson Fisher, Teresa Peterson Miller

**The Shetland Bus**
David Howarth

**Occupied: A Novel Based on a True Story**
Kurt Blorstad

'The Germans were the best lovers'
Bjørn André Widvey
2021
Skeivt arkiv

## Germany in the immediate post-war period

**DPs**
**Europe's Displaced Persons, 1945-1951**
Mark Wyman

**Postwar: A History of Europe Since 1945**
Tony Judt

**Beyond the Wall**
Katja Hoyer

***The Soviet Occupation of Germany: Hunger, Mass Violence and the Struggle for Peace, 1945–1947***
Filip Slaveski

***Aftermath: Life in the Fallout of the Third Reich 1945–1955***
Harald Jähner

***Berlin: The Downfall: 1945***
Antony Beevor

Printed in Dunstable, United Kingdom